HIT AND RUN LIKE HELL . . .

They were thirty yards away from the last bunker when it blew.

The explosion jolted the four men ahead six feet and then drove them into the ground. The gushing, roaring blast disintegrated the roof of the bunker and its three feet of dirt cover, showering the mass into the air and driving some of the debris a hundred yards away. It kept roaring and exploding and then small-arm rounds began cooking off in the fire and the four attackers leaped up and charged away from the area as fast as they could run. They overshot Murdock by fifty yards, but he and Ching kept up with them. They were all panting when they dropped to the ground and caught their breath.

"What the hell was in that one?" Sergeant Per asked.

One of the Israelis grinned. "Sarge should have warned you. We found two open cases of C-4. Must have been fifty pounds to the box. Dumped out the quarter pounders and set our small contribution on top . . . nice bang, what?"

SEAL TEAM SEVEN
COUNTERFIRE

KEITH DOUGLASS

BERKLEY BOOKS, NEW YORK

Special thanks to Chet Cunningham for his contribution to this book.

SEAL TEAM SEVEN: COUNTERFIRE

A Berkley Book / published by arrangement with
the author

PRINTING HISTORY
Berkley edition / March 2002

All rights reserved.
Copyright © 2002 by The Berkley Publishing Group.
SEAL TEAM SEVEN logo illustration by Michael Racz.
Cover art by Cliff Miller.

This book, or parts thereof, may not be reproduced in
any form without permission.
For information address: The Berkley Publishing Group,
a division of Penguin Putnam Inc.,
375 Hudson Street, New York, New York 10014.

Visit our website at
www.penguinputnam.com

ISBN: 0-425-18400-5

BERKLEY®
Berkley Books are published by The Berkley Publishing Group,
a division of Penguin Putnam Inc.,
375 Hudson Street, New York, New York 10014.
BERKLEY and the "B" design
are trademarks belonging to Penguin Putnam Inc.

PRINTED IN THE UNITED STATES OF AMERICA

10 9 8 7 6 5 4 3 2 1

*To those untiring, determined,
and uncompromising
397,000 U.S. Navy men and
women on active duty, who stay
the course and defend
our nation with pride
and honor.*

FOREWORD

Some of you have written to me with regrets about the loss of some of the old hands in the Third Platoon of SEAL Team Seven. It happens in combat more often than we would like, but we have to be realistic. In this line of work, men get wounded and killed. There are also replacements needed due to training accidents and the unusual and tough wear and tear on all of our Navy SEALs. That's why there are always new SEALs coming up through BUD/S training program. If you've ever wished that you could be a SEAL, and are in the Navy or want to join the Navy, now might be a good time to talk to the Navy people about the program.

It isn't an outfit that you can automatically join. You must apply, then pass a series of tests, including tough physical and psychological testing. That's how the SEALs get the best and toughest men in the Navy. Just a thought.

So, how is it going with you? How did you like this SEAL adventure? Let me know. Hey, I can take your criticism and even weather a pat on the back. If it's okay with you, I might use a quote from your letter in a special page in one of the books that show what you think of the series. Write to me at: Keith Douglass, SEAL Team Seven, 8431 Beaver Lake Dr., San Diego, CA 92119.

You have a good day now.

Keith Douglass

Rear Admiral (L) Richard Kenner, Commander of all SEALs.

Commander Dean Masciareli. 47, 5'11", 220 pounds. Annapolis graduate. Commanding officer of Navy Special Warfare Group One's SEAL Team Seven.

Master Chief Petty Officer Gordon MacKenzie. 47, 5'10", 180 pounds. Administrator and head enlisted man of all SEAL Teams at Coronado.

Lieutenant Commander Blake Murdock. Platoon Leader, Third Platoon, 32, 6'2", 210 pounds. Annapolis graduate. Six years in SEALs. Father important congressman from Virginia. Murdock recently promoted. Apartment in Coronado. Has a car and a motorcycle, loves to fish. Weapon: Alliant Bull Pup duo 5.56mm & 20mm explosive round. Alternate: H & K MP-5SD submachine gun.

ALPHA SQUAD

Timothy F. Sadler, Senior Chief Petty Officer. Top EM in Third Platoon. Third in command, 32, 6'2", 220 pounds. Married to Sylvia, no children. Has been in the Navy for fifteen years, a SEAL for last eight. Expert fisherman. Plays trumpet in any Dixieland combo he can find. Weapon: Alliant Bull Pup duo 5.56mm and 20mm explosive round. Good with the men.

*Third Platoon assigned exclusively to the Central Intelligence Agency to perform any needed tasks on a covert basis anywhere in the world. All are top secret assignments. Goes around Navy chain of command. Direct orders from the CIA.

David "Jaybird" Sterling. Machinist Mate First Class, Lead Petty Officer. 24, 5'10", 170 pounds. Quick mind, fine tactician. Single. Drinks too much sometimes. Crack shot with all arms. Grew up in Oregon. Helps plan attack operations. Weapon: H & K MP-5SD submachine gun.

Luke "Mountain" Howard. Gunner's Mate Second Class, 28, 6'4", 250 pounds. Black man. Football at Oregon State. Try-out with Oakland Raiders six years ago. In Navy six years. SEAL for four. Single. Rides a motorcycle. A skiing and wind surfing nut. Squad sniper. Weapon H & K PSG1 7.62 NATO sniper rifle.

Bill Bradford. Quartermaster First Class. 24, 6'2", 215 pounds. An artist in his spare time. Paints oils. He sells his marine paintings. Single. Quiet. Reads a lot. Has two years of college. Platoon radio operator. Carries a SATCOM on most missions. Weapon: Alliant Bull Pup duo 5.56mm & 20mm explosive round.

Joe "Ricochet" Lampedusa. Operations Specialist Second Class. 21, 5'11", 175 pounds. Good tracker, quick thinker. Had a year of college. Loves motorcycles. Wants a Hog. Pot smoker on the sly. Picks up plain girls. Platoon scout. Weapon: H & K MP-5SD submachine gun, alternate Bull Pup duo 5.56mm & 20mm explosive round.

Kenneth Ching. Quartermaster First Class. 25, 6' even, 180 pounds. Full-blooded Chinese. Platoon translator. Speaks Mandarin Chinese, Japanese, Russian, and Spanish. Bicycling nut. Paid $1,200 for off-road bike. Is trying for Officer Candidate School. Weapon: Colt M-4A1 rifle with grenade launcher.

Vincent "Vinnie" Van Dyke. Electrician's Mate Second Class. 24, 6'2", 220 pounds. Enlisted out of high school. Played varsity basketball. Wants to be a commercial fisherman after his current hitch. Good with his hands. Squad machine gunner. Weapon: H & K 21-E 7.62 NATO round machine gun.

BRAVO SQUAD

Lieutenant Ed DeWitt. Leader Bravo Squad. Second in command of the platoon. 30, 6'1", 175 pounds. From Seattle. Wiry. Married to Milly. No kids. Annapolis graduate. A career man. Plays a good game of chess on traveling board. Weapon: Alliant Bull Pup duo 5.56mm & 20mm explosive round. Alternate: H & K G-11 submachine gun.

George "Petard" Canzoneri, Torpedoman's Mate First Class. 27, 5'11", 190 pounds. Married to Navy wife, Phyllis. No kids. Nine years in Navy. Expert on explosives. Nicknamed "Petard" for almost hoisting himself one time. Top pick in platoon for explosive work. Weapon: Alliant Bull Pup duo 5.56mm & 20mm explosive round.

Miguel Fernandez. Gunner's Mate First Class. 26, 6'1", 180 pounds. Wife, Maria; daughter, Linda, 7, in Coronado. Spends his off time with them. Highly family oriented. He has family in San Diego. Speaks Spanish and Portuguese. Squad sniper. Weapon: H & K PSG1 7.62 NATO sniper rifle.

Colt "Guns" Franklin. Yeoman Second Class. 24, 5'10", 175 pounds. A former gymnast. Powerful arms and shoulders. Expert mountain climber. Has a motorcycle, and does hang gliding. Speaks Farsi and Arabic. Weapon: H & K MP-5SD submachine gun.

Tracy Donegan, Signalman Second Class, 24, 6' even, 185 pounds. Former Navy boxer, tough, single, expert tracker and expert on camouflage and ground warfare. Expert marksman. Platoon driver, mechanic. Frantic Chargers football fan. Speaks Italian and Swahili. Weapon: H & K G-11 with caseless rounds.

Jack Mahanani. Hospital Corpsman First Class. 25, 6'4", 240 pounds. Platoon Medic. Tahitian/Hawaiian. Expert swimmer. Bench-presses four hundred pounds. Divorced. Top surfer.

Wants the .50 sniper rifle. Weapon: Alliant Bull Pup duo 5.56mm & 20mm explosive round. Alternate: H & K MP-5SD submachine gun.

Frank Victor, Gunner's Mate Second Class, 23, 6' even, 185 pounds. Two years in SEALs. Radio, computer expert. Can program, repair, and build computers. Shoots small-bore rifle competitively. Married. Wife, Phyllis, a computer programmer/specialist. No children. Lives in Coronado. Weapon: Alliant Bull Pup duo & 20mm explosive round.

Paul "Jeff" Jefferson. Engineman Second Class. Black man. 23, 6'1", 200 pounds. Expert in small arms. Can tear apart most weapons and reassemble, repair, and innovate them. A chess player to match Ed DeWitt. Weapon: Alliant Bull Pup duo 5.56mm & 20mm explosive round.

1

Sierra Leone
Africa

Ground fire ripped through the night sky, leaving glowing red tracer patterns, as the big VTOL Osprey came in fast, turned its engines into the vertical position, and lowered gracefully to the ground where two red flares burned. Two rounds hit the bird near where Lieutenant Commander Blake Murdock crouched. He swept back the door and the moment the wheels touched the soft black Sierra Leone soil, he jumped to the ground with Quartermaster First Class Ken Ching and Electrician's Mate Second Class Vincent Van Dyke right behind him.

Murdock pointed to the left, where they saw muzzle flashes a hundred yards away. They all hit the dirt, and Murdock and Ching brought up their Alliant Bull Pup duo rifles and each sent a 20mm high-explosive round into the trio of gunfire flashes. The twenties shattered the Sierra Leone darkness, and the fire from that sector cut off just after a wailing scream.

Three U.S. Marine Recon fighters followed the SEALs out of the plane. Murdock motioned them to the left, and he and his two men darted to the right and charged out forty yards, then went prone with weapons pointing outward. They were on perimeter defense for the VTOL birds. Now Murdock saw the other five Osprey craft where they had landed in a rough triangle about thirty yards apart. Six men from each bird were deployed outward as security.

Sporadic rifle- and machine-gun fire blasted from the other side of the aircraft. Murdock heard three twenties ex-

plode and the small-arms fire stopped. Ten Sierra Leone
soldiers dashed past the perimeter defense and to the birds,
now with doors wide open. They began unloading their payload of rifles, submachine guns, rockets, RPGs, and
thousands of rounds of ammunition from the birds. Murdock
had had a chance to check the cargo over on the short ride
from the U.S. aircraft carrier *Carl Vinson,* CVN 70, just off
the coast of the small African nation.

Enough weapons and ammo to start a war, or to finish
off a group of sadistic rebels the current regime had been
battling for six months. Now the government forces of President Ahmad Tejan Kabbah had a chance to deliver the killing blow if they had enough weapons and ammo. This was
it. Three SEALs from Third Platoon, Team Seven, were on
each of four birds, and two on each of the other two, for
security.

Murdock sensed movement to his right and pulled down
his night-vision goggles. A squad of rebels about a hundred
yards out crept forward through the black night that was
turned into a light green shooting ground by the goggles.
He lasered the troops, fired an airburst, and cut down six of
the eight men with the shattering 20mm round. The other
two men in the rebel squad limped away into the heavy
growth near the edge of the field.

Behind him, Murdock could hear the native soldiers panting as they rushed to unload the arms and ammo. There was
supposed to be a force of over two hundred government
troops in the area, to sweep it clean of rebels, but several
small groups of rebels had penetrated, and now Murdock
heard more firing to the left on the other side of the VTOL
birds. He signaled to the Marine sergeant to keep his men
there, then he spoke on the Motorola personal radio. They
were now using shoulder mikes, which had proved to be
sturdier and easier to work with.

"Ching, Van Dyke, let's hit the other side of the birds
and see who we can scare. Move. Now." The three lifted
up and raced under the wing of the big Osprey, across the
open space, and under the next VTOL being unloaded. They
went out thirty yards beyond it, then dove to the ground

seven yards apart. More muzzle flashes showed directly in front of them.

"When ready," Murdock said, and dropped a 20mm HE round on the flashes of two guns he saw out two hundred yards. The shooters must have fired and moved. "I've got them right ten yards. Ching, do a twenty at ten to their left." They waited, and at the first flash of new firing both SEALs launched a laser 20mm. They exploded over the target, and this time there was no counterfire.

All was quiet for a moment; then they heard the rumble and clank of what could only be a tank. Murdock hit the mike. "SEALs, perimeter. I hear a tank. When you see him, blind him with some rounds of WP, then try for his tread with the twenty HE. Who has him?"

"Sounds like he's coming my way," Frank Victor, gunner's mate second class and new to the platoon, said.

"Victor, is that you?"

"Yes, sir."

"Anybody near Victor down there?"

"Nearby," Mahanani said. "Critter is coming up on us fast. Any more support in here? Jefferson?"

"Yeah, man," Jeff said. "I've got him. Big sucker, coming up fast, then he slowed down. Don't think he's gonna shoot yet. Maybe a hundred yards out there in the dark. No NVGs. Anybody else see him? Has he got ground troops following him?"

"Can't see him, Jeff. I'm charging out there a ways to blind him, then try for the treads," Mahanani said. "Who else over here has the twenties?"

"Got one," Jefferson said.

"Yeah," Franklin said. "I'm with a twenty. Where are you guys?"

"On the point of the triangle heading north."

"Don't leave home without me," Franklin said. He sprinted across the open space. Two rifles made tries for him from the woods, but missed. He slid in beside Victor.

They ran doubled over and ten yards apart to the woodsy edge of the clearing, and hit the dirt. Now they could hear the engine of the big tank, but it wasn't moving.

"How do we know it's not a government forces tank?" Murdock asked on the net.

"Damn, didn't think about that," Victor said. "If he shoots at the birds, we'll know."

Just then a machine gun on the tank stuttered out two ten-round bursts of fifty-caliber.

"Go," Murdock said. "He hit one bird. Not sure how bad."

"I've got smoke in," Franklin said. He aimed ten feet in front of the tank, a huge dark blob among the dark trees, and fired. Then he put another one in front of the tank.

As he did, the other two SEALs sighted in on the side tracks of the monster and both fired about the same time. The tank lurched forward to get out of the smoke. Franklin put two more 20mm smoke rounds in front of it, and Jefferson and Victor both fired the twenties again, two rounds each. The last two rounds found a weak spot on the churning tracks and blasted off the motive force of the tank. It spun around as if it had fully braked one tread. Then the engine whimpered to a halt. The lights snapped off, and the SEALs heard the hatch open but couldn't see anything. Both SEALs fired an HE round at the tank; then they retreated to the fringe of the woods.

"Coming in, three friendlies," Victor said on the Motorola. "Don't get your rocks off on us. We're on your side."

The three charged into the triangle of aircraft, then found their defensive spots again, and bellied down, aiming their weapons outward at the heavy growth of trees and brush.

"Trouble from this other side," Murdock said. "At least a company of rebels moving up. No firing yet. I've got them on the goggles. Anybody else with goggles see them?"

"I've got them," Lieutenant Ed DeWitt said. "Looks more like two companies. Where the hell are all those government troops supposed to be? This hardware gets into rebel hands, it's good night, Irene."

"I need three more Bull Pups on the east side," Murdock barked. "Sound off."

"Sadler coming."

"Jaybird on the move."

"Fernandez almost there."

The SEALs found their leader in the murky half-light of the moon and spread out along the east side.

"We've got six or seven Pups over here. For those who can't see the target, the lieutenant and I will put airbursts on the rebels, then each one of you fire three rounds and hold. Ed. When you're ready."

Murdock sighted in with the laser on the slowly moving group of men still bunched up out about two hundred yards. He fired. The resulting crack of the airburst was quickly followed by a second; then moments later six more exploded in the air over the first firing point.

Murdock checked through the NVGs. A few of the troops took cover behind trees. Dozens turned and ran.

"Raise twenty-five yards," Murdock said, and fired again. More rounds exploded as they tracked the men running away.

"Murdock, Marine Sergeant Nelson. There's a jeep coming hell-bent for leather through the west side. I've got two Marines here and M-16's. We can't stop him. Tried tires and windshield. He's into the clearing heading for the first VTOL bird."

"I see him," Tracy Donegan, signalman second class, shouted into his shoulder mike. "He's too close to the bird for me to use the twenty. Shit, he's going to crash into the nose of the plane." They heard the explosion. The large Osprey erupted in flames; some small-arms ammunition still inside began cooking off and firing in every direction. Moments later the fuel tanks went up in a gigantic, roaring fireball.

"Suicide mission," Donegan said. "Damn, I couldn't stop him."

"Lieutenant, how close to unloading are you?" Murdock asked on the mike. The Navy officer had been given a Motorola.

"Almost done. We're taking off the second two birds now. Marines and SEALs grab the next bird you can. Make your man count. We lost the pilot and copilot and two crewmen in that fire. They were about ready to leave. Let's move it. Two and three, get out of here."

"Head for the birds, Marines and SEALs," Murdock bellowed. His mike caught it, and so did half a dozen Marines who had been firing into the target with their M-16's.

"Ed, take one bird and count," Murdock said.

He sprinted to the closest VTOL bird and found a SEAL and two Marines inside. Two minutes later he had five SEALs and eight Marines. He reported his numbers to Ed and Sergeant Nelson.

"We've got all the Marines, Murdock," Ed said. "We have thirteen SEALs in this one."

"We're short two SEALs," Murdock said.

The crew chief of the bird ran in and closed one door. Murdock moved to the other one. "Get out of here. No telling what else the rebels have out there. I'll see you when I see you." Murdock jumped down from the Osprey and ran for the fringe of brush as the engines wound up and kicked up dirt and dust while the VTOL slowly lifted off straight into the air. Two rifles picked up Murdock on his run, but missed hitting him. He crashed into the growth a dozen feet, then bellied down in the brush and touched his shoulder mike.

"SEALs, time to come home. Where the hell are you two?"

"Hiding," the whisper said in Murdock's earpiece.

"Yeah, I hear you, take it easy. Lots of rebels around you? Click once for yes." One click came. Murdock waited. He had no idea which direction to go. Then the earpiece spoke to him.

"Van Dyke. Bastards all around me. Most of them from that company you shot to hell. They're mad. Cheered like wild when the bird blew up."

"They pulled back a little?"

"Yeah, some."

"You seen Lam?"

"He was nearby. I think he got hit. We come off the line to backside these fuckers. Should have told you."

"Can you find Lam?"

"Yeah. I think so. I got a scratch, but it's nothing. The bad guys have pulled back to reorganize. I figure they knew the shit was coming in here tonight. Heard one truck back there somewhere."

"Could be the government trucks. I see two coming in now. They have some troops with them. We'll try to hook up with them and get out of here."

"Birds all left?"

"Right, too dangerous to stay any longer. RPGs would kill them from this woods-to-plane range. Look for Lam."

Murdock watched the two trucks move up to the stack of boxes of rifles, machine guns, and ammo at the site near the first VTOL, which was still burning. They pulled the ammo out first so it wouldn't explode. He wanted to run that way and bring back some help, but he didn't know the language. Strike that. English was the official language here in Sierra Leone. But he knew they would shoot first and talk later.

"Got him," Van Dyke said.

"How bad?"

"Not good. Looks like one in the arm and another one in his leg, up high. He's almost out of it."

"Where are you from the burning chopper?"

"Yeah, see it. To the east, maybe twenty yards in the brush. About opposite that second stack of ammo on this side."

"I'm moving up that direction. Don't the fuck shoot me."

Murdock moved slowly and silently. He had this routine down to an exact science. Never put your foot down until you were sure it wouldn't break something and make noise. He found the two SEALs about five minutes later.

Van Dyke had bandaged Lam's upper right arm and his lower leg. The in-and-out on his leg was no problem.

"I can walk, I can walk," Lam kept saying.

"The shoulder isn't so good," Van Dyke said. "I think it's a ricochet and it's still in there."

"So what?" Lam asked. "Let's move. The last chopper ready?"

Murdock checked the two bandages. They would stop the bleeding even when Lam walked.

"We move quietly around to the side where the trucks are

coming in. I'll try to talk to one of the Sierra Leone soldiers without getting my head blown off."

"Where are the choppers, that new funny VTOL one?" Lam asked.

"They had to leave, too much danger," Murdock said. "We're on our own for a while."

"My fucking fault," Lam said. "I got hit and couldn't move there for a time. Why didn't you use the radio?"

Murdock stopped and looked closely at Lam. His earpiece hung down his back on the thin wire. Murdock pushed it back in place, and they glided slowly through the thick growth toward the road where the trucks were coming in. So far Murdock had seen three come, load up, and leave. The workers who unloaded the planes were gone. He saw no one. Each truck must bring its own work force. He stopped opposite the fourth stack of ammo and weapons. The truck would come to them.

They sat down to wait in the fringe of woods. Murdock looked at Van Dyke. "You said you picked up a scratch?"

"Oh, nothing to worry about. Place on my arm. I think it was some shrapnel from one of our own twenties. So no Purple Heart."

Murdock pushed back Van Dyke's jungle-camouflaged shirtsleeve and checked it. A jagged line two inches long oozed with a line of blood that ran down his arm and dripped off his fingers. Murdock used his first-aid kit and put some ointment on the gash, then wrapped it tightly to stop the bleeding.

"Some damn scratch," he said. Van Dyke grinned.

A truck came five minutes later, ground to a halt, and left its lights on aimed at the stack of weapons and ammo. Four men got out of the truck and began taking the goods to the truck. Murdock watched the loading. He could come up on this side of the rig without being seen.

"Stay," he said, and brought his Bull Pup to port arms and slid across the twenty yards to the side of the old van-type truck without a sound. He paused at the near side, then crept around the front until he could see the men working.

One soldier stood to the side evidently directing things. English, they spoke English.

He tried the direct approach without showing himself.

"Lieutenant, I need to talk to you," Murdock said loud enough so the man could hear him, but not the workers. The soldier turned sharply, a submachine gun coming up.

"What the hell. Who is there?"

"A friend. I just helped bring in this stack of guns and ammo. I'm a United States Navy SEAL and I need your help."

"You could be a rebel."

"If I were, you'd be dead by now, right?"

The man twisted his face into a frown, then nodded. "Yeah, guess so. I saw the strange planes leave. How do they do that?"

"Vertical takeoffs and landings. After takeoff, the whole engine turns until it's level with the wing and the plane flies forward like any plane."

"Yeah. Okay, come out, but keep your hands up."

Murdock did as he stepped out and moved forward.

"Stop, close enough. You say you're with the U.S. Navy?"

"Right, the SEALs. We're specialists in covert projects like this."

"So, the U.S. brought in these weapons?"

"Yes, but nobody is supposed to know about it."

"Yeah, but I know about it." His sub gun came up and centered on Murdock's chest from six feet away.

"We're on your side, the government's side," Murdock said.

The man with the submachine gun laughed. "You don't say, brother. Got news for you. We're not on your side. Knew right away that you weren't a rebel. Guess why. 'Cause we're the rebels, and we thank you for the fine weapons and ammunition." He laughed again, and Murdock saw no chance to get to him or to use the Pup.

"Stand steady, SEAL. Since you're a warrior, I'll give

you a choice. You want me to kill you quick, or slow? One in the head or two in the belly, so you can moan and scream and go out of your mind with pain? Which one, American Navy SEAL, which one?"

2

Murdock's mind blasted into hyperspeed selecting and evaluating every move he could make, anything he could do to reverse the situation. Every move and method he thought of came up negative. He was facing death down the barrel of a submachine gun and there wasn't a thing he could do. Dive left and bring up the Pup. Not a chance he could beat an aimed weapon. Throw the weapon at the rebel? Wouldn't work, bullets fly faster than a hurled rifle. He stared hard at the smirking rebel.

"Kill me and get promoted to colonel in your ragtag outfit, is that what you want?"

"Better than being a captain. You trying to talk me to death? Won't work, United States SEAL. I should keep you so we can prove to the world that your country is against us. Might do some good. No, not a chance. Bring me much more pleasure to cut you in half with about twenty rounds." His white teeth gleamed in the moonlight as he grinned.

"Oh, yeah," he continued, "and I think the time is about now."

Murdock heard the horrendous sound of a weapon firing, but he didn't feel the bullets slam into his body. Then the rebel in front of him grew a splash of blood on his forehead as his body began to jolt backward, his finger still on the trigger of the submachine gun. Murdock dove sideways and rolled as the sub gun fired from a spasming trigger finger as the rebel died. The weapon in the man's hands lifted as he fell until it pointed skyward, and ripped off another dozen rounds before the man hit the ground.

Murdock rolled once more, came to his feet, and without

a glance at the men loading the truck, charged back into the brush twenty yards away. Now he heard the rifle fire coming from the woods he had left. Van Dyke, he decided. The kid would get a gold star. He crashed through some brush and went flat on the leaf-mold-covered ground, his Bull Pup cradled in his arms.

"Van Dyke, where are you guys?"

"About ten yards north. Figured you might need a hand out there. I take it they weren't friendly."

"They are the rebels. Somehow they got the upper hand here. Suggest we put some twenties into the truck and those stacks of weapons and ammo that are left. Fire when ready."

Murdock crawled to the edge of the woods and sent his first shot into the truck engine. It erupted, blowing off the hood and sending parts of the engine over half the clearing. Another twenty hit the rear of the truck setting off some sympathetic explosions, and a minute later the whole rig was one mass of flames and detonations.

Murdock moved his sights to the stack of ammo and weapons still in front of the truck where its headlights had been shining. He found the black mass and triggered a round. The 20mm HE round detonated on a stack of ammo boxes and blasted them into kindling. Another round from Van Dyke shattered boxes containing the small arms, and set off a packet of plastic explosive that splattered the rest of the weapons and cartridges over half the world.

"Good shooting," Murdock said. "Anybody see the other piles of goods?"

"Too damn dark," Van Dyke said.

"Send out a WP in the middle of the place," Lam said. "I might be shot but I'm not out of it."

Murdock dug a marked WP 20mm round from his ammo stash and chambered it. "Good idea, Lam. One WP on the way." He fired into the middle of where the Osprey planes had parked. It blossomed in white streamers and outlined two of the piles of boxes.

It took them another four minutes to find and explode the remaining ammunition and cartridges. A lot of it would be salvaged tomorrow, but the rebels would have to come back and do it in the light. Maybe by then the government forces would be on hand.

Murdock heard small arms firing to the south. None of the rounds were coming their way.

"Lam, how's it going?" Murdock asked.

"Hanging, man. I can hike with the best of you. Where we going and when?"

"Working on that. The maps I saw put us just south of Freetown, the capital city. We're also about five miles from the coast. Our best bet is to work our way to the coast, then up to the big town, and find some of the government troops."

"Why weren't the Sierra Leone troops here to pick up the goods?" Van Dyke asked.

"You can bet a lot of folks are going to be asking that same question," Murdock said.

They had grouped together, and watched the last of the loading crew from the truck run back down the road they had come on.

"Not a good idea to use that road," Murdock said. "We crash brush and head for the coast. Still wonder where the hell the government troops are. Uncle Sam spent a pile of dough for nothing here. Fact is, we gave a bunch of weapons to the rebels. The shit is gonna fly over this one. Let's take off and see what we can find."

Just as they pulled back into the woods, a small vehicle jolted into the clearing and a pedestal-mounted machine gun began chewing up the brush and trees around the edges of the clearing. It started well away from the SEALs and before it came their way, the trio was two hundred yards into the brush and trees.

Murdock led the way, with Lam in the middle and Van Dyke tail-end Charlie. They hiked through the thinning woods for five minutes, then came to a thick swamp with mangrove trees, sand, and clay.

"Not going through that mess," Van Dyke said. "Didn't they tell us that along here there were about twenty miles of swamps and lagoons and rivers and such? How the hell we gonna get through them?"

"We don't," Murdock said, making an instant decision.

"We go back to the field and follow that road. It must be the only piece of solid ground in the area. Once the rebels cut it, they controlled the landing zone. Damn poor planning by the federals; no wonder they are losing their war."

"I'm pumping some out again," Lam said. "Damn bandage came off my leg."

They stopped and Van Dyke put on a new bandage, wrapping it tight.

"Sorry about this, home folks. Usually I don't get myself shot."

"No sweat, beach boy," Van Dyke said. "Fuck it, I'll carry you if I need to. Let's chogie."

Murdock led them carefully up to the lower end of the LZ. The glow of the fire still showed on the downed VTOL. They saw no vehicles or men. The rebels should have left someone close by to protect their loot.

"We're going to stay in the brush near the road," said Murdock. "If it's clear, we'll use it. First a long look. The rebels have to be down there somewhere. A camp, a patrol, something."

A mile down the road, the land on both sides gave way to an evil-looking swamp, and the SEALs had to move out to the road itself. They hiked cautiously, watching all sides, with Murdock monitoring the area ahead with his NVGs. They were just across the stretch with no firm land on either side when Murdock swore.

"Company up front about three hundred. Looks like a small camp. They have a fire and guards on the road. Must be a vehicle there somewhere but I can't see it."

Murdock looked at Lam. He had been limping badly the past few minutes.

"I'm fine, just fine and dandy, Commander, sir," Lam said. "Just figure how in the hell we get out of here."

Murdock grinned. If Lam was bitchy he must be making it. Hurting, but weathering the fucking storm. "Back into the woods," Murdock said. "We work toward them and do some recon, see exactly what we have to work with. How are we on ammo?"

"Twelve more of the twenties, lots of 5.56," Van Dyke said.

"Plenty of both kinds, Skipper," Lam said.

The three SEALs worked through the woods near the side of the road on what turned out to be a long spit of solid ground in the middle of the twenty-mile-wide swamp. They saw the wet places more and more at the sides of the road. The mangrove trees flourished in the murky environment. Then Murdock held up his hand and they stopped. Through the brush he'd spotted the camp.

"Looks like a blocking position," Murdock said. "But all of their weapons are aimed the other way, down the road to keep anyone from coming up this way. I see four men on duty. One on a heavy machine gun, and the others behind sandbags. Could be a backup platoon sacked out in the brush on that side of the road."

"Or on this side," Lam said. "Wish I could go take a look, but I don't have the potatoes right now."

"I'll check it," Murdock said. "Hold here, be back in five."

He had only to go another fifty feet to see that the area on his side of the roadblock had no rebel residents. He used the Motorola and called the others forward. They worked past the guards without a sound. The last dozen feet they had to move into the edge of the swamp to find cover at a brushless area next to the road.

They came out wet to the knees, but without drawing any attention from the rebels.

"How far we have to go?" Van Dyke asked, nodding at Lam.

"Can't say. We take it easy. We've got all night. Before the sun comes up we should run into some government troops. If they planned on picking up these munitions and arms, they should have had a bunch of people around."

"Why out here in the middle of a twenty-mile-wide swamp?" Van Dyke asked.

"Hard to get into, easy to defend," Murdock said. "Just depends who was here first."

They kept hiking. Twenty minutes later, Lam went down and Van Dyke called to Murdock.

"Give me ten and I'll be moving again," Lam said. "Don't know why I'm so fucking weak."

Murdock checked the bandages and found out. Both were bleeding, had been for some time. They treated the wounds again, then wrapped them with the last of their bandages and had Lam lie down and relax. Murdock had two ampoules of morphine in his kit. He opened one and gave the shot to Lam, who nodded.

"Yeah, Cap, I needed that. Sorry to be such a wipeout. Shit, this isn't me."

"Take it easy. We'll have you out of here before daylight and on the way to that big floating island off the coast and their hospital. We move out in ten."

It was almost twenty minutes before they could get Lam up and walking. Then he leaned on Murdock's shoulder and Van Dyke carried his weapon and most of his ammo. They saw no more rebels.

"Hope to hell all the bad guys are behind us by now," Murdock said.

An hour before sunrise, Murdock heard laughter ahead. He left the other two and worked up cautiously. Looking past a large mangrove tree, he saw a fire with half a dozen men around it. They were relaxed, and had out no security that he could see. He watched them for ten minutes. No one came to or left the fire. They all had on uniforms, and some had weapons slung over their shoulders muzzle-down.

Murdock moved up slowly until he was just outside the light from the fire. Looking at the fire so much, they would be night-blind looking into the dark.

When he was thirty feet away, he lifted up and sent a burst of three rounds over their heads from the 5.56.

"Don't move or you're dead," Murdock bellowed. "Who's in charge?"

One man lifted his hand.

"Rebels or government troops?" Murdock roared.

"Government troops, sir. Sergeant Tejan."

"Were you supposed to pick up weapons and ammunition tonight from some helicopters?"

"Yes, sir. Supposed to. Rebels cut us off and we missed it."

"Where are the rest of your troops?"

"We're an outpost, sir. We have a thousand men a half mile down the road. No way we could get to the landing field."

"Lay down your arms and hands on your heads. SEALs come on up," Murdock said to his shoulder mike.

They both came in with weapons leveled.

Murdock had moved up to within six feet of the sergeant.

"Prove to me you're who you say you are. An ID card?"

The sergeant slowly lowered one hand, took a folder from his shirt pocket, and extracted two cards. One was a Sierra Leone Army Identification Card. The other a credit card. The name was the same on both.

Murdock nodded and lowered his weapon.

"Good. We have a wounded man. Do you have a medic here?"

A man stepped forward with an over-the-shoulder medical kit. He went to Lam and nodded. He put him down on some grass and using a flashlight, began treating both wounds and bandaging them.

"You have any transport?" asked Murdock.

"No, sir."

"Any communications with your main body?"

"Yes, sir. Radio." He took a handie-talkie-size radio off a holder at his side.

"Get a jeep up here as soon as you can. Tell them that we're part of the force that brought in the munitions."

Twenty minutes later, the SEALs sat in a large tent on a solid piece of ground beside a blacktopped road.

Colonel Limba smiled as he gave his guests a breakfast and cans of Coca-Cola. "We are glad to know that you destroyed most of the weapons and ammunition. We will have trouble enough salvaging what is left. The rebels have an amazing network of spies and methods of travel in the swampy area. They knew you were coming, where the goods would be unloaded, and how to block us from getting to it. Sometimes their intelligence is better than ours."

"Can you help us get back to our ship, or at least communicate with the carrier off your coast?"

"It has been done already, Commander. As soon as it's light and we have total security, we will send you to Freetown, where a Navy helicopter is waiting for you. Within two hours you should be back on board the carrier."

3

Lieutenant Commander Blake Murdock settled behind his desk at Third Platoon, SEAL Team Seven, and tried to relax. It had been a week since they had returned from the ammo delivery mission into Sierra Leone, and he still wasn't sure what the final outcome was. From what Don Stroh told him, the government forces had charged up the road the next morning, blasted through the weak force at the roadblock, retaken the landing field, and recovered about half of what had been sent to them.

At first the government forces had been furious that so much of the equipment and ammo had been destroyed. Then their field commanders explained to them that the rebel truck would have hauled away all of the weapons and ammo and shipped it out on small boats through the maze of waterways in the swamp by morning.

When the SEALs burned down the rebels' truck, they'd stopped the looting of the goods. The SEALs had had no way of knowing what other transport the rebels might have had. As near as anyone knew now, the government army got half of the shipment, the rebels about an eighth, and the rest was blown up. Also, Uncle Sam lost one Osprey aircraft, two pilots, and a crew chief. A copilot on another of the Ospreys was wounded in the shoulder. Third Platoon had only one wounded. Lam was clamoring to get out of Balboa Naval Hospital over in San Diego. He wanted to get back with the platoon. The doctors had not been kind. They told him he'd be there for two weeks and then on limited duty. Turned out the bullet in his leg had been a ricochet and had done little damage, but they wanted to watch it. One of the doctors told Murdock when he was visiting that they routinely kept SEALs in the hospital longer than usual so they wouldn't try to get back on duty too quickly and hurt themselves further.

Ed DeWitt had worked out a new training schedule, and now on Monday morning when Murdock looked it over at 0630 in his office, it seemed about right. They had to totally integrate the two new men. Frank Victor had performed well on the shoot-out at the Osprey drop. The other new man, Tracy Donegan, hadn't been as involved, but had done nothing to hurt his position. Training was what they needed. More conditioning, more live firing in the hills, and more all-night problems all aimed at teamwork, each SEAL supporting and protecting every other SEAL.

He looked at the schedule again. Monday, they would start with a run through the "O" course with their times recorded. Then they would take a six-mile swim underwater with full combat gear. When they got back it would be rubber-duck time, with each squad in a duck working on surfing in to the beach. Too often they had to come in through high surf on foreign shores so they could hit the beach at the exact place they needed. It was a fine art to time the wave exactly right. He'd have his best surfboard riders working the boats today. They had the right feel for the Southern California waves, and could tell when they were washing out or breaking up. Last year on a similar training workout, one boat had flipped and knocked out one of the SEALs. They'd found him just in time to keep him from drowning.

"Morning, Skipper," Senior Chief Petty Officer Timothy Sadler said. He slid into a chair across the desk from his boss and sipped at a cup of store-bought coffee. Sadler was the top EM in the platoon, and at six-two and 220 had the size to do the job.

"My guess the workouts get tougher today," Sadler said.

"You win the million dollars, Senior Chief. We need to

get that edge again. We had it before Sierra Leone. We need to sharpen it up and push the men."

"Aye, sir. Can I see the schedule for today?"

Murdock handed over the write/wipe board that had the day's schedule on it in green ink.

"Yes, sir, looks good. Only, before the O course, let's start with fifty sit and push."

Murdock looked up and nodded. "Easing them into it?"

"Yes, sir, but we'll soon be at a hundred three times a day. Sharpens the muscles and the mind." Damn yes, they can do it, Sadler sniped at himself. He was the oldest guy on the platoon. If he could handle it, the rest of the kids could too. They did or they got the hook back to the regular Navy.

Lieutenant Ed DeWitt came in and dropped into the chair that the senior chief quickly vacated.

"Where's the coffee?" Dewitt growled.

"And a good morning to you too, Ed. Sounds like you got up on the wrong side of a minefield this morning."

"You should see it from inside my eyeballs," Ed said, scowling. "I'm never civil until after 1100. How do you like the training sked?"

"Looks good for a start," Murdock said. Ed could be a slow starter when he wanted to be. They'd handled the platoon together now for going on three years. A long time for the officer team in the platoons. Ed had married his lady, Milly, and he had mellowed out a little this past year. "How's my favorite married lady?"

"Milly has had another job offer out at Deltron Electronics. Some hyperfink wants to raise her salary to sixty-five thousand and send her up to Silicone Valley. She asked me about it, and after Milly unglued me from the ceiling, she said she'd already turned down the job."

"She's a classy lady, DeWitt, and twice as smart as all three of us put together." Murdock looked at the senior chief. "Milly is way up there high in the computer stratosphere," Murdock said. DeWitt grinned at the compliment to his lady. Then Murdock turned to his top EM.

"Senior Chief, is there any reason we should continue to

use the Colt M4Al carbine?" Murdock asked.

"The Colt?" Sadler asked. "Well, what we use it mostly for now is the forty-mike-mike, smoke, and HE. Hell, we've got both of them now on the Bull Pup. Like we saw in Sierra Leone, the smoke from the twenties isn't as much as you get from a forty grenade. But you can put two or three WP twenties into the target and get the same result." He furrowed his forehead a moment and wiped one hand across his face.

"Then too, Cap, we can use the smoke now out to a thousand yards with the Bull Pup," DeWitt said. "I'd think we can phase the Colt right into the armory."

"The only problem is getting enough of the Bull Pups," Murdock said. "It isn't fully developed yet to the manufacturing stage. The military won't be issued any until 2006. How many do we have on hand now, JG?"

"I'm not sure. Seven that I can think of. I'll talk to my men and our armorer and get an exact count."

"If we don't have enough, we'll fill in with the MP-5's," Murdock said. "Let's get the new look in weapons as soon as possible. Only Lam and Ching have the Colt in Alpha."

"Did I hear something about a new vehicle we were going to be able to test?" Sadler asked.

"News travels fast," DeWitt said. "Fact is, Senior Chief, we're going to check it out this afternoon. It's called the Turtle right now. The Defense Department calls it their Combat Entry Attack Vehicle, or CEAV. Somebody called it a Humvee with fins, but it's more than that. I saw it this morning for about five minutes. Three company engineers are with it and they said they'll give us a ride. Basically it's an amphibian, something like the old ducks of World War II. Only small enough to be inconspicuous, a true amphib that holds eight men and can make fifteen knots in water and do up to forty miles an hour on land."

"This I got to see," Sadler said. He shook his head and chuckled. "You know, this could knock the IBS in the head. If she's small enough to get on an Osprey . . ."

"Doubt that, Senior Chief," Murdock said. "Get me a final

count on how many Colts we have and who uses them in Ed's squad."

Promptly at 0800 Murdock heard a whistle blast in the assembly room outside his office. He took a look out the door.

"Fall in, you tadpoles, do it by squads, let's have an official roll-call count this morning," Senior Chief Sadler barked.

The twelve enlisted SEALs grumbled and scurried to the two squads facing the senior chief.

"Alpha Squad all present or accounted for," Jaybird bellowed.

"Bravo Squad all present or accounted for," Miguel Fernandez shouted.

Sadler looked over at Murdock and saluted. "Third Platoon all present or accounted for, sir," he barked.

"Carry on, Chief," Murdock said, returning the salute. He turned to DeWitt, who had been watching out the door as well. "Starting to sound like the regular fucking Navy around here."

Sadler looked at his team. "At ease. Can anyone tell me why the hell we're still packing along the old Colt M-4A1?"

"Shit, we shoot it," Jaybird shouted, and the squads laughed.

"Yeah, yeah, I know. This is my rifle, this is my gun. This is for shooting, this is for fun. Besides that, what can the Colt do that the rest of our weapons can't?"

"Fire the forty-millimeter grenade," Fernandez said.

"Right, give that man a cigar. So can we replace that forty in any way?"

"Hail, yes, Senior Chief," Signalman Second Class Tracy Donegan said. "We put two, maybe three of the twenty-mike-mike smoke rounds in there and that takes the place of the forty."

"Another cigar," Sadler yelped. "True. And we can kick that smoke out a thousand yards, not two hundred. As of today the Colt is remanded to the armory. Anybody packing one should get it turned in. If we don't have enough Bull

Pups to go around, which we don't, you'll be drawing an MP-5 sub gun. Any questions?"

"Yeah, when do we get more of the Bull Pups?" Kenneth Ching, quartermaster first class, asked.

"Soon as we can. We'll evaluate any future missions. If it looks like we'll need more long guns instead of sub guns, we'll go back to the Colt. Okay, spread out a little, we'll get the day started off right. Drop and give me fifty good ones, and I mean the chest hitting the fucking floor. Do it."

The chief did it, as well as Murdock and DeWitt, who had come up to the formation. Sadler liked that the officers did all of the training and physical workouts that the EMs did. That absolutely cemented unit loyalty.

Sadler wasn't the first finished with the fifty. When he did finish, he stood and watched the ones slower than he was. "Stand when you're done. The last man finishing gets to do another fifty."

Jaybird caught the honor, and shouted a different swear word between each push-up.

When he was done, he stayed on the deck.

"Next, ladies, we do fifty bent-knee sit-ups. Let's go, now." Sadler dropped to the floor and started the gut-tightening exercise that had always been hard for him. He had to push to beat half of the platoon.

He watched the last ones finish. "Not bad. I beat two more of you than normal. Means we have to do more workouts. We're moving up to a hundred of the big three soon, so you might want to do a little extra training on your own." He looked at the two officers, who had finished their sit-ups.

"Ready, sir?"

"Lead out, Senior Chief."

Sadler led them at a steady trot out of the building and past some structures to the O course. Obstacles at about twenty stations were situated in a square plot of sand. They all knew the spot well.

"Lieutenant, sir, you will be timer at the end, and Commander, you start Alpha Squad off at thirty-second intervals. We haven't been here for a while, but anything over nine minutes will get you another try. Alpha Squad lead out."

Sadler watched the men go. He figured it was the toughest obstacle course in the world. If there was a worse one, he hadn't seen it.

This one had a course record of four minutes and thirty seconds. BUD/S trainees had to do the course in ten minutes or they didn't move onto the next step to becoming a SEAL. Most of his men could do it in from six to eight minutes, Sadler guessed. The course began with the parallel bars, the stump jump, and the low wall. Then came the rope climb and the high wall to go up and over. Next the thirty-foot-long barbed-wire crawl with the wire down to three inches off the sand at one point, the five-story cargo-net climb, the balance logs, the log stack, the rope transfer, and the two consecutive hurdles five and ten feet high. That was the toughest one. The men had to jump for the top of the five-foot hurdle and land on their belly on the crossbar, then muscle up until they stood on the five-foot bar, then lunge for the top of the ten-foot bar four feet away. There were more obstacles, but Sadler figured he'd know them when he saw them this time.

Long ago Sadler had learned that this course ate up upper-body strength for a snack. The best way was to attack each obstacle using as many muscle groups as possible to spread the workload. Those who tried to simply muscle their way through usually didn't finish.

The men groaned, sweated, ran, and climbed. Sadler went after the last man in Alpha Squad, and came out the other end with a time of eight minutes and thirty-two seconds. He would have the times of each man, and hoped that he wouldn't be the slowest. He took over the timing from the lieutenant, and the officer hurried out to take his turn through the course monster.

As each SEAL finished the course he dropped and did twenty-five push-ups, then rolled over and tried to relax.

Sadler checked the men's times. So far Jaybird was the fastest with six minutes and ten seconds. When it ended, Sadler found two of the platoon members were over nine minutes. He'd have a talk with them and suggest they do the course every day for a week on their own time.

Ed DeWitt came boiling in as the last man through, and checked his time. Seven minutes and forty-two seconds. He grunted in surprise and turned away. The O course played no favorites.

Sadler walked over to where most of the SEALs sat on the sand. "On me. I want a column of ducks by squads, let's move it. Yesterday was the only easy day."

"Hoo-ha!" the men bellowed in unison.

The senior chief led them back to the platoon area at a six-minutes-to-the-mile run through the sand. At the home base he barked out the new orders.

"We're going on a little swim. Water's warm, so we'll use only our cammies and the new Draegr Auto-Mix units. I want full combat vests and with the usual ammo and your assigned weapon. Let's do it. In ten minutes we have to be in the water."

The swim with combat gear to the tip of the North Island Navy Air Station went as planned, with Ed DeWitt leading them with the plastic compass board to give them the right direction. They went down to fifteen feet and using visual contact, and two-man buddy lines, the platoon swam at the lieutenant's direction toward the end point. They came up once at the two-mile mark, barely letting their eyes break the surface of the blue Pacific Ocean to check on their angle. DeWitt adjusted his azimuth, and went down and swam the rest of the way to the marker buoy.

They surfaced and gathered around the JG. "Moving back, we'll put Donegan on the board. Donegan, I want you to take us down to forty feet and lead us back to the BUD/S beach. It'll be a good check on the new automatic control Draegr we're breaking in. If anyone has any trouble, yank your buddy's tie-line and get to the surface at once. Everyone understand?"

When no one objected, DeWitt handed the compass board to Donegan, the newest member of the platoon. He and his buddy on the tie-cord swam to the head of the line and promptly duck-dived, and the rest of the platoon followed. The senior chief knew the new rebreather was supposed to calibrate the right amount of oxygen and nitrogen mix in the rebreathed air. If they went to a hundred feet, the computer in the Draegr compensated with more nitrogen. When they came back up to fifteen feet, the mix had the required amount of oxygen. This would be their first full-scale, combat-simulated check on the deeper swim.

The Draegr worked fine at forty feet and the SEALs were pleased with it. When they came up on the home beach, they attacked it in the usual fashion. Two men charged in swimming hard and using a wave to surf in the last few feet, then lay log-still in the surf and sand watching the beach for any enemy activity. When they were sure it was clear, they charged into the dry sand and went into a defensive position with their weapons pointing shoreward. Then the rest of Alpha Squad stormed into the beach the same way, followed by a line of SEALs from Bravo Squad.

Murdock waved at the men and they all stood, now lathered with dry sand on their wet cammies. A black-shoe lieutenant commander came toward them, but stopped just short of the dry sand.

Murdock saw him and ambled that way, not flicking a grain of sand off his face, hands, or uniform. He held the Bull Pup in front of him at port arms, ready to bring it down to fire in the flick of an eyelash.

"Sailor, I'm hunting Lieutenant Commander Murdock. Is this his platoon?"

"It is, Commander. Point of fact. We're not sailors, we're SEALs. A good thing to remember. I'm Murdock. What's happening?"

Ten minutes later the SEALs had washed the sand off their cammies in the surf and run by squads a half mile down the strand to where a strange-looking vehicle stood with a dozen regular Navy officers and men milling around it.

The black-shoed lieutenant commander rode a Humvee down the strand, and arrived only a minute before the SEALs.

A three-striper stepped out of the crowd and grinned at the dripping SEALs.

"Murdock, I don't how you do it, but we have a package

for you. Came air freight this morning at North Island with your name on it. No explanation, just deliver it to you for evaluation. Not to be used on any real operations, but simulated ones are fine. That's all I know. What the hell is happening?"

"A new toy to play with, Commander Eckert."

"This one came under the signature of the CNO," Eckert said with a touch of awe. "You have friends in high places."

"All in a day's work. It's called the combat entry/attack vehicle. We had a hand in the general design and capability, and made some suggestions about what we hoped it would contain."

The commander moved closer. "It's an amphibian, Murdock?"

"Looks that way. That's what we asked for. Is your entourage ready to get back to the regular Navy? We usually don't train with an audience."

Eckert grinned and waved. "All except the two civilians. They sent some engineers along to check with you. You have fun with your toy. It's yours sink or swim, as the saying goes. I'll get these people out of here. Good luck."

The SEALs had dropped to the hard sand in squad formation, since no order had been given otherwise. They watched the regular Navy types get into vehicles and drive up the strand to where they could get out on the road and head out to wherever they came from.

Murdock went back to the SEALs and waved. "Our baby has arrived. We talked about this a year or so ago. Some of you were in on it. We call it the Turtle. What's a turtle?"

"Hell, something we make soup out of at home," Mahanani said. He drew two laughs.

"Yeah, it's also an air-breathing amphibian," Frank Victor said.

"This creature swims?" Jaybird asked. "Underwater or on top?"

"Not do us much good if it were a submarine," Murdock said. "From what I remember, we wanted a rig that could be hoisted onto a destroyer, then launched ten, fifteen miles off target and we move onshore with it, then right up a beach

and toward our land target. A true entry vehicle and, we
hope, with some firepower."

Murdock watched his men. They were interested, eager
to learn more about this new weapon. "Okay, let's move
over and check it out. Nobody inside yet. Be nice to the
civilians. They can't help it. Move out."

4

The two civilians standing beside the Turtle wore brilliant Hawaiian print shirts, Bermuda shorts, and sunglasses. One was tall with a beard, the other one short and wearing a SEALs cap. The SEALs didn't pay any attention to them.

Murdock took his first close look at the machine. It was about twice the size of a rubber duck. Sat on four tires that were twice as wide as most car tires and that looked under-inflated. Reminded Murdock of sand tires on a dune buggy. It had a bow, hull, and closed front end that stopped with a slanted steel panel that extended up two feet where the windshield should be. There were four view slots in it. The whole outside of the rig was made of dull green steel with no sharp corners.

Ed DeWitt came up rubbing his chin. "Damn thing is sixteen feet long and has twin screws aft. Crazy-looking tub. Didn't we ask for a fifty MG up front? Where the hell is that one?"

The tall civilian with the beard came up to Murdock and grinned. "You must be Commander Murdock, the honcho of this outfit. I'm Dunwoody, helped create this mutha."

Murdock took the offered hand. "Mr. Dunwoody, I'll get the men corralled here and you can give us a rundown on the Turtle. Take it from the top, we're in no rush."

Murdock bellowed, and the SEALs came to one side of the Turtle where the civilian stood.

"Gentlemen, at last we have a prototype to show you," said Dunwoody. "Hear you call her the Turtle. Good as any. First some statistics you don't need to remember. She's six-teen feet four inches long from bow to the propeller. No headlights, she's not road-certified. She has a beam of six feet and four, which means she will roll a little in a rough sea.

"Yes, she swims, but leaves little more than eighteen inches of freeboard to present the lowest possible profile to give radar operators fits. She buttons up tight on top and stays dry inside. Room for eight and a driver. She's unsinkable. Has built-in buoyancy panels so she can fill up with water and still stay afloat.

"She has Cadloy steel armor plate overall that protects her against 7.62 rifle fire. Power is a liquid-cooled Cummins V-504 diesel with two hundred and two horsepower. Her top road-cruising speed is fifty-five miles an hour, slightly less than that cross-country. The wheels gyro down when she hits the dirt to give you two-foot-obstacle clearance. Water speed has been pushed up to twelve knots with the least possible engine noise.

"To give you firepower, a turret raises hydraulically just behind the driver's chair. This Turtle is fitted with a .50-caliber machine gun with a three-hundred-and-sixty-degree field of fire. Any questions?"

"Yeah, how does it switch from propeller to wheel power when we get it on land?" Frank Victor asked.

"Good question. It's automatic, all done with sensors on the wheels. Once the wheels hit the sand or shore, the computer signals the drive shaft, which switches in half a second from prop to wheels and you're off and driving."

"Has she got a steering wheel, or do we just drag one foot to turn?" Jaybird cracked.

"Steering wheel, and gearshift for the automatic transmission. Not even a stick. Another thing might surprise you, electronic brakes with brake pedal and all."

"Has this one been wet?" DeWitt asked.

"Took a joyride this morning in the bay and then into the ocean," the shorter civilian with the cap said. "You won't be doing any waterskiing behind her, but overall, we're happy with this machine."

The tall engineer opened a swing-up door on the side of the craft. "Take a look inside," he said.

The SEALs crowded around it and gave their approval. Inside, it wasn't a bare-bones metal can; it had bench seats along both sides, room for gear in back, and a swivel chair for the driver/boatman up front. Just behind him was the raised turret and the handles of a mounted .50-caliber machine gun where a man could stand and see out viewing slots on the side of the turret.

"I need seven men for a demo ride," the bearded civilian said.

"Alpha Squad," Murdock barked. "We've only got seven. Front and center and board. Who drives?"

The tall one was already inside and in the driver's seat as the SEALs stepped on board. They quickly realized they had to bend over so they wouldn't clunk their heads. They looked over the inside closer. It had racks on the short walls to tie down gear, and a large first-aid kit. They sat on the benches, and found them to be wider than usual and with foam padding on them. Murdock took the spot behind the driver and looked at the console of instruments. The dashboard looked more like a car than a boat. It had the usual auto readouts, lights for overheating, low oil, generating, and a fuel gauge. The steering wheel was about two thirds the size of that on a car and heavily padded. The bearded man swiveled his chair around.

"Ready back there?"

He got a chorus of ayes, and pushed a button on the dash to close the side hatch.

"She has hatches on both sides, manually or electrically operated. Most every system on board has a backup. Two power shafts to the twin screws. If one goes out, all the power is automatically switched to the one operating." He looked back. "Ready to move?"

Without waiting for an answer, he pushed a starter and the diesel engine growled into life. He let it warm up for thirty seconds, then pushed the gearshift lever into forward and the Turtle rolled down the slight incline, across the soft sand, and into the receding froth and salt water of the Pacific Ocean.

"We take the breakers head-on," the engineer said.

"We've got enough weight to smash through most of them without much of a surge. This baby has never tipped over, and never filled with water, but we might get some splash through the turret. Here we go."

Murdock bent over and looked out the view slots. They were three inches wide and twice that long and made of inch-thick Plexiglas. He could see a breaker just cresting and crashing down as the Turtle took it head-to-head, breaking through and coming out on the other side.

"I never felt it switch from wheels to screw," Murdock said. He was amazed how quiet it was inside.

The driver bobbed his head. "No way you should know when it switches coming out. More obvious going into land. There's a lurch when the wheels hit and dig in to move you up the beach."

By then they were through the breakers and into the calmer ocean beyond them. The driver touched another control on the panel and the left hatch swung up.

"Hey! It could get wet in here," Luke Howard yelped.

"Usually it won't," the bearded one said. "You can lift the hatches on both sides if you need to for putting firepower on an enemy." He hit the switch again and the other hatch went up.

"Hey, this is living," Jaybird sang out. "Can I check it out for a date I have Saturday night?"

"If you want to pick up the tab," the engineer said. "Cost of this first prototype was a little over three hundred and twenty thousand dollars."

"No sweat, put it on my Visa Card," Jaybird said.

"Cut the speed to five knots and I could do some good trolling out the side here for yellowtail," Senior Chief Sadler said. "I could catch dinner for us on the way home."

After that it was just a boat ride. Murdock signaled for the driver to take them back to shore.

When the Turtle came back, DeWitt took his squad out on a run while Murdock talked with the engineer.

"How long do we get to keep it and who do we send our design changes and suggestions to?"

"That would be me," the shorter man with the cap said.

He handed Murdock a card. "Bill Spencer. E-mail me any suggestions that you might have. About how long you get to keep it, all we have to do is have your CO sign off on some papers I have and it's yours. We have another prototype at the factory we'll work with. We want you to give this some field evaluation. The specs say no enemy-fire missions, but who is going to know? We want you to check out everything within two months so we can move ahead. We have a contract to build ten of them. They are designed to work in pairs, with transport for a full platoon."

Murdock grinned. "Sounds good. You have an operator's manual?"

"Two of them in my bag back by the gate."

"Good. We'll also want you to train two of our men in each squad to be the drivers. Eventually we'll want every man in the platoon able to drive the rigs."

"We can give your men all the training they need in two hours. From then on, it's your baby."

A Humvee boiled up and stopped abruptly ten feet from the two men. Commander Dean Masciareli steamed out of the passenger's seat and marched over to Murdock.

"Why in hell wasn't I informed that this vehicle was on base?"

"Just came, Commander. This is Engineer Bill Spencer from the factory. He's about ready to take you on a private demonstration drive."

The Turtle came sliding through a breaker, coasted up to the sand, and the wheels dug in and it half-floated, half-rolled on in with the surge of sandy water; then the wheels took over and without a pause or hesitation, it rolled up the dry sand to the top of the slope and stopped. SEALs popped out both sides of the craft.

Masciareli seemed to cool down as he watched the Turtle come in. "Damn, that was smooth, Spencer. It ever been stuck?"

"Yes, sir, once in some thick mud holes where we pushed it, the wheels couldn't dig us out. That was a manufactured hazard, and it won't find them often."

"Mr. Spencer, why don't you take the commander for a ride?" said Murdock.

"Do you have time, Commander?" Spencer asked.

"Well, I had an appointment. Think I can squeeze this in. I hear we have this as a permanent part of our operation here on base."

Spencer said that was true as the two walked away and stepped into the Turtle.

Murdock motioned to DeWitt, who came up. "When they come back, get Victor and one volunteer and have them checked out on driving the Turtle. Keep them on land for a while, then work out to sea. The rest of us will go on a little hike. Make your pick."

DeWitt looked at his squad and picked Franklin. He sent the rest of Bravo Squad over to Murdock.

"Time we get back to work, SEALs," Murdock said. "We'll do six miles down the sand and back. I want a seven-minute-mile pace. Bradford, lead us out in a column of ducks. Let's move it."

Five minutes later, well down the beach, Murdock ran to the head of the line.

"We're not out to break the four-minute mile, Bradford. Slow it down and maybe the guys won't kill you."

"Aye, aye, Commander. I'm slowing down."

They used the wet sand for easier footing, and made it to the far end of the Navy Communication Station antennas where it met the Imperial Beach city border. When they came to the turnaround, Murdock took the con and led the way back up the beach. He moved the pace up faster.

Halfway back to the O course they met DeWitt and the two Turtle drivers slogging through the sand toward them. Murdock waved at the trio and kept moving.

Back at the platoon area, Murdock had the men fall out and clean and oil their weapons. "We'll cancel the rubber duck drills, Senior Chief. We're as good as we're going to get on them, and we might just not have so much use for them in the future. I need to talk to the commander about where we house the Turtle and what kind of security we need on it. I should be back in a half hour."

Twenty minutes later, Jaybird had his H & K MP-5 bright, clean, and oiled. He put his gear in his locker and found Sadler in the platoon office.

"Senior Chief, remember I told you about that community service work I'm doing, coaching Little League?"

Sadler looked up with a frown.

"This is Thursday and it's practice day," Jaybird said. "The team has a practice at 1630. I sure would like to get over to the field, if there isn't anything pressing here."

"Did you beat me on the O course today?"

"I didn't see the times, Senior Chief."

Sadler grunted. He remembered the time when a SEAL ate, drank, and pissed SEAL life twenty-four hours a day. "Yeah, the old man said we should encourage this sort of thing. Take off now, but be back here for 0800 tomorrow."

"Right, Senior Chief. I'll be here. Thanks."

Sadler watched him leave. Jaybird was one of the best men in the platoon, and had been around the longest. He had avoided getting shot up too bad to get discharged and too little to die. The senior chief shrugged. Jaybird would be on the line when they needed him. He looked at the training chart for tomorrow. Yeah, that workout would be no problem. What about tonight? If Sylvia didn't have anything planned, he was going to polish up the trumpet and sit in with the Dixie Five. They were playing at some dive in Chula Vista. Sadler grinned just thinking about it.

5

Little League field
Coronado, California

Jaybird wore shorts, T-shirt, and a baseball cap with the bill in front, and shook his head when a ball from the coach rolled right past the shortstop.

"Willy, you run over in front of the ball, then bend over and reach for it. You bend your right knee and it's right in front of the path of the ball. Then if you miss the ball with your glove, it hits your knee and stops. You grab it with your right hand and throw it to first or second."

"Show me," Willy said. He was eight years old, had played one season in the Caps league, and moved up to the minors. He was the worst shortstop Jaybird had ever seen. Jaybird waved at the other coach, Harley Albertson, to hit him a grounder. Jaybird got in front of the ball, bent down with his right foot and leg in the path of the ball, and lifted up his glove at the last minute and let the ball hit his shoe. He grabbed the ball and flipped it to the second baseman, who made a stab at it and missed.

"See, Willy. If you don't get the ball in your glove, it still is stopped nearby and you can grab it and throw. If you don't almost kneel down, the ball will go through your legs into left field."

"So?" Willy asked, his sharp brown eyes challenging.

"Then, Willy, I'll have to tell your father that you can't play shortstop, and you'll have to go to right field, where nobody hits the ball and you can grow roots waiting out there for the inning to end."

Willy grinned. "Hey, I don't want to grow no roots. Let me try again."

Jaybird moved back twenty feet and rolled the baseball toward Willy. He had to move only six feet to one side. His knee came down and he missed the ball with his glove, but it hit his leg and stopped. He grabbed it and threw it to the second baseman, who was so surprised to see it coming that he threw up his glove and caught it.

"Good play," Jaybird called. "Good play, Willy, you to Joe. Now we're getting somewhere."

Jaybird watched the rest of the practice. It was before the season started, they hadn't had their first game yet, and they were still a long way from being a team. Eight-year-olds were simply not that coordinated. Some of them did well. But Jaybird had yet to see a ball hit to the outfield that was caught. Their pitcher had trouble getting the ball all the way to the catcher without bouncing it. Jaybird grinned. Still, it was a load of fun. His kind of baseball. There were two other coaches, both older than he was. One was the pitcher's father, Harley Albertson, the head coach. He was short and pudgy, wore glasses, a baseball cap, suit pants, and a white shirt. He always came directly from his banker's job to the practices. He sweated like an overworked horse, and was given to making up words to use in place of swear words.

"You gimbleshakled marsnest, Phil, you missed that easy grounder." He was gentle and easy with the kids, and they seemed to try harder when he made suggestions to them.

The other coach was Rusty Ingles, an insurance salesman in his late thirties, married but with no kids. He was a slender six feet tall, with thinning red hair and lots of freckles. He knew baseball rules inside out, and said he'd played for a junior college back East somewhere for two years. He handled mostly the outfielders, trying to teach them how to judge a fly ball and then to catch it. He wasn't having anything like good results.

Jaybird had lettered in baseball three years at his high school, playing shortstop, and loved the game. He followed the Detroit Tigers, not the Padres in San Diego.

"Good throw," Jaybird yelled as the third baseman gloved

a slow roller off Coach Albertson's bat and threw it all the way to first base. It arrived after only one hop. "Way to go, Pete. Way to throw, guy. Keep up the good work."

"The infield is your job," Coach Albertson had told Jaybird the first day when he found out he'd played in high school. "Show them how to play the positions and how to field and throw the ball. That's all there is to it. I'll run the pitchers and catchers and try to teach these little wonders how to hit the ball." It was the first year for most of the boys to try to hit a thrown ball. Last year those who played had been able to hit the ball off a T-Ball stand in front of the plate.

This was their third practice, and the coaches were still moving players around. First they asked what position each boy wanted to play. So far they had no girls on the team. Jaybird was glad about that. Nobody wanted to be catcher. Coach Albertson drafted one kid who could throw pretty well. After the second practice he liked it.

"Okay, infield practice," Jaybird called. "Rusty will hit some ground balls and I'll call which base you throw it to. First round will all be throws to the first baseman. Okay, Rusty, hit some."

Rusty's grin popped out, and he made a vicious swing at the ball he tossed up. He missed it by a yard. The boys all howled with glee. Then he began batting the ball gently directly at the players in turn. Jaybird nodded as Rusty hit the ball almost exactly where he wanted to. All the boys liked Rusty. He was never harsh with them, and half the time told them jokes to get a point across.

He hit a slow roller to the second baseman playing between first and second. The boy ran toward the ball, missed it, and threw his glove on the ground, then ran for the ball and threw it toward first base. It missed the first baseman by ten feet.

"No problem, Joey, you'll get the next one," Jaybird called.

Twenty minutes later they called a halt to the fielding and went up to the plate to practice hitting. Coach Albertson tossed the balls in easily for the hitters. Rusty watched for a minute, then headed for the rest rooms. They were city-built, made of concrete block, so they were cold and spartan. Jaybird felt a calling as well and walked to the facility. He had just started around the double turn into the boys' bathroom, which eliminated the need for doors, when he heard a boy yell from inside.

"Hey, don't do that," the boy called.

Jaybird frowned and edged around the concrete-block wall so he could see inside the small room. Joey, the second baseman, stood near the urinal with his pants down. He backed away from Coach Rusty Ingles.

"I just want to see where the ball hit your leg," Coach Ingles said, squatting beside the boy.

"Told you it didn't hurt me," Joey said.

"Let me check." Coach Ingles moved forward, caught the boy's leg, and rubbed it; then his hand moved up to Joey's crotch and fondled it.

"No!" Joey shouted, and jumped back.

"Hey, that didn't hurt, did it?" Coach Ingles said. "Hey, I bet it felt good. Look what it did for me." Coach Ingles's back was to Jaybird then, but he could see the man unzip his pants. Joey jerked up his pants and ran for the door. Jaybird stepped away from it and around to the side of the rest room. Coach Rusty didn't leave the bathroom for five minutes.

Jaybird scowled. What the hell was going on? Was it what it had looked like? Rusty Ingles was a pedophile? Had he been bothering other boys on the team? Before Jaybird could think it through, Coach Albertson called.

"Hey, Jaybird. Get your fanny over here. I can't do this all by myself. Both of you vanished on me. You pitch some soft ones. I need to do some batting coaching here or we'll be last in the league again this year."

Jaybird pitched underhanded for a half hour, and then the practice was over. Rusty bailed out early, saying his wife had a special event planned for that night and he had to get home. Jaybird helped the boys put away the equipment in the big bat bags, and then loaded them in Coach Albertson's van. Jaybird was trying to decide if he should tell Coach

Albertson when they were done, but before he could the
man waved and drove away. It was Jaybird's turn to wait
at the diamond until the last boy's parents came to pick him
up. Joey had left, and didn't seem affected by what Jaybird
had seen. So what should he do? Call the cops? Cause a big
flap in the league? Accuse Rusty privately and tell him to
quit coaching this or any other team of small boys or he'd
wind up floating facedown in Glorietta Bay?

Jaybird thought about it on the way back to his apartment.
He lived only ten minutes from the field. Everything in Coronado was close at hand. He could take Ingles out in a half
a second if it came to that. How did he keep it from happening again somewhere else? The only way was to get
Ingles convicted as a pedophile. Then he would be on record
and wherever he moved, the cops would know he was a sex
offender. Yeah, easy to say, but how to get evidence good
enough to stand up in court?

He turned around and drove back to the bathroom and
checked it out. Yes, it would work. Six months ago he had
bought a small video camera. Hadn't used it much. He
looked at the overhead. No ceiling, just an open area and
beams to the roof. Over a small storage area he found a
place where he could put the camera and it would record
everything that went on.

All he had to do was get to practice early in two days,
plant the camera, and turn it on. It would run on the battery
for two hours. Then he'd pick it up and see what he had on
the tape. With any luck Rusty Ingles would try it again with
a different boy. It was an ideal setup for Ingles. The kids
would be afraid to tell anyone, and he could take advantage
of them. If this didn't work, Jaybird had about decided he
would break Ingles's leg, and then maybe an arm, to con-
vince him to stay away from the kids.

After training on Thursday, Jaybird set up the camera a
half hour before practice started. He turned it on and went
out to the diamond. Twice he saw Rusty Ingles go to the
bathroom. Each time one of the boys was already in the
small building. Practice was just about over, and Jaybird was
ready to go pick up the video camera, when his beeper went

off. He read the message. "Alert. We ship out in three hours."

The SEALs had a job. He yelled at Albertson that he had to go, he didn't know when he'd be back. Active duty. Albertson knew about his wild schedule and waved.

"Good luck, man. Stay safe and come back. We need you."

Jaybird ran for his car. He was only ten minutes from SEALs headquarters on the Coronado strand. He was the last one to report in.

Senior Chief Petty Officer Sadler growled at them as they gathered around him.

"Oh, yeah, we've got one. Orders are for your desert cammies. Two pair, regular weapons. We've got seven Bull Pups for this run, so they will be spread around. We'll want the MGs and the rest of you come with MP-5's. Your usual mix of goodies for your vests. We will have available all the combat weapons, munitions, and supplies we need on the other end. That's all I can tell you now. Get cracking. We fly out of North Island in two hours and twenty minutes."

"What plane?" Jaybird asked.

"Like to throw you each in the rear seat of an F-14 and get you moving at Mach two-point-five. But we can't do that. You'll be in the usual fast-delivery aircraft, the Gulfstream II. Slam us along at five hundred and eighty-one miles per hour max, cruise at forty thousand. Nice and quiet up there. Now move it."

Everyone was medically cleared to go. Lam swore up and down that his arm wound from Sierra Leone had healed and his left leg was damned near back to normal. He demonstrated for the senior chief and walked, then ran without any limp. Everyone knew it must hurt Lam, but they also knew he'd never admit it and get canceled out on this mission.

They were twenty minutes early getting to North Island, a ride in the Navy bus of about six miles from their home base. Lieutenant Commander Blake Murdock sat the SEALs down on the tarmac to wait for the final fueling on the plane. His grin spread all over his face.

"Want to tell you that we won't have the JG to kick around any more. Ed DeWitt's papers came through today. He's now officially a full lieutenant, and I want you deep divers to show him proper respect."

"Hooooooo-yah!" the SEALs shouted in unison.

"Where is the lieutenant leading us this time?" Kenneth Ching asked.

Lieutenant DeWitt held the twin silver bars in his right hand, the railroad tracks glistening in the bright sunshine. He looked at them, then up at his men.

"We know where, and something of the why. We'll be getting a printout on the plane with more about the what. We're going to merry old England. Our destination is London, to a military airport just south of London actually, near the town of Crawley. Why? This is now a top-secret, ultra-secret operation. The British people don't know about it. The American people don't know about it. I doubt if more than five people in Washington, D.C., know about it. But we are legal. The CNO called Commander Masciareli about four hours ago, and told him the assignment. He called the master chief, who called me."

"So what's it all about?" Lam asked.

"Big trouble. Really, really big trouble. The kind of trouble the Western capitals have been fearing might come someday. Well, it's here. Some Islamic militants or some extremist Palestinians have smuggled a nuclear warhead into London. We know where it is, on board a hijacked mid-sized Japanese freighter now anchored in the middle of London's harbor."

"Somebody wants us to go in and get back the boom-boom?" Jaybird asked.

"Precisely," Lieutenant DeWitt said. "However, they don't want it to go boom. That would spoil a lot of afternoon English teas in London."

"What about the hotshot SAS?" Bill Bradford asked.

"They have requested us to come in on a joint operation," Murdock said. "They will let us handle the water end of it, and anything else that we work out."

"Time," DeWitt said. He pointed to the plane that stood

with the passenger door open. The SEALs stood, moved into two squad ranks, and jogged to the business jet and walked on board. The Gulfstream is a large executive jet used as a military VIP transport. The Grumman Aircraft/Aerospace plane has a crew of three and carries nineteen passengers in first-class-type seats. Two Rolls-Royce engines kick out 11,400 pounds of static thrust. It has a ceiling of 43,000 feet and can take jumps of 3,712 miles on one drink of fuel.

"Oh, yeah, this is the way to fly," Paul Jefferson said, easing his two hundred pounds into the luxury seat. "Beats a Gooney Bird or a COD Greyhound any day."

As they settled into the seats, a dress-blues Navy lieutenant commander in a regulation but tight skirt came out of the cockpit area. She was trim and more than pretty, with soft brown hair framing her face, showing high cheekbones and bright green eyes. She frowned a moment, then nodded.

"They told me I'd have a full load. Usually I get a better-dressed class of passengers." She chuckled. "Hey, I'm kidding. I know what you SEALs do, and I'm proud to be a part of this mission. No, I don't know what it is, and I don't want to know. We take off in two minutes. We tried to get Navy box lunches for you for your evening mess, but we couldn't. So the Hotel Del Coronado stepped in and provided you with twenty dinners, served on china. So don't drop anything. We'll stop in New York for fuel and take off right after we're topped off. Any questions?"

"I don't suppose a phone number would be available?" someone piped up from the back.

The pilot smiled. "The only one I give out is my husband's."

Half the SEALs groaned.

"Welcome aboard. If I can find some tailwinds upstairs, we should hit New York in five hours." She went back into the cabin and seconds later, the jet engines revved up, the chocks were pulled away, and the sleek jet rolled toward the takeoff runway.

A half hour later, the crew chief, a yeoman second class, pressed Colt Franklin into helping him, and they served the Hotel Del Coronado dinners: three-quarter-pound top sirloin steak with all the side dishes on huge platters with stainless-steel silverware.

"Why don't we eat on this airline all the time?" Vinnie Van Dyke yelped.

After the meal, the yeoman cleared the dishes; then Murdock took the floor. "We don't know what we'll do on this one. My guess is they want us to move in and take down the freighter so we can free the captive nuclear bomb."

"How big is it?" Miguel Fernandez asked. "I mean, is it a warhead out of an ICBM like we worked before, or is it a stand-alone? Maybe they bought it from China, so it could be a large thing."

"We don't know about any of that," DeWitt said. "All we know is that the British Prime Minister called the President. He called his Secretary of Defense, who called the CNO, and we're in business."

"Grappling hooks up the side of the freighter?" Tracy Donegan asked.

"Could be," Murdock said. "Or we could go up the side out of a rubber duck with hand and foot magnets."

"I'd guess there is some kind of a quid pro quo that goes along with the terrorists not setting off the bomb," Senior Chief Sadler said.

"True," DeWitt said. "They want Israel to agree to the immediate evacuation of all Jews from the West Bank and the Gaza Strip, both civilian settlers and Israeli military."

"They don't want much, do they?" Jack Mahanani asked. "Just rip out twenty years of colonization by the Israelis. It'll never happen."

"Trade that for, say, three million dead Brits?" Frank Victor asked. "That's quite a price to pay."

"But it's second-hand blackmail," Luke Howard said. "They threaten England, and tell them to tell Israel to pull out their people or the Brits get nuked. Doesn't make logical sense. Why would the Israeli government react to a second-hand threat? Now, if the bomb was in Haifa Harbor, it would be a direct threat to Israel."

Murdock spoke up. "We don't have to sweat the politics. All we have to do is find the damned bomb, throw a lead blanket around it so it can't be triggered by remote control, and turn it over to the Brits, who will de-fang it."

"Sure, but then what?" Jaybird asked. "While the threat is there, the Israelis and the Brits can't lift a rifle against the Arabs. But as soon as the bomb is grabbed and the threat is gone, you think the English and the Jews are going to sit on their hands? They'll go after the Arabs like wildfire. The killing fields will be bloody red."

"Not our concern," DeWitt said. "We do our job and when it's done, we're out of there."

"Maybe," Jaybird said. "What if Mossad and M-6 ask us for just a bit more help in taking down some of the Arab militants?"

"Unlikely," Murdock said. "But, like everything else in this old world, it's an uncertain place, strange times, and you can't really count on knowing how any of our little explorations are going to turn out."

messenger to the Israeli government at exactly the same time.

"The SAS was assigned the responsibility of eliminating this threat to the heart of London. We know of the SEALs' skills in and around the water, and we asked for your help. Our job is to capture the ship and seize the bomb before it can be triggered. The message, which has not been released to the public, warns us that the Arab men with the bomb are ready to sacrifice their lives at any time, and will detonate the bomb on orders even if they can't get away. Commander, your thoughts on the situation."

Murdock introduced his team by last name only and with no rank; then he stood.

"Gentlemen, this is a problem that has haunted the Western world since the advent of Arab terrorism forty years ago," said Murdock. "Now it's a reality. I'm sure in the terrorists' demands there is some warning that if any attempts are made to attack or try to take control of the Japanese freighter, the bomb will be set off immediately. Standard terrorist rhetoric.

"Still, we must take down the ship, and do it quickly before they have a chance to trigger the bomb. There are several factors to consider.

"One, that there actually is a live bomb on board that can be triggered by the terrorists.

"Two, there is a live bomb on board, but the terrorists have not been trusted by the Arab extremists to know how to trigger it.

"Three, that there is no bomb. But we can't assume that it is a bluff.

"If we knew which situation we're facing, it would be simpler. Since we don't, we have to consider that there is a bomb, it is live, and the terrorists know how to trigger it. With that factored in, it means we have to move swiftly, aggressively, and we must win the fight quickly or simply die in the process along with millions of residents and visitors to London."

Captain Brainridge nodded. "Yes, Commander, we agree. We must take the threat seriously, and consider it a viable bomb that can be exploded by the terrorists on demand. So, what's our first step?"

Murdock looked at his team. "We have had no advance planning on this one. If we may now?"

Brainridge waved his permission.

"Suggestions," Murdock said.

"How about a chopper landing," Jaybird said. "Lots of open space on most freighters over holds where a bird could come down and dump out thirty men. We spread out and capture the ship and the bomb."

"If the bird couldn't land, we could rope down thirty of us from a chopper in sixty to ninety seconds," Lam said.

"Up the sides with grappling hooks and ropes about 0100 sounds better," DeWitt said. "This way, no noise to alert the Arabs. A chopper is going to be a warning even before we could get on deck, and the Arabs would have every man ready with submachine guns for us and RPGs for the choppers."

"We could use limpet mines on the hull and sink her into the harbor bottom," Senior Chief Sadler said. "Even so, they could trigger the bomb as she was sinking or even when it was underwater. I withdraw the suggestion."

Murdock looked at the English captain. "How long is the freighter, Captain?"

"About a hundred and twenty meters, about four hundred feet long."

"Could we consider an airdrop with the square steerable chutes we all use? It should be easy to hit a four-hundred-foot-long ship that's about sixty or seventy feet wide."

The SAS men at once huddled, whispering. A moment later Captain Brainridge looked up.

"Commander, we like the idea. We do bull's-eye skydiving for practice. No reason why a hundred percent of our team couldn't hit the cargo hatches of that ship at night. Almost no wind at night. She has running and navigation lights on, plus some floods to help keep her safe from boarders. A perfect target. You brought your chutes?"

"No," DeWitt said.

"No problem, we can provide them. All of your people are jump-certified?"

"More combat jumps than we want to remember," Murdock said. "No problem there. How many men? We can put sixteen on board."

"We'll jump sixteen as well, giving us thirty-two. We'll jump by twos so we don't clobber the deck with bodies. One pass with two planes should do it. Jump from about a thousand feet so we can get down fast."

"Sounds good," Murdock said. "I'd think that speed is the most important factor here. Do we go out early tomorrow morning to hit the ship about 0100?"

Captain Brainridge nodded. "We have carte blanche from the Defense Ministry. Anything we want. How are you on weapons?"

"We have our long guns, but probably could use some more sub guns, H & K MP-5's if they are available, plus more ammo. Senior Chief Sadler can get together with your ordnance man and work it out. Can we fly out of here?"

"I'll get in two jump planes for sixteen each. No sweat."

"Lead blanket," Murdock said. "Do you have available a lead blanket that your nuke men use to mask bombs? The lead keeps out any stray or intentional signals to trigger a bomb. As soon as we nail the bomb, we shroud it with the blanket to prevent some bad-ass from setting it off."

"Yes, capital idea. We'll get two brought in. After we secure the bomb the lead blankets will be brought in by a chopper to us."

"Do you have a man who can defuse a nuke?" Murdock asked.

"No. We should have one along. I'll see if there is one who is jump-qualified. If not we'll have to ferry him on board by chopper with the lead blankets as soon as we secure the ship and capture the bomb."

"Good. Have him close by on shore in the chopper waiting for your radio signal. Timing here could be critical. We have no idea how they might trigger the bomb. It could be done with a remote-control radio signal of some kind."

"We'll have it covered," Brainridge said.

"Do we have a schematic of the ship?" Murdock asked. "Where might they hold the nuke?"

"We've talked to the company in Tokyo. They faxed us some schematics, but they don't help much. There are no locking compartments on board. Mostly open holds. They said the bomb could be kept in the forward crew quarters."

"If any of the crew are left, they might help us find the bomb once we take down the ship," Murdock said. "We have a man who speaks Japanese."

"That should cover it, Commander," Captain Brainridge said. "Send your man with our ordnance expert for your supplies. Let's get together again at 1800 and see what else we need to do."

"Right here?" Murdock asked.

"Right here."

"What about the chutes? You must have expert packers."

"The best in the world. We've never had a chute fail on us," Captain Brainridge said. "I'll put in an order for thirty-two chutes to be brought here. We usually keep over a hundred ready to go in our stockroom."

"Good. If you people use them, we can trust them too. How can we keep in touch?"

The captain signaled, and one of his men brought over two cell phones. "They're mates. My phone number is on the back, and I've got the number of your phone on the back of mine. These will keep us in touch anywhere on the base and for a wide area."

"Good, we might just need them. See you back here at 1800."

Murdock walked out of the room, and saw Senior Chief Sadler shaking hands with one of the SAS men. They headed in a different direction, evidently to work out the need for weapons and ammo.

Back in the assembly section of the barracks building, Don Stroh had shown up with pictures of the ship in the harbor in London.

It was big, but not one of the huge ones.

"Too many men," Ed DeWitt said. "We can't have thirty-two men parachuting into that one small area all at the same time. We'll be clobbering each other, hitting cranes and hatch covers. Why don't we let the SAS chute in and we go up the side on ropes. Got me a bad feeling about all those chutes in that little deck."

"That's it," Murdock said. "As soon as he said thirty-two, something started rattling around in my head. I couldn't pin it down. Yeah, you're right. Let me see if this phone works."

They talked on the phone for five minutes. The captain agreed that his men would parachute in and Murdock and his men would come up the sides of the ship from the water. Captain Brainridge could supply a quiet running boat for them that would hold the platoon. They would have radios in the plane and in the boat to coordinate their arrival. The SAS would drop in as soon as the SEALs were up the side of the boat. They both would take down the ship and find the bomb.

Murdock grunted and put down the phone.

"I don't know, it doesn't seem right. Why would the terrorists let us know where they are with the bomb, and then just sit there waiting for something to happen? Doesn't seem reasonable to me."

DeWitt frowned. "They've only been anchored in that position for less than twenty-four hours. Their ultimatum is only twelve hours old."

Murdock lifted his brows and shook his head. "Hey, I'm probably just tilting at fantasy windmills. When I see the blades going around, then it'll be time to get concerned. What else do we have to do to get ready for that climb up the side of that freighter?"

Murdock found the sedan the SAS had left for his use, and the driver took him as close as they could get to the Japanese ship in the harbor that they would try to take down. Murdock got on his phone and called the SAS captain.

"Brainridge, Murdock. We don't need your boat. We'll swim out to the ship underwater to insure surprise. We have that gear, rebreathers, and we can take what we need in drag bags. We will need a bus to get us to our PD by 0030. Figure about fifteen minutes to swim out, then up the side and be on board by 0100, when you and your guys will drop in for a visit."

"You're full of surprises, Murdock, but I like this plan the best. That way no snoopy lookout could see the boat and give the alarm. Yes, it works. I'll have a bus for you at your quarters at 2300. Everything else going on plan?"

"So far, so good, Captain. See you at 1800."

The SEALs took the change in plans in stride. To them it didn't matter how they arrived at the ship, just so they were undetected. Then nobody got shot going up the side of the ship.

Murdock, DeWitt, Sadler, Jaybird, and Lam filed into the conference room five minutes before 1800. The SAS team was there, but the general and the two British civilians were not. Don Stroh waved at them, but didn't talk. Murdock wondered why he was so distant on this mission. Maybe he'd gotten chewed out by his boss.

Captain Brainridge carried the meeting. "Any more changes? We still go in at 0100. That's exactly seven hours from now. Did you get the weapons and ammo you need?"

"We did, Captain," Senior Chief Sadler said. "We also drew six lines eighty feet long with grappling hooks. We're ready."

"The bus has arrived and the driver knows the route to the ship," Lieutenant DeWitt said. "We'll leave a half hour earlier than suggested to give plenty of time for him to get lost once."

"Our equipment has been checked and rechecked," Murdock said. "We're ready to go. Any word of change of plans from the politicians?"

"No, it's still in our lap. There was another radio message that indicated the Arabs are getting restless. They want some action before dark tomorrow night."

"We can guarantee them that," Murdock said. "Oh, if by any chance we get on deck before you do and we run into a firefight, we'll give you a red flare so you can hold off until we get the deck clear and safe."

"Sounds good," Captain Brainridge said. "No fun dropping into cross fire on a restricted area like that one." He looked around. "If nothing else, I'd suggest a short sleep period before you motor out. Never know when we'll get any more sleep."

The captain stood, and the rest of the men came to their feet. The captain and his SAS men walked out.

Stroh drifted over to Murdock. "This is a nasty one. You are totally covert on this one. Only four or five men in Washington know that you're here or know about the nuke blackmail. I'd bet not even your father knows, Murdock."

"Might be a bad bet. He has sources all over town." Murdock looked at the CIA handler. "You know anything more about this? Is Israel set to move on the Arab extremists once this mess is over?"

Stroh shook his head. "Honestly I don't know. I'd bet my last Microsoft stock that they will move viciously, but I have no intel on it."

Murdock waved the group out the door. "Good idea about having a sleep period. Senior Chief, get the men down for three hours. Then we make final prep and we'll get moving."

"Aye, aye, sir. Three hours. Consider it done, sir."

For the SEALs a sleep period like this didn't necessarily mean going to sleep. Anyone who wanted to could. It did mean no talking, no singing, no music. Contemplation, relaxation, and meditation were encouraged.

Senior Chief Sadler wanted to call his wife. He'd only had a quick talk with her before they left Coronado. He'd caught her between customers at her real-estate sales job in Coronado. It wasn't fair to her, all of this sudden activation, the long training runs and then being gone so much. He'd promised her that after his twenty-five they would open their own real-estate agency and he'd learn the business. Hell, a guy couldn't keep up with these damn kid SEALs until he was fifty-five. Admin maybe. He wanted to keep working with the SEALs even if he wasn't on a team. He had no desire to go back to the black-shoe Navy. He'd done his time there. Before he knew it, his wrist alarm went off. It was time to get ready. In two hours they could be in the middle of a huge gun battle. Oh, yeah, once more into the fray. He loved it!

7

London, England

Sixteen SEALs from the Third Platoon of SEAL Team Seven slid into the water a quarter of a mile from the *Sendai Maru*. When Murdock was sure all were in the water and had their buddy cords tied around their wrists, they submerged to fifteen feet and followed their leader on a compass course directly for the Japanese-flag freighter.

Murdock counted the strokes. He felt a small boat race over the water above him; then when he figured he was within fifty yards of the ship, he surfaced cautiously, letting only his eyes break the surface of the water. Yes, there she was, the target freighter. She had lights on, more than usual, but the near side was dark from the waterline up the side thirty feet to the rail. Murdock tugged his buddy cord and Jaybird came up beside him. Soon there were sixteen faces looking at the ship. Murdock waved down, and they vanished under the cold waters of London's harbor to complete the swim to the black side of the *Sendai Maru*.

Murdock felt the rough steel side of black paint, and moved to the surface. Three SEALs were already there. Luke "Mountain" Howard had one of the grappling hooks out of his drag bag, and tied the loose end of the line to his wrist. Murdock knew that throwing a grappling hook that high when a man was in the water was a tough assignment. They had practiced this in San Diego Harbor on several friendly freighters. The secret was the next two largest men came alongside the thrower, and each caught a foot for him to stand on, then treaded water like crazy as the thrower made his try.

Jack Mahanani and Bill Bradford felt the lunge upward as Howard threw the hook, driving them two feet deeper into the water. They came up a moment later to see the result. Howard was swearing softly and pulling the forty feet of line up from the bottom of the harbor with the grappling hook attached.

On the third try the hook went over the rail and held Howard's 250 pounds. Jaybird was the first one up the rope. He left his drag bag with flotation collar with another SEAL, and went up hand over hand, walking up the steel side as he powered to the top. When Jaybird was halfway up, Ken Ching went up the rope.

The trio of SEALs tried another grappling hook ten feet down from the first one. Howard made this one hang up on his second try. Murdock told them that two would be enough. With the two it took the SEALs four minutes for everyone to climb the rope and get on board. They tied their drag bags with flotation devices onto the lines they had climbed, and left them next to the freighter's side.

Jaybird went over the rail and flattened on the deck. He saw four lights on this part of the freighter. A huge crane stood to one side; beyond that he could see four hatch covers. He saw no guards, lookouts, or gunmen. He prowled toward the bow of the craft and the superstructure that rose from the deck near the middle of the ship. Where were the damned Arabs?

Behind him he heard muted sounds as the other SEALs came over the rail. Murdock surged up beside Jaybird as he looked around a second crane.

"Where are they?" Murdock asked.

Jaybird shrugged. The two SEALs charged along fifty feet of deck and ran hard for their objective, the bridge. They found the first door unlocked. They went through it silently, their MP-5's ready. No one was in the small room. It had steps leading upward and they took them soundlessly.

Three minutes later Murdock and Jaybird found the bridge deserted. They made a sweep of the captain's cabin directly below and four more cabins. Nobody. Where were the Arabs?

Murdock ran back to the long deck. He used the Motorola, the SEALs' personal communication radio that was good for about two miles.

"Check in when you have your objective. We found nobody on the bridge. Has anyone seen any Arabs?"

"None here," Van Dyke said. "Nobody in forward crew quarters."

Four more men checked in with negative answers.

Murdock heard a plane. He took out the second radio and keyed it. "Flight SAS, this is Deckhand. Abort. I say abort jump. We are in place and so far haven't found a single Arab or Japanese crewman on board. I say again, abort the jump."

The radio sputtered, then came on clear. "Did you say abort? Murdock? Abort? We're ready. No Arabs? Christ, where did they go? Where did the fucking nuclear bomb go?"

"Sorry to spoil your fun, but no use taking the risk of a jump here. This is a washout. It must have been a decoy. Now we really have to find the bomb."

It took them twenty minutes, but at last they found the Japanese crew. They had been locked in a forward hold, but had been given a supply of food and water. The Japanese shouted and screamed in delight when they were released.

Ken Ching was soon with them and getting the story. There were twenty-four in the crew. They went back to their usual posts and positions and were all smiles. They even lowered a boat with a motor and ferried the SEALs, and the floating drag bags they had tied to the lines, back to shore.

Murdock used the cell phone and called for the bus to come and pick them up. He talked to Captain Brainridge on the cell, and Brainridge said he'd get the bus to them.

"What the hell happened?" Brainridge railed.

"We got snookered, outfoxed. The Japanese said that there was no bomb on board, never had been. The Arabs boarded their ship at sea ten miles off the harbor when their own boat was sinking. Then they took over and made the captain sail the ship into port and tie up at an anchorage rather than at the dock where she was expected.

"Ching said the Arabs told the crew that they would leave before it was daylight, but the crew would be locked up. The Arabs said someone would rescue them within two or three days."

It was just after 0300 when the SEALs got back to the small military base near Crawley. Captain Brainridge and his three SAS men were waiting for them.

"No wonder our intel men with hundred-power telescopes didn't see any Arabs on board the ship," Brainridge thundered. "They weren't there. Now our huge problem is trying to find out where they and the fucking nuke bomb are."

Murdock slumped in a chair and nodded. "Oh, I agree, absolutely agree. You must have some kind of a clue. The crew said they never saw anything that could have been a bomb. In the small boat that was sinking, they saw only a few suitcases, which the men salvaged before the boat sank. No bomb."

Brainridge sank into a chair and shook his head. "I'm not used to this kind of shit. Usually I get an assignment, a mission, and I go and do it and come home and take a week's furlough. This hide-and-seek is no fun."

"Did you report our raid to your Home Office or whoever is in charge of this?"

"I did. They yelled at me for five minutes, then apologized for ten minutes. Then they asked me how we find the bomb in a town with seven million souls?"

"Hope you had some suggestions," Murdock said.

"Actually I didn't. They said to just hold on here. They have a committee of twenty of the best detective minds in Scotland Yard working on the problem right now."

"Good, maybe by morning I'll have some ideas. Right now I'd just as soon have a few hours of sleep. Teacher, may I be excused?"

Brainridge laughed. "That you can, old sot, that you can. Let's convene class again about 1000 in the conference room."

Murdock waved, walked over to his bunk, and flopped on it. He got up only long enough to take off his wet cammies, then dropped on the bunk again and pulled the light Army blanket over him.

Murdock had breakfast in the morning before he went to the meeting with Brainridge. The SEAL was thirty minutes late getting there and offered no excuse.

"I've been catching it all morning from four different agencies," said Brainridge, "each of which thought we should have caught the Arabs and found the bomb last night."

"The committee come up with anything?"

"Zilch. They've been up all night talking, arguing, suggesting, and negating. I think we may have at least one duel coming up."

"What about the Arab boats in port?"

"What? Say again?"

"What about the Arab-flag boats in London Port? Any one of them could have a nuclear bomb on board."

Captain Brainridge's eyes snapped, his brows raised, and he jolted out of his chair and grabbed his cell phone. He dialed and waited.

"Yes. How many ships are there now in the Port of London flying Arab flags?" He listened a moment. "Well, find out. I need to know in ten minutes. Move it!"

He hung up and nodded. "Oh, yes, now I think we might have something." He paused and his eyes hooded. He rubbed his face with one hand and scowled. "Only how do we board a foreign-flag-ship without causing an international incident?"

"Easy," Murdock said. "Health inspection. Your National Board of Health, or whatever agency you have, has had a report that this boat has a case of bubonic plague on board. The health inspectors take precedent over any national sovereignty considerations. Hey, it works. They also take on board the most sensitive Geiger counters they have to look for any radioactivity they can find. I've done it before in Greece."

Brainridge grabbed his phone again. He dialed and listened. "You have those Arab ships yet? Ten. Good, here's what I want you to do. No questions, get it done in the next hour. I don't care what kind of strings you have to pull. Now listen carefully."

After he finished on the phone, Brainridge looked at Murdock. "Thanks, I've got some ships to search." The captain ran out of the room, and tires squealed as he drove away.

Murdock went back to his bunk for a nap before noon chow.

By 1600 the ten Arab-flag ships had been searched, scrutinized, taken apart with a magnifying glass. They found no bomb, and no crew that was the least bit nervous worrying about the inspectors finding a bomb.

Murdock's phone rang when he was getting his gear cleaned and ready for shipment.

"Hey, Commander. Great idea about the ships. The health inspectors didn't find any bubonic, but they came up with one case of diphtheria, three of measles, and two of rabies. They're happy. My boss isn't and the Home Office isn't. They still want us to find the bomb. Any more good ideas?"

"What about pleasure boats? Do they register at the port or anything like that?"

"Not that I know of. They just sail in and tie up somewhere. Marina space is getting hard to find."

"What about the big ones, the seventy-, eighty-, hundred-foot yachts? Where do they tie up?"

"A yacht club somewhere."

"You have a speedboat?"

"I can get one."

"Let's take a boat ride and see if we can find any boats with Arabic names and maybe even a flag or two. Can't hurt."

The line was dead for a few moments. "Yeah, SEAL. I just got a go-ahead to test the waters. That sedan you were using should still be there. Tell the driver to bring you to Pier 12. He should be able to find it. Bring another set of eyes with you. See you in about an hour. Oh, the terrorists have been talking on the radio again. We tried to triangulate it, but the message came in a quick burst and no time to get a fix. They have given Israel another twenty-four hours to get their military out of the West Bank."

"We'll talk. I'll see you at Pier 12."

Before Murdock and Lam left for the pier, Don Stroh came in. He was grinning.

"Hey, SEALs, I just got you another week's vacation with pay for you guys in London Town. The Brits want you to hang around a while and see if there's anything more you can do to help. They are grabbing at any straws they can right now. Panic is soon to set in. In another twenty-four the story is going to leak to the press. Then all hell is gonna break loose in London."

Murdock told Stroh about the ships. He remembered Greece.

"Heading out now to look over the pleasure craft from the Arab countries," Murdock added. "Hope we have some luck." He looked over at Ed DeWitt, who had just come out of a nap.

"Lieutenant, you have the helm," Murdock shouted. Ed waved. Murdock and Lam hurried out to the sedan and headed for Pier 12.

London's waterfront is a massive affair, with miles of piers and wharves and docks. It looked like an impossible job, but Captain Brainridge had his bulldog face on as the twenty-four-foot powerboat slid away from the dock. Also on board was a man who introduced himself as James Anthony.

"This gent is from Scotland Yard," Brainridge said. "Figured we might need some law authority from time to time, if we find anything worthwhile, or if we get a lot of flack from some of these snobbish, closed, members-only clubs." He turned the boat back toward shore.

"Have a list of thirty yacht clubs and tie-ups," Brainridge said. "We might just get lucky on one of them. By bringing in the bomb on a small craft, the terrorists would have complete control. They could also use their radio and move from one spot to another."

Murdock and Lam held on as the captain drove the boat

into a large marina where there seemed to be no craft smaller than seventy feet long.

They trolled along, slowly watching boat names on the sterns in the head-in slips. Now and then they had to angle out to miss the larger ships. Only one had a non-English name, and Lam said it was a Greek moniker.

The second and third marinas they went to failed to show any Arabic names. The fourth one was smaller and looked more exclusive. There was a guard at the entrance, and he waved them over. The Scotland Yard man talked to the guard.

"Do you have any transient boats here?"

"A few, but this is private property."

The Yard man showed a badge. "Anthony of Scotland Yard. We're looking for a yacht from an Arab country. Have you had any that docked here in the past week or so?"

"This is official?"

"As official as it gets without a warrant, and we are in a rush."

"Yes, we've had one boat from Saudi Arabia. Husband and wife. Nice folks."

"We'd like to meet them," Anthony said. "Is their boat here and are they on board?"

Five minutes later the entire crew from the small boat stood on the slip outside the seventy-foot yacht. The owners said hello from the deck and asked what the visitors wanted.

"Ma'am, sir. Anthony of Scotland Yard. We've been watching for some illegal and banned material we heard is being brought into the country via pleasure craft such as yours. We don't have a search warrant, but we assure you that this is a vitally important matter. Could we look around your ship?"

The Saudi man nodded. "Absolutely. We'll cooperate. We have nothing to hide. Welcome aboard. We'll show you every nook and cranny and compartment."

Twenty minutes later the search team was back in its boat heading for a new marina.

They went through four more moorages before they found another Arab yacht.

"It's Arabic for *Sundowner*," Murdock said of the name on the yacht. The search crew tied up and walked up the slip to the side of the yacht. Captain Brainridge called out, "Hello the ship. Permission to come aboard."

Two men appeared quickly at the rail of the ship, which had its deck four feet above the slip. The men looked down.

"I am Hamdani, boat owner. What do you wish?"

"I'm Inspector Anthony with Scotland Yard. We want to do an inspection of your ship. We're looking for illegal cargo brought into England."

"You need the search warrant," Hamdani said. He was about forty, slender, with a full beard and mustache. His eyes gleamed darkly from under heavy brows.

"Not if I think there is just cause that a crime has been committed and I'm in pursuit of a suspect," Inspector Anthony said. The Arab scowled. He said something softly in Arabic to the man who stood beside him. Neither one showed a weapon. Then Hamdani looked at Anthony. He spoke rapidly in Arabic then.

"You are a pig, a scoundrel, an asshole of camel shit." The words in Arabic rolled out and he watched the men in front of him carefully. None showed signs of understanding the words.

Hamdani shrugged and spoke in English. "We do nothing wrong. You must have the search permit." To the man beside him he said softly in Arabic, "Use the telephone, tell Andwar to leave the slip at once and head for the channel."

Murdock understood Arabic, and he had followed the words the man had said from the first. He had steeled himself not to react to the insulting line. Now he grabbed for the ankles of the man who was about to leave. The Arab pulled away.

"No," Murdock said in Arabic. "You will not tell Andwar anything. But you will tell us everything we want to know."

"That won't happen," Hamdani spat. He drew an automatic pistol from his clothing, and at once two Arabs stepped out from behind him on the boat, each holding a submachine gun. Both were pointed directly at Murdock and the search party.

8

"Don't shoot them yet," Hamdani told his men in Arabic. He scowled at the four men in front of him. "You have heard too much. You all must come and be our guests on board. In another three or four days it will be over and we will release you. Now, all of you come up the steps and on board."

Murdock pointed toward the shore. "What about our man right over there with his machine gun trained on your backs?" he asked. The men with the sub guns looked that way.

"Over the side," Murdock shouted, and he and Lam dove off the slip into the empty slot next to it and stayed underwater. The submachine guns chattered, but the water deflected the bullets upward and they missed the swimmers, who dove deep.

Instinctively, Murdock and Lam both turned and swam underwater to the slip they had been standing on. The solid planks protected them and they could hear what went on above. Their heads came out of the water with a foot to spare below the planks.

A short time later they heard the SAS man and Anthony go on board the yacht. Murdock pointed back where they had left the speedboat, and he and Lam went underwater and swam that way. It was less than fifty yards. They both surfaced about the same time, showing only their eyes. The Arabs had not yet found the speedboat. Murdock remembered that the keys had been left in it in case it had to be moved. He and Lam slid over the side of the craft and crouched low in it. Lam reached out and cast off the two lines; then Murdock started the motor and they raced away from the dock and back into the wide waters of London Port.

Well off the marina, Murdock idled the craft and found the cell phone he had left on board the boat when they had gone to check on the Arab yacht.

"Will 911 work here?" he asked Lam.

"No. Here in England you call 999."

He did. It worked.

"Operator, this is an extreme emergency and I need you to connect me with Scotland Yard at once."

"That's highly irregular, we have procedures."

"Lady, I know that. I must get to Scotland Yard at once. Break the rules this time. It's of utmost national importance."

"I may get in trouble, but I'll try. You're a Yank, right?"

"Yes, please, hurry."

It took him only two minutes to get the right man. Then Murdock mentioned Inspector James Anthony and his assignment today.

"The inspector and an SAS captain have been kidnapped at the Watertown Marina aboard an Arab yacht called the *Sundowner*. Go get them. More important is for the harbor patrol or someone to watch for an Arab yacht leaving the area. I don't know how big it is or what its name is, but a man on board is called Andwar. It has to do with the extreme emergency we're dealing with. I'm Murdock of the U.S. Navy SEALs. We're working with the SAS."

"Yes, we copy, you're recorded, and we'll put teams on both cases at once. We know who you are and what you're doing. Do you think the . . . the package might be on that Arab pleasure craft?"

"I'm sure it is. Call out the Navy. Have them check every Arab boat heading out of port."

"Will do, Murdock. We're moving."

Lam looked at Murdock. "We're going back, right? The only weapon I have is a .38 hideout on my right ankle."

Murdock grinned. "My .38 is on my left ankle. Damn right we're going back. We don't leave any of our own behind, and right now those two are part of our operation."

Murdock turned the boat around, and they came up slowly to the marina and docked at the first slip. The Arab yacht was in the second tier of slips. There was no easy way to get to the target. It was big enough that the bridge looked out over most of the other boats, which made for a perfect lookout spot.

The SEALs surveyed the problem and both agreed. They would go down the first line of slips. Drop into the water between boats, and cross over to the other line of slips so they could come in at the stern of the target.

"They shouldn't be watching in that direction even if they think we might come back," Murdock said. "Hell, we're wet anyway. What's a little more water."

They met two boat people going down the first row of slips, but nobody was around to see them slide into the water between two fifty-foot sailboats. They did a heads-up crawl across the narrow channel between the slips, and came up on the stern of the *Sundowner*. She was tied up on the port side. There was no good access on the starboard. With the deck four feet above the slip planks, the SEALs had room to lift up on the slip beside the hull of the craft and stay out of sight of anyone on board. They did. Murdock stood up and looked across the deck. They were aft, and he could see only the walkway along the cabin and the door leading inside. He looked to the stern and found no guard or lookout.

A diversion. On the slip were two buckets half filled with water and with washing gear nearby. Murdock pointed to one of the buckets, and Lam pulled it back out of sight.

"Toss it up forward and I'll be at the steps and try to nail whoever comes out to investigate." Murdock grabbed the other bucket and dumped out half of the water. He hefted it by the handle and grinned.

The steps on the slip were the movable kind used at many marinas to allow the people to walk up them to board higher-riding boats.

Murdock moved to them, crouching next to the ship, holding the partly filled bucket in his right hand, and nodded. Lam threw the metal bucket high and when it crashed down on the deck, it made a smashing metallic sound. Murdock heard voices from inside; then he heard footsteps come out of the cabin and stop. Murdock surged upward leaping high and swinging his heavy bucket hard just over the rail at the man's back. It slammed into him, jolting him forward. He fell on his hands and knees, the sub gun clattering out of his hand.

Murdock jolted up the steps and dropped flat on the surprised Arab. He slammed his fist into the man's cheek twice and saw the Arab pass out. Murdock dropped the man into the water beside the boat, picked up the submachine gun, and moved toward the cabin door.

"What's going on out there?" someone inside yelled in Arabic. Murdock didn't respond. Lam crept up the steps, his .38 out. Murdock and Lam surged through the cabin door into a salon twenty feet long with plush furniture, a big-screen TV, and two Arabs sipping drinks. Both looked up in surprise.

"The party's over," Murdock said in Arabic. "You, Hamdani, on your feet and take me to where your prisoners are." The Arab lifted off the couch slowly, then charged Murdock. The SEAL lowered the muzzle and fired one shot into Hamdani's right leg. The Arab stumbled and went down on the thick carpet. He swore and stood slowly. Murdock frisked him, found a handgun, and tossed it to Lam, who had the second man covered.

Twenty minutes later they had found the prisoners, and had the three Arabs tied and lying on the forward deck. Murdock had fished the first man out of the water. He was alive and swearing. Three official-looking cars drove into the marina, and six men surged down the dock to the slips. Anthony waved, and the Scotland Yard men came on board.

Ten minutes later, the SAS captain, the Yard inspector, and the two SEALs were back in the speedboat patrolling the port. They powered toward the ocean end of the bay as fast as they could. Anthony now had a Yard radio. There had been no sightings of an Arab boat moving toward the ocean. Scotland Yard had the help of four eighty-foot Navy patrol craft that could do thirty knots.

"They say they have spotted only four pleasure craft of any size heading outbound," Anthony said. "Two American, one French, and one Israeli."

Murdock laughed. "Yes. Think the way the terrorists would," he said. "They would figure that if anything went wrong, the Navy would be looking for Arab flag-boats. How to avoid this? Fly a different flag. What would be most ironic? Fly an Israeli flag on the boat with the bomb on board."

Anthony radioed the idea to his men with the Navy boats. They liked the logic. "Two cutters are heading for the Israeli boat now. We should know in ten minutes."

They kicked the boat up to top speed and slanted toward the mouth of the port. Long before they got there, they had a report.

"Yeah, Anthony, you had a good idea. We tracked down the Israeli boat. They saw us coming and tried to run, but we nailed them. We boarded her and found the whole crew and passengers were Arabs. We saw a big splash just before we boarded, and know something went overboard. Below we found two sets of scuba gear and tanks. So we don't know what happened."

"Tell him to get an exact spot where they splashed," Murdock said. "Use a satellite tracking device. Must have one."

Anthony tried, but they didn't have anything like a Mugger with them. They got coordinates as closely as they could.

Anthony looked at Murdock.

"They dumped it. Get your Geiger counters out and go over that boat. It's got to show radiation. First call the SEALs in Crawley. Tell Lieutenant DeWitt to get all the men with their diving gear and outfits for Lam and me, and take the bus to the bay where they were before. A boat will meet them there."

"You're going to try to find the bomb in the bay?"

"If it's there and we have some help, we should be able to give it a good try. Get talking on that radio."

The Navy had anchored the Arab boat in place and called for the radiation detection team. It was more than an hour before the other SEALs raced up on a British Royal Navy patrol boat. An ensign on the first patrol boat on the scene talked to Murdock by radio.

"Yes, sir, Commander. We saw the splash. I figure the ship here moved about forty to fifty yards downstream before we got her stopped and anchored. Best we can do."

"Did you see any divers go in the water?"

"No, didn't see any. We watched her close after that splash."

"Good. Now one more question. Does the Royal Navy have a minesweeper in port? Anything that can search the bottom of the harbor here for metal?"

"I see what you mean. I don't know. I'll call the admiral and ask him at once."

"One more thing. Can you anchor one of your patrol boats over the spot where we think the splash occurred?"

"That I can do right now. You diving?"

"As soon as we can get where you are."

The Navy patrol boat that picked the rest of the SEALs up at Pier 12 rushed them to the spot, which was toward the outer part of the London harbor. The Navy team on board the Arab yacht found definite traces of radiation on deck in three places.

Murdock put down Alpha Squad first. "We want a complete search. On the bottom we'll go hand-in-hand and make sure we don't miss anything. Not sure of the visibility, but it'll be better now than tonight. Over the side."

The harbor at this point was only about sixty feet deep. The new Draegrs automatically adjusted the air/nitrogen mix so they could stay down at that depth for extended lengths of time.

Murdock stared ahead through the murky water. There wasn't enough river flow to really clean out the harbor. They were over a mile from the North Sea, so that didn't help. He stumbled over something in the muck of the bottom, kicked it, and saw an old piece of what could have been an aircraft wing. Maybe a wartime Spitfire that didn't quite make it back to the airdrome.

They crisscrossed the area for an hour, then swam to the

surface. Murdock went back down with Bravo Squad and Lieutenant DeWitt.

After a two-hour search the SEALs came up for a breather in the clean air.

The ensign reported that they had no minesweeper ready for work in the area. The closest one was in Portsmouth. It would need twelve hours to get under way, then another six hours to get on site.

Anthony came on board. "We have been questioning everyone on that Arab ship and can't get a thing out of any of them. It's a pleasure cruise. They know nothing about any bomb on board. I do get the idea that two of the people who were on board are not there now. One woman let slip a name, another woman another name, and neither one is on the passenger list."

Murdock frowned. "They wouldn't just dump the bomb and forget it," he said. "They had to have a fallback plan. Dump it overboard with a neutral flotation device. Put two divers in the water with it and they could swim it to shore or to another boat."

"It didn't come to another small pleasure craft," the ensign said. "We've been monitoring everything that comes in or out of port ever since we saw the splash."

"Then it has to be the shore. Ensign, can you haul anchor and get us to the closest landfall to this point?"

"Aye, can do, Commander."

Five minutes later, the SEALs kicked out of their flippers, shrugged out of their Draegrs, and stepped on shore. The area was only partly built up, with a series of mud flats and shallow water. It took only a half hour of working both ways along the shore from their landing point for the SEALs to find the track.

Some large object had been pushed, dragged, then looked like it had been rolled through the soft mud flat for fifty yards to a now-and-then dirt road that meandered around the mud flats. More footprints showed in the mud near the roadway. Then they found tire tracks. By that time there were a dozen Scotland Yard men all over the place.

"Pickup with a lift gate would work here," Murdock said.

"They roll it on the lift gate and if it's strong enough, it lifts the bomb up and into the body, where it's braced and they simply drive away."

A shout went up six hundred yards inland. Anthony, on his radio, asked what they had found. He listened and grinned.

"Some luck after all. The blokes ran into a muddy spot they couldn't get through with the pickup. Mired down to the rear axle. They left the pickup. We have license plates to check. The boys up there say looks like they off-loaded something into a larger truck, probably with four-wheel drive and lots of engine. They've had four hours to get it out of here."

The SEALs jogged up to the transfer point. Anthony went with them, and said the Yard had checked the license plate and had a home address on the pickup owner. Two teams were on the way to talk to the owner. The SEALs and Anthony followed the road out of the flats and to the first paved road. An old man with a dog on a leash stood there watching.

"Ain't been this much activity around here since that Spitfire crashed into the flats during the winter of '43. What the hell happened out there?"

"Nothing you need to know," Anthony told him.

Murdock smiled at the old man. "What kind of a dog?"

"Terrier. I used to show him before he got too old like me."

"You live nearby?"

He pointed. "About twenty rods that way. Strange. First two men ran up the road and to a phone, I'd guess, on the corner two blocks down. Then the pickup came. Got me curious."

"The men who ran up the road. What did they look like?"

"By then I'd come out with Roger here and walking. Seen them up close. A-rabs, no doubt. Then a big truck came. Had huge tires and a cab high off the ground. Even had some kind of a crane on the back, you know, to pick up things with.

"I came back not ten minutes later. By then I was real

curious. Wrote down the make of the truck. It was an Atlas, and the license place was Atlas 44. Remember that. One of them personalized or maybe business kind of plates."

Anthony had stayed to listen; he gave Murdock a thumbs-up and took out his radio. He moved away and talked. The SEALs waited.

He returned grinning. "Yes! Atlas is a producer of specialized trucks, fairly small operation. Their trucks all have license plates from Atlas 1 to Atlas 234. Atlas 44 is owned by a man with a small business and we have his address. We have cars coming over here we can use to make a raid on the place. Want to come along?"

The SEALs all had their MP-5's, which had been slung over their backs during the search. They had worn their combat harness loaded with the usual combat essentials, and were ready to kick ass. They jammed into six cars that arrived and sped away.

It was a two-hour drive to find the place. It was just north of London near the small town of Hertford. The sun had set sometime before and Murdock's watch showed just after 2045. The cars stopped a block away, and Scotland Yard set up a command post. They had twelve Yard men and the sixteen SEALs.

"Your firepower is better than ours," said Anthony, who was in charge of the operation. "We'll have you surrounding the place, but be careful you don't shoot any friendlies."

The main building was about twice the size of a good house. It had two windows in front, two sedans parked out front, and a truck with a crane attached at one side.

"We'll put two flash-bangs through the windows, then smash down the front door and charge inside," Anthony said.

"Inspector Anthony, did you bring those lead blankets?" Murdock asked.

Anthony nodded. "Indeed we did. In one of the cars. We'll bring it up close. Any other questions?"

"We won't fire unless some bad guys come boiling out the back doors," Murdock said. "Single shots only."

They deployed. Murdock was with Alpha squad in front

of the building. He watched the flash-bang grenades blast inside, and at the same time two big Scotland Yard men hit the front door of the place with a leaded battering ram and the door caved in. Six Yard men boiled through the smashed-open door. Murdock heard four shots, then all was silent. Anthony came out and signaled to a car, which drove up directly to the front door. Three men carried the lead blankets into the building.

Murdock ran up to the door, but held the rest of the SEALs back. He stepped inside and saw two dead Arabs. Both had submachine guns and bandoliers of ammo across their chests. A third Arab sat on the floor, his hands trying to hold blood in his chest. He coughed and blood flew from his mouth.

"We almost made it," he said in English.

Murdock saw the men shaping the lead blankets around a three-foot-high muddy wooden box in the middle of the room. It was made roughly in the shape of a squared-off ball. The lead blankets were doubled.

The Arab didn't notice them. He looked at the nearest Scotland Yard inspector and asked him something.

"What?" the inspector asked.

"Could you get my watch? It has a picture of my wife and two daughters in it. In my pocket. One last look."

The inspector looked at Anthony. He nodded. The Yard man fished out the gold-plated pocket watch with a chain. The man opened the top of it and looked at the inside of the cover.

Then he laughed. "Fools," he yelled. "Damn fools. I've won after all. All I have to do is press the stem and in ten seconds the bomb detonates and half of London and all of us simply vanish from the face of the earth as we vaporize in a glorious atomic explosion."

"Don't do it," Anthony said.

The Arab laughed and blood sprayed out of his mouth. He looked at the red stain on his hand and his watch, and said something in Arabic that Murdock figured was a prayer. Then he screamed and pushed the stem on the pocket watch. He screamed again and counted on down from seven to zero.

Nothing happened.

The Arab opened his eyes and stared in disbelief at the bomb. Then he began to cry.

"The lead blanket prevented the signal from getting to the bomb," Murdock told him in Arabic.

The dying man looked at Murdock and shouted something, but this time nothing but a froth of blood came out of his mouth. His eyes glazed; then the blood stopped and he tilted to the left, then fell over dead before he hit the floor.

By the time Murdock left the building, an armored truck with siren blasting pulled up outside. Men were equipped for the job. A ramp opened in back and a small forklift rolled out and into the building.

Murdock called the SEALs around and told them what had happened inside.

"That wraps it for us then, Cap?" Bill Bradford asked.

"We'll have to wait and see."

Inspector Anthony came out and found the SEALs. He wiped a line of sweat off his forehead.

"Too close in there. We'll never know if that was a real trigger that he had in that watch or not. Oh, we'll check out the watch, but would it have set off the bomb without the lead shield around it?"

"Ours is not to wonder why," Jaybird said.

Anthony laughed, and it broke the tension for him. "True, how true. Now, let's get you men back to Crawley and some dry clothes and lots of good chow."

His radio came on and he listened to his earpiece. A moment later he nodded. "Yes, sir. Yes, I'll tell them. Good night, sir."

He looked over at Murdock. His grin grew to cover his whole face. "That was my boss. He said to thank you for your help on this little project. Without you we probably would never have found the damned bomb. We've had a message for you from Mr. Stroh."

"Oh, boy," Paul Jefferson said. "This can't be good."

"Mr. Stroh says that you should get some food and then a good night's sleep. However, just because this little game of hide-and-seek is over, you won't be going home. He says he has a new project for you that starts bright and early in the morning."

"Oh, yeah," Frank Victor said. "Just exactly what we need—another surprise."

"What the hell is it?" Colt Franklin asked.

"It's a surprise," Senior Chief Sadler said. "If we knew what it was, it wouldn't be a surprise. Let's shag ass out of here. I'm hungry."

9

The next morning Murdock and DeWitt met with Don Stroh at the small officers' mess on the military base. Murdock wasn't quite sure what kind of a base it was. There were Royal Air Force planes there, also Royal Naval units, and he had seen companies of soldiers marching around.

There were only ten tables in the mess. Three of them were occupied. The Americans feasted on bacon and eggs, hash browns, and cups of scalding coffee. After the dishes were cleared away, Don Stroh put a folder on the table from his slender briefcase.

"This may seem slightly unusual, but I'm telling you this before it's official. It's still just a suggested plan by a foreign power, and the President and the CNO and even the Secretary of Defense have not given me a report on it, or a decision."

"The British want to strike back at the extremists who they think orchestrated this nuclear blackmail," Ed DeWitt said.

Don Stroh looked at him with a jolt of surprise. "Ed, how could you know something like that? You're right to a degree. That's the general idea; however, they want to go about six steps farther. The Brits are furious with the terrorists and want to annihilate the three or four elements of the Arab extremist movement that have been causing the world so much trouble over the past forty years. They want to blast them into hell, to ruin them so completely and so thoroughly that they never will be able to reorganize or ever have any power again.

"The President told my boss that he didn't have any real

objection to a payback strike, something to tell the extremists that we know what they did and we want to hurt them. He is worried about taking it the next few steps, in effect conducting a war of attrition against the various Muslim hate groups. They include the Arafat Palestinians, the Fatah movement in Ramallah on the West Bank, and even the Mohammad Medein originally thought to be active only in Chechnya and Dagestan. Plus Hamas, the Shiite Muslim Hezbollah, and even the London-based Al-Muhjiroun. Now it is believed the Medein had a major hand in the bombing of the destroyer *Cole* in Yemen, where those seventeen U.S. sailors were killed and the billion-dollar state-of-the-art missile destroyer was seriously damaged and put into a repair dock for a year."

"Just the U.S. and the Brits would be in this?" Murdock asked.

"Oh, no, in fact we would be junior partners. The main cog in the machinery would be Israel, who has the most to lose here and the most to gain."

"The West Bank and the Gaza Strip," DeWitt said.

"What are the Brits planning?" Murdock asked.

"We're not sure. They haven't told us. We know that once this story of the nuclear blackmail breaks, it will be documented within an inch of its life. There will be pictures of the dead Arabs, the complete scenario of what happened. The dead Arabs and the two who were caught alive will be tied to certain terrorist organizations by the British right up front. Once the story breaks, Britain will hit them quickly. We think it will be an air strike that will pulverize certain known headquarters. Beyond that, we have no idea what their plans might be."

"What is Israel saying?" DeWitt asked.

"We know they are planning something, but we don't know what. They have strongly urged that we should handle it on a triad basis, sharing equally in the planning, financing, and personnel. They have been feeling out our people on the idea. It would be scalpel-clean; it would be pinpointed at certain headquarters and people. It would be continuing until those involved in terrorism were blown off the face of the Middle East."

"What about the U.S. no-assassination rule?" DeWitt asked.

"Technically these would not be assassinations. They would be military strikes in response to warlike activities by the enemy."

"But we don't want to take a reinforced regiment into the Gaza Strip to take down Arafat's headquarters and his summer house?"

"Precisely. These strikes would be anonymous. There would be no footprints left or equipment lost to identify any of the attackers. No personnel would be left in the field, dead, wounded, or alive. It would be clean, probably not quick, and would take a lot of resources."

"Do you think Washington will take on a job like this?"

"In view of the destroyer *Cole*, there is a certain feeling in the air that there should have been a response long before now. From what I hear, we were just not sure enough of the terrorists to tie them down to a nation and a headquarters we could pulverize with a response."

"Any timetable?" DeWitt asked.

"None, but it has to be soon. Britain has been putting together a response since the start of the nuke threat. They have a plan by now, and are tying down the country and the area to hit. Israel isn't that far along yet, but they have contingency plans for all kinds of retaliation against a number of targets."

"So, Uncle Sam is the holdup here, dragging his size-sixteen feet," Murdock said.

"As I hear it. A decision is due to come down within the next two days." He paused. "Any wounds or injuries during the current bit of training maneuvers?"

"Well put, Stroh. We didn't have much to do. No serious physical problems that I've heard about."

"We're solid and ready to go," DeWitt said.

"I'd say we're in for some training during the next two days," Murdock said. "No firing, but we can do a lot of roadwork."

"Can we tell the men what's brewing?" DeWitt asked.

Don Stroh took a drink of coffee and pushed it away. "Not this time. This is more than top secret. If it doesn't come off, we might talk about what might have been. If it happens, they men will know soon enough, and they always understand anything they do has to be top secret."

"Fair enough," Murdock said. "As long as you're picking up the check here. You know we don't travel with any money."

Stroh looked at Murdock and snorted. "Don't I always. When are we going fishing again? I'd even settle for some bottom fish, some sculpin, rock cod, and a few mackerel."

"As soon as we hit Coronado I'll give you the fishing report," Ed DeWitt said. "Come out anytime you're free. There's always something to catch around the kelp beds off San Diego."

For the first day, the SEALs used the temporary quarters and made a fifteen-mile run through the immediate area. They saw a lot of this semirural part of England up close and intensely personal. The locals had evidently seen a lot of military around, since they hardly glanced at the SEALs as they went jogging down the narrow English roads.

The second day, they did a ten-mile run in the morning with full combat gear except for the Draegrs. In the afternoon it was another ten-mile jaunt with only their cammies and primary weapons. They all chose the MP-5.

That evening, Don Stroh came into the barracks and waved at the SEALs. They hurried up around him and he gave them a tired smile.

"I've been up for almost thirty-six hours mother-henning this project, and I'm tired as hell, so no cracks and no comments," Strohl said. "You have an assignment. A general assignment but with no actual action involved, yet. Tomorrow morning at 0800 you will board a British military transport jet and you will be flown to Tel Aviv, Israel, where you will quartered at an Israeli Army facility pending further orders."

"Hey, Stroh, we gonna kick ass on some of them fucking

A-rab terrorists who brought over the bomb?" Lapedusa asked.

"I'd say that's a possibility," Stroh said. "You'll have to wait and see what your orders say."

Tel Aviv, Israel

The SEALs' quarters in Israel were much like those in Britain, a twenty-man barracks with an attached common room for gear and meetings, and a small dayroom with Ping-Pong and pool tables. They would eat at the general mess about a block away. The Army post had heavy security all around, and the interior guards carried loaded weapons.

Don Stroh was there to meet them at the military airport and rode with them on the bus to the Army post just north of Tel Aviv. He gave them some facts about the country as they rolled along.

"Israel is a small nation of not quite six million people, which is about the population of the state of Missouri. Israel has a land mass of a little over eight thousand square miles, which is the same size as New Jersey. It's a fairly new nation, being created by the United Nations when it partitioned Palestine into Jewish and Arab states in 1948. The Arab nations have never recognized the partition, and have been at war with Israel almost constantly from that date to this.

"Israel is surrounded on three sides by mostly belligerent Arab nations many times its size. For example, Syria has sixteen million people, Lebanon has four million, and Jordan has five million, for a total of twenty-five million Arabs who are for the most part belligerent and would like nothing better than to drive all Jews into the Mediterranean Sea. Egypt, on Israel's southern border, is less belligerent and sometimes almost friendly, but Egypt has a population of sixty-nine million people. You can see why Israel can be paranoid at times."

"We're not here to fight all those different countries, are we?" Mahanani asked.

"Absolutely not. If this goes down, it will not be a war against a nation; it will be one or more strikes against certain

terrorist organizations that have preyed on Israel and many
other parts of the world, including the United States."

The SEALs had been in the barracks for almost a day. They
had cleaned and oiled their weapons twice, been on a five-
mile warming-up march around the perimeter of the base,
and had two excellent meals.

The call came at 1000 for a meeting. Don Stroh brought
the message.

"Only three of you can go," Stroh said. "It's a planning
session and to get some areas of concern ironed out."

Murdock looked at his men. He pointed to DeWitt and
Jaybird. They went in the military sedan Stroh had com-
mandeered, and rode to the headquarters building. This was
an Israeli Army post and well manned. Murdock guessed at
least two regiments must be posted here. The GHQ was
large but businesslike. They were ushered into a conference
room that had a huge table with eighteen chairs around it.
Each place had a pad of paper and a ballpoint pen, a glass
of water and two pieces of chocolate fudge.

Twelve men sat at the table. Murdock and his team came
in, followed closely by three men Murdock recognized as
being British SAS, wearing their famous beige berets with
the winged dagger on them. They kept their berets on, but
the rest of the men were uncovered. All wore versions of
desert cammies.

A man at the end of the oval table stood when the last
six were seated.

"Good, we're all here. I am Colonel Assaf Ben-Ami with
the Israeli Army Department and I'll lead the discussion.
We all know why we are here. I'm pleased with the three-
nation cooperation on this project. We have the SAS delegation from England. We have the U.S. Navy SEALs here.
We have also the Israeli Special Forces from the Air Force,
the Navy, and the Army. We welcome all of you. We are
here to talk about our first strike against the terrorists. The
diplomats have had a hand in our negotiations. They have
stipulated that our first action will be on the Gaza Strip, at

Gaza City, and concentrating on the headquarters of al Fatah and its military wing, Tanzim.

"The HQ of these groups is the same as that of their parent group, the Palestine Liberation Organization, which is directed by Yassir Arafat. Our first target will be the seashore headquarters of Arafat and the PLO. This is in the form of a mission assigned by our governments and is not open to discussion.

"Beyond that point everything is open. It has been suggested that the strike come as soon as possible. I know that all of our organizations are used to working rapidly, and I suggest we do so now. We'll start by opening the floor to methods for reducing this target." He looked at a man halfway down the table, who stood. "Yes?"

"Sir, one way would be to use a Naval bombardment. We can use guided rounds with good accuracy. A Naval action would be without risk to manpower, could be done quickly and with massive destructive power."

Another man stood. "Sir, we could drop twenty SAS men by parachutes onto the beach in a silent attack. Surround the HQ and on signal use grenades and explosives and take over the building in five minutes. Then we would clean up, use explosives on any remaining structures, and egress into the water for a small-boat pickup."

"How big is this headquarters building?" someone asked.

"As I understand it from looking at intelligence photos," said Ben-Ami, "it's three stories in parts, two in others, with side structures as well. So it's going to take a massive attack to knock down a building that size."

Heads nodded around the table.

"Any comment on the Naval attack?" the colonel asked.

"Too much chance for error," one Britisher said. "We want this to be a scalpel operation, with pinpoint accuracy, so we don't kill any civilians or blow up their houses."

Several men nodded and some said yes.

The SAS man stood again. "Sounds like it's too big a target for us to destroy. We could take out the personnel, but not the whole building without a lot of extra charges."

Murdock recognized the men from the Israeli Special Forces units. There were four of them at their end of the table. None showed any sign of rank. All were young and lean with short haircuts and intense faces.

"So how do we attack this seaside villa?" the colonel asked. "The PLO headquarters is well known. We've hit it before. This time our mission is to totally demolish it and to waste as many of the upper-echelon leaders as possible. Any more suggestions?"

"Yes," a tall, slender man with blue Israeli Air Force tabs on his shirt said. "I'd suggest an attack by four aircraft using laser-aimed air-to-ground missiles. That should do the job."

"As a good start," Murdock said. "Within two minutes after the missile strike there should be a landing party moving into what's left of the building eliminating any surviving or wounded personnel, setting charges to reduce the structures to a three-foot level, then egress to sea for pickup by boat well out of range of shore fire."

"How could the timing be kept down to two minutes?" the Air Force man asked.

"Position sixteen SEALs fifty yards off shore in underwater rebreathing gear," Murdock said. "When the first missiles hit, the sixteen swim hard for shore, drop their rebreathers, and charge into the HQ within two minutes after the last missile explodes."

"Yes," another Israeli said. "Our underwater units can do the same thing. It's a good plan."

"A thirty-two-man attack force including the Israelis would make it easier," Murdock said. "Some for security in a perimeter, some to do the blasting and cleanup."

"We have the rebreathers?" the leader asked.

"Yes, Colonel, we use them all the time," the Israeli UDT man said.

"One complication," a British SAS man said. "We understand this is not a one-structure HQ. There are at least six smaller buildings mixed in with the civilian population residences within two blocks of the main unit. We have them pinpointed and identified beyond all doubt. Mossad has confirmed the units."

"So, we have a wider target," the colonel said. "Any suggestions on these units?"

There was a moment of silence. The SAS man spoke again.

"Colonel, if the attack comes at night, we could have a low-profile insertion boat a quarter of a mile offshore. When we know the jets are making their firing run, we charge at full throttle into the beach and put thirty men on the sand within three or four minutes after the missiles hit. We then split into six teams and charge to the targets, putting five men on each building. We blast in the front doors and clear the building of all terrorists, then set charges and leave incendiaries to go off after the blast. This turns the rest of the rubble into ashes."

The colonel nodded. "And what of PLO personnel found in the six organization buildings?"

"They would be eliminated," the SAS man said.

The colonel looked around the table. "The plan sounds good. It takes a minimum of synchronized work dependent on another unit. It puts the manpower where it can best be used. Now, any other ideas how to get at the HQ building?"

"We could send teams of sappers in through the surf after dark," one of the Israelis said. "Take out the sentries and blow up the place. We wouldn't have enough personnel to clear the building."

"We could drive a remote-controlled truck filled with explosives against the side of the GHQ," Jaybird said. "But then that would take a week to set up, and get the explosives on site and the radio control for the truck. Forget it."

The colonel looked over the group again. "I think we have a good plan with the Israeli jets and their missiles. They may need more than four; we'll let their planners figure that out. Then the SEALs and the SAS hit the beach. Egress will be by the same SAS boat if it can maintain its position, and the SEALs would be picked up offshore after a swim. Now timing.

"I can get the Air Force to make this hit with four hours notice. SEALs, what kind of lead time do you need?"

"We'll need to arrange with the Israeli Navy for a boat

to carry sixteen SEALs to within a quarter of a mile of the target. Navy?"

"Our regular patrol boats can do the job. It's now about 1100. They patrol near Gaza every three or four hours. It's routine and would bring no alarm. We have units at Ashdod south of here, which is only twenty miles from Gaza City. They can do twenty knots, so it's a little over two hours from Ashdod to the insertion area. We can also move the SAS men via the same patrol boats."

"Both the SEALs and SAS men can be flown by chopper from here to Ashdod," the Israeli Air Force man said.

Colonel Ben-Ami smiled for the first time. "Yes, it's coming together. What time should the attack come?"

"0200," one of the SAS men said. "Their people will be asleep, their guards will be getting tired, and it gives us plenty of darkness to get into position."

Colonel Ben-Ami looked at Murdock. "SEALs?"

"Fine. All we need is more ammo and charges and the Air Force to get us down the coast."

"SAS?" the colonel asked.

"Plenty of time, sir. We like to move quickly. We will want extra ordnance if it can be supplied."

"Ordnance is no problem," one of the Israeli Special Forces men said. "Both of you see me as soon as we're done here."

"Good," Colonel Ben-Ami said. "I'll make the contact with the Air Force and get clearance for the attack and the choppers for transport. Moshe, you handle the Navy. Be sure those patrol boats are big enough to haul the needed men. We'll meet back here at 1400 to see that all of the details have been worked out. The choppers will be here by then to fly the forty-six men to Ashdod. That's all, gentlemen." The colonel stood, and the men around the table jolted to attention while he walked out.

The three SEALs huddled together. "Weapons?" Murdock said.

"We'll need three of the Bull Pups," Jaybird said. "No chance to get more rounds for them here."

"I'd say the rest MP-5's except for one 21-E machine gun," DeWitt said.

Murdock nodded. "I agree, only just two of the Pups, and one more MP-5. We'll be mostly close-in work. I'll get to the local ordnance guy."

Murdock sought out the Israeli ordnance man, and he and the SAS trooper went with him to work out the details for more ammunition and plastic explosives.

10

Gaza City, Gaza Strip

Omar Rahman sat behind his plain desk in the PLO headquarters building in Gaza City, staring out at the sea and rubbing his left knee. Where did the cartilage go? The X-ray showed almost none left between the bones in his left knee joint. Sometimes it hurt like a knife going deep into his thigh. He had felt knife wounds before. At those times he simply could not walk, couldn't bend his knee. He sighed. Old age creeps up on a person. It certainly had on him. He was only sixty-two, and already he had the feeling his body was falling apart. He had been sturdy all his life, almost never sick, no broken bones, no heart problems, not even prostate difficulties as some of his friends had.

He looked out at the surf again past the gentle sloping sand. It was always a worry to him. They were naked here. Their leader, Yassir Arafat, was exposed and vulnerable. For a time they had planted mines in the inviting sand of the beach. Then two young girls ignored the warning signs and ran into the sand toward the inviting cool of the water just a few yards away. One of them died. The mines were taken out the next day.

Omar looked back at his desk. Why was there so much paperwork? He adjusted his store-bought magnifying glasses and read the letter again. More troubles on the West Bank. Didn't they think the Leader had enough trouble here, and with his worldwide jaunts to promote Arab unity and the glory of Allah?

Darkness slipped up on Omar like an angry woman. He pushed his feet into his sandals and eased away from the desk. Standing was no problem as long as he had something to push up on with his hands. He did so now and tested the left knee. Easy, easy, now full weight. Yes, it was not painful right now, he could walk, he could check the guards. They were loyal to the cause and to Yassir, but still they needed reminding sometimes. There was always danger. The Jews could come creeping out of the water at any time. The guards were on one-hundred-percent alert all night, every night.

He worked around inside the complex of rooms to the four open sentry windows. The men with their automatic rifles sat well back in the rooms so they couldn't be seen outside. The rooms were nearly dark. As light faded completely, the guards moved up to the windows where they had better firing lines. Nothing. Good.

Omar waved at the four, then went on to the rest of them. Ten guards every night. Only three times had they been needed, but they had saved several lives those nights.

After his rounds, Omar went to the former formal dining room. It had been changed into a mess hall where forty soldiers and workers could sit down at once. Tonight there would be visitors. More than twenty of the best of the leaders of the al Fatah and the Tanzim wing would be there for a conference, then an all-night planning session. They wouldn't leave until at least three A.M. It would be an historic occasion. Yassir Arafat himself would chair the meeting until midnight. Then he had to take his armored car to the small airport where a plane was waiting for him.

Omar saw some of the early arrivals. He knew most of them. Shook hands, then picked up his evening meal from the line and ate at a table by himself. He knew the chef on duty tonight. Omar would send half a dozen rolls home to Hinda, his wife of forty years. He pushed stringy white hair back from his forehead. His beard was almost white now as well. If he trimmed it he would look elegant, but he preferred to let his wild hair have its own way, making him look unkempt and dirty. Dirty? Omar snorted. He took a bath every night.

Just before he left the compound, a messenger came with

a letter for him. Omar opened it quickly. It was in writing, so it must be serious. He read it, then again. It was from Arafat, who said he would be late and might not get there at all. He asked Omar to stay for the meeting, and to help all he could until the session closed at three A.M.

Omar nodded to himself. A person loyal to the great Arafat did not even think of refusing a request from the great man. He would stay. Omar went back to the dining room, where the meal was almost over. He took another helping of the lamb stew. He would need the extra strength for the session tonight. Hinda would have to wait for her rolls. He put them in the white paper sack the cook had given him and took them back to his office. When he arrived home late the next morning, he would awaken Hinda and they would heat the rolls and eat them with strawberry jam. Hinda loved strawberry jam.

Back in the assembly room the meeting had begun. Nabil Oweida held the floor. He would fire up the members of the groups and urge them on to more and more action against Israel and the Americans. The young man hated the Americans almost as much as he did the Israelis.

"I tell you again, my fellow warriors for the glory of Allah. We must strike first, we must strike hard, we must strike every day of the year. We must kill the Americans, we must push the infidel Jews out of our holy lands." Nabil Oweida paused and took a sip of water. He was young in Omar's eyes. Young and idealistic, with that firebrand fervor that Omar had once projected himself. Oweida wasn't tall of stature, probably no more than five feet six inches, but when he spoke, when he warmed to his subject, he came across to the faithful as twenty feet tall.

"Tonight we will make plans to coordinate our efforts. We will strike the Jews wherever we find them. We will not allow peaceful coexistence. The very term shall be banned from further use. We will push the evil Jews into the sea and let their god rescue them.

"Do you remember Article One of the Palestinian National Covenant? Palestine is the homeland of the Arab—" He stopped and stared hard at the thirty leaders who sat in straight rows in front of him. "All of you who remember it, recite it with me. You all had to memorize it. Don't let me down this early. Let's try it again. Palestine is the homeland of the Arab Palestinian people; it is an indivisible part of the Arab homeland, and the Palestinian people are an integral part of the Arab nation."

By the time they were halfway through, almost all of the men in the room were barking out the words. When they ended, there were shouts and screams of vengeance from every man there.

"This is our mandate, our responsibility, to drive the hated Jews out of Palestine where they have no business being in the first place. The United Nations made a great and horrendous blunder in 1948 when they divided *Our Great Land* into two sections, Israeli and Palestinian. Half of our homeland is now in enemy hands. We will continue to fight to regain it.

"Article Two, you must remember it: Palestine, with the boundaries it had during the British Mandate, is an indivisible territorial unit."

Again a great cheer went up from the thirty-two Arab throats, and Omar felt his blood surging, felt the old hatreds surface, knew that he could go out tonight and, damn his knee, attack a Jewish settlement, fire a machine gun, plant a bomb in a Jewish market. Omar wiped sweat from his face, and realized that his whole body had responded and he was sweating like a he-goat chasing a female in season.

Nabil continued. "Perhaps you didn't memorize Article Three, but you know what it says: The Palestinian Arab people possess the legal right to their homeland and have the right to determine their destiny after achieving the liberation of their country in accordance with their wishes and entirely of their own accord and will."

The cheering this time didn't last as long, but it gave Omar chills up his back. His hands flexed, and he could only imagine how strongly the leaders of the al Fatah and Tanzim were reacting. Tomorrow would see the launching of many new headaches and deaths for the Israelis and as much trouble for the Americans as possible.

Oweida stopped reciting the Palestinian Covenant, and swung into his special skills: organization and carrying out battles and campaigns against their enemies. He quickly divided the group into four parts, each with a specific set of targets. Their job was to devise ways that would not be defensed by the enemy, or even thought of. Oweida moved from one group to the next, listening, making suggestions, helping them refine and pinpoint targets that would have the most lasting effects against all of their enemies.

Omar slipped out and talked with the head cook. There was a new shift of cooks on hand to make a midnight supper for the planners. They would eat and then continue their discussions at thirty minutes into the new day. Omar was satisfied that the meal was progressing, and went back to the assembly room.

Omar looked with pride at the fourth man in the first row. He was one of the top three leaders in the al Fatah movement. He was also Omar's second son. His firstborn had been killed while delivering a bomb into the heart of Jerusalem in the Jewish quarter. The bomb had gone off prematurely, but it had killed over fifty Israelis including ten soldiers. As soon as they knew that Esam had died, Jamil, his second son, had quit his job as a banker in Gaza City and charged into the al Fatah with a zest and ambition and talent that Omar had not been aware he possessed.

Now Jamil was third in line for the top al Fatah leadership spot. Even Yassir Arafat himself had commented on the talent of the young man, much to Omar's pleasure. Jamil would be coming home with him after the meeting before he went back to his post in Jerusalem, where he was in deep cover and working hard with new ways to frustrate and injure the Israelis. Currently Jamil had the toughest and most dangerous job of any in the PLO.

Omar stood slowly, tested his left knee, nodded, and left his chair at the back of the assembly hall and checked on the guards. He had put on four extra tonight. This was no time to let down, not with the finest leaders in their entire organization here for the planning session. Nothing was going to disturb them, absolutely nothing. Omar dropped back in his seat near the back of the big room. It was going well. They would break at eleven-thirty for their supper, then start again an hour later for the last part of the work session.

Omar bent and rubbed his knee. The doctor had told him to take pain pills to deaden the hurt. When that didn't kill the pain and the cartilage wore down even more, they would have to use cortisone shots. After that the doctor wouldn't tell him what they would do.

Omar frowned, then rubbed his knee. It seemed to help. Tomorrow he would get some of the pain pills.

11

Mediterranean Sea
Off Gaza City

Murdock looked out the cabin of the 105-foot Israeli patrol craft at the lights of Gaza City. They were over a mile off-shore and the lights were fused together into a glow. The Israeli Navy lieutenant checked his watch.

"Twenty minutes until 0200, Commander."

"Move in slowly at five knots. Plenty of time. Get us to a quarter mile if you can, then we'll swim."

"Aye, aye, sir." The Navy man made a transmission on his radio and both the patrol crafts moved toward shore. The second boat held the sixteen Israeli underwater forces.

Murdock checked his watch. "Better gun it up to ten knots, Lieutenant. This is one party I don't want to be late for."

The boat captain nodded at his man on the throttle, and the boat moved ahead faster. The Israeli team in the second boat caught up quickly.

"Quarter mile, sir," the lieutenant said.

"Dead stop," Murdock ordered. DeWitt had been check-ing the SEALs at the bow of the ship. He had been over every bit of gear and straps twice. Murdock walked in beside them, with the flippers giving him trouble on land or deck as they always did. They had decided on wearing their cam-mies and no rubber suits. They wouldn't be in the water long enough to make up for the clumsiness the wet suits produced on land. They had also decided not to go with the Draegr rebreathing device. They would swim in on the sur-face. Nobody could see them in the dark anyway, and they wouldn't have to worry about finding the Draegrs or dragging them along on the firefight.

"We'll go overboard in three minutes. Gives us ten to swim in and get ready for 0200. Everyone ready?"

Murdock saw the dim outline of the second patrol boat, which was without lights, forty yards away. He looked back at his boat driver. "Tell the other boat we get wet in two minutes."

They dropped in by squads, surfaced quickly, and powered toward shore. They had decided to stop just outside the surf line and wait until two minutes before attack time. Then they would swim directly through the breakers and head for the sand. If nothing happened at 0200, they would play wet logs on the beach until the jets came in.

Murdock had seen a few floodlights around the PLO headquarters, but not as many as he'd figured. Now as he waited just beyond the breakers, he could see there were more lights than he first thought. He knew he wouldn't hear the jets coming. The first sound they would hear would be the detonation of the missiles, with the jets flashing overhead seconds later. He had no idea what type of missiles the Israelis would use, but he was sure they would be big ones that could get the job done. Four missiles had been planned. The SEALs would be moving up on the sand after the first two, then wait out the second pass.

His watch glowed that it was 0200. He didn't hear the missile, more sensed it, and he snapped his head around to watch the big building. One side of it suddenly exploded in a huge ball of flames, the sound crashing over them a moment later. The second missile came then, producing flames and a brilliant flash and roar as it exploded on the other end of the complex. Murdock could see the center of the three-story building slowly sag, then crash down into the second story, and then all of it collapsed onto the ground floor.

The sixteen SEALs on the surface began their crawl stroke into the breakers and through them until they could feel the sand under their feet. They hesitated in the waist-high water as more waves broke over and around them. The third and fourth missiles came into the firestorm of blasted rubble a moment later, both hitting almost at the same time. It was overkill, but Murdock didn't worry about it. He waved the men forward and they charged up the beach, splashing through the waist-high, then knee-high water as it surged back at them from the sloping beach. They kicked off the troublesome flippers and surged ahead.

Murdock didn't see them until they began running up the beach. The underwater men from Israel were on his right and exactly on time, heading for the right half of the big bonfire. Murdock and the SEALs took the left-hand section for any mop-up needed and to run down any escaping terrorists. Behind somewhere, Murdock heard a high-speed engine whining toward him from the sea. That would be the SAS men coming in to attack the six off-site targets.

Murdock's SEALs charged up the sand and over a decorative low fence toward the structure. What was left of it standing was burning. There was no chance to get within fifty feet of the flaming mass. They had just started to circle to the left end of the place, when a secondary explosion caught them all by surprise. The pounding, roaring blast came at the far left end and put out part of the fire, but sent burning boards, roofing, and other debris high into the air.

"Hit the deck," Murdock bellowed. He hadn't even had time to get his Motorola working. The burning boards dropped all around them, some sailing as far as the sea. When everything stopped falling, Murdock sat up.

Jaybird slid in beside him. "Secondary? Their stash of boom-boom?"

"Must be. Let's get on the rest of the way round here and see what's on the other side."

The SEALs regrouped and circled their end of the complex. What had once been a series of connected buildings, some of them three stories high, now was nothing but a burning mass of rubble not over three feet high. The SEALs went back to the water side.

One section, six feet wide, near the middle was not yet burning. They moved up as close as they could. Murdock stared through the blown-out window and saw what he decided had been an office. A desk remained and a chair in front of it. On top of the desk sat a white paper bag about the size of a lunch sack.

"Some terr is gonna miss his late-night snack tonight," Jaybird said. They found two men crawling away from the building. The MP-5's chattered and the crawlers stopped moving permanently.

Murdock pulled out his Motorola and called the Israeli team.

"Yes, Yanks, I hear you. Not much left on this side. We've found two survivors who we dispatched. We've circled our end and it looks like we're about done here."

"We've found the same situation. You see those SAS men come in?"

"Heard their boat. Haven't seen them."

"So where are these other six targets?" Murdock asked.

"Not the slightest. Figured the Brits would do them."

Murdock heard someone coming from the beach, and looked over. There were two of the SAS men, one limping badly. They saw Murdock and headed his way.

"Fucking boat flipped on us. Lost a lot of our lads. We need some help. Can we team up with you blokes on this one? I know the targets."

"Let's go," Murdock said. The word passed to the last SEAL in the area, and they jogged forward with the Brit. They went down a block, past curious residents on the sidewalk looking at the firestorm near the beach.

"Fifth house down," the Brit lieutenant said. "Frame house with yellow trim."

They sensed no opposition from the civilians. A block later they came on the house. The front door stood open. Two men in the yard looked up, saw the military unit converging on them, and ran into the house.

"We'll take the back, Ed, you go in the front," Murdock said on his Motorola.

"Got it," Ed said.

Murdock led his seven men to the side of the house. He saw two lights snap off inside the building. At the last window he threw a fragger grenade hard through the glass, then kept on going to the rear of the structure.

The small bomb went off with authority inside. Murdock put his men on the ground and they watched the rear door a moment. One man came running out, and six Parabellums drilled through his body, dropping him into the dirt of the backyard.

Murdock heard two grenades explode inside the house; then the radio came on.

"Going inside," DeWitt said. "Don't fire into the place or use grenades. We'll clear."

Alpha Squad remained on the ground and waited. They heard a half-dozen shots fired in the house, then another grenade and more shots. A short time later the rear door opened and a voice bellowed.

"Friendlies here, SEALs coming out the back door."

The troops moved to the front of the house, and the SAS man pointed on down the street.

"Second and third targets are half a block down this way. We have two houses side by side. They must know we're coming by now."

"DeWitt, take the far house with our SAS man. We'll get the near one. Go."

"Your house is concrete block with no paint, small tree in front, no sidewalk," the SAS man said.

"Hey, Brit. You have a name?" Murdock asked.

"Yeah, I'm Trent-Jones."

"Okay, Jones it is. I'm Murdock. Concrete block with small tree. We're moving."

Both houses were dark when they came toward them. At once a rifle fired from one window, and the SEALs took cover behind two parked cars and three good-sized trees. "I'll cover you," Murdock said "Jaybird, Van Dyke, and Ching, move to the back door and cover it. Go on my fire."

Murdock moved his Bull Pup to 5.56 and fired three rounds into the nearest window, then three more rounds into the next window. He worked down the side of the house until his three men were safely past the windows and to the rear. He pushed the selector on the Bull Pup to 20mm and fired one round into the front door. It blew the whole wooden door all the way inside the house. Murdock sent one more twenty round inside; then he and the rest of the squad charged the front of the house.

There was no answering fire. The SEALs pressed against the front of the concrete structure and waited. "Jaybird, hold it back there, we're going in," Murdock called on the radio.

"Roger that."

"Howard, you and I. I've got the left."

They charged through the door, covering their sides of the large room they found. It was so dark they couldn't see anything. Murdock used his penlight, holding it three feet from his body. The powerful but small beam showed two dead bodies on the floor, both holding submachine guns.

"Two terrs down here," Murdock said on the radio. They charged through the rest of the house, and found one more man in the rear room. He was wounded. He screamed at them and lifted an Uzi in Murdock's beam of light. Howard put four rounds of Parabellums into his chest, and he dropped the weapon and met his ancestors in half a second.

"All clear," Murdock said. They went back outside just as DeWitt and Jones charged the front door of the other house. Murdock heard firing from the rear.

"We've got two downed terrs here," Donegan said on the Motorola. "Little bastards thought they could outrun a bullet."

"Two more dead inside," DeWitt said. "We're done here."

They could hear sirens—fire, police, or the Palestinian Authority military police, they didn't know which one.

"Let's haul ass out of here," Murdock said. The SEALs jogged toward the sea, cut back a block, and then down another deserted street until they could see the dark waters of the Mediterranean. Trent-Jones went with them. "You swim?" Murdock asked the SAS man.

"Like a salmon, but I should go find my mates."

"Was there another officer with them?" Murdock asked.

"Yes."

"He probably has most of them in tow. The sirens will push them back to sea. We'll try to find them once we get out a ways. Can you strap your weapon over your back?"

"Quite, regular procedure. How far out do we swim?"

"I'll contact the patrol boat before we hit the water. He should come in to a quarter mile and key in on our light sticks. At least that's the plan. We'll see how well he can follow orders."

Murdock told the SEALs to stash their Motorolas in waterproof compartments on their cammies. He called the boat.

"Patrol One, you should have men in the water in two minutes. Can you read me?"

"Surfers, we have you. We're a mile off. Are you north or south of the target? We can still see it burning."

"We're north now about three hundred yards. Have you heard from the Israeli swimmers?"

"They have been picked up by Patrol Two."

"We're moving. Did you know that the SAS boat flipped? You might ask Patrol Two to watch for survivors. We have one SAS man, Lieutenant Trent-Jones, with us."

"Will relay. We're looking for seventeen?"

"Right. We know of one wounded Brit on shore. Do your best."

Murdock put away his radio. "Let's get wet, men," he said, and led the way into the water. Without their flippers it was harder work swimming out, but nobody complained. They had no wounds that Murdock had heard about, and it was only a quarter of a mile.

When Murdock figured they were far enough, he had each man take out a signal stick, break it to start it glowing, and hold it up as high as he could and still tread water.

Trent-Jones stayed near Murdock.

"This is a bit cold, isn't it? But better than waiting on the beach. Were those the Palestinian Authority sirens we heard?"

"Probably. They held off long enough so the danger had passed. They don't like to get involved, I've been told."

"Hear something coming," Lam shouted. The rest of them listened, but it was a full minute before Jaybird let out a yell. "Starboard about two hundred," he bellowed. They all waved their light sticks.

"Be a damn shame if this is a Palestinian patrol boat,"

Jaybird yelped. "Hope to hell they don't have any out tonight."

Two minutes later they recognized the Israeli patrol boat, and it cut power and slid up to them through the calm Mediterranean. Once aboard, Murdock asked about the SAS boat.

"The report we have is that it capsized on a rough wave near shore and went down. The other patrol boat heard their Mayday and rescued twenty of the SAS men out of the water and the three crewmen. Five were found on the beach by a search party including the one with the broken leg. Four of the SAS men are missing and presumed drowned."

Trent-Jones slumped in his seat in the cabin. "Four of my men gone. How could it happen? We train in small boats. We dump boats and know what to do."

The Israeli patrol boat captain looked at the notes he had taken on the radio transmissions. "One explanation I heard is that two of the men may have been trapped belowdecks and couldn't get out. The other two could have been knocked unconscious when the craft went upside down, and drowned."

"We lose anyone else on the operation?" Murdock asked. "The Israeli underwater men?"

"All accounted for, Commander."

"Then we missed the other three house targets," Trent-Jones said. "I don't even know where they were. The SEALs took down three of them; at least we did that much."

For Murdock the twenty-mile boat ride was a long one. He was feeling the British SAS man's loss, his pain at the way he and his men had fared in the attack. They had been lucky to lose only four men. Could have been the rough wave caught the boat broadside when it was turning for the run to the beach. Long damn ride.

Murdock was exhausted by the time they hit the dock at Ashdod. Then came the wait in the cold wet cammies for the chopper ride up the coast to Tel Aviv. By the time they were back in their quarters at the Army base, the sun was starting to shatter the blackness of night. Murdock couldn't get out of his mind the look on the SAS man's face when the lieutenant learned he had lost four men. That man's agony would be with Murdock for a long time.

12

Tel Aviv, Israel

Most of the SEALs slept in until 1400 that afternoon. Don
Stroh had been around twice, and the third time he found
Murdock up, dressed, and hungry.

"Breakfast at two in the afternoon?" Stroh asked. His
round face had darkened a little lately from sunshine duty.
His hair was thin and brownish, over ears that were too big
for his head. Blue eyes danced as he escorted Murdock to
the small officers' club where they ate. Murdock had sau-
sages and a stack of eight pancakes. Stroh had coffee.

"Reports are coming in from agents in Gaza City," Stroh
said.

Murdock went on eating.

"Good reports. Your team did a bang-up job last night."

"Why we get the big bucks, Stroh."

"Modesty won't get you promoted, sailor."

Murdock gave him the don't-mess-with-me look, and
Stroh chuckled.

"Always the tough SEAL. Like Arafat was just another
walk in the park during business hours. Another day at the
office. Well, your team totally demolished the Arafat GHQ.
The word we're getting is that there were thirty of the top
leaders of the al Fatah and Tanzim groups in a conference
in the building when the missiles hit. There are no known
survivors. Four cooks and a group of guards are also listed
as KIA."

"We didn't know about the conference. No Arafat?"

"He was supposed to be there, but was delayed by a mal-
functioning aircraft somewhere."

"Our group didn't have much to do. The missiles took care of the matter rather well. We did nail three of the separate units."

"Sorry about the SAS and their losing four men."

"It's a dangerous game we play. Usually some of the good guys get hurt. It just didn't happen to be us this time."

"The local command says there is no sense trying for the other three satellite buildings. Anyone who was there has been moved as of six A.M. this morning and all records taken with them. That's a closed book. We take what we can get, which is about a ninety-percent completion of the mission."

"So we're released here and can go home?"

"No."

Murdock scowled. "Just a plain unpregnant no? Why not? What more do they want from us? What are the new plans? Give me something more than just a two-letter answer."

Stroh sighed and took a long draw on his coffee. He looked at Murdock over the rim of the cup. "I can't tell you a lot more. You are on U.S. Navy TDY orders with an open end. The powers are interested in more than al Fatah. There are several more deadly groups around. This one was the easiest to take down, so it was first. My guess is that there will be three or four more hits. I don't know if you SEALs will be involved in any or all of them. We wait and see."

"Is that huge planning group going to be making the decisions?"

"Probably, but I've suggested that they cut it down to not more than ten people. Two from each of the three nations and four overhead from Israel. They might go for it."

"Whatever, we'll be here. I should get back for our after-mission debrief."

He groused to himself on the way back to their quarters. Sure he loved this job, and he was doing something extremely worthwhile, but sometimes it was frustrating. The platoon could use some good solid teamwork training. He had new men, and they hadn't been fully integrated into the procedures. Every man had to know instinctively what the man on his right and left would do in any firefight situation. That was the way they saved lives. That was the way they lived to be old SEALs who could muster out and flop around on the beach in the sun and not worry about anyone shooting at them.

Maybe after this current project, or three or four, from what Stroh had been hinting, they could get some time to themselves and spend it alone out in the California desert. Do some concentrated squad and platoon drills and firing sequences and realistic training. Some of the older hands were getting a little complacent. Murdock couldn't put up with that because it would cost them a KIA on one of these shoots. He'd be damned if he was going to bury any more SEALs.

Senior Chief Sadler had the men working over their weapons and gear when Murdock came into the assembly room next to their quarters.

DeWitt nailed him when he came in the door. "So, does Brother Stroh have any good news for us? Like when we go home?"

"Not likely. Most likely we'll get some more assignments while we're here. Might as well tell everyone at once."

Murdock called the men together and went over what Stroh had told him.

"So the nut of it is that we're here, and we'll be in more hits against some of the terrorist groups before we leave," Murdock concluded. "We don't know who or what or when, but we'll be ready when it comes."

There were a few groans.

"This is why we get the big bucks," Jaybird said.

"What Navy are you in, sailor?" Mahanani brayed.

"Whatever Navy we are," Murdock said, "we'll probably be doing ground duty for the next mission or two. Most of the bad guys are on the West Bank, which, if you don't know, is the west bank of the Dead Sea, which is between Jordan and Israel. So get out your slogger boots. Right now we do our after-action critique. Bravo Squad, what went right and what could have been better?"

They worked over the mission from top to bottom, and found little to pick on that could have been done better. One suggestion was that on swims of less than a mile, they didn't wear fins. Usually they would be lost when the SEALs hit the beach anyway. A half hour later they had it all thrashed out, and Murdock looked back at DeWitt.

"Lieutenant DeWitt, didn't I see you pick up some books on Israel and the Arab problem that first day we were here?"

"That I did, oh, great one, our Commander."

"They enjoy that rank shit," Joe Lampedusa whispered loud enough so everyone could hear.

"You'd enjoy it too, Lampedusa, if you'd ever get off the pot and go for second class," Senior Chief Sadler snapped.

"Hey, easy on me. I might be wounded again. Anyway, I struck for second a week before we left."

Murdock turned to him. "You did? Get out of here, find a computer you can use to send, and e-mail and check with Master Chief MacKenzie and see if you made it. Move, sailor."

Lam grinned and ran for the door.

"Now, getting back to the important stuff. Lieutenant, how about a half-hour lecture on Israel, its historic place in our society, and how it got the Arabs just mad as hell?"

DeWitt stood, polished the new railroad-track bars on his shoulders, and grinned. "Usually a scholar of my standing doesn't lecture before such a motley and unlettered crew as this. However, this one time, I'll break with academic standards and try to enlighten you."

"What the fuck did he say?" Ken Ching asked. Everyone roared with laughter.

DeWitt went to his bunk and brought back a book. "Actually I was going to lecture to you, but I figured I better just read some of this since I'm not sure if all of you know how to read."

That brought a chorus of catcalls and hoots.

"Listen up: Occupying the southwest corner of the ancient Fertile Crescent, Israel has some of the oldest known evidence of primitive town life and agriculture. A more advanced civilization has been found from 2000 B.C., and the Jews probably arrived here around 1000 B.C. with King David and his successors. From there to about 590 B.C. Judaism was developed."

"So, okay, these guys ain't no Johnny-come-latelies," Fernandez said. "You'd think they'd have their ducks in a row by now."

"They did have a few troubles," DeWitt said. "First the Babylonians, then the Persians, and then the Greeks conquered them. It wasn't until 186 B.C. that the Jewish Kingdom was revived. For a hundred years things went well. Then Rome marched in and took over and put down the Jewish revolts of 70 A.D. and 135 A.D. During this time they renamed Judea Palestine after the first inhabitants of the area, the Philistines.

"The Arabs first took over Palestine in 636. The Arab language and Islam prevailed for several centuries, but there remained a stubborn Jewish minority with its own customs and religion. About the year 1000, foreign empires again started conquering Palestine, including the Seljuks, the Mamluks, and the Ottomans. Ottoman rule lasted for four centuries, until the British took over in 1917 pledging to support a Jewish homeland in Palestine. By 1920 the land east of the Jordan River was detached and Jewish immigration began. Hitler and the Nazis spurred a flood of immigrants, and at the same time Arabs from Syria and Lebanon surged into the area, and it turned violent with fighting between Jews and Arabs. Then in 1947 the U.N. partitioned Palestine into a Jewish and a Palestine state, and Britain withdrew the next year."

"We really having a test on all this?" Bill Bradford asked.

"Absolutely, and anyone not passing has to stay after school," Jaybird yelped. That brought a laugh.

"Now we come to the fun part," DeWitt said. "In 1948 Israel was invaded by Egypt, Jordan, Syria, Iraq, Lebanon, and Saudi Arabia. That put twenty to thirty times as many Arabs in those countries fighting tiny little Israel, which had been a nation for only a year. Israel was not smashed, but she did lose some territory. Egypt occupied the Gaza Strip and Jordan took over a long chunk of former Israeli land on the West Bank of the Jordan River.

After one small stalemated war, Israel went into the Six-Day War in 1967 and smashed the whole neighborhood.

They took over the Gaza Strip, occupied the Sinai Peninsula all the way to the Suez Canal, captured East Jerusalem, Syria's Golan Heights, and Jordan's West Bank. The U.N. arranged a cease-fire.

"Since then there have been minor skirmishes and one-day wars, and raids that have left the whole area unsettled and volatile. Israeli Special Forces made the daring raid into Entebbe, Uganda, in 1976 to rescue one hundred three hostages seized by Arab and German terrorists. It was a textbook raid, perfectly executed, planned in detail, and deadly where needed. We've studied it. We should do so again.

"In the next few years there was some improvement. Israel signed peace treaties with Egypt and Jordan, the later ending a forty-six-year state of war between the two. But terrorism and fighting by Arabs against Israel's military occupation of the West Bank and the Gaza Strip continue to this day."

"And we're right in the fucking middle of it," Jefferson said. "Bet you a buck we're heading for the West Bank on our next mini-vacation to the Holy Land."

"That's enough culture for today, gentlemen," DeWitt said. "I've checked with the locals. There's a ten-mile course laid out to the north of us that we can use for training. If the commander has no objections, we'll do it with full combat gear and weapons, minus the Draegrs. We move out in twenty minutes." DeWitt looked at Murdock, who gave him a thumbs-up.

"All right, people, let's shag ass."

They took the first ten miles at a slow jog, covering a mile in exactly eight minutes. They had done the eight-minute jog so often that it was routine, ingrained into their muscle patterns and brain tissue until they could come within twenty seconds of the time nine times out of ten.

At ten miles, Murdock stopped them and let the men look around the Israeli countryside. They were in a semi-residential area, with some businesses but mostly houses. Even on this fertile plain along the sea, there was little room for farming. Houses had taken over, as they had so much of the world's best farmlands.

Murdock turned the SEALs back. "Van Dyke will lead us out. I want a seven-minutes-to-the-mile pace for the first five, Van Dyke, then move back to eight minutes for the last five. Move out."

When they puffed into the camp and on to their barracks, they found a delegation waiting for them. Colonel Ben-Ami didn't look pleased with the wait. Murdock recognized three of the six men as ones from the first planning session.

"SEALs, good. Murdock, wasn't it? Glad you're back. We have a new assignment. Timing is not so vital, but we need to do some work. Can we all use your dayroom?"

13

At the door to the dayroom, Colonel Ben-Ami motioned to Murdock. "We've cut the size of our planning group. We need just two SEALs."

Murdock nodded and pointed at DeWitt, who moved over with Murdock, and they followed the rest into the dayroom. There were twelve of them standing around the Ping-Pong table. There weren't enough chairs for them all.

"Getting right to the point, gentlemen, our next mission will take us deep into the West Bank. A little background for you on the West Bank. This is often confusing to non-Israelis, and even to some of us. The West Bank is located west of the Jordan River and the Dead Sea. On the east of it is Jordan, and Israel is on the north, west, and south. The sacred city of Jerusalem is on the very west edge of the West Bank. The Palestinian Authority administers and polices several of the major cities in the area, but not all of the West Bank.

"Israel maintains military control over much of the land including several Jewish settlements. There is an estimated population on the West Bank of just over two million. This includes both Jews and Arabs. The size of it is 2,270 square miles; that's about twice the size of the state of Rhode Island, and a quarter of the size of the state of Israel.

"Israel captured the West Bank from Jordan in the 1967 war. A 1974 Arab summit conference designated the PLO as the sole representative of the West Bank Arabs. In 1988 Jordan cut legal and administrative ties with the area. Jericho was returned to Palestinian control in May 1994. An accord between Israel and the PLO expanding Palestinian self-rule in the West Bank area was signed September 28, 1995. Later agreements give Palestinians full or shared control over forty percent of West Bank territory.

"With that foundation, we move on to the project at hand. We have an Israeli presence in most of the major areas of the West Bank. What we don't have is total and complete control. However, when we operate in the West Bank, we can rely on some friendly forces and many safe areas.

"We have a group called the Israeli Land Corps Special Forces. We call these *Mistaravim* units. This Hebrew word simply means becoming an Arab. These units speak and dress like Arabs and act like Arabs do as well. This is not a secret force, neither is it an elite unit. Rather, they are a regular special force unit trained for specific jobs.

"We have a sizable military force at Rama Army Base in the city of Ramallah, which is in the occupied territories. Ramallah is about fifteen miles north of the city of Jerusalem. Remember, Jerusalem is not a huge metropolis. It has about six hundred thousand people, while Tel Aviv has almost four times that number.

"Our Mistaravim units have intensive training for fifteen months concentrating on basic infantry drills, advanced infantry work, and helicopter assault skills. Then come two months of counterterrorism and hostage-recovery work. This is first as individuals, then in advanced operations with units. One of the last training periods deals with learning Arab traditions, the Arabic language, and how Arabs think. Then come civilian camouflage, looking like an Arab with hair dying, contact lenses, Arab clothing, and other elements of undercover operations.

"I'm telling you this because you'll be working with some of these men in the coming mission. This is one that we've been planning for several months. We probably could do it by ourselves, but on this one we want it to be carried out by the combined forces of Britain, the U.S., and Israel.

"Needless to say, we will be in territory controlled by the Palestinian Authority. We will be the invaders. We will wear uniforms of a different type. Some of us will wear the outfits that the Authority police wear. They really are a small army of over thirty thousand men, but their training is spotty and sketchy. On a one-on-one basis, an Authority cop wouldn't have a chance with one of our Mistaravim men. We will wear none of our own traditional uniforms. Arab clothing, brown contacts, even black wigs for some and dyed hair for others. The mission is scheduled to last for three days. That means one day moving to the target, one night to take down the target, and the third day to return to friendly territory, where Mistaravim and Regular Army troopers will be on hand to cover us and welcome us.

"Security will be unreasonably tight. We have a continuing fear that there could be a traitor among us, reporting regularly to the Authority leaders and directly to the terrorist organizations. The leaders of our various units will have sealed orders that will be opened only at the last possible moment.

"I can tell you this much. We will be taking down a terrorist training college, where young converts and enthusiasts get their training in advanced terrorism. We will also be digging out more than forty trainers and cadre, about a hundred students, and blowing up enough ordnance and explosives to flatten a square city block of four-story apartment houses. We know of three such areas, and we will undertake the job of demolishing this one and putting as many Arab terrorists in immediate contact with Allah as possible. We take no prisoners.

"For the next two days the SAS and SEALs will be issued their costumes, get their hair adjusted and their faces and hands tinted to a proper Arab shade. The third day we will be moving into the immediate area, going to Arab towns, in threes and fours, and viewing Arab life. The fourth day will be for transport."

Colonel Ben-Ami turned to where Murdock sat. "Commander Murdock, I understand you have a newly developed shoulder weapon that can fire various types of twenty-millimeter rounds. Is that right?"

"Yes, sir, Colonel. The twenties come in HE, armor-piercing, and smoke, and any of them can be detonated as an airburst up to about a mile."

"Airburst?" The colonel frowned.

"Yes, sir. The round is laser-sighted. The feedback from the laser in a hundredth of a second sets the fuse in the round for the number of rotations the round needs to make until it hits the target. When the spinning round reaches the correct number of turns, the round explodes. It's great for shooting around corners, over buildings, and hitting the reverse slope of a ridge."

"Bring along all of those weapons you have and as many rounds as you can carry."

"Yes, sir."

"Now, any general questions?"

One of the SAS men held up his hand. "Sir, will we be working in our units or will we be dispersed among your Mistaravim specialists?"

"Undecided, Captain. We like both ideas. Your units have been trained in teamwork, cooperation, knowing what the buddy on your right and left will do in most situations. That's hard to break up. However, we believe that some mixing of our specialists in with those units will give us the most effective fighting forces."

"Sir?" Murdock said.

"Commander."

"Will there be time for any fieldwork with live firing in this mixed-team operation? I believe that it would greatly benefit my SEALs to have such a cooperative training run."

"Been some talk of it. Would that be beneficial to the SAS troops as well?"

"Yes, sir," the SAS captain who spoke before said. "It would give us a firmer operational level when we get into the actual mission."

"Then it's done. We'll work it out. That will come at the end of the sessions, when you're in your new uniforms and costumes and Arab civilian camouflage. Yes, I think that will be good."

"Transport?" one of the SAS men asked.

"It will not be a long trip. We will be going in as regular troop rotation replacements at the Rama Army Base near Ramallah we talked about before. We'll go in at night in closed trucks, so no notice will be taken of your disguises. Transport to the mission area will be by civilian sedan in staggered and random routes so we don't alert anyone. Radio control will be strict and timing will be decisive. That's as much as I can tell you about the actual mission."

The Israeli officer looked around the group. "If there are no more questions, we'll be meeting at Building 187 tomorrow morning at 0800 to get our preliminary operation started. Now, one word of caution. This is not a competition between the services or nations. This is a cooperative mission. I know both SAS and SEAL men are highly trained and kept at razor-sharp efficiency. I have read after-action reports on many of your amazing missions. What our instructors will do in the next three days is to try to enhance your current skills, and get them slanted into this unique situation you'll soon find yourself in. We will appreciate the intense cooperation of every man in this operation. That's all. You're dismissed."

Murdock and DeWitt watched the rest of the men go through the outside door, then went to the connecting door into their equipment room. Six SEALs stood there with grins all around.

"Hot damn, we're gonna get some action after all," Canzoneri said.

"Eavesdropping?" Murdock asked as he came through the door.

"No, sir," Jaybird said. "Just watching the TV from way over here. That colonel has a parade-ground voice, doesn't he?"

"Yeah, we're going into the West Bank," Donegan said.

"Holy shit, we're gonna kick Arab ass," Frank Victor shouted.

"Holy shit?" Lampedusa asked. "The Pope been using our latrine again?"

Bill Bradford whacked him with his floppy hat.

"So what do you think, Commander?" Senior Chief Sadler said. "We going to get into some heavy action here?"

"Looks like it, Senior Chief. We better be sure we're

ready. Like the man said, 0800. You guys get chow? Did DeWitt and I miss it?"

"Oh, we chowed down, Commander," Franklin said.

"Figured," DeWitt said. "Can we run a tab on Stroh at the officers' club?"

"Let's try."

14

Desert training area
Near Tel Aviv, Israel

Murdock lifted up at the edge of the wadi until the soft gray, civilian-type hat showed enough so he could get his eyes up and see over the sand and rocks. Ahead of him were two houses, both with hundreds of bullet holes in them. He saw someone in one window and no other sign of occupants. He dropped down and used his Motorola. "Force One, I have one terr showing in the window of the first house. That's just one terr that I can see."

"This is Force Two," his earpiece responded. "We see more than a dozen armed men behind the first house. They're trying to suck you into a trap. Abort scouting mission. Instead, open fire with three of your twenties with airbursts at each side of the house. Weapons are free."

"Twenties one and two take the port side, three and four the starboard. Fire when ready, one round each."

Murdock waited a moment. "Simulating the firing of four twenties on the first house. Over."

"Half the force behind the house is down. Let's move out Force One and Two with assault fire on the first house. Over the top, now!"

Murdock waved his arm forward and his mixed Force One of Six SAS men, sixteen SEALs, and ten Israeli Special Ground Forces charged over the top of the wadi, formed into an assault line, and began firing as they walked forward with a relatively straight line. After fifty yards, and when they were fifty yards away from the first house, the com-

mand came on the radios to charge forward running and
firing.

They ran, and the line bent and angled and then straight-
ened. Quickly the men came to the house, stopped their
assault fire, and used fragger grenades through empty doors
and windows. Then on radio command, the two forces of
thirty-two men each surged inside the six-room, two-story
house and cleared each room in order using flash-bang grenades, then rushing into the rooms. Murdock waited for the
report. He had it twenty seconds later.

"House one clear," Ching reported.

"Four minutes and thirty-two seconds," a new voice said
on the Motorola. They had been reprogrammed to the Israeli
personal radio frequency. "Not bad, a bit off our usual standard, but we didn't kill any of our own chaps. So, good
show. We'll assemble in the living room for a final critique."

Murdock went into the large room with the others. He
looked at his hands and arms. They and his face had been
given an instant three-week suntan, a soft shade of brown
the makeup artist said would fade out and be gone in six
weeks.

The critique by Colonel Ben-Ami took fifteen minutes
and covered everything from the way they entered the sedans, to the timing on the flash-bangs and the assault fire.
When it ended, Murdock decided he hadn't learned anything new and that he and his platoon could work well with
the other professionals they would be fighting beside. He
had hardly recognized some of the SEALs when they put
on their Arab clothes. They had been wearing them for two
days now. None of his men had on wigs, but half of them
had their hair dyed dark black. It would grow out, the hair-
dresser said. Or if they washed their hair every day after the
current assignment was over, the black dye would fade out
in two weeks.

Murdock looked back at Colonel Ben-Ami at the front of
the room.

"This is our last training session," the colonel said. "I
think the past four days have been worthwhile. Gives us
practice working in our new uniforms if nothing else. Some

of you still look a little self-conscious about your Arab clothes. That will be gone when you're on an Arab street with lots of Arabs around you. So, we will have a briefing at 1900 in Building 54. Our civilian transport will leave just after 2200. Remember, no wallets, papers, letters, anything that could identify you on your person. Each of you will have well-used Arab identification papers, the usual for this area, and three hundred in used dinars in case you get cut off or somehow entangled. For you Yanks, a dinar is about the same as a U.S. dollar, worth a little more actually. Are there any questions?"

"Once the target is taken down, how do we find our transport back to Ramallah?" an SAS man asked.

"Your six- or seven-man squads will each have a designated sedan. The sedan will be left near the target. After your independent mission is over, move back to the sedan for a ride home. There shouldn't be any real trouble. If there are roadblocks, you will be dispersed enough going home to prevent any connection. Just use your identity papers, and you should be fine."

"If not, do we shoot our way through the roadblock?"

"That will be a field decision that the senior officer or man in charge in each sedan will have to make. We've been over the assignments of each squad and the timing of each of the actions. Is there any man who does not know the number of his squad, who his squad leader is, and what his squad has as its primary mission?"

No hands went up. There were seventy-six men crowded into the room. Thirty Israeli special ground forces, thirty SAS Britishers, and the SEALs. Two Israelis went with each of seven four-man SAS squads. Three Israelis went with each of five SEAL groups. Four groups had three SEALs each, and one had four SEALs. It made up twelve fighting units, each with its own target and commander.

"No one has asked about wounded," the colonel continued. "We have inclusive medics; however, there are not enough for each six- or seven-man squad. If you have a medical emergency, use your radio and give your location and ask the closest medic to report to you. Best we can do. Remember this, we leave no one behind. We leave no wounded, no dead, and certainly do not allow ourselves to be taken prisoner.

"We have been over our assignments a dozen times. They should be memorized and letter perfect. This is not a sequential type of attack. No one squad depends on another doing a task before it can do its work. Once your job is done, ask if anyone nearby needs help. If not, haul ass and return to your transport and drive out of the area. We do not expect any concentrated resistance from the Arabs.

"You have seen the mix of our squads. This is for security reasons. Six SEALs with no one speaking Arabic would be totally lost in the middle of this situation if, for example, their transport failed. We have put three Israelis with each SEAL squad, and we have also put two Israelis with each of the SAS squads. So far, it has worked out well. Our Israeli Mistaravim members are adequate to fluent in Arabic, and that could be a lifesaver for a squad that is cut off or in trouble somewhere. We hope that it is a precaution not needed."

Colonel Ben-Ami stopped and looked around. "Very well, we'll see all of you later at our briefing at 1900."

The rides back to the Army base were in the same nondescript and much-used sedans that they would use that night to get to the PLO training site. Murdock had no idea how far it was. He dozed off, not sure when he'd have time to sleep again. Before he nodded off, he thought about how he had become a cog in a machine again, a fighter in a squad instead of leading the squad. He shrugged. This was his job, he'd do it the way the hosts wanted it done. If he had reason to take over the squad, he could do that too. He slept.

The briefing at 1900 that evening came after showers and chow and a short time on their bunks. They learned little new, except that the SEALs should bring all of the Bull Pups they had plus all of the rounds they could reasonably carry. At least one of the twenties would be in each mission squad as far as they went. Murdock counted out seven of the twenty-millimeter blasting rifles. He figured twenty rounds per gun, but when he hefted the special ammo pouch that looped over the head and rested on his chest, he cut the rounds to fifteen per man.

Colonel Ben-Ami wore Mistaravim Arab clothing now as the rest of them did. The SEALs had become accustomed to it. Most of the clothing was loose and it helped to hide their weapons. Their combat vests, with all the ammo pockets, were hidden by the outside layer of dark Arab shirts and robe-type clothing.

"We've made one small change of plans," the colonel said. "All of you are ready. We will push off in exactly fifteen minutes. The drive will be about three hours and we will keep in touch by radio, so the cars are never more than a mile apart but not next to each other. All cars have specific parking spots that your drivers know. We will leave the vehicles and move up to the objective on radio orders. Our hope is that we will be on site and ready to attack at 0100. Questions?"

There were none.

"All right, gather up your squads, your equipment, and your ammo and explosives, and we'll move out as soon as every squad leader signals that he is ready to drive."

No one had been told the exact destination, except the drivers. They weren't talking. Murdock settled down for the drive, and came alert when the car stopped. He checked his watch. It was just past 0030. A half hour to attack time.

"We there?" he asked. The Israeli driver chuckled.

"Almost. Another quarter mile. Now I can tell you. This is an arid section of the West Bank in a range of hills about a mile from the Jordan River. The combined PLO-Intifada training camp is located here. We have known of it for about six months and have been working on an attack. With you specialists, it's an ideal time.

"Our target and mission is a set of bunkers at the far south end of the camp where ammunition, explosives, and RPG rounds are kept. It will be heavily guarded. First we have to breach the wire around the camp, which will set off alarms. But identical alarms will be going off at twelve points around the camp at the same time or within seconds."

The driver looked around. His name was Sholomo Per; he was a twenty-eight-year-old career soldier and a leader in one of the Mistaravim units. Per brought the car to a stop at the end of a road. There were barriers there with signs Murdock couldn't read.

Per used the radio. "Squad Bunk in position at parking."

"Good, Bunk. Hold there."

The men eased out of the car. Murdock had SEALs Ching and Vinnie Van Dyke with him along with the three Israeli special forces men. They waited.

Three minutes later the orders came on the radio.

"All units move up toward the wire. Hold thirty yards off for the attack signal."

They formed a line silently, and on Per's arm swing began to jog forward. They had roughly a half mile to go according to the plan. Per spread them out when they came in sight of the boundary fence that marked the southern end of the Arab training camp. They went up within thirty yards and eased to ground and waited.

Four minutes later the word came from the radio. "All units, move up to the wire now and place charges. You have two minutes."

"We have two minutes," Per said. "Ching, you have the C-4. Move up to the fence now and plant three charges that will blow a man sized hole in the barbed wire and single-apron. We want to be able to run through. You have two minutes."

Chin nodded and ran forward. He slowed twenty feet from the wire and crawled the rest of the way. He tied two charges six feet high on the heavy fencing, and then two more down from the top to bottom. He inserted preset timer-detonators, looked at his watch, and waited. When it was twenty seconds to 0100, the radio spoke to them.

"Activate the charges on the fence, now."

Ching pushed in the timers, lifted up, and ran back to where the other men waited thirty yards away.

"Eight, nine, ten," Per counted. The explosions came a second later, four of them almost on top of one another. The three SEALs were in front as they charged the wire. Far off Murdock heard other faint explosions. The blast had done a fair job on the fence, but one segment of the single apron fence on the far side was nearly intact. It stretched out for six feet and started at the three-foot-high level nearest the fence. The main vertical wire had been blown away.

Ching was first man through; he held his MP-5 on his chest and dove into the apron wire, smashing it down within a foot of the ground. Right behind him came Van Dyke, who stepped on Ching's back and leaped over the rest of the wire. Murdock followed, and then the three Israelis. When the last one was past, Ching eased up from the wire, pulled away some of it sticking into his right arm, and came to his feet. Then he ran to catch up with the others.

They ran forty yards directly into the camp toward a soft light over a structure that looked only four feet tall. It was. Vinnie used his Colt M-4A1 Israeli copy and lofted a white star shell over the structures ahead. Now they could see four of the low-lying buildings that were dugouts, with the ammo and explosives underground.

As soon as the star shell blossomed, half a dozen defenders tried to hide. Murdock powered in a twenty round that exploded in the air between the first two buildings. The rest of the squad fired into the area with their small arms. Ching put down one man who tried to run out of the light. Murdock fired two more airbursts between the buildings, and Sergeant Per used his radio mike.

"Right, lads, good work. Now let's go up and greet the bastards face-to-face."

They charged forward in a running assault line, holding fire until they saw any targets. A machine gun opened up to the left next to one of the buildings. Murdock fired a lasered round at the edge of the building, and it burst in the air just over the corner. The machine gun stopped firing.

Twenty yards farther and they hunkered down behind the first of the buildings. Per pointed to the left, and he took that side with his two mates. Murdock and his SEALs moved to the right. When they came around the side of the structure, they saw only two bodies. One lifted up and tried to fire, but Ching cut him in half with a six-round burst from his MP-5.

They looked across at the other two buildings. A door slammed and Murdock frowned. Per slid up beside them. "That far bunker with the door that just closed. Can you take the door off with a twenty, Commander?"

"No problem." Murdock aimed at the door and fired one round. The door disintegrated. He fired one more round through the door and they waited. Nothing happened. Per motioned to the nearby bunker.

"This one first. Two grenades through the door if it's open." He pointed to his two Mistaravim buddies. They charged the door. One swung it open outward and they both fragged it. When the hot shrapnel stopped flying, they charged inside with flashlights on and held away from their bodies. A moment later they came out.

"All clear," one said. "About a hundred tons of explosives in there. Blow the top right off this box when it goes up." Per left them to guard the outside of the closed door. The rest charged the next bunker to their right. The door stood open. Murdock and Ching threw in fragger grenades. When they exploded, the two SEALs charged inside, with their small flashlights on and held away from their bodies. One submachine gun chattered at them. Ching swore and answered with six rounds from his MP-5. Both Murdock and Ching dodged behind wooden crates that usually held rifle ammunition. They heard movement beyond them. Murdock threw a box across the bunker and lifted up with his Bull Pup on the small bore. When the box hit, two weapons fired from chest high toward the back of the bunker. Both Ching and Murdock fired at the muzzle flashes, four sets of three rounds each. When the tremendous sound died down in the cavelike area, neither SEAL could hear a thing. They touched, and shone their small flashes on grenades. Murdock nodded. They both threw the hand bombs at the far end of the forty-foot-long bunker. When the blast sound died away, Murdock thought he heard a groan, then a scream.

They moved forward down an aisle in the bunker through stacks of boxes that could be holding mortar rounds, grenades, or more small-arms ammo. Halfway to the back they stopped. They were moving by feel now, not using the lights.

Murdock touched Ching, held up his flash over a stack of wooden crates, and aimed it at the back of the bunker. There was no response. The two SEALs both used lights and charged down the aisle between the closely stacked boxes. At the back of the bunker they found four men, three of them dead. One man lifted up his hand; his other hand held his bloody chest. Ching put one round through his forehead. They made a careful inspection of the whole bunker using the lights. No more terrorists.

Out front, they found that Per and his other Israeli had cleared the third bunker. They met outside the fourth one. Another Israeli guarded the cleared bunker. Ching leaned against the one he had just helped sanitize.

Per asked Murdock what was in his bunker, and nodded when he heard. "That leaves this last one to hold their C-4, sixty-percent dynamite, and a whole mess of RPG rounds."

Vinnie Van Dyke moved out and checked the door. It was locked from the inside. The three moved back thirty yards, and Murdock put a twenty round into the door, blasting it back inside the bunker. A half-dozen shots snarled from inside the bunker and hot lead slanted through the door.

"Could be a dozen in there," Murdock said. "Maybe we don't have to go in."

Sergeant Per looked at him. "You have your two pounds of C-4?"

Murdock nodded. He took the C-4 out, wrapped the quarter-pounders together with all-purpose green tape, and pushed a timer detonator into the pliable plastic explosive.

"This should give enough bang to set off everything else in that cave," Murdock said. "If the RPG rounds are in wooden boxes, they might survive, unless there's a fire hot enough to burn the boxes and set them off. You ready, Sergeant?"

The Israeli grinned. "Been waiting six months to get

ready," he said. "Blow it when you're ready. We'll be over behind the other bunker."

Murdock ran up beside the fourth bunker with the live terrorists inside. Sergeant Per used his radio.

"We're blowing bunker number four. Get in back of the other bunkers and watch your heads. It will be a real whammer."

Murdock set the timer for ten seconds. He hoped the terrorists were far enough in the rear of the bunker so they couldn't find the bomb and throw it outside. He took a deep breath, figured his retreat line, and punched the activation lever on the detonator. He held his arm out and threw the bomb into the bunker, then ran like hell for the next bunker and slid around the side of it. No sweat. The big boys could do a hundred yards in ten seconds.

He counted down in his mind without knowing it. "Three, two, one." The first explosion was dwarfed by a thunderous, billowing, shattering roar as the top of the bunker shattered and blew out in all directions. The giant explosion sucked into its maelstrom all the air in the vicinity, leaving the six men gasping for breath. Then in a fraction of a second, the vanished air was replaced with a massive, swirling tornado of hot gases, smoke, and air as the explosion surged outward in one stupefying avalance of horrendous blasts that spun the attackers around and dropped them into the West Bank sand and rocks.

Murdock shook his head to clear it, then lifted up on his hands and knees and picked up the Bull Pup he'd dropped. He peered around the side of the bunker when the final gusting blasts passed it and tried to see the exploded bunker. All he could see were a few vertical concrete columns towering over a hole in the ground that was now twice as deep as it had been seconds before.

Sergeant Per slid up beside him and took a look.

"Bingo. Won't have to worry about that C-4 in the middle of Jerusalem. Now about the other three."

Just as he said it, he saw a column of three headlights racing toward them over the desert. They were still a half mile away.

"My meat," Murdock said. He steadied the Bull Pup, put it on the twenty barrel, and lasered in on the first oncoming lights. They were moving at a narrow angle toward the bunkers. Murdock lasered again, then fired. The first round was slightly to the left and hit where the vehicles had been. Murdock adjusted, lasered into the path of the lead rig, and fired another twenty. This time the airburst was close enough to send the rig spinning off the road and crashing into the shallow ditch.

The second and third rigs had wider-set lights. The trucks both slowed and Murdock's next round nailed the second one, killing it in place and blocking the road. The third truck moved cautiously into the shallow ditch to go around it. Murdock aimed directly at the headlights and fired. The contact round hit just at the top of the radiator and exploded with a fury. The rig stalled, then the engine caught fire, and a moment later the fuel tank exploded.

Sergeant Per shook his head. "Sweet Mother, when can I order a hundred of those rifles? We need them. It makes any walking soldier into a slow-moving tank. We could use about a hundred of them and twenty thousand rounds of ammo as soon as you release it for sale."

He shook his head again. "We have three more bunkers to blow."

Before any of them could move, a machine gun rattled out two bursts of nine rounds each, slamming through the bunker area and thudding into walls and roofs.

The team of six dug into the ground.

"Well, now," Murdock said. "Looks like we've run into a small complication we didn't figure on."

15

Murdock looked up from where his face pressed against the sand and rocks of the West Bank ground. The machine-gun firing paused, and the six men darted for cover behind the nearest bunker.

"Sergeant, we've still got three bunkers to blow," Murdock said. "You get them done and I'll slow down the visitors."

"Right, Commander. You used your C-4. We have plenty. Don't get yourself shot up."

Murdock ran to the far corner of the bunker, and saw the machine gun firing at them again. He could see the muzzle flash, and now more small arms joined in. Sounded like AK-47's, heavy, harsh, and deadly. He lasered in on the MG flashes and fired one round. A moment later he saw the killing airburst. The gun fired again, and he lasered it once more and fired. This time the machine gun didn't fire again.

He motioned to Ching, and they went toward the gunmen.

"Must be some of those from the trucks," Murdock said. "We need to slow them down or stop them. What are you shooting?"

"MP-5. Way out of my range."

"Might not be for long." They ran forward for thirty yards and hit the dirt. They waited and listened. They could hear a chorus of dogs barking somewhere to the north. The Israelis had warned them about the dogs. There were packs of them roaming wild all over the West Bank. Also, many homeowners kept them for watchdogs. The Israelis always carried a second handgun to shoot dogs with; otherwise their missions were often blown.

Murdock figured it was three minutes since they had come out this far. He heard an explosion in back of him, and then a sympathetic roar that lit up the night sky into daylight for a hundredth of a second. He looked to the rear and saw the bright flash turn into the reddish glow of a fire.

That brought more shooting from in front of them. Murdock figured the rifle flashes were about two hundred yards away. A dozen of them, maybe more. He fired two quick laser rounds hoping he had the range. One round burst long, the second one came over the flashes, and he fired again, lasering the exploding twenty round.

For a moment there was total silence. Then Murdock could hear talking. Arabic, but he couldn't be sure of the words. One man began to scream, and a gunshot sounded, stopping the human voice.

"Pistol shot," Murdock told Ching. They waited. Ching cocked his head listening.

"Moving," he said. "I'd guess they are going the other way. Bugging out. Now they're running."

Behind them near the third bunker, Vinnie Van Dyke taped two quarter-pound sticks of C-4 together and pushed in the timer detonator.

"A minute, Sergeant Per?"

"Sounds good. Take it into the bunker and put it in the middle of anything that looks like it could explode. Not the ammo boxes. Then shag your ass out of there."

"Aye, aye. I can do that." Vinnie had used his flash to set the timer on the detonator; now he carried the potent bomb inside the third bunker and used the flash to find something dangerous. He found a dozen five-gallon cans that could be gasoline. Nearby were boxes of hand grenades. He found one box open and laid his bomb on top of the hand bombs. Vinnie pushed in the plunger on the timer and ran out the door. He sprinted for the fourth bunker, and was there with time to spare. He and the three Israelis looked around the edge of the fourth bunker as the bomb went off. It was a pounding roar, with smoke and debris shooting out the door of the bunker like it was a rifle muzzle. The roof didn't blow off, but sagged in places. Then they heard the

fire and how it cooked off one box after another of hand
grenades.

"Oh, yeah," Vinnie shouted. "I love it."

Two Israelis took bombs into the last bunker. Sergeant
Per used his radio. "Commander, any luck with the visitors?"

"They gave up and took off for home," Murdock said.
"No action from up ahead of us for five minutes."

"We're three bunkers down, one to go. Hold your spot
and we'll move that way after the final boom-boom. Any
casualties?"

"No cuts or scrapes here, Sergeant."

"Good. See you in about five. After this next blast, give
us some flashes with your torch, if you would. Oh, flashlight."

"That's a roger."

Sergeant Per saw the two Israelis run out of the last bunker, and he pointed to Vinnie and they all ran in the direction
that Murdock had gone. They were thirty yards away from
the last bunker when it blew.

The explosion jolted the four men ahead six feet, and then
drove them to the ground. The gushing, roaring blast disintegrated the roof of the bunker and its three feet of dirt
cover, showering the mass into the air and driving some of
the debris a hundred yards away. It kept roaring and exploding, and then small-arms rounds began cooking off in
the fire, and the four attackers leaped up and charged away
from the area as fast as they could run.

They overshot Murdock by fifty yards, but he and Ching
kept up with them. They were all panting when they dropped
to the ground and caught their breath.

"What in hell was in that one?" Sergeant Per asked.

One of the Israelis grinned. "Sarge, should have warned
you. We found two open cases of C-4. Must have been fifty
pounds to the box. Dumped out the quarter-pounders and
set our small contribution on top and lit the fucking fuse.
Nice bang, what?"

As the secondary explosions died down and the small

arms kept cracking, they could hear half a dozen choruses of dogs howling.

"Hurt their ears," Per said. "Surprised we haven't run into any dogs before now. The Arabs like to keep them on their sites as watchdogs. These are wild ones, roam in packs, and can kill a man if he isn't well enough armed to fight them off."

He looked around. "Anybody hurt, injured, sprained ankle, anything?"

Nobody responded.

"Good." He took out his radio. "Seekyou, Seekyou. This is twelve far south. A knockout here. Anyone close want help?"

"Yes, twelve. We're ten south here, I figure about a mile north of you. We saw and heard your work down there. Good fellows. We ran into about fifty terrs on a night-training problem. Evidently it is a live-round firing test and they have caused us serious problems. Could you put a run due north and say twenty degrees to your left?"

"On our way. We have one twenty. Do you have one of the big ones?"

"No twenty here, would have been a huge help. Actually, they have us pinned down. Our mission was the pumping station, the water tanks, and the wells. Quite a sophisticated setup. Look Russian to me but no names on equipment. We were here and set to get started when a pack of dogs attacked us, and when we fired on them, that brought in the terrs. Don't know how well trained they are, but we're now about a hundred yards from the target and in a wadi with good cover, but no chance we can take on fifty of their AKs and come out ahead."

"We're moving up. Should be there in about eight minutes. Put a star shell over the hostiles and radio us where you are from them. We're gone."

Everyone had heard the radio talk. Sergeant Per led the run to the north and twenty degrees to the left. They covered the first half mile quickly, then came to a series of wadis. They had to dip into the wadis and climb up the other sides. It slowed them.

Per used the radio. "Pinned, give us another three minutes. Damned wadis are killing us."

"Looks like the terrs are organizing some kind of an attack. I can hear them moving units to each side of us. Any speed will be appreciated."

"Star shell now on them," Per said. They had just climbed up on a wadi ledge, and Per motioned to Murdock. "When that star shell goes off, send a round up that way. Could be a half mile. Let them know more trouble is coming for the students."

Murdock nodded and watched to the north. When the bright flare lit the sky to the north, it wasn't as far as they'd figured. Murdock lasered on the star shell itself and fired. He didn't know if that would send back a response on the laser. He waited a second, then two, and saw his round airburst somewhere near the flare. He got off another shot before the flare burned out. They ran up a small rise, and could see the shadows of some small buildings ahead and lights around a large round water tank. To the north of that they spotted some muzzle flashes.

Murdock sent one round that way, and then counted his ammo.

"Hey, twenty, that indeed is a tremendous weapon. One of your rounds burst right over the biggest group. They hadn't bothered to disperse, and that round must have put twenty men wounded or dead. The men to the sides have been pulled back. They are increasing their small-arms fire, but that can't hurt us. How is your ammo supply?"

Per looked at Murdock.

"I'm down to ten. Don't know where they went."

"The terrs know," Per said. "Let's find the wadi our mates are in and work up it to find them. Look alive now; we could start taking fire at any moment."

They ran another hundred yards north, and could see the fire from the terrorist students. Murdock wanted to fire again, but that would give away his position and they were in the open. Another fifty yards and they found a good-sized wash that led to the left.

"Could be it," Per said. They ran along it out of sight for

a hundred yards. It petered out to the surface. There was no sign of the other men.

"Light sticks," Murdock suggested. "Do any of the other squad's men have light sticks they could break and show just to the rear?"

Sergeant Per sent the radio message, and a moment later they spotted three blue light sticks one more wadi ahead and again to the left. They charged up there, radioing where they were and that they were coming in.

"No friendly fire, mates. This is the squad that's come to help you."

They found the six, three Israelis and Senior Chief Sadler, Bill Bradford, and Mahanani.

"Where's your Bull Pup?" Murdock asked Sadler.

"Hell, I didn't rate one. Must be two of them in another squad. Glad you made it."

Murdock and Per talked to Lieutenant Moshie Hadera. He had been in the planning group.

"Commander. We've got one wounded man. They evidently sent out a pair of scouts to check out this facility they must have been making a mock attack on. Caught us by surprise and one of my men took a round through his leg before we got under cover. Thanks for the twenties. Really shook them up. They must think we have a tank in here somehow."

"Glad to help. I need to discourage them some more. I've got ten rounds. I can use up three more. That should do it."

The lieutenant nodded, and Murdock moved up to the top of the wadi bank where he could see the occasional muzzle flash. When he spotted the next one, he lasered it and fired. The round exploded only two hundred yards away. In the flash, Murdock could see the troops in a shallow wadi. He could hear screams of pain when the sound of the round died.

He fired again and then waited. Lieutenant Hadera came up and used his binoculars.

"Yeah, looks like they are moving out. Maybe some damn cadre will form them up into a company and march them away."

"Let's hope," Murdock said.

They waited.

"How about a star shell?" Murdock asked.

The lieutenant nodded and fired one from his rifle. It burst two hundred yards downrange and began to float slowly to the ground. Murdock knew he had twenty seconds. The terrorists had not formed into a company, but were in what looked like squads that were not dispersed the way they should be. He saw a group of three seven- or eight-man squads, and fired a round over them. It exploded with a devastating effect. He sighted in on another group of two squads and fired again.

He got off one more shot as the flare faded. He thought he saw some silver bars on the collar of one of the men just as he fired. It was a direct-impact round and hit five yards in front of the squad, and the shrapnel sprayed them with deadly effect. With the flare, the men in the squad beside him with long guns had been firing as well, cutting down more of the terrorists.

"Let's go get them," Sadler said. He looked at the Israeli Mistaravim officer.

He nodded. "We'll leave my wounded man here and come back and blow up this facility. Spread out in a line of skirmishers ten yards apart. We'll go at a steady jog. No firing until we run into them. At the site they stayed at, we'll look for wounded to dispatch. Let's go."

At the shallow wadi they found ten packs, a rifle, eight dead bodies, and two wounded who were put out of their misery.

"Ten down, we estimated fifty of them. Forty to go, with a bunch carrying your shrapnel and in no mood to fight. Let's catch them."

The attackers ran then with their weapons at port arms. Within a hundred yards they caught two stragglers limping. They were gunned down without a missed step as the eleven men charged forward.

Another hundred yards and Bradford stopped them. "Listen," he said. They did.

No sound of movement ahead. "I heard bolts clicking on

rifles. They have stopped running and are in a wadi waiting for us. Scouts?"

He looked at Lieutenant Hadera. The Israeli pointed to his two men, who slid out of the group and worked ahead silently. The rest of the raiders settled down in a four-foot-deep wadi out of harm's way and waited.

"Fifty yards and all clear," the Motorolas chirped.

"A hundred yards, yes, voices ahead. I can see the wadi. It's a deep one and long, almost straight. We could cut fifty yards to the right and hit the wadi. I'll be there waiting. Then we take them from the flank. They'll have no protection."

"Will do," Lieutenant Hadera said. He motioned to the rest of the men. "Absolute silence. No talking, coughing. At a walk."

They moved like shadows in the faint moonlit night. First they went to the right fifty yards, then turned north. They found the wadi and the two Israelis waiting for them.

"The troops are up there about forty yards," the scout whispered. "A little bend, then we can see them."

The lieutenant arranged his firepower. He put Murdock in the middle of the twenty-foot-wide wadi, then ranged men on each side of him, some to stand, some prone so they all could fire at once. They crept forward, careful not to make a sound.

A murmur of voices came to them; then they were at the bend and Per gave the order with a whisper into his mike. "Now."

The men fired at once. Murdock got off two 20mm rounds, then switched to the 5.56 barrel and emptied a magazine. Around him men were firing. A few return rounds came; then the survivors stampeded down the wadi to a bend and out of sight. Murdock put another twenty round at the bend in the wadi, and hoped he had some shrapnel angling up the channel where the men must still be running.

They moved up slowly on the killing field. Two wounded were dispatched with single shots. They counted twenty-four bodies. There were thirty backpacks abandoned. Murdock checked out one. They held only clothing and a meal carton.

Lieutenant Hadera gave the order quietly. "Pick up all weapons and ammo you can find. We'll put it in the next fire we set. Let's move back to our target."

By the time they had scoured the area, they had twenty-six AK-47's and over three hundred rounds of ammo. They divided up the weapons and marched back to the watering hole.

Lieutenant Hadera had worked out his assignments on blowing the water facility before they left. Now he made the duties known, and the men went to work planting charges. They worked the cover off the well. It was a six-inch drilled well, and they couldn't get into the pipe. They set charges to mangle the pipe and blow up the diesel engine that powered it. The pumping station took several charges to demolish the pumps and the engines that ran them. They set off the pump charges first. The diesel blew and caught fire, and when the diesel fuel spilled out, it began burning. The men threw the AK-47's into the fire to ruin them.

The pipeline from the water tower was hit next with charges pasted on the big pipe downstream a hundred yards, then each twenty yards up to the tank. The blasts were set off in sequence. The terrorists would have to lay a whole new pipeline through this stretch toward the main facility.

Mahanani helped set charges on the pair of huge water tanks. He had no idea how much water they would hold, but he had seen smaller tanks on standpipes in good-sized towns in Mid America. They put charges on one side, under the legs on the far side, and then two more charges, setting up both tanks the same way. The men activated the charges on signal by the radio, each set for thirty seconds; then they all ran uphill so they wouldn't be caught in the flood of water.

"Damn shame to waste the water," Lieutenant Hadera said. "But there's no way we can get it to the Israeli settlers who need it."

The explosions came then, sharp cracks of brilliant sound and light. The big tanks wobbled; then the water gushed out of them at four ruptures on each one. When the water was gone, flooding downhill into a wadi, the tanks tipped all the way over and rolled down the slope a hundred yards as the twelve men cheered.

Hadera used the radio. "Water pump squad. Done here. Anyone need help?"

"Well done, water pump. You're too far down there to be of help to us. We're nearest you. Things in hand here. Report back to your transport and get out of town before they report this raid to their highway units. Go."

Murdock looked north. He had ten more men up there somewhere. He wasn't going to be able to do a damned thing to help them.

Lieutenant Hadera thanked them and said he would see them back at the Army base. Sergeant Per gathered his men and they began their hike back to their car.

"About two miles, so shouldn't be a strain," he said. When they were a half mile from the spot where they'd left the car and well past the blown-up bunkers, Murdock touched the sergeant's sleeve.

"Maybe it would be good to send a scout out and check around the car."

"Good idea," Sergeant Per said.

"I'll go," Van Dyke said. He waited until the rest of the men had dropped to the ground, then jogged forward, careful not to make any noise. He slowed as he came to within fifty yards of the car. Then he stopped and studied the area. Nothing looked out of the ordinary. He couldn't see much, but there seemed to be no black bulges around the car where there shouldn't be.

Van Dyke moved forward slowly, one easy step at a time. He made sure his foot did not break a twig or kick a rock before he put his weight on it.

He was thirty yards away when he heard a man near the car cough. Then he saw the glow of a cigarette at what could be the other end of the car. Two of them. It had to be a roving patrol outside the fence. They must have heard the explosions half a mile away. Van Dyke knelt on the sandy soil deciding what to do.

16

Van Dyke knew two terrorists waited for them at the car. There was no cover or concealment. He went to the ground silently, turned his head away from the car, and whispered into the mike, "Skipper, two visitors at car. Hold there."

Van Dyke remembered a fringe of stunted brush on both sides of the narrow road where they'd parked the car. He lifted up and faded at a forty-five-degree angle away from the car and toward the brush. It would put him about thirty yards from the car. He watched every direction, made sure he didn't make any noise when his feet hit the sand and stones. The men at the car didn't move. He saw the cigarette glow again, and the cougher hacked four more times. Good.

Van Dyke made it to the fringe and stepped into the concealment. It was sparse. The two men should be watching the area in front of the car toward the border fence.

After five minutes of hard and careful movement, Van Dyke reached the dirt road forty yards behind the car. He slid in and out of the brush along the road as he advanced. He could see neither of the terrorists. One was near the rear wheel. The cougher must be at the front of the sedan. Which way would he be looking? Outward, toward the fence. That was what he protected.

Van Dyke moved faster then. He held his MP-5 at port arms, ready to bring it down and fire quickly. He wanted to do it all silently if possible. When he was ten feet from the front of the car, he could see the coughing guard clearly. He had one foot on the front bumper staring toward the fence. Van Dyke drew his KA-BAR fighting knife and held it in his teeth as he took the final six quick steps.

The terrorist guard turned just before Van Dyke got there, but he was too late. The butt plate of the MP-5 was already six inches from his skull and descending rapidly. It hit with a ripe-melon sound and the man collapsed. Van Dyke grabbed the fighting knife from his mouth by the blade, drew it back, and threw it at the smoker, who had turned at the sound the first man made when his head banged against the fender on his way down.

The chest was the perfect target and Van Dyke's throw sailed true, turned over halfway, and the blade plunged six inches into the startled terrorist's chest. It entered just below his heart. He tried to yell, but couldn't. He held onto the door handle for a few seconds, then sagged as a large severed artery coming out of his heart pumped all of its blood into his body cavity, and sank to the ground, both hands grabbing at the big knife.

Van Dyke butt-stroked the unconscious man at the front of the car a second time, smashing in his skull, then dragged his body into the brush. When he got back to the smoker, he ground out the still-burning butt on the ground, withdrew his KA-BAR from the dead man's chest, wiped it clean on his shirt, and pulled the body behind some low-growing shrubs.

Van Dyke used the radio. "All clear. I have a sedan leaving from this point to Ramallah in four minutes. Hustle, you guys."

"All clear?" Sergeant Per asked.

"Clear as the midnight ride of Paul Revere. In a word, yes."

"Be there in five," Per said.

Van Dyke checked the car. They'd had time; they could have booby-trapped it. He used his flash and checked underneath on the muffler. No heat-sensitive bomb. Nothing wired under the hood to go boom when the starter kicked over. He picked up the dropped AK-47's and pushed them into the car's trunk. Van Dyke slid into the brush out of sight when he heard the five men coming.

"Friendlies coming in, hold your fire," Ching called out.

"Welcome on board," Van Dyke said, stepping out of the brush. "Let's get this act on the road."

Murdock looked north as the car turned around and headed back to the Army base at Rama. He wondered how the other ten SEALs were doing.

Jaybird, Jefferson, and Victor had slept most of the way to the target from the Rama Army Base. One of the Israelis with them nudged them awake.

"Close by now," the squad leader said. He was Sergeant Jacob Epstein, and he told them he'd been on over twenty killing missions into the Palestinian territory. The SEALs could tell a bloodied trooper when they talked to one. Epstein said they were less than a mile from their parking spot. "Let's get ready."

The SEALs pushed magazines into weapons and charged rounds into the chambers. Their car edged to a stop near a pair of small buildings on a dirt street that ended in an open field. They could make out a security fence not far beyond the end of the road.

They had been briefed on their target. Their two six-man teams would go after the barracks for trainees, visitors, and workers at the learning center. The driver and squad leader told them there should be about 150 trainees and workers at the site. They should be mostly in the barracks. Epstein's team would launch a surprise hit on one of the two units precisely at 0100. The other team would hit the near by second barracks in the complex. Both buildings were new and had been in use for less than a year. This secret facility had been exposed after a PLO prisoner captured by the Israeli forces had talked his head off in exchange for his freedom. He'd given them a detailed description of the facility, personnel, and scheduling of classes.

Both Jaybird and Jefferson had 20mm weapons. They would start the operation with white phosphorus through the windows on the ground floor, then HEs through as many windows as they could hit. There should be three or four other strikes by the combo forces in the main area of the camp at the same hour, so any opposition would have to choose what to defend.

The second sedan rolled to a stop not far away, and its six men got out. Jaybird and Epstein's squad left its car and assembled near the fence.

Sergeant Epstein motioned them to the side. "We'll cut this fence. Too close to use explosives. Cut it and get through at fifteen minutes after midnight. Gives us thirty more to get in position above the barracks for the 0100 attack. Everyone ready? We have ammo and plastique, right?" They all murmured their assurances.

"The other lads will cut the fence; we'll follow them through," Epstein said. "No quick triggers. We don't fire until I give the order. Jaybird and Jefferson, you'll start the party. Let's move out."

They worked through the fence cut, then to the left and up a slight hill past a dark and silent building to a cut-bank above the first barracks. It wasn't as large as Jaybird thought it would be. Three stories and maybe a hundred feet long. Housing for fifty students, probably on double-deck bunks. Jaybird hoped they all were home when the party started. There was a good chance that the trainees would not have ammo for their weapons in the barracks.

He waited.

Victor fingered his MP-5. He might not shoot until they were closer or inside. The range was almost a hundred yards. He screwed on the silencer, thinking it might help inside.

The growl came from the right.

"Dogs, damn, fucking dogs," Epstein said. "They use them for guard dogs. But usually they're just packs of wild things. Might be only one or two or a dozen. We can't fire our weapons at them. Knives?"

A dog lunged through the darkness directly at Victor. In a reflex action he lifted the MP-5 and drilled three silent rounds into the dog's chest. The large dog angled to the left of Victor, pushed by the high-velocity 9mm Parabellums. It whined a moment, then rolled over and didn't move.

"Nice shooting, Victor," Epstein said. "I didn't even know

you had a silencer for that little squirt gun. There could be more dogs, so keep alert."

They had moved up another forty yards when three dogs leaped at them without a sound. Victor got one; the other two went down with KA-BARs slicing into their throats and hearts. Jaybird pushed a big black dog off him where it had knocked him down. The dog gave a low growl, and Jaybird drove the KA-BAR into the dog's throat and slashed it out.

"Damn dogs," he said, wiping canine blood off his blade and his right hand.

The squad paused and waited for the other unit to catch up with them. Then they eased along the last quarter mile until they were at their two assigned firing points.

Jaybird checked his watch. He pushed the light on the dial and saw that they were ten minutes early.

"We wait," Sergeant Epstein whispered to the men. The six men were spread out at five-yard intervals watching the target. There were still a few lights on in the rooms.

Three minutes later a ragtag unit came into the security lights at the back of the building. One man kept shouting something.

Epstein came past each SEAL. "He's screaming for a medic. Claims he fell down and broke his leg and he needs attention."

"He'll have a lot more than a broken leg to worry about in about four minutes," Jaybird whispered back.

The two Bull Pups would start the action with WP rounds into the ground-floor windows. Then move with HEs, or more WPs, on any targets the two SEALs could see.

Jefferson and Jaybird sighted in on their targets. Jefferson had the left side. Less than a minute later the word came in the earpieces.

"Twenties, give them hell."

Jefferson had been waiting with his finger on the trigger. He fired. Jaybird's round came out a moment later. The smoke rounds both went through windows on the ground floor. At once the rest of the squad began firing into the barracks. Jefferson and Jaybird put four more WP rounds each into the barracks' ground floor, and at once could see the smoke of the fires they had started.

Men poured out of the building, caught the rifle and automatic-weapons fire, and promptly scurried through doors toward the front of the structures where they would be out of the direct line of fire. There was no return fire.

Jaybird got in one airburst before the screaming students found their way back into the burning building or out the front.

"SEALs hold here and continue firing at targets of opportunity. I'm taking the SAS and moving around so we can get some shots at the front of the place," Epstein said. He scowled. "Jefferson, bring your twenty and come with us."

They left at once, running down the hill and across a lighted area to the darkness and around the side of the building, keeping fifty yards away from it.

Jefferson got off a round as they ran. He saw thirty or forty men, clad mostly in underwear, milling around the front of the burning building. His first shot airburst over them and a third of them went down.

The Israelis fired automatic weapons, and what was left of the group scattered. Jefferson tracked a group of ten and lasered them and fired. Only four of them kept moving after the airburst that sprayed them with deadly shrapnel.

"Jefferson, put some HE into the front of the building. Windows if any are left." The words came over the Motorola.

Jefferson fired two contact rounds. The first hit the window frame and smashed it inside as it blew. The second went in a third-floor window and exploded inside.

Jefferson watched a car race into the area and slam to a stop. He put a twenty-millimeter round into the car before the men inside could get out. The car exploded, then the gas tank went, and the whole thing was a funeral pyre blazing into the night.

"Move back," the radio in his ear told Jefferson. He lifted off the ground where he had been firing from, and ran with the three SAS men back the way they had come.

Jaybird was still slamming twenties into the second and

third floors. "You got any more WP?" he asked.

Jefferson said he had four. "Give me two and let's light up the second floor," Jaybird said. "Damn box isn't burning fast enough."

They fired the last four WPs' and the phosphorus started more fires. Jaybird had a view of the second barracks. It too was now on fire, burning brightly.

"We're done here," Sergeant Epstein said on the radio. "Let's hook up with the other squad and move back. Other squad, where the hell are you?"

"In your hip pocket in case you hadn't noticed," the radio chirped. "Be there in two. Going your way."

The other squad jogged in out of the darkness, and they all left for the parking area.

"Scout out front?" Jaybird asked over the radio.

Epstein thought a minute, then the radio came on. "That you, Jaybird? If it is, take the lead. Keep within forty yards of us. Hard to see anything in this damn half-moonlight. Use your radio and keep us up to date."

Jaybird said he would, and jogged ahead on the route back toward the cars. At first it was just a walk in the park. He kept his eyes watching forward, and nearly missed the movement to the right near the fence.

He dropped into the sandy rocks and used the mike. "Company. Something next to the fence behind me about twenty and twenty in front of you. I think I smell exhaust, so it could be a jeep or an armored rig. They have any?"

"No armored. Maybe a jeep. We're down and waiting."

"How about a star shell straight up? I'll nail the bastards if it's them. Couldn't be any of ours, could it?"

"None of our people are within half a mile of us," the whispered words said. "Star shell coming."

Jaybird found some thick weeds to lie in with the Bull Pup aimed at the suspect. He heard the rifle report; then seconds later the flare blossomed two hundred feet above. He saw the rig at once, an open jeep with four men. All had rifles. He had already aimed, and he fired less than a second after the flare burst. The HE round hit the small vehicle in the engine area, blew it off its wheels, and turned it over, disintegrating the engine. His second round found the gas tank, and the whole thing went into a fireball that lighted the area for fifty yards around. He could see no movement. Then he did.

One man crawled away from the fire directly toward Jaybird, who switched to 5.56 and drilled six rounds into the crawling form. The terrorist flopped over once, then never moved again.

"Welcome to hell, bastard," Jaybird whispered.

"Light or no, we've got to move." The radio brought Epstein's words. "We'll circle and find you, then get away at a fast run. Moving."

Jaybird saw them come out of the fringes of the light. He jogged out to meet them; then they angled for the fence, and the two miles they had to cover to get to their parking spot.

Jefferson and Victor pulled alongside Jaybird.

"Good shooting, little buddy," Jefferson said.

"Yeah, but I'm down to one more twenty."

"I've got four more in case we hit trouble. Glad to share."

They kept running.

Just over twenty minutes later they hit the dirt and checked out the hole in the fence they had cut an hour ago. It would be a perfect trap for anybody watching for them.

One of the SAS men slithered toward it, used night-vision goggles, and tapped his mike three times.

"All clear," Epstein said. "But we still go through one at a time, twenty yards apart. Move."

Five minutes later they slid into the two cars and headed for Ramallah.

"Nice night's work," Jaybird said where he sat next to the driver in the front seat.

"Beautiful," Sergeant Jacob Epstein said. "We've got to get some of those twenty-millimeter slammers if we have to steal them."

"Amen to that," Jaybird said. "I voted to have each of our men carry one, but seven is all we could wrangle."

"Don't make me jealous. Now let's settle down and get

some sleep before we hit home. I'll let you know if we run into any trouble."

It took Jaybird five minutes to get to sleep. He wondered what the rest of the SEALs were doing. Was it target practice like they'd had, or did some of the guys come up against some real opposition? He looked north, where more SEALs were in operation around the headquarters of this training complex.

17

They had a seven-man squad with four SEALs and three Israelis. Fernandez checked the scene. They had just hiked in two miles from their transport, and were on a small rise behind what they were told was the general headquarters building of the training complex run by the PLO with some assistance from Osama bin Laden.

Fernandez frowned. Ahead was a concrete-block building, two stories, with only one window on the rear and no rear doors. From his vantage point it looked like a fort. SEALs Donegan, Franklin, and Canzoneri dropped beside Fernandez.

"We going to take that place down?" Canzoneri asked. "Looks like the outside of a tank."

Sergeant Menuhin slid into the dirt beside Fernandez. "Looks pretty tough, doesn't it? But we take it from the front. We have ten minutes before 0100. By that time we'll be in front of it with half the squad on each side. We have one of the twenties. You'll fire it to start our operation. Then after five or six rounds inside, we throw grenades through the windows and charge in and clear it out room by room."

"How many rooms?"

"Twenty-eight if our spy is correct. Shouldn't take long. Your long-range artillery should soften them up considerably."

"Who will be there this time of night?"

"It's a combination office and living space for the top officials in the training division here. If we're lucky, we can wipe out their top cadre and training officers. There are supposed to be twenty-two men quartered and working here. We better move."

The Israeli Mistaravim had split his seven men into two details, one on each side of the block house. They expected no guards walking outside. It was a secure area. Fernandez and Canzoneri went with the sergeant and another Israeli around the right-hand side of the building.

The three with the sergeant walked toward the building as if they belonged there, especially in their Arab civilian clothes. They paused at the side of the building, and Sergeant Menuhin checked his watch.

"Two minutes to wait," he said.

They took a quick look around the corner of the building, and saw four men leave the complex. All had on civilian clothes since that was what they wore when they went on raids. Menuhin let them go. He looked at his watch again, then saw two quick flashes of light from the far side of the building.

"Let's move. We get out front far enough for Fernandez to use that twenty. Now." They sprinted out thirty yards and went to the dirt in what looked like a parade ground. Fernandez put the first round through a second-story window, the second one through the front door, which he blew off the hinges. He tried a WP round on the first floor to the left, and by the time he got off one more WP round to the second floor left, men began pouring out of the building.

He lasered one round over the heads of a dozen, then shifted to his 5.56 barrel and with the rest of the shooters began picking off individuals who darted out of the building. They couldn't get out the back.

Some return fire came. Fernandez saw muzzle flashes from the end of the second floor. He triggered a twenty into the room, where it exploded, and the firing stopped. He searched other windows for shooters, but found none. No more men came out the door.

"Move up," Sergeant Menuhin said into the personal radio. "We go in two at a time. SEALs pair and you Army types take it. First team goes in and works down the left-side hallway clearing the rooms as you go. Grenades or gunpowder. Next team in takes the right-hand side and we do the same routine. When the first floor is clear and there isn't a battalion out front firing at us, we work the second floor. SEALs, inside."

Fernandez and Franklin hit the hole where the door had been, and darted to the left through a small lobby. They saw no one alive. Two bodies had been blown across a desk and another one was sprawled beside it. They ran to the first door in the hallway. Fernandez kicked it open and jolted to the wall beside the opening. No reaction. He looked inside. The lights were still on in the building. No one was in the room.

Franklin went to the next door on the other side, and turned the knob and pushed it open hard. Two rounds blasted through the opening. Franklin reached around with his MP-5 and hosed down the room with nine rounds. He looked in from floor level, and found two men in civilian clothes, both dead against the far wall.

They checked seven rooms on the ground floor left, found four empty, and killed four more terrorists before they reported the floor clear to Sergeant Menuhin. They had heard firing to their left, and soon Donegan and Canzoneri came on the radio reporting their section clear.

"Stairs center," Menuhin said. "We'll meet there and take on the upstairs."

They met and moved up the stairs slowly. The sergeant poked his head over the top step and then jerked it down. Three rounds blasted through the space where his skull had been.

Donegan jerked the pin out of a grenade, let the handle fly off, and cooked it two seconds before he threw it down the hall. It exploded when it hit and they heard some yells. By that time the sergeant had a grenade ready, and he threw it farther down the hall.

When the shrapnel stopped zinging down the hallway, Canzoneri lifted his MP-5, pushed it over the top step, and sent three bursts of three rounds down the hall. He took a look.

"Nobody showing," he said. "I'll crawl to the first door left. Cover me."

Canzoneri dropped to the floor and slithered forward, his MP-5 in one hand and a grenade with the pin pulled in the other hand. He kicked in the door.

Down the hall a head poked out of a room. Donegan chased the man back inside with a three-round burst into the door frame. There was no reaction from the first room. Canzoneri looked inside, then jolted into the room and fired two shots, and came out nodding.

Donegan took the next room. Before he could open it, two rounds slammed through the door. He jolted the panel open and flipped inside a grenade that exploded with a roar. Donegan rushed into the room the minute the bits of deadly steel stopped singing. He fired two three-round bursts, cutting down the man at the window who was trying to get outside.

They worked the rest of the rooms. Only two more were occupied, and the terrorists tried to give up, but the Mistaravim men gunned them down. The Israelis had seen firsthand what these terrorists could do in a crowded marketplace with a car bomb.

Sergeant Menuhin gave the men a thumbs-up and waved them down the hall. They encountered no more hostiles as they went outside and ran around the back of the building and up the slope nearly to the fence. Then they paused.

Menuhin gathered them around. "That's our first objective. Now we have time to hit the secondary. It's their training rooms, assembly room, mess hall, and kitchen. This one is supposed to be wooden construction, so our plan is to burn the sucker down. About a quarter of a mile more north. Let's do it double time."

They ran north along the fence, and found one place they had to zig down closer to some small single-unit buildings. Fernandez figured it might be officer country. They angled into the camp itself past two small buildings that were dark and closed.

Sergeant Menuhin stopped them at the corner of a concrete-block building. "Just past this is the area we want.

Let's get some of your WPs into the place if you have any
left, Fernandez. Then we'll hit what's left with C-4 on one-
minute timers. Spread out after the WPs, and don't push in
your detonator activator until you get word by radio."

Fernandez went to the prone position and slammed one
round through a set of windows nearest them. The WP exploded inside and a fire began. He had three WPs left. He
spread them around the complex, then waved at the Israelis.

They all ran to the building, kicked in doors to get inside,
where the bombs would do the most damage. Fernandez and
Franklin found themselves in the assembly hall. It was big
enough to hold two hundred. They found the basic roof sup-
ports and put bombs on them. They planted four bombs,
then gave a ready to Sergeant Menuhin on the Motorola.

"Hold until I get everyone covered." The SEALs waited,
watching for anybody to come in and challenge them. Nobody moved.

Three minutes later the signal came. "Punch in the one-
minute timers now, and haul ass out of there and back to
the fence. We'll group up there. Go."

Franklin and Fernandez punched in the timers and ran for
the door. They could smell smoke all over the big building.
At the door they paused and Franklin looked out.

"Shit, we got trouble. Looks like fifteen fuckers out there
with their automatic rifles, in a line of skirmishers, like
they're waiting for us to come out."

"Fifteen to two," Fernandez said. "And we have about
thirty seconds to figure it out before those bombs go off."

"Any twenties left?" Franklin asked.

Fernandez checked the magazine. "Empty," he said. He
pulled the bolt back a half inch. "Yeah, one in the chamber.
What are they, forty yards out there? I'll laser one over their
heads and as soon as it goes off, we hose them down with
everything we have left, then get our butts out of here."
Fernandez aimed the twenty Bull Pup and fired.

After that the two of them fired their weapons as fast as
they could. Fernandez didn't figure out if the twenty did the
damage, or the automatic fire from the 5.56 and the 9mm
rounds. About ten seconds later, he realized it had worked.

Most of the fifteen were down, and not by choice.

"Go, go, go!" Fernandez bellowed.

They came out the door just as the charges blew behind them, giving them an added boost. Franklin's magazine ran dry, but he didn't have time to put in a new one. He and Fernandez set a new record for the two-hundred-yard dash as they pounded down the street, arms pumping, breath coming in desperate gasps. They rounded a building and slowed; both jammed in new magazines and then tried to figure out where the fence was, the boundary fence for the meeting.

"Nobody behind us," Fernandez said.

"We shot the shit out of them fuckers, but we got to keep going. To the right up that slope to the right in the dark, that's the fence. Come on."

Five minutes later they lay in some tall weeds on the slope next to the fence. Two of the Israelis had shown up. One used the radio and guided in Sergeant Menuhin, who brought along Donegan and Canzoneri.

They were halfway back to where they had left their car when Franklin moved up to Fernandez and hit him on the shoulder. "Hey, we walk through any water anywhere? I got some strange wet squishing in my left boot."

Sergeant Menuhin heard the words and stopped them. He used his pencil flash and looked over Franklin's left leg.

"You took a round about halfway up your thigh, Franklin. Didn't you feel it?"

"Hell, we was running so fucking fast I couldn't even feel the ground. One of them bastards shot me?"

"Looks that way, went right on through. Let me put a bandage on it and a pad on both sides. I won't even take your pants off. Hold steady now." The Israeli wrapped the wound with a white bandage that stood out in the darkness.

"Oh, yeah, now I can feel it," Franklin said.

"Can you walk, little buddy?" Fernandez asked him.

"Can an eagle fly? Let's get moving."

"Better have a shot of morphine, sailor," Sergeant Menuhin said. "That leg could go out on you at any time."

"No way, Sarge. I'm fine. Lets chogie."

The Israeli frowned. "Chogie?"

"Yeah, haul ass, get out of town, move it."

Menuhin grinned. "Yeah, okay, we can always carry you if you pass out. Let's chogie."

Fifty dark yards farther along the fence, Canzoneri stopped the squad.

"Hey, I feel naked. We don't know what's out front. I'm moving out as a scout. That way we won't all get clobbered if they're waiting for us."

The sergeant nodded, and Canzoneri jogged out thirty yards until he could just barely see the shapes behind him. "I'm at thirty, let's move," he said on the radio.

When they passed the headquarters building, they could see the fires still burning. A few men idled around. Nobody was trying to put out the fire.

"Fuckers planned everything but a fire department," Franklin said.

Canzoneri found nothing to hinder their movement along the fence. Twenty minutes later they came to the cut-open place. He stopped the squad and watched the area for five minutes. Nothing, no trap waiting for them.

"Yeah, the hole in the fence looks like a virgin, but better spread out to twenty yards between you and then run like hell through it. I'm first. Hey, this scout shit is okay."

Fifteen minutes later the seven men squeezed into the sedan they had left parked less than three hours before. It was just after 0315.

"Let's get this show on the road," Franklin said. "I need a two-hour nap." He frowned, then his face twisted and he groaned. "Damnit, Sarge, you still have that little shot of morphine? I think I need it now."

18

Lieutenant Ed DeWitt, Lam, and Howard lay in the sand and rocks just inside the fence up a half mile from the head-quarters building that Ed knew was a target. He worried a little about coming back this way past the HQ once it had been hit by a squad. He was with three Israelis. Corporal Zared led the team. He had briefed them in the car.

They were hitting the small ammo and explosives bunker that was at the north end of camp where terrorists could stop by and pick up weapons, ammo, or explosives on their way to missions. It was restocked from the big ammo bunker that another squad would attack far to the south end of the camp.

"If we have time, we double back about a quarter mile and take out the small motor pool they have. Our reports show ten two-ton trucks for personnel, ten or twelve sedans, six jeeps, and four SUVs."

DeWitt felt his palms get moist, the way they did some-times just before a mission. It was a little strange taking orders from a corporal, but he was just another cog in the machine now, doing his job. Get it done and get away with-out losing a man. That was his purpose.

"We move in five minutes," Corporal Zared said. "We hit the ammo at exactly 0100 to coordinate with the other strikes. Any questions?"

"Yeah," Lam said. "Will there be any C-4 in that bunker we can team up with on our bombs?"

"Let's hope so. We'll send two men in. It's a relatively small bunker dug half underground with a concrete base and sides and three feet of dirt on top of the roof. It will be locked, but we'll shoot the lock off. I have a forty-five automatic I brought along to do just that. Then we put two men inside; the rest of us are security. Lam, you and my man will go in and set the charges. Rig them with one-minute timers, but don't start them until I give the word on your radios. Okay, time to move.

"The mound is that third blob to the left up there. I've been watching it and there aren't any guards of any kind. I haven't seen any interior guards anywhere in this camp. Sloppy, and a dangerous way for them to operate. Let's go, now."

They worked down the slight slope and into the main camp, past two small buildings and around a streetlight of sorts. Then they came to the ammo bunker. A shadow moved by the sunken door. Ed DeWitt pointed to it, and the Israeli took out a thin-bladed knife and worked up silently.

The guard sat on a chair that leaned back against the bunker door. He was sleeping. One slash with the sharp blade across the man's throat, severing the left carotid artery and the jugular vein, and the terrorist guard slept forever. Ed dragged the guard to the back of the bunker. Corporal Zared fired twice at the heavy padlock on the door, and it jolted off into the dirt. One Israeli and Lam went inside with their two pounds of C-4 each. They used the radio two minutes later.

"We've got the charges set, the timers for thirty seconds, and we're ready to rock and roll," Lam said.

Howard, DeWitt, and Corporal Zared moved to one side of the door.

"Push in the timers and get out of there," Zared said. He pointed in the back toward the brush along the border fence, and when the two came out of the bunker, all six men ran for the brush. They were halfway there when the charges went off. It didn't blast the roof off the bunker, but smoke and debris gushed out the doorway and blew the door fifty feet across the compound. In one area the roof sagged; then the dirt began to sift into the bunker.

"No way we can look inside," DeWitt said.

He had just said it when they heard an explosion, a roaring crackling sound far to the south.

"Must be this one's big brother down at the main ammo dump," Zared said. "They lit off a big one."

"Let's find the motor pool," DeWitt said. "Which direction?"

It was about a quarter of a mile back the way they had come. On the way they heard rifle fire and what Lam was sure were the twenties sounding off.

"Our buddies are busy too," Lam said.

It took them five minutes to find the motor pool. Most of the trucks and cars and SUVs were parked outside. They broke their quarter-pound C-5 bars into three pieces and took off gas- and diesel-fuel tank covers. They pressed the C-4 halfway into the filler tank tube and when half of all the rigs were ready, they set the timers for thirty seconds; then the six men pushed down the fourteen timer devices on the detonators and ran for the fence.

The first C-4 went off in a six-by-six truck's filler tube and blasted the burning gasoline over four other trucks, which caught fire at once. Then the rest of the charges went off in random order, demolishing the rigs bombed and spreading burning fuel on those cars and trucks without any charges on them.

The squad stopped and looked back at the devastation. Every vehicle in the small compound burned fiercely. The motor pool building itself caught fire and began to burn furiously. Barrels of gasoline and diesel heated up inside and exploded, showering parts of the building a hundred feet away; some of the boards were still burning when they landed.

They saw several men rushing around the area where the trucks burned, but it was far too late to salvage anything, even a spare tire.

"You jokers won't be driving anywhere for some time," Lam said. The rest of the team nodded, then moved forward toward the fence.

They had run past two small buildings and across a street when a jeep skidded around a building and the headlights bore straight down on them. They didn't have a chance to move before a machine gun stuttered out three five-round bursts. One of the Israelis went down.

The five other men left jerked up their weapons and zeroed in on the headlights, blasted them out, and riddled the vehicle before it came within thirty yards of them. It veered off to the side and rammed into a building. The squad blasted the wreck with a hundred more rounds.

Corporal Zared knelt in the dirt beside the road. He touched the throat of his buddy. His face took on a sharp expression and he slung his rifle over his back, then picked up the Israeli Mistaravim and walked with the others toward the fence.

The squad took turns carrying the dead man. He had two machine-gun rounds in his chest, one through his heart. He had died instantly.

They used a fireman's carry, with the body over one shoulder, holding onto arms on one side, the legs on the other.

DeWitt tried to talk to Corporal Zared, but the Israeli waved him off. They met no resistance as they moved along the fence to the spot where they had cut the hole. Their car was in the same place and had not been tampered with.

The third Israeli, Eleazar, drove. It was the longest drive that Lieutenant Ed DeWitt could remember. Nobody said a word. Ten miles from the Army base at Ramallah, they saw a Palestinian Authority police checkpoint ahead. There was no chance to go around it. Eleazar said he could talk them into letting them through without an inspection.

"Everyone just stay calm," Eleazar said. "It's late and these cops are tired. Let me handle it."

There were only two Palestinians on duty when the car came to a stop as the Police Authority man held out his hand. He came up to the window and spoke in Arabic. He carried a submachine gun.

Eleazar, in the driver's seat, answered him in Arabic. He said they were part of a soccer team returning to Ramallah after a hard game way up north.

The guard was skeptical, and ordered the driver out of

the car. He looked at him and patted him down. He found no weapon.

"One of our players took sick. I'd appreciate getting him on to the hospital in Ramallah."

The Palestinian policeman shook his head. "I want all of you to get out of the car. Right now."

Corporal Zared had been listening closely. When the policeman ordered them out of the car, he leaned out the window and shot the cop twice in the chest with a pistol, then pushed across the car and fired twice, hitting the second policeman in the chest.

Eleazar jumped back in the sedan, slammed the door, and drove forward with tires squealing on the blacktopped road. Eleazar was grim-faced as they rocketed down the road. He pushed the old sedan as fast as it would go.

Corporal Zared reloaded the magazine in his pistol so it was full, and pushed it back in place.

"It was the only thing to do," he said to the group. "In another two or three minutes he would have seen our dead body and we'd have been in big trouble. Forget it. We'll be back in the Rama Army Base before anyone even finds those two."

"Let's hope that you're right, Corporal," DeWitt said.

They drove for five minutes and saw only two other cars. Then, ahead, the driver spotted a flashing red light.

"Could be trouble," Eleazar said. "Everybody lock and load. If we have to shoot it out we should far outgun this police car squad."

The flashing light came closer. Then it loomed right in front of them and rushed past. It was an ambulance.

"Might be going to tend to those cops," Lam said.

"At least they weren't looking for us," the driver said. "We'll be at the Army gate in five minutes."

At the gate of the Army base tight security was in effect. All five of the men had to get out of the car and be inspected. The guard stared at the dead man and then let them pass.

Colonel Ben-Ami was there to meet them. He ushered the three SEALs to a temporary barracks.

"You'll be housed here until tomorrow night, when you will be driven back to Tel Aviv. Your car is the last one to return. I'm sorry about the one man we lost. One dead and three wounded. Good, but we don't like to lose any on a mission like this. From my reports so far, all twelve of the strikes went well and we enjoyed outstanding success. We'll get our reports from our man inside the complex later today."

Murdock welcomed his three SEALs at the door, checked for wounds, and pointed at bunks.

"You're the last ones back, glad to see you. No injuries, that's good. We only had one so far, a bullet hole in Franklin's leg. He's over at the base hospital getting treated. Lam, how is that leg of yours holding up?"

"Stings a little bit, but it never was that bad. I'm fit for duty."

"Good. We made it through this one in good shape. Let's get some sack time and see what we do tomorrow."

Just before Murdock dropped on his bunk, Colonel Ben-Ami came in. Nobody shouted, "Attention." He looked like he expected it. He saw Murdock and went over by his bunk.

"We've changed some plans. We have our force in place here at Rama. No sense in going back to Tel Aviv. We have some small one-squad projects here in the West Bank that need taken care of. We'll have a planning session in the morning. No, make that about 1300, Commander."

"Yes, sir, Colonel. We'll find it."

The colonel walked out and Murdock frowned. Some one-squad projects. He wondered what they would be.

19

The following afternoon, Murdock, DeWitt, and Lam sat in a meeting room at the Rama Army Base in Ramallah. Colonel Ben-Ami led the group of planners from the three services.

"I'll come right to the point. We have several targets in the West Bank that we have been wanting to strike at. One of particular urgency has seemed to be out of our reach.

"This is a man known only as El Cuchillo, which is Spanish for The Knife. You may have heard of him. He was one of the top planners in what we Israelis still call the Munich Massacre at the Olympic Games in Germany on September 5, 1972. Most of the weightlifting team was killed in the botched attempt at rescuing them from where they were kept hostage in a dormitory. Eleven Israeli athletes, five members of the Arab Black September gang, and one German were all killed in the rescue try. The Knife planned and directed the hostage takeover, but was not on the site at the time of the attack. He also carried out three deadly terrorist bombings and submachine-gun attacks at the Jerusalem airport. He has been the leader in at least twenty bombing attacks on Israel and her people in which more than three hundred have been murdered.

"He is now in his late seventies, says he is retired from his 'police' work with the PLO and that he is no longer interested in politics. He is also a rich man from what most experts agree are terrorist attacks on other nations that were probably paid for by OPEC.

"With his money he has bought a whole village. He is the mayor, the chief of police, the master of everyone who lives there. He is now known as the King of En Gedi. Technically, En Gedi is outside of the West Bank, in the territory of Israel. But it's so close to the Palestinian Authority area that they in fact control it. Most of the people there are Arabs, intensely loyal to Cuchillo.

"Israeli citizens or Army personnel can't move about there freely. Besides the PA, the whole town's residents devote themselves to his protection. We have lost two three-man squads going in there deeply undercover to take him out. He's a blight on the face of mankind. We would like to remove him from this earth by any means possible.

"Which brings us back to En Gedi and the Dead Sea. As you know, the Dead Sea is not a sea, but a lake which is fifty miles long, eleven miles wide at points, and at the deepest over thirteen hundred feet down. It is the lowest body of water on earth. It is truly a dead lake, with no fish or wildlife strong enough to live in it. Its only life is a few strains of bacteria. Salinity is three hundred parts per thousand, which is from two to five times as salty as the Great Salt Lake in Utah, where they have a commercial brine shrimp operation.

"Why am I talking about the Dead Sea? We now believe it's the only way to get to The Knife. His defenses are in a semicircle around the palace he has built on the very edge of the Dead Sea. That's one of the reasons we have the U.S. Navy SEALs with us. You have much more practical experience in saltwater operations than our men do, and you have simply been trained to a higher level of aquatic efficiency.

"That is our first target for the day. We won't leave you out on a stick. We will carry out helicopter raids on another known terrorist who lives nearby. The attack should pull a lot of resources from the protection around The Knife, and make your attack on him at least possible. I don't want to delude you SEALs. This will be one of the toughest missions that you've ever undertaken.

"With some arm-twisting and cooperation, we think we can insert you into the Dead Sea about twenty miles below En Gedi. At night you should be able to walk along the shore at most points. We'll get into that when we do our detailed planning.

"Now, for the rest of you we have some projects that are dry. Last night one of our cars was stopped by Palestinian Authority officers. For some reason, one of the officers became suspicious. Both cops at the checkpoint were killed and our car made it back with no further incident. However, the Authority has tightened greatly the movement by car and truck in their controlled sectors. It will make it harder for us to move through their zones by car for probably six months. We may have to utilize helicopters at times, which draw too much attention. We're working on that."

Murdock stood. "Sir, could we be excused to work with our planning group on our target situation? If you send along one of your men to help us with planning details, that would help. I'd guess there is no tremendous hurry on this one."

"No time line, correct, Commander. Yes, go work on your planning. I'll send two men who know the area to your quarters."

"Thank you, sir."

Later, the entire Third Platoon gathered around a table in the big room at their quarters where the two Israelis had laid out a large-scale map of the lower half of the Dead Sea. The Israelis introduced themselves. The first was Lieutenant Ebenezer, the second, Corporal Almon. The officer was tall and thin, ramrod straight, his uniform pressed and perfect. The corporal was short and a little heavy, with eyeglasses and a thin mustache. Ebenezer used a pointer and located En Gedi, and then moved the wand to the darker-colored area to the west.

"These are the Judean hills. They are not exactly the Alps, but they do present some difficulties. We've sent one team through them, but ran up against outposts of The Knife as far away as fifty miles. The closer the team made it to the sea, the heavier the protection became, until they were unmasked and butchered before they even saw the Dead Sea or the large palace where The Knife now lives."

"Salinity in the sea was what again?" Jaybird asked.

"On the surface and for fifteen feet down, it's a regular thirty-three percent, winter or summer."

"Wow. I swam once in the Great Salt Lake, and I remember they said it varied there from five to sometimes fifteen percent. Won't it be hard just staying underwater out there?"

Ebenezer smiled. He was about thirty, and had the underwater badge on his blouse. "Yes, it can be. When we dove in the Dead Sea, we used additional five-pound weights to help keep us just below the surface. Depends on your basic weapons package and how much ammo you carry."

"Can you get us closer than twenty miles?" Lam asked.

"That is a problem. The Authority ranges over that area down there. They provide an outer ring of protection for their hero El Cuchillo."

"We'll have to use the rebreathers," DeWitt said.

"So, you get us into the sea down twenty miles and we make it to the target and do him," Murdock said. "Then how do we exfiltrate?"

"We've heard that the Authority has power boats that can patrol the sea near their area," Lieutenant Ebenezer said. "The boats in that salinity float extremely high in the water and can go thirty knots instead of twenty."

"Boats would not be a big problem," Mahanani said. "We've tangled with some of the toughest."

"No chance to get overland to that town over there, Yatta?" Bill Bradford asked.

"That town is also in an area where the Palestinian Authority has a lot of control," Corporal Almon said.

"So if we have to go back down into the Dead Sea," Murdock said, "can you pick us up at the same point you dropped us off?"

"That depends," Lieutenant Ebenezer said. "We'll be in the Authority's unofficial zone. We might disturb them some when we take you in, and then as we get back to our safe house or home country. If we do, it will be tougher to get you out."

"Hell of a lot easier than walking," Luke Howard said.

"We've been left high and dry a time or two," Murdock said. "The men like to see the extractors do their work after we've done ours. Why not a chopper pickup? I don't remember the Palestinians having an air force."

"Possible, possible. We'll need communication with you. The small radios won't do for that. We need something with a hundred-mile radius. I'll provide two for you before you leave."

They talked about weapons, and decided on one Bull Pup since this should be an up-close operation.

"Yeah, oh, yeah, maybe," Jaybird croaked. "Hey, I'll carry a second twenty over my back. I say we take some long-range protection just in case we need it."

They moved on. Timing. How long would it take the SEALs to move twenty miles up the beach and in the water after drop-off? They decided on a night raid.

"We work best at night," Franklin said, who had just come in from the hospital.

"Who's that *we,* Franklin?" Fernandez chirped. "Not what your girlfriend tells us." Everyone laughed.

"What's the shoreline like?" Senior Chief Sadler asked. "Is it swampy and marshy, full of salt brine, or hard and firm for hiking?"

"Much of it's on the mushy side, no plant growth, salty mud I guess I'd call it," Corporal Almon said. "You'd have to move away from the water fifty feet to get solid footing."

"Any people in that desert?" Jefferson asked.

"Almost none until you get to the immediate area around the little town of En Gedi. It has developed into a minor farming zone with small plots of fertile ground under cultivation and most truck garden crops for easy sale.

"Last we knew, there were about three hundred people in the little town. About half are farmers and the rest earn their daily bread by protecting The Knife."

"He's retired by now?" Bill Bradford asked.

"Not a chance," Ebenezer said. "He works every day, helps maintain a PLO web site, has e-mail and a satellite phone. He's sharp, vindictive, active. When he was asked by some of his followers when he was going to retire, he said he would quit when the U.S. and the Jews all got out of all of the Arab lands, including Israel."

"How many men will we need?" DeWitt asked. He looked at Murdock.

"One squad should be able to do it, but we may need the rest of the platoon for backup and security once we get to the target. I'd say we take both squads, unless that presents some transport problems for the Israelis."

"Eight or fifteen, not much difference," the corporal said. "I assume that your wounded man will not make the trip."

"I checked with the hospital last night. He's restricted to the post for a week, so he won't be going. Tough luck, Franklin."

"Hey, Skipper," Franklin bellowed. "I'm fucking ready for duty. I hardly even limp anymore."

"Sorry, sailor, the medics have spoken."

Corporal Almon watched the interchange with a grin. Then he went on. "We'll either go in to the bank by sedan or chopper. Just how will depend on the situation in the surrounding territory and the temperature of the terrorists and their scale of attacks during that week. A chopper would be my first guess here."

"Any timing?" Senior Chief Sadler asked. "Like any holy days where they would be less vigilant?"

"Do unto them," Lieutenant Ebenezer said, laughing. "I know what you mean, but their holidays don't offer much help, and I don't know of any coming up soon."

"We'd want an early start in the afternoon from our Initial Point, so we can hit any inhabited areas just after dark so we don't tip our hand," Murdock said. "We'd want to get to the water as soon as possible after full dark. Will it be all desert down there that we'll be going across on this side of the Judean hills?"

"Our only IP is here at Rama; we'll figure out the time-table for the aircraft we use. We can bring in a chopper here. We do from time to time, and the locals are used to seeing them come and go. No problem there. Yes, we leave at all times of the day and night."

"How far and how much time do we need to get from Rama to the insertion place?" Jaybird asked.

"A direct line between the two is a little over fifty-two miles," Corporal Almon said. "A flight line to take advantage of the Jordanian hills would be about fifty-seven miles. Remember, this isn't Texas. We're a small country."

"Flight time for the forty-six would be about fifteen minutes," Commander," Jaybird said. "That's at a hundred-sixty-five-miles-per-hour max speed."

"I'd guess your Israeli choppers would have about the same speed," Murdock said.

"Maybe five minutes more," Corporal Almon said.

"Are we ignoring moving up the water by IBS?" DeWitt asked.

Murdock looked around the group. "Oh, for our Israeli friends. The IBS stands for Inflatable Boat Small, a Zodiac-type rubber boat that can do eighteen knots with a fifty-five-horsepower motor. Carries eight, so we'd need two of them."

"I'm sure we could get them quickly from the U.S. Navy if you request them," Lieutenant Ebenezer said.

Murdock looked around.

"Beats hell out of walking twenty miles," Luke Howard said.

"Stand a better chance against their patrol boats if we had the ducks," Jaybird said.

"So we lose them going in, we can always run back down the bank or swim if we have to," Mahanani said.

"Request the IBS and motors operationally ready from the U.S. Navy," Murdock said.

Lieutenant Ebenezer nodded at the corporal, and he hurried out. "Done. We'll give you a time line on when we can have the two boats here on site." The Israeli looked down at his notes and a map.

"One more thought," he said. "We try to confuse the PA folks when we can. Our people will probably want to fly straight past En Gedi, stay in the mountains, and touch on the small community of Arad, which is about eighteen miles below En Gedi and inland some. That way the Palestinians there will report that our chopper flew over their town and the Palestinian Authority will be totally confused about where we're heading. We'll swing around and drop you at a point maybe three miles north of the village of Newe Zohar, which is also right on the Dead Sea and on the only road south along that body of water. This may increase our flight time by two or three minutes."

"Sounds like a good idea," Murdock said. "Have we missed anything?"

"Special ammo and charges?" Senior Chief Sadler asked.

"I'll have an ordnance man talk to the senior chief about that as soon as we're done here," Lieutenant Ebenezer said. "We can furnish you with anything you need except the special twenty-millimeter rounds you use. I don't suppose regular twenties would work."

"Never tried them. No reason they shouldn't work as contact rounds," Jaybird said.

"So we wait on the confirmation by the Navy on the IBSs," Murdock said. "I think we're through here."

"One point," Ebenezer said. "How many of you speak Arabic?" He said the last sentence in Arabic.

Murdock replied in kind. "I do, but not well."

Franklin spoke up also in the Arabic tongue. "My Arabic is a little better than the skipper's, but not much."

"You'll have no need for your Arab clothes, but another Arabic speaker could be handy. I've been authorized to accompany you, if it meets with your approval."

Murdock looked around at his men. Most nodded or grinned. Jaybird settled it.

"Oh, yes, nothing like a local native guide in a terrifying foreign country."

"Yes, Lieutenant," said Murdock, "we'll be glad to have you on board, but your rank will be negated. In the field we're all yardbirds, buck privates, working as a team. You'll be attached to Lieutenant DeWitt's Bravo Squad. Glad to have you on board."

The Israeli smiled. "Great, glad to be with you. I know how to take orders, Commander. All of your men outrank me on this mission. I'm so pumped up I can hardly wait."

20

At the last minute they decided not to wear wet suits.

"Won't be in the wet long enough to make them worthwhile," Lieutenant Ed DeWitt said. "That water is warm anyway if we do get damp."

They would take no rebreathers either, just their cammies and a full load of combat gear and ammo. Two men carried ammo "collars," the rigs that packed goods in pouches front and back with a hole in the middle to push your head through.

They had modified their weapons stance a little. Vinnie Van Dyke would keep his H & K 21-E machine gun, and Fernandez would take along his PSG1 71.62mm NATO round sniper rifle. They would take two Bull Pups, and the rest would handle the familiar MP-5 submachine gun.

"Gives a better balance in case we run into some long-range problems before we actually get into the town," Murdock said. "There's a road that hugs the west bank of the Dead Sea, but we don't know how close. We don't want to get into any confrontations down there fifteen miles from the target. We'll make every attempt to stay out of any trouble before we hit the palace."

They were suited up and all set to go, waiting in a ready room near the small airfield at the Rama Army Base. The helicopter had been loaded with the two IBSs and two drag bags with extra ammo and explosives.

"Just saw the bird again," Jaybird said. "She's a converted U.S. forty-six. Looks like she's been updated all the way and has a spit and polish on her that shows the Israeli thoroughness. No worry about this old bird not making the round trip."

DeWitt nodded. "Good." He turned to Lieutenant Ebenezer, who now wore cammies and rubber boots like the
rest of them. He had told them to call him Eb. "What do
we know about the inside of the palace or the grounds?"

"Nothing. We have aerial shots of it, which you've seen.
The general layout, but we don't know what or who are in
which of the buildings. On that score we'll have to play it
by ear."

An Israeli Air Force officer looked into the room. "Time
to load up, gentlemen. This way."

They followed him, looking a little like overloaded mountain climbers. The troops stepped into the familiar form of
the forty-six and settled against the sides. The two fully
inflated IBS boats were wedged into holders at the aft end
of the craft, just in front of where the hatch would swing
down for their quick departure.

"Same deluxe seating arrangement, I see," Lampedusa
cracked as he settled down on the cold metal floor.

"A fuck and a half better than walking," Bradford said.

"Was the half that floozy blonde we saw you with a cou-
ple of weeks ago, Bradford?" Jaybird yelled.

"Hell, no, that was no floozy blonde, that was his own
dear mommy," Mahanani said. That brought a laugh.

Murdock had been first on, and he enjoyed the banter
among the men. It showed him that they were loose and
ready, sharp and set to put everything on the line to accom-
plish their mission. He looked over at DeWitt, who nodded.
Yes, everyone was ready. They had an even sixteen men
again with Franklin out of action and Eb taking his place.
It should work.

The chopper's crew chief came into the big belly of the
craft. "We have a flight time of twenty-two minutes depending on what kind of winds we run into. There almost
for sure will not be any enemy ground fire directed against
us. We'll land about fifty yards from the water to be sure
we have a firm footing. The captain asks that you check
your radio with him now, and again just after you get on
the ground and away from the aircraft."

Murdock keyed in his handheld radio.

"Grounded One calling Bird One."

"This is Bird One. Read you loud and clear. Grounded Two?"

DeWitt had given the other Israeli radio to Eb, who responded.

"Grounded Two to Bird One, over."

"Yes, loud and clear. Check again once we're parted."

The top rotor picked up speed, and soon they could hear little except the engines and rotors. The SEALs, used to this excess noise, settled down for a short rest before they moved into action.

Jack Mahanani eased back against the side of the chopper with a resignation that he had developed early in his life on Maui in the Hawaiian Islands. He was a hospital corpsman first class, but didn't come to the SEALs as a corpsman, rather as a SEAL. The six-month training had been easier for him than most, since he had lived in the water since he was old enough to breathe.

He thought back to the islands as he often did when there was a hint of stress. He mellowed out this way, got ready for what was coming. This one was a mystery. Nobody was quite sure where the man they wanted was, or even if he was in his Dead Sea palace. Usually they had better intel than that. Still, a strike at his HQ would be productive whether they nailed the top man or not.

Mahanani had been good in school. High grades came easy for him, and that left more time to swim and fish and surf. He did a lot of all three, and specialized in free diving with his spear gun. He told his classmates they could order the type of fish they wanted for dinner and he'd go and dive and bring it back to them squirming on his spear.

His senior year in high school had almost undone him. She was sleek and slender, attractive but not beautiful, and had a smile that turned Mahanani into mush. He had first met her when she sat behind him in American history. After that he began spending less time in the water and more hours in the library and in study halls. Almost always she would be there, Betty Yakamora. Her soft voice and Asian eyes captivated him.

He had been captain of the basketball team that year, and they won the state championship. Betty came to every game. Raging hormones combined in them one night on a moonlit beach, and they made love furiously, then gently, and now Mahanani was really hooked.

Two months later they found out she was pregnant. Mahanani told her that he would marry her as soon as they were out of school and he had a job. But Betty had other plans. She told him she wasn't ready to be a mother. She had applied to go to the University of Hawaii and had been accepted for the fall. She had no room in her life right then for a child. They stormed and argued and screamed at each other for a month; then one day she told him that she had aborted the child and that he didn't have to marry her.

Jack had been the furious one. Family was important to him, and to have his child suddenly yanked away from him was a monstrous affront. Mahanani never saw her again. He joined the Navy and left a week before graduation. He put Betty behind him and stormed through boot in San Diego at the Naval Recruit Training Station, and then applied to be hospital corpsman and went for his training in San Diego at the old Balboa Naval Hospital in Balboa Park.

He'd been in the Navy three years and had made second class when he was assigned as a backup corpsman at a SEAL exhibition on San Diego Bay and Harbor Island. What he saw the SEALs do that day caught his imagination: the rope airlifts, the fast boats, the parachuting, the chopper insertions, and the fast-boat pickups from the water.

The next day he applied to transfer to the SEALs. It was a year and three tries later when he was accepted as a SEAL tadpole and began his six-month training. Murdock had grabbed him as soon as he'd interviewed him for an opening in what the rest of the SEALs considered to be the most active of the platoons in all of the SEAL Teams.

Now Mahanani did double duty as a SEAL while also packing the regular corpsman's gear. He had fallen into the job by accident when the platoon's regular medic was wounded and went down. Murdock had not applied for a new corpsman, and nobody upstairs had thought to ask how the platoon got along without a corpsman of record. Mahanani shrugged. It wasn't that much more work, and if he could take care of both jobs, he was happy.

Mahanani looked up through the dim light of the chopper. He felt more than heard the men moving.

"Red light," Murdock bellowed so he could be heard. "Land in five minutes. Final check on gear now."

The men went into the patrol order and each man inspected the man ahead of him, then turned around and checked the man behind him.

They could hear the chopper's engines take on a new tone as the big bird came around and lost altitude.

Murdock looked out the side entrance door. Absolutely black. Not even a campfire or a taillight. Black on black. He could paint a picture on it.

They felt a small bump as the big bird settled on its landing gear and the red light on the rear hatch went to green. The big hatch swung down and hit the ground.

The two men assigned to the job quickly untied the IBSs and pushed them out the rear hatch. The two squads exited by the side hatches, and grabbed the boats and ran them toward the water that they could see twenty-five yards away.

Murdock ran with them, checking his long-range radio at the time. He could hear and be heard. He put the radio in a waterproof package and tied it to his combat vest.

The shoreline here was a little mushy as they carried the rubber boats down to the water. Bravo Squad loaded in the first boat, and Alpha took up the second one. Before they pushed off there was a check of equipment.

"Two drag bags?" Senior Chief Sadler whispered. Two ayes came back. "Eight men per boat?" Murdock and DeWitt answered aye. Two men in each squad had out their Motorolas. They would be the contacts as the SEALs moved through the Dead Sea to the north. If they did get wet for any reason, there would be plenty of reserve units in waterproof pouches.

"Let's move," Murdock said. He heard the chopper's engines gear up, and the big craft lifted off and vanished into the night. Then there was no sound, no lights, only blackness and the Dead Sea.

"Start motors," DeWitt said on his Motorola. The motors caught on the second pull and the two boats, latched together with a sixty-foot buddy cord, angled north up the blackness of the Dead Sea.

Murdock studied the area. The pilot had told him they would land eighteen miles from the target and that there were no settlements of any kind between there and the target. He also said the road along there was near the water, but usually forty to fifty yards away. They might see the headlights of an occasional car or truck on the road, but the sound of the IBS motors would be no problem.

The Zodiacs revved up to eighteen knots and slid through the salt-brine sea with little effort. The men on the engines and tillers soon felt the difference in the much more buoyant water. They had to slow down a little to help maintain control.

When they left on the boats, Murdock had checked his watch. The luminous dial had shown him it was 2010. With any luck they would have ten hours of darkness. By the end of that time, the plan was that his SEALs would have completed their mission, returned eighteen miles south along the west coast of the Dead Sea, and be ready for pickup. Murdock hoped that it went exactly that way.

"Cap, I hear something," Lam said.

Murdock used his Motorola. "Let's go dead in the water. Turn off both engines now."

A moment later the silence overwhelmed them. Lam stood in the second boat looking north, then toward shore, then back to the north again.

"Can't be sure, Cap, but if I was a betting man, I'd say there is a motorboat coming this way. Okay, I am a betting man. I'll put a thousand up that there's a boat headed our way, not fast, maybe fifteen knots."

Murdock tried to listen, turned so his ear was open to the north. He didn't hear a thing other than a gentle slapping of the water against the sides of the rubber ducks.

"I want one star shell loaded and ready to fire," Murdock

said. "Two Bull Pups at the ready with impact rounds. If this is a patrol boat, we want to take it out fast before they can radio. Star shell, bang, bang, they're dead."

"Ready with the star," Fernandez said.

"Ready with a Bull Pup," Jaybird added.

"I'll be the other Bull Pup," Murdock said. "We wait." He turned to Lam. "Anything new?"

"No, just a continual sound coming from them. Getting louder. On the water sound travels twice as fast. I'd put them at no more than two miles and closing."

They waited. Another two minutes.

"Oh, yes, I can hear it now," Murdock said. "Try to nail him at two hundred yards, Fernandez. You might need two or three flares. Once one goes, we're committed and we have to take him out. There's no commercial traffic on this Dead Sea, so it has to be a Palestinian Authority patrol boat. Hold steady, Fernandez, don't fire until I give you weapons free."

"Roger, Cap."

They waited. There was almost no noise from the water, no waves, no wind, just dead all around them—the Dead Sea. Murdock frowned and looked north. Did he see running lights?

"Yeah, Cap, running lights. Sometimes the chemicals on the water give off a kind of fog that sloshes around and confuses the visual. So our look at him may come and go. But that is the bad guy up there."

"How far?"

"Six hundred yards and closing about ten knots."

"Radar?"

"Probably," Lam said. "Depending who they bought it from. Most patrol boats these days have radar as a given."

They waited.

"Three hundred yards tops," Lam said.

"Fernandez, can you see the lights?"

"Oh, yes, I'd say maybe three-fifty."

"Good, Fernandez. In twenty seconds I want you to fire one and have a second ready immediately."

"That's a roger, sir."

A few moments later, the sound of a shot came. "Firing one, Commander. One round off and away."

"Everyone down. Bull Pups fire as soon as we get a target. We're committed now, people. Let's make this count."

21

A fraction of a second after the star shell bloomed over the Dead Sea, the SEALs could see a medium-sized patrol boat heading toward them from a little over two hundred yards away. Two trigger fingers squeezed and two twenty-millimeter rounds blasted out of the short barrels heading for the slow-moving PLO craft.

Murdock steadied the telescopic sights of the Bull Pup on the craft after the recoil, and watched as his round punched into the cabin of the boat and exploded. At nearly the same instant another round hit lower down on the side of the boat almost at the waterline, exploding with a furious blast of metal and water.

"One more twenty round," Murdock said, and sighted in again after working a new round into the chamber. His second shot hit near the bow two feet over the waterline, and blew a large hole in the port side just under the water. Jaybird's second shot hit the cabin, blasting into junk anything left after the first round. The craft slowed, and then coasted to a stop. She was dead in the water.

"Waste any personnel in sight," Murdock said. The sniper rifle cracked once, then twice, then again.

"Two terrs down, one went over the side," Fernandez said.

The two rubber ducks slowed and stopped about fifty yards off the stalled patrol boat. It was listing badly to port. The bow deck was almost at the water level. A sudden burst of rifle fire came from behind the cabin. Ten SEAL weapons answered it.

"Don't think we nailed him, Cap," Jaybird said. "Too much cabin there protecting him."

"Jaybird, put an AP round right at the waterline, now," Murdock said. "Eb, will a ship sink in this water?"

"Oh, yes, quite a few down there. Depends how deep it is here, but there should be no trace."

"Good," Murdock said, and sighted in on the waterline about amidships and fired an armored-piercing round. Jaybird's hit first, and the explosion seemed to continue inside the craft. It heeled over more to port then, and came to a twenty-degree list. Murdock's AP round hit about midway along the forty-foot craft, just as the parachute flare sputtered and went out.

In the sudden darkness, they could now see a small fire burning in the cabin area. It grew larger. An explosion deep inside the patrol craft made it shudder. Then the flames leaped higher as if fueled by diesel or gasoline. The large explosion came a moment later, shattering the upper structure of the boat and dumping it on its side. The stern settled; then water sloshed over it and without a cry or a whimper, the patrol boat sank by the stern and nothing was left on the surface but a few boards and an empty one-man life raft that had automatically inflated.

They heard no splashing after the boat went down. Murdock moved the two ducks into the area, looked around a minute, then hit the Motorola. "Let's move on north. Anybody hit by that counterfire?" Nobody spoke up. They settled into their eighteen-knot trip to the north.

They had figured a run of about an hour and ten for the trip north to a landing spot where they could hide the boats. Now they were ten minutes behind that schedule.

"Let's move a little closer to shore and watch it," Murdock said on the Motorola. "Looks like there won't be anyplace to hide these ducks. My suggestion would be, as soon as we see any sign of those small farms, that we stash the boats and do the rest on foot."

An hour into their run they spotted lights ahead. Just a few, as if in scattered houses. The closer they came, the more evident it was that they had reached the small farming operation. Murdock wondered where the farmers found fresh water, but knew they did.

"Lam?" Murdock asked.

"Yeah, the farmers are at it here. Looks like it's walk time. Not much activity over there."

They had seen two cars or light trucks move along the roadway next to the Dead Sea. Now they saw a few more cars driving around. Murdock checked his watch. A little after 2130. Not even bedtime for farmers.

"Let's hit the shore," Murdock said on the radio. "We'll beach the ducks and hope to be back here ready to use them again before anyone finds them."

They landed, pulled the ducks up out of the water, and knelt down waiting. Lam came back five minutes later.

"Just a few farms right along here. Nothing that reaches out to the highway and north for maybe two miles. Then we'll have to be more careful."

"Right," Murdock said. "Lam out front by a hundred. Everyone have on his ears? Radio check, Bravo?" All eight men checked in, even Eb. The seven men in Alpha came on the horn.

"All right, Lam, take your hundred. We don't want any surprises. We're plenty early, so there's no rush. If we get to the palace by midnight it should be about right."

Lam moved out ahead of the troops. He had his MP-5 with the silencer on it for quiet work. He moved along the bank of the Dead Sea where it was solid ground, keeping every one of his senses alert. He could smell the salt mist coming off the sea. To the far left, away from the water, he noticed the "green" smell of growing things. Vegetables, from what they had been told.

A dog barked. The damn Arab habit of keeping dogs around to sound the alarm. The platoon should be far enough away from the farms to avoid the dogs. Unless there were packs of wild ones running around here too.

Lam moved up another five hundred yards and paused. Something to the left. The roadway curved closer to the water here, and when a vehicle came along it toward him,

Lam went to the ground and became a dark blob. The lights swept past and were gone.

Lam reported how the road curved closer to the water, and moved ahead. Another two hundred yards and he saw a building to the left with lights on. It looked to be near the road, and Lam studied it carefully. He moved up slowly for a better look, then used his 7-×-35 field glasses. Yes, a checkpoint on the road. He could see two armed men standing just outside the structure. Now, did they have any motion or vibration sensors stretched across the road and on down the beach to the water?

Lam walked across the spot where he figured any such sensors should be. Nothing. He moved back and forth across the point several times. No response. He used the radio and reported the checkpoint to Murdock.

"Looks like just a check on the road," Lam said. "Should give us no problems."

Two more cars came at just the wrong time, and the SEALs had to wait for the cars to pass before they ran through the narrow strip of land between the water and the highway. Then they were past that and moving up to the checkpoint.

Lam had waited for them there, and hustled them past it before he moved out ahead again by two hundred yards.

There were a few small buildings well across the road and into what looked in the dark like green fields. There must be fresh water from somewhere to irrigate them. He saw no activity, and most of the small houses didn't have lights on.

Two minutes later Lam went down on his stomach in the sandy, dry ground and stared ahead. This one was more than a checkpoint. A splash of light showed in a large square ahead where some type of building hovered near the road. A lift gate extended across the width of the highway, and two cars had been stopped and uniformed men inspected the rigs. He heard the talk, but didn't know Arabic.

"Cap, better come up and take a look and leave the troops down there. We've got a bigger post across the road."

Two minutes later, Murdock bellied down beside Lam and used his binoculars. He swore softly.

"Fucking roadblock won't bother us, but look at the wire that extends out into the brine. No telling how far it goes. It's a good old-fashioned double-apron barbed-wire fence. Four feet high in the middle on steel posts and with razor and barbed wire. Then slanting-up aprons on both sides, also of razor wire. Not a thing of beauty to get across without making a hell of a lot of noise."

"Or getting wet," Lam said. "Trouble is, the wire might extend twenty feet into the water. At least until it rusts off in the brine."

"How far are we from the town?"

Lam had been watching the growing brightness of the lights ahead. He'd figured about a mile before he found this blockage. He told Murdock.

"We either get wet now or take out the roadblock."

"Getting wet is best; then we still have surprise at the palace. I'll go check on the end of the wire. Hell, we're not afraid of a little bit of water."

Lam ran to the wire where it vanished into the blackness of the Dead Sea and wiggled it. Solid. He stepped into the water and eased out three feet. The muddy bottom sloped gradually. He probed with his foot and hit the wire a foot under the water. Lam stepped on the wire construction, and it sagged to the bottom of the sea in the salty mud. With his hand he searched where the four-foot upright should be, but there was none. Just the tapered-down end of the typical double-apron defensive fence. He went back the way he had come to where Murdock lay in the sand.

Ten minutes later, the SEALs had waded around the end of the barrier fence and were wet only to their waists.

"Easy," Jaybird said. "Why didn't they have some noise-makers on the fence? Some old beer cans tied together works great, or here in Muslim land some Coke cans would do the trick."

Murdock now went with Lam on the point. They came to a half-fallen down building that at one time might have been a bathhouse for a retreat or hotel. Now it was almost collapsed and shattered by the elements. They used it for cover for a moment. Murdock took out his NVGs and scanned ahead. The light green landscape showed him no bodies, no movement. He saw two cars parked ahead on the other side of the road. Houses were now in regular rows of blocks across the highway. They had at last come to the town, Murdock decided.

They saw the lights in front of them twenty feet later. The four-foot-high beams of light from giant searchlights daggered across the black sand of the Dead Sea and vanished in the darkness well out into the wetness. Murdock saw the source of the light at once. A pair of huge searchlights that sat about fifty yards inland. They evidently were aimed down a street so they had an unobstructed shot at the beach and the water.

Murdock and Lam went to the sand again and watched, but could see no change in the steady beam of the lights. No rotating, no flashing on and off, just a steady beam that would immediately bathe anyone in their light the nanosecond a crossing was tried.

"Around the bitches," Lam said. He pointed. "We can get across the road here, go down a block inland this side of the lights, walk around them, and come back to the wet on the other side."

Murdock checked it out with the glasses. He could find no roving guards along the light beam, and nobody working the other end of the lights. He did see three submachine gun guards walking around the pair of giant, smoking searchlights as the arcs gave off their smoke and odor.

"Move up," Murdock told the troops on the Motorola. He explained to them on the air what they would do and why. By the time they were in position a block from the light, Murdock and Lam had already crossed the street, walking and fading down the dirt street with occasional houses on both sides.

The rest of the platoon filtered across the road, then into the houses, and detoured around any that had lights showing. Murdock and Lam went fifty yards beyond the smoking-arc searchlights and dropped down to study the area for guards.

"Dogs," was all Lam could say before two large animals came out of the darkness and without a sound hurtled through the air with snapping jaws searching for their victims' throats. Murdock rolled to the left and clubbed one of the animals with the butt of his Bull Pup. He hit it in the neck and it went down, then sprang up. Murdock got out his KA-BAR and on the next lunge of the animal, he drove the blade into the dog's throat and slashed it sideways. Blood flew, and Murdock rolled away from it as the dog came down hard where he had been. It gave a short whine, then turned over and died, half its throat torn away.

Lam had spun to his back, jerked up his knees, and lashed out with both feet as the slightly smaller dog snarled and dove on him. Lam's boots caught the animal in the chest and lifted the dog and threw it over his head. That gave time for Lam to draw his KA-BAR and slash twice at the animal's head as it charged him again. The blade tore across a cheek and through one eye, and the dog bleated in pain, dropped its long tail between its legs, and ran into the darkness.

"Watch for dogs," Murdock said on the radio. "Stay in place while we finish our recon."

It took them ten minutes to be sure there were no human sentries around the back side of the lights. They floated across the danger zone and filtered back through the streets to the wet. Murdock had no way of knowing where the palace was except that it was facing the water. So they would stick with the salt brine until they found the target and could recon it.

Another block and the lights from ahead increased in brilliance by a factor of four. They moved up as close as they could and not be in the splash. This well-lighted place had to be the palace. Huge floodlights bathed the beach and water in front of the palace. They also highlighted guards. Three worked a fifty-yard post in front of the palace and in a foot from the Dead Sea. Another rank of guards passed each other on the dry sand, and a third line of four more guards hovered around the chalky whiteness of the building that had to be the palace. It was three stories, pure white in the glow of the floodlights, with a large portico-type rear entrance and what could be thirty windows facing the sea.

Murdock brought up Eb and he checked the situation.

"Yes, about what we figured, only more guards. If we try to take out one or more, the rest collapse on us and we're in trouble. Too damn many to go around. From the lighting pattern, I'd guess all four sides of the palace have guards, about the same number and positions."

"What the hell can we do now?" Lam asked.

"The oldest one in the book," Murdock said. "Joshua used it in the Battle of Jericho several thousand years ago."

"Diversion," Eb said, grinning.

"Let me check around two more sides just to be sure," Lam said. Murdock nodded. Lam vanished to the left, still in the dark, heading round the left side of the palace as it faced the water.

"Will he be all right?" Eb asked.

"Best man I have for land warfare. He's got elephant ears and a sixth sense that has pulled us out of more than one tough spot. Yeah, he'll be all right."

Murdock used the Motorola to fill in the rest of the men on what they'd found, what Lam was up to.

"Jaybird, Sadler, and DeWitt, front and center," Murdock said in the radio mike. Moments later the four men lay in the sand looking at the searchlights.

"Suggestions," Murdock said.

"Yeah, diversion," Jaybird said. "Shake them up, move about half of them off their usual position. Something that will last for a while."

"Like a firefight?" DeWitt asked.

"Bombs and a firefight. Bombs to start it off. Maybe a fire. An old building with a WP into it. Then a firefight over their heads to pull them back down this side of the lights."

"Possible," Eb said. "Not a chance we're going to get past them without a fight of some kind. That would bring out the reserves. We've heard he has fifty men guarding him here."

"Just what we need," Murdock said. He scowled. "We can get half the force to the south, then use airbursts on those left, and put five or six twenties through the windows. Any idea where the boss sleeps or works?"

"Not a clue. We can't get a man inside here. It has proved impossible for three years."

"Could we burn it down?" Senior Chief Sadler asked.

"We've heard that a lot of the palace is made of stone, some marble. But the interior should burn like a torch."

Murdock frowned as Lam materialized out of the darkness and slid in beside them.

"About the same all the way around. Lights and more men. Must be twenty, twenty-five that I saw."

"No diversion," Murdock said. "No good place for it, wouldn't work. Too many guards. DeWitt, bring up the troops and spread them along this side of the lights. Some will be across the road and in behind some of those houses. Ten yards apart, at least. Where's Fernandez?" He used the radio. "Fernandez, get your weapon up here." He looked at the rest of them. "Spread out, ten yards, let's lock and load. We're going to put down one central guard with the silenced sniper rifle. When half a dozen guards rush to his aid to find out what happened, we'll put two laser rounds over them, then take out the rest of the guards in a weapons-free. As that's starting, Jaybird and I will plaster as many twenties through the windows as we can. WP, AP, anything that we have. If we can reduce that guard force enough, we can assault the fucker and get inside and track down our man.

"DeWitt, you have the rest of the platoon in its spaced-out positions?"

"Not yet, Cap. Hate to tell you, but we've run into one small problem over here. Better hold off your sniper fire."

"What the hell is it?"

"You better come over just across the road and have a look, Commander."

22

Murdock dropped beside Ed DeWitt where he lay in the dirt beside a house that looked out on the side of the palace. Directly in front of them not twenty yards away, a palace guard made a turn at the end of the post and walked back toward the brighter lights.

"You're right, Ed. No way to hide the facts of the matter. Ebenezer, you on?"

"Yes, Commander."

"Have you noticed anything different about these guards?"

"Look routine, sir."

"I'm at the side now and Ed and I have seen at least four guards who are women."

"That too is routine. They use women in combat. Nothing new for them. They can kill us just as easy as a man can. They pull the trigger on a submachine gun and you die just as quick."

Murdock frowned. He didn't like killing women. He had done it two or three times, but only in extreme situations. Like this one. He touched his mike again.

"Listen up, men. We have some women guards walking posts out here. They are soldiers just like the men. We're nondiscriminatory when it comes to them. We snuff them along with the other guards. Fernandez, pick one guard and drop him with your muffled shot. Now."

Murdock scanned the guarded area ahead. Slightly to the left he saw a guard stumble and go down. A cry went up from two guards, and five or six of them rushed to see what the downed guard's trouble was. Jaybird's lasered shot exploded directly over the group of eight men and women, blasting shrapnel into four of them, killing two and putting the other two down.

At once the rest of the SEALs opened up, pinpointing the guards in the glaring lights. Murdock and Jay turned their weapons on the palace. Murdock's first 20mm round hit the wall, missing the window on the first floor. The WP round sputtered and showered the wall and grounds with the brilliant display of the exploding phosphorus. His next three rounds went inside. He had alternated high-explosive rounds with WP, and worked his way along the windows on the left front wing on the first floor. Jaybird took the right.

Murdock stopped firing the twenty and looked at the guard force. Half of them were down and not moving. There were still more than fifteen running around looking for cover. Half a dozen more men came around the side of the palace. Murdock put an HE round in front of them, spraying the 20mm into a deadly hail of shrapnel that slammed four of them to the ground.

Jaybird and Murdock put the 20mm rounds of HE and WP into the big building. Murdock could see two fires burning through the windows. He checked the grounds again. He could see only three guards still shooting. A moment later their weapons went silent.

"Frontal assault," Murdock ordered on the radio. "Assault fire on the run. Let's get out there and get inside. Move. Now."

He stood with the rest of them and ran forward. They formed a long curved line from the side, bending it so they all could fire at the palace without hitting each other.

Some counterfire came from the palace, but not as much as Murdock had expected. It was one of those killing missions where he knew he would take casualties.

They fired a deadly rain of hot lead as they ran forward. It was only forty yards across the sand to the front of the palace. Every window in the place had been shattered. Lights came on and went off inside. Murdock fired one 20mm round at the large double doors at the center of the first floor, and they jolted open.

Ed DeWitt and Guns Franklin stormed through the big doors into the darkened interior. Ed saw dim movement to his left and drilled the shadow with three rounds. He heard a moan and a body falling. Lights showed down a hall.

Ed used his NVGs and checked the rest of the entrance room.

"Clear entrance," he said on the net.

Six more SEALs charged inside. Murdock and Jaybird ran into a hall on the right. They kicked open doors and found lights on, but no people. A submachine gun with a higher voice than the MP-5's chattered its deadly sound. Murdock figured it came from the second floor. They kept opening doors along the hall and clearing rooms. Four more SEALs backed them. They found no people, only offices, living rooms, and a well-equipped recreation room with a beautiful pool table.

They came to an open stairway at the end of the hall. Murdock and Jaybird went up the steps in surges, covering each other as they moved. Jaybird peered over the top of the steps. He smelled fire and found smoke on the second floor.

"Right wing, first floor clear," Murdock said. "One man stay there to keep it clean. Rest move up."

"Left wing first is clear," Ed DeWitt said. "Found four men, all wasted. One computer wing, which we will demolish with a quarter pound of C-4. Moving to second floor. Watch out for friendly fire, we'll be opposite each other."

"Ed, take the second, I'll take some men to the third," Murdock said. He motioned and Jaybird, Ching, Lam, and Bradford went with him up the stairs to the third floor.

Again, they smelled smoke but saw no fire. The rooms here were smaller, mostly bedrooms. In one room they found two women sleeping. They came up bleary-eyed and groggy. Murdock bound their wrists together with plastic strips and told them in Arabic to stay where they were.

The rooms became larger as they worked toward the center of the building. At the middle of the floor, the room's door was locked. Murdock kicked it hard, but it didn't open. He moved to the side and waited. Two hot lead slugs bored through the door and dug into the wall opposite. Jaybird put four 5.56 rounds into the lock area, and one of the big doors creaked and swung inward. More rounds slammed through the opening as the SEALs hugged the wall out of the line of fire.

Ching held up a flash-bang grenade and Murdock nodded. They both threw the small nonlethal bombs into the room about the same time. When the series of piercing high sound blasts and then the blinding flashes of light subsided, the four SEALs charged into the room.

It was a huge bedroom and office. One side had ceiling-high windows that looked out on the Dead Sea. Now they lay shattered all over the room. To the left in the bedroom side stood a huge king-sized bed with a canopy. A nude woman sprawled on her back on the bed, her body lathered with blood from hundreds of glass cuts from the shattered windows.

A man lay on the floor, his hands over his ears. He wore only white pajama bottoms and he too had been slashed by the glass, but not fatally. Lam jerked his hands away from his ears and bound them behind his back. He was not The Knife.

"Eb, third floor center," Murdock said. "We've got a live one to question. Send Ebenezer up here."

The rest of the room was sprinkled with the exploding window shards. The office held four computers with twenty-six-inch screens. Murdock blasted all four and their screens with a dozen rounds of 5.56.

No one else was in the room. "This isn't our boy. We move down the hall," Murdock said.

Lieutenant Ebenezer came in and went to the Arab who lay on the carpeted floor. He spoke sharply to the man, who groaned and turned away. Ebenezer kicked him in his left kidney, and the Arab howled with pain. Ebenezer told him to sit up. He did, and Eb began questioning him.

Murdock and his team moved down the hall. As soon as they left the big room, an automatic weapon fired at them from the end of the hall. Bradford swore and dove back into the big bedroom. He leaned against the wall and felt his side. His hand came out red with blood.

"Fucking A-rabs, dirty sonsofbitches, goddamned fuckers."

Ebenezer heard him, went over, and saw the blood. He looked inside Bradford's cammy shirt and put on a pad, then wrapped gauze around Bradford's chest inside his shirt.

"That'll stop the bleeding. You hang with me here. We'll talk with our small Arab friend over here."

Bradford swore again, then hit the radio mike. "Cap, Bradford. I picked up a slug. Not helping much for a while. Sorry."

"Take it easy there. Can Ebenezer help?"

"He has. Go get 'em."

As soon as the fire came from down the hall, all three SEALs returned with counterfire and drove the gunman back into one of the rooms. But which one? Lam lay in the hallway, his MP-5 covering the hall and the doors. He provided Murdock and Ching with the cover they needed as they checked on four more doors with windows looking out at the broad expanse of the Dead Sea.

All were elaborate suites, but had no people in them, Murdock found out. At the first sound of gunfire, the whole complex must have been evacuated. With a few exceptions. Where was the man with the machine gun?

Murdock kicked open the last door and stopped. Three men stood there; none held weapons, but a submachine gun lay nearby on the floor. He and Lam stormed through the door at the same time. The three men didn't move. Behind them stood an oversized bed with a solid wooden canopy.

"Stand aside," Murdock said in Arabic.

"No, we protect our master with our lives," one of the men said.

Murdock waved his weapon at them. "Stand aside, or I'll shoot."

A voice in Arabic rumbled from behind them. Slowly the three men dropped to their knees, turned, and put their heads on the foot of the bed and waited.

For the first time, Murdock saw the man in the bed. He looked nothing like the pictures they had of El Cuchillo. This man was thin, not well, with a festering sore on his cheek. His eyes were dull and slow-moving. One hand, more skin and bones than flesh, lifted and pointed at them.

"You have come at last," he said in Arabic with the same rumble of a diseased voice.

"Ebenezer, down the hall to the last door, quickly," Murdock said.

The Israeli came in the door with his MP-5 sweeping the room. He took in the scene in a second, dropped the muzzle, and rushed to the bedside. He turned in surprise and looked at Murdock, who nodded.

"I'd say that's our man, but he's been hiding behind this facade of vigorous activity to cover himself."

"And I speak English," El Cuchillo said. "I am The Knife, but I am about as dangerous as a half-blind kitten."

"You have killed many of my countrymen," Eb said. "You have been a terrorist drenched in blood, yet you show no remorse."

"I am a soldier in the Army of Allah. I do only his will."

"You are a murdering bastard who should die slowly," Eb said.

He stared at the old man, whose eyes were deep-set, with brittle white skin stretched tightly across his face by the protruding bones.

"You killed in Munich in 1972 and outraged the world."

"A soldier in Allah's Army."

"You butchered women and children in eight distinct car bombings in Israeli town markets."

"The work of Allah continues."

"You killed two good friends of mine in Haifa."

The old man shrugged.

Lieutenant Ebenezer lifted his MP-5 and slammed three rounds into the pasty-white legs that lay on top of the white sheet. The old man screamed, but the sound came out as only a whisper and a gargling, frothy rumble. Tears crept down his cheeks. He shook his head a moment, then looked up.

"That didn't hurt me a bit. I am Arab, I am a soldier of Allah."

Two of the guards kneeling at the foot of the huge bed lifted up in protest. Ebenezer swung the MP-5 around and shot both of them in the chest. They slammed backward in sudden death.

"You are like vermin on the face of decent human beings," said Ebenezer. "You are gutter trash, the spawn of pure camel dung."

Murdock understood a little of the Arabic. He moved back and used his radio.

"Report in. DeWitt, what's happening?"

"The palace is clear. We found four more bodies. Took out three more guards. Found a locked room in a structure behind the main building. We're not sure what's inside. Could be an explosive bunker or a magazine of some kind. Holding on that. You find anything?"

"We have The Knife. He's an old, old man. Eb is questioning him."

"How old?"

"Old and sick, looks like he could be eighty-five, maybe ninety. Skin and bones, in bed and dying."

"What about the locked room?"

"Hold, we should be down shortly. Post your guards. We don't want to be surprised."

Eb stared at the ancient one on the pillows.

"Why the deception about your still being an active terrorist?"

"Often the fear of a potential act is as effective as the act itself." The old voice came in spurts, raspy, shaky, and it was hard to understand every word. When he finished the sentence, he closed his eyes and took deep breaths. A tremor of pain darted through him and his face contorted, then relaxed. His dazed eyes sought out the Arabic speaker.

"Why don't you kill me? I'm ready. Allah is waiting to welcome me. He tells me I've suffered long enough."

"I won't do you any favors, El Cuchillo." Ebenezer looked away and in a fraction of a second, the third guard at the foot of the bed lifted up and in one soaring movement, hurled himself backward at the Israeli officer. Eb looked up to find the body coming at him. He jolted to one side, jumped out of the way, and triggered a three-round burst at the guard.

Two of the rounds burned into the man's neck, spilling him to the side, cutting his right carotid artery, which pumped blood out in a huge spurt with every heartbeat, jetting the raw red blood eight feet across the room.

The third round in the burst missed the guard, slammed over the bed, and hit the old terrorist in his forehead, hammering him back onto the bed, spreading blood, brains, and chunks of his brittle skull over the pillows.

Lieutenant Ebenezer's eyes went wide. He lowered the weapon slowly, went forward, and took one last look at the man.

"I think we're done up here," Murdock said. "Let's go see what Ed has found downstairs."

Murdock stopped by the first room they had entered on the third floor, and saw Bradford standing and taking a few steps.

"How you doing, Bradford?"

"Not the best, Skipper, but I can walk. Hell, I'm about five minutes from fit for duty."

"Let's go downstairs and find DeWitt."

Murdock held his arm as they went down the steps. That put a strain on the shot-up side, and Bradford winced with every step but didn't utter a sound.

They found DeWitt with most of his squad at a building attached to the main house but with a separate entrance.

"No windows and only one door," DeWitt said. "Figured it had to be something special. Nobody has gone out or tried to get in since we found it. Big padlock on the door hasp."

"Easy. Put about six rounds around the hasp and blow it out of the wooden door," Jaybird said. The others stood back as the big mouth of the platoon went to work. It took him only three rounds before the hasp spun out of the wood and the door hung ready to open.

Murdock nodded to his second, who reached out, stayed against the wall, and swung the door open. Nothing happened. The inside was dark. DeWitt shone his flashlight past the doorjamb from the ground level and into the dark room.

They heard some jabbering from inside. Lieutenant Ebenezer pushed up beside DeWitt and shouted something into the darkness.

An answer came back, and Ebenezer grabbed the flashlight and charged inside the room. A moment later he found a light switch and turned it on.

Murdock and Jaybird had surged in right behind Ebenezer, their trigger fingers ready.

More shouting, and Murdock tried to get his eyes used to the sudden light after the darkness. He saw three cots with men on them. Ebenezer was embracing them one by one, and shouting in a language not English or Arabic.

He turned, and his face billowed with a smile.

"These men are Israelis, we thought they were dead. They are a special Mossad team sent in two months ago to find a man ready to flee this land and bring with him some vital information."

23

"Let's get these guys out of here and in a friendlier spot," Murdock said, looking at the three Israelis on the cots.

"Chained down," Ebenezer said.

"Bolt cutters, who is packing?" Murdock said on his Motorola.

"Yo," somebody said, and a moment later Fernandez came into the room and worked on the chains. He cut the loops in the medium-thick chain and had the men free quickly.

"Clothes?" one of them said. They all wore only underwear shorts and T-shirts. The SEALs searched the room and found the Israelis' clothes in a big wooden box.

Each man asked for a weapon. Jaybird gave up the spare MP-5 he had carried. Bill Bradford gave up his sub gun, glad to get rid of the weight. He gave the Israeli six extra magazines. Jefferson handed over the .45 auto he carried under his left arm and four filled magazines.

"How you doing?" Murdock asked Bradford. Mahanani had redone the bandage and given him a shot of morphine.

"I'll make it, Cap. You just point me in the right direction."

Murdock talked with Ebenezer. "We have the three men. You want to go after the target they came after?"

"Absolutely. We've accomplished our main, let's give this a try. Plenty of time before we head back to the boat."

"Where are the reserves they should have here? Will there be a counterattack of some kind?"

"Doubt it. We wasted enough out there on guard duty so

the rest are hiding their tails anywhere they can until day-light."

"Where is this turncoat?"

They talked with the three Israelis. Two spoke good English.

"His name is Najjar Hanieh. He had been a shoemaker, but he had such a perfect drawing skill that they used him to illustrate and draw diagrams for their terrorist plans. He has a small shop in the business area and lives behind his store."

Ebenezer held up his hands a minute. "Names. This is Commander Murdock and Lieutenant DeWitt. These three lucky men are Adir, Yehudi, and HADERA. That's enough to remember. Adir, you know how to find that little store?"

"With my eyes closed."

"DeWitt, you take the lead with Adir and your squad. Alpha will back you. Let's move."

They left the area like ghosts in the night. In ones and twos, slipping from one building to another, they worked two blocks to the main business street. Halfway down it they went into an alley. Murdock held his men at the mouth of the alley, spread out in a defensive position. He didn't believe that the Arabs here would roll over so easily once they saw a little blood.

DeWitt and his squad led the Israelis into the alley, and were almost to the back door of the turncoat's shop when gunfire sounded ahead of them and they dug into the dirt of the alley, behind one old truck parked there and in some building offsets.

The squad returned fire, aiming at the muzzle flashes less than fifty yards ahead.

"Cover us," Ebenezer said. Then he and Adir lifted up and dashed ten yards ahead and behind a building. Then they ran up to a smaller one beside it. All were made with common walls. The shorter one had a door that Ebenezer kicked in. He ran inside. Adir charged along right behind him.

"This is the right place?" Ebenezer asked. They were in a storeroom, and saw steps leading to the left.

"Let me go first," Adir said. He slipped up the steps quietly and tried the door at the top. It was unlocked. He edged it inward and called softly.

"Najjar. Najjar, wake up, we are your friends." His Arabic was excellent. He repeated the words again, and this time they heard some sounds inside. Then steps came toward them.

"Adir? Everyone said you were dead."

"We've come to take you out of here. Get ready to travel. You have ten minutes to get your clothes together and what you can carry in your pockets. I'll handle the briefcase filled with terrorist plans and targets that you promised me."

Najjar struck a match and studied the face in front of him for the time it took for the match to flame out.

"Yes, I can come. They told all of us that the three Israeli spies had been caught and were beheaded." He paused. "Yes, I am glad to see you. Wait."

In the alley outside, Ed DeWitt kept up fire at the gunmen at the far end of the alley as long as they fired back. When they stopped, his men stopped.

At the other end of the alley, Murdock looked at the street and buildings. There could be a company of Palestinian Authority policemen out there. But were there? He figured not. There'd been no advance hint that anyone was coming. The Israelis said they had been captured two months ago. The PLO would tend to let down their guard after two months. But who were the gunmen at the other end of the block? How did they know that the attackers would come here?

Then he knew. Somehow they'd found out about the three spies being rescued, and they must know who the spies had come to rescue in the first place. Now all that mattered was how many men the Arabs had been able to throw together to stop them. It wasn't a good feeling. He got on the net and told the others what he had figured out.

"So we play it carefully from here on. We double-check every building before we go past it. Better exfiltrate out this way on the alley with the prize, but keep a rear guard to get off some last rounds. How is our man doing?"

A dog ran across the street, but didn't pay any attention

to them. A cat screeched on a fence and then jumped off. Murdock's radio came on.

"Skipper," DeWitt said. "We're in contact and the man is getting dressed. Should be out in a minute or two. Wilco on the getaway. Will be your way in about five. Yes, here they come now. We'll lay down some cover fire, so don't be alarmed."

Murdock heard the firing from familiar weapons, but little counterfire. Where had the gunmen gone? He told Lam to recon out toward the water to see what he could learn. "Don't go more than a block, and be careful."

Two minutes later Bravo Squad came up and spread out. Lam called in.

"Looks free and clear up here, Cap. Had one car, but it turned off and is gone. Few lights on, no streetlights. Nobody on the street. I'd say it's a go up here for a block. I'll wait. This is still about a hundred yards to the water."

"Roger that."

Murdock looked around at the dark shapes. "Alpha Squad up front, our visitors in the middle, and Bravo bring up the rear. Spread out at least five and let's move." Murdock took the point and led out, checking every building, every window as they faded along the dirt street toward the Dead Sea.

Nothing.

The hairs on the nape of his neck stood up. What? Where? He scanned the buildings again. He felt like he was in a huge trap and the killer hammer was jolting down to squash him.

Lam came out of the gloom. "Still looks good ahead, Skipper. Some traffic to the south of us, two whole cars."

"Could they be moving men and guns south to block us?" Murdock asked his head scout.

"Possible. I can take a run down that block and check."

"Do that, and we'll move south on this street. Last one before the highway, then the sand and the water. Go. Don't get yourself shot, and report back on anything. If all is well, we'll meet you a block south of here on the wet sand."

Lam gave a curt signal with his hand and vanished into the night. Murdock kept the platoon moving. He was halfway through the block to the east when Lam called in a whisper on the radio.

"Trouble, Cap. I'd say about twenty men with long guns. They have formed a blocking line from the near side of the highway down to the water's edge. Look like some of them have uniforms, maybe the Palestinian Authority guys."

"Thanks. We'll change plans and go the way you went. Ed, you hear that? Reverse march and lead us south down that street we just passed. Go south, be careful. Put out a scout. We might be able to go around that bunch up there. If not we'll be in a tough firefight."

"Roger that, we're reversed. Fernandez is out as scout."

Murdock acknowledged the call, then went to find Bradford. He was beside Ching, who'd grabbed his combat vest and was holding him up by one arm.

"I can make it, damnit!" Bradford growled.

"Sure you can. Now just keep going this way for another block; then we get a rest or you can pack me a ways."

Murdock fell in behind them and watched their rear.

Ed came on the radio. "Okay, I get the picture better now. Lam is with me. We're maybe fifty yards from the end of the picket line out to the west. We keep going here without a sound, we should outflank them and be gone."

"Let's get south of them, then get some protection and hit them with the twenties," Murdock said. "Otherwise they'll be chasing us all the way down the sea. Jaybird, how many twenty rounds left?"

"Five in the magazine and five more."

"I've got seven left. We can discourage them to hell and back with those rounds. We'll move down out of range of their guns, say five hundred yards, laser them and let fly. Now let's get past the end of their line without a damn whisper. Go, Ed."

The line of SEALs, with ten yards between them, moved agonizingly slow as the men worked their way across the silent dirt street and in back of the buildings on the continuing street. The Israelis and their Arab guest were in the middle, with Alpha Squad bringing up the rear.

They were almost across the exposed area when a dog

charged out of the darkness and attacked Luke Howard, the third man from the end. Luke heard it coming and swung his sniper rifle like a club. The heavy butt of the weapon pounded into the side of the dog's head, and it went down without a whimper.

The last two men stepped around the dog, and Murdock did the same, giving a little sigh of relief when he was behind the building. They moved faster then, still as silent as a ghost company. One more block and they ran out of buildings. Fernandez angled them east toward the water. They were still thirty yards from it when they crossed the black-topped highway in a rush, then melted into the darkness of the shoreline.

"How far?" DeWitt asked.

"Two hundred yards more due south," Murdock said. "Jaybird, back here with me for the shoot." Murdock had spotted a building with a light in a second-story window on the cross street where the Authority guards had set up their ambush. He kept track of it as they moved, and when he figured the building was five hundred yards away, he called a halt. Jaybird had been walking beside him for the last two hundred.

"See that light, first one on the left? Laser on that. We can move right after we see how we do."

They both fired. The two twenties went off in airbursts with a cracking roar. Some small-arms fire followed from the line of troops, giving both Jaybird and Murdock new targets to laser. One of the next two rounds was a WP, and Murdock stared a moment at the perfect circle of death dealing smoking white phosphorus before it fell to the ground and brought screams of agony from the shooters below.

Murdock heard the two SEAL sniper rifles join in the fight as the long guns found the range from the muzzle flashes.

Jaybird put one contact round on the highway twenty yards in front of where they figured the troops were, and he saw the flash and the swath of shrapnel that tore into the thin line of Arabs. Four more shots each with the airbursts, and Murdock called a cease-fire.

"Enough, let's chogie out of here. Who is helping Bradford?"

"Ching," DeWitt said. "I've sent four men ahead to the checkpoint we saw on the highway. They will take it down and bring back a vehicle to transport Bradford."

"Good. Any more casualties?" Murdock asked. Nobody replied. "Ebenezer, how are your four friends holding up?"

"All doing well. The prisoners were treated fairly well. Their captors said they were being held to trade with Israel for some Arabs in jail."

Gunfire sounded to the south of them. The SEALs and guests had closed up to four yards separation, and Murdock had moved to the front along with Lam.

"Our MP-5's," Lam said. "No other weapons fired that I could hear. Our boys must have won the day."

Ahead a quarter of a mile, Senior Chief Sadler went to ground in the shallow ditch of the highway, and with the other three SEALs drilled the checkpoint with a deadly hail of hot lead.

"Don't harm those two vehicles," he had warned his three men. Victor, Mahanani, and Jefferson all kept their rounds away from the two sedans. Two guards had been on duty near the pull-down barrier when the shooting started. Neither one left the area, both down with multiple bullet wounds.

They had planned to come at the roadblock from two directions, but now Sadler changed the order. "We'll all move up on this side until we can see behind the barricade and the small building. Watch for any movement."

They ran forward, bending over to make a smaller target. There were no rounds fired at them from the checkpoint. They went to ground again and watched the structure. One of the sedans had a large wet spot under it.

"Damn, a ricochet must have hit the gas tank," Sadler said. "Six rounds each into the little shed over there. Might be one more of them on the floor."

They fired, then all lifted up and charged across the highway and thirty yards to the checkpoint. Sadler kicked in the door to the small building and fired six rounds.

"All clear roadblock," he said on the radio. Victor ran to the undamaged sedan and looked inside. The keys hung in the ignition. He got in, fired up the engine, and without lights drove back up the highway north until one of the SEALs there waved Victor to a stop. He turned around carefully, then opened the rear door and helped Bradford slide into the rear seat. He was groggy again. He was in need of help, and it should be soon. As agreed, Jefferson climbed in the front seat to ride shotgun. They rolled down all the windows.

Murdock came alongside. "Drive down about a mile and a half to where we left the boats. Blast your way through that other checkpoint. It might not even be operating this time of night. Stop at the boat, let Jefferson find it, and wait for us there. We've got to make some decisions here soon."

Murdock went back to his men and led them down the side of the Dead Sea on the hard ground. He took out the long-range radio the Israelis had given him and turned it on, then pushed the send button.

"Grounded, calling High Bird," Murdock said. He let up on the transmit button and waited. No response. He tried it three more times, then checked the batteries and switches with his penlight.

"Lieutenant Ebenezer up front," he said on the Motorola. "Get out your long-range radio and see if you can contact High Bird."

Ebenezer came jogging up a minute later. "I tried it five times, but I get no response. These sets should reach back to Rama Army Base easily. Are they off the air, or did we ruin both of these radios?"

24

Murdock looked at the Israeli Army man. "I heard your transmission, so that part works, and my receiver works," Ebenezer said. "Let me transmit and you listen."

He did. Murdock's receiver worked.

"So, must be some problem on the other end," Ebenezer concluded. "Maybe they don't expect to hear from us this quickly and they don't have their set turned on. These are special radios, so the signal doesn't come in on the regular base radios."

"Let's hope," Murdock growled. "How far to the boats?"

Fifteen minutes later they came to the spot where they had left the boats. Both were still there and in good condition.

Senior Chief Sadler came up. "Commander, we launch the boats now?"

"Hold for a while, Chief. Mahanani, go up to the road and check on Bradford."

"Aye, Cap," the medic said on the Motorola.

"Any reason that chopper can't pick us up here instead of eighteen miles down-water?" Murdock asked Eb.

The Mistaravim soldier shook his head. "Not that I can see. No problem if they heard the bird now up at En Gedi or not. That was a major concern coming in. I'll try the radio again."

There was no response from Rama.

Mahanani came on the Motorola. "Skipper, the Brad here looks lots better than last time I checked. Gave him another ampoule of morphine. No fever. Slug must have missed his kidney and his intestines, so no peritonitis. Says he can walk, but I wouldn't count on more than a hundred yards. Know he's feeling better. He called me an ignorant, stupid, beach-bumming half-breed Kanaka bastard."

"You two going steady?" Murdock asked.

"Naw, just a little contest to see who can call the other one the worst name. He's one up."

"Bring him back to the boat, we've got to push off. Too damn close to the action here. Tell Victor to stay with the car. Drive it down a quarter mile when we push off and wait for us. We might need the rig later. He's got his Motorola?"

"Got it on, Skipper," Victor said.

"Let's move to the boats and get them ready to launch. Bradford will be in the last one out. Move it."

Bradford made his way slowly across the sand to the boat. Mahanani hovered nearby, but didn't touch him. The big man let out a sigh as he sat down in the rubber duck and it slid into the black salt brine. Lam started the motor and took the tiller, and the two small craft began working their way south along the shore.

Four times Lam had signaled with his flashlight, and Victor moved the car along the road to match their progress. By that time it was 0112, and Murdock tried his long-range radio again.

"Grounded calling High Bird. Grounded calling High Bird."

He waited, and was about to try the call again when the speaker came alive.

"Yes, Grounded, read you."

"High Bird, looking for a ride. Mission accomplished."

"Launching in ten, Grounded. Same pickup point?"

"No, closer, about ten miles north of drop-off. No GPU with us, but we'll give you a white flare for an LZ when we hear you coming in."

"That's a roger. ETA your position, about thirty-five. Out."

The darkness seemed to deepen on the black water of the Dead Sea as they sailed south. The Motorolas came on.

"Victor here, Cap. That first checkpoint is coming up.

Looks like one light on. My lights are off. Should I run it, blast it? What?"

"Slip up on it, then blast through as fast as you can go. No bar, right? If you see any bodies, fire at them as you go past."

"That's a roger, Skipper. Getting ready to blast through." The air went silent.

"Oh, yeah, I'm through. Just one guard on the driver's side. I put four new buttonholes down his chest. I'll stop a mile ahead and wait for your signal."

Three miles north of En Gedi along the Dead Sea west bank, the Palestinian Authority had established a strong point. Captain Khadar smiled as he patted the Israeli long-range radio that they had captured from the three Jew spies two months ago. He understood English and a little Hebrew and he grinned. He knew exactly when an enemy helicopter was coming in. He'd had telephone warnings from En Gedi about the raid on the palace and the dead comrades there. This would be his chance for a great victory. It wasn't often that the Authority had a chance to shoot down an enemy helicopter.

Since he'd had a report of a helicopter coming toward the Dead Sea early that evening, he had been listening on the Israeli radio. He had to move fast. Ten miles from where they had been dropped off. Easy, ten miles up the Dead Sea bank. He was furious about the attack on the palace. There was a report that The Knife was dead. The killers would pay.

He roused four of his best men and put them in the truck with the stake body. Each of his men had four shoulder-fired RPGs and their AK-47's. They would drive without lights north along the highway for seven miles, and wait and see what happened. The helicopter would be coming in, probably from due east. As it came down to land, they would shoot it out of the air, then search for the killers who had murdered their hero.

Yes, it would be a glorious day for Allah!

The four Palestine Authority policemen grumbled when

they were awakened and told of their task. But they brightened when told they would soon have the chance to shoot down an Israeli helicopter. They cheered as they left the garage where the truck had been kept ready. Now all they needed was some good fortune and they would strike a deadly blow for Allah.

Murdock estimated they had come ten miles from the strike, and pulled the boats into shore. The men towed them onto the sand and spread out in a perimeter defense around the location. Victor parked the car on the shoulder and came in with the others.

It had been twenty minutes since the Israelis had given them an ETA of thirty-five minutes. Murdock hunched over where he sat, staring south. There was nothing but black on black. One unending bit of sand and black water after another. Not a light or a car or a building.

Lam lay in the sand on the north side of the defense watching and listening for any pursuit by the Arabs. Any trouble would come from that direction, but so far nothing.

Five minutes before the promised ETA, Lam sat up and frowned. Had he heard something from the south? He listened again, concentrated, closed his eyes, and poured all of his strength into his hearing. Yes, faint, but there it came again. The slow grinding of a truck, getting stronger, coming his way.

"Cap, we may have a problem," he said on the Motorola.

Murdock stirred, shook his head, and answered.

"Something moving this way on the road from the south," Lam said. "A truck if I hear it right. Moving slowly, maybe trying to sneak up on us."

"Who would know we are here?"

"That radio transmission you made with the chopper was in the clear, wasn't it? You gave him our location."

"Yes. But who else but the Israelis would have a radio that could pick up the signal?"

"Got me, Commander. I just do the listening. Want me to roam south a half mile and see what I can find?"

"Go, be careful."

Lam came off the sand and ran south along the shore. He carried his MP-5, and wished he had something longer. He ran hard for two hundred steps, then slowed for fifty more. Then he stopped, let his racing heart settle down, and listened.

Yes, the same grinding motor, as if it were crawling along in low gear, making more noise than if it were rolling at ten miles an hour in second.

"Definitely a truck, Skipper. Coming our way. I'm about a quarter up. I'll do another quarter and see what I can hear."

He ran again. Had to be a truck creeping up on a known location. How known? Oh, damn.

"Skipper, did the three Israelis we freed have a long-range radio like yours when they were captured? If they did it could be bad news and we're pinpointed."

Murdock swore softly. "Ebenezer, did you get that last Motorola?"

"Yes, I just checked with the men. They said they had a radio exactly like ours, but they disabled it before they were captured."

"Disabled, not destroyed."

"Correct."

"Disabled can be repaired. Some friends from the town to the south could be coming to meet us and the chopper. Talk to the High Bird in Hebrew, maybe the A-rab won't understand. Tell him there could be a problem at the LZ."

Murdock listened to the exchange. He didn't understand a word of it.

"Commander, Bird One says he's five minutes off the Dead Sea. He wants a white flare now."

"Cap, I've got a stake truck with men in the back," Lam said on the radio. "The road swings wide here; he's out of range of my MP-5. I can't stop him. He's rolling at about forty miles an hour. Be at your position in two minutes."

"Fernandez, a flare to our south, white, now. Jaybird, get south a hundred and watch and listen for that truck. Use any twenties you have left. Stop the sonofabitch."

"Roger, Cap. I've only got two twenty rounds."

"Snipers, go with Jaybird. We can't let that truck get near the chopper."

The flare popped and floated down. Murdock could hear the bird coming in from due east; then he heard a new sound, a truck engine racing as it drove forward. Jaybird heard the truck and saw a dim outline on the road. He lasered it and fired. The twenty sailed over the charging truck and exploded in the air thirty feet behind it. The truck kept coming. The SEAL sniper rifles began firing.

The dark blob of the truck came closer, and Jaybird fired his last twenty. Just as he triggered it, the truck made a screeching turn to the left away from them, and the round burst slightly in back of the truck, but some of the shrapnel hit the rig.

Landing lights flared from the chopper as it came in closer. The truck skidded off the road into a field away from the gunfire. Lam swore when he saw the rocket whooshes coming from the truck.

"RPGs away," Lam shouted into his Motorola mike.

"Abort, chopper, abort," Murdock called into his long-range radio mike. But he was too late. The chopper had found the flare and was powering down on the big rotors as it began to settle in for a landing from a hundred feet.

Three more whooshing sounds came from the truck. Then three more as the RPGs slanted into the air tracking the chopper. The big bird was still fifty feet off the ground, and coming down slowly in a controlled descent, when one of the RPGs hit the fuselage just in back of the side door. The explosion ripped the side of the ship open. Shrapnel from the round blasted through to the cabin, and riddled the pilot where he concentrated on his landing.

The CH-46 turned sideways; then the rotors stopped as the engine blew apart, and the CH-46 crashed straight down and burst into a huge fireball as the fuel exploded.

"Get the truck," Murdock barked into the Motorola. "Don't damage it. We need it for transport over the Judean hills. Ed, get your squad out there. Rifles, can you see any personnel? Nail them, but don't kill the truck."

Bravo Squad ran toward where they'd last seen the truck.

Lam was out there somewhere as well. "We have four people out here besides us," Ed said into his Motorola. "No friendly-fire casualties. Watch the truck."

They ran two hundred yards across the highway and east. Well ahead of them, Lam had seen the RPGs fire, and surged toward the truck to get in range for his MP-5. Now he was less than a hundred yards behind it as it crawled forward. He stopped and sent two three-round bursts into the stake body, then ran again. He heard the sniper rifles cracking ahead and to his right. How did Fernandez get way up there? He heard glass break, and saw the taillights on the rig signal a stop. The driver. Somebody got the driver.

Lam stopped and watched the rear of the truck. He saw one man drop down and crouch beside the back duals. Lam put three rounds into him and waited. Another man went down the other side of the truck, and Lam nailed him with the second three rounds of 9mm Parabellums. He watched, but saw no other movement.

"DeWitt. Two down from the rear of the truck. I think somebody nailed the driver. The rig is dead on the ground. I'm ahead of you somewhere, so don't target me."

"That's a roger, Lam. Move up and clear the truck."

Lam sprinted the last thirty yards. He found one body in the back of the stake body, then eased around the right-hand side. If the driver was down, there could be someone in the passenger's side. Just as he reached for the door, it pushed open and a man in a khaki uniform stepped out. He carried a submachine gun in both hands. Lam triggered six rounds into the man's back from six feet away, and he slammed into the door, dropped the weapon, and slid to the ground dying as he fell.

Lam lifted over the side of the truck and looked into the cab. One body lay draped over the steering wheel. The windshield had shattered and exploded inward.

"Clear on the truck," Lam said. "Five men down. Any survivors on the chopper?"

Murdock had just walked away from the fire that still raged where the CH-46 had crashed. There was no chance of survivors. Small-arms rounds continued to explode as they cooked off from the heat of the blaze.

"Lam, does the truck still run?"

"Give me two."

Lam pulled the dead driver out of the cab. The keys were still in the engine. He hoped none of the rounds had hurt the motor or the fuel supply. He used his pencil flash, moved the transmission lever out of gear, and found the starter. The engine ground over four times, then sputtered, then came to life and ran smoothly.

"One truck up and running," Lam said. "Moving it back to the road."

The SEALs gathered around the truck as it rolled over the sand and onto the blacktop. In back they found three unfired RPGs, lots of blood, and two MREs. In the cab, Murdock found an Israeli long-range radio exactly like the one he and Eb carried. He grunted and went to see the Israeli.

"Ebenezer, are there any roads to the east across the Judean hills?" Murdock asked as he looked back at the still-blazing wreckage of the chopper and the funeral pyre for its three men.

"No roads up this high. We're back in Israeli-controlled land, and we can drop south on this road for fifteen more miles to the town of Newe Zohar. Then we can drive east."

"First we should see if we can talk with anyone back at Rama. Do they monitor this frequency back there?"

"They should know that they have a chopper out," Ebenezer said. He made the call, but had no response. "When the chopper is overdue on its run back to the base, they may start getting curious and monitor this frequency," Eb explained. "We'll try again in two hours."

"We're back in Israeli territory, right?" Murdock asked. Eb nodded. "So we should have no trouble driving to where we can call in a new chopper."

"Depending on the fuel situation," Eb said. "This is a gasoline-powered truck. Petrol isn't always easy to find down here, and where it is available, it can cost dearly. Do any of you have any cash we can spend on gas?"

"Weren't issued any money," Murdock said. He looked at Lam behind the wheel. "How much gas in the tank?"

"Looks about half full."

"Siphon all the gas out of the sedan. We can all fit on the stake. Let's get ready to roll. Use the tubes we have over our backs to hold the weapons for the siphon. Go."

It was twenty minutes before they started moving. Bradford was lucid and seemed to be hurting less. He sat against the cab of the truck in back and sang a little song he hadn't thought of in ten years.

Three rode in the cab and seventeen in back. It was a full load. Lam drove, and they rolled down the highway at forty miles an hour. They pulled into the small village of Newe Zohar just as it was getting daylight. Ebenezer had an idea. He had Lam drive around until they found the police station. One Israeli cop on duty quickly called his superior, who came in ten minutes later.

Lieutenant Ebenezer showed the man some documents, and the chief of police kept nodding. Ten minutes later their truck's tank was filled with gasoline from the police pump and they had two ten-gallon cans full in the back.

"Now maybe we can get somewhere," Ebenezer said. He tried the radio again, but had no luck getting a response.

Eb rode in the cab with Murdock and Lam. "Our only worry now are Arab marauders. They roam over the underpopulated hills and sometimes hit small towns. They are well armed and take what they want. Usually they drive old military jeeps, decked out with ten-gallon cans of gasoline. We watch for them and when they see our guns, they will race away as fast as they can."

Before they left town, Eb had Lam stop in front of a small store. He came out with four large sacks filled with pastries, fruit, and sandwiches. He passed them out to the men and then they began their eastward journey. "I always carry money with me just in case of an emergency like this," he told them.

Lam looked at the map the Israeli showed him as Eb said, "First we go south on this same highway for ten miles; then we make a right turn into the only road. I'm not sure if there are any more settlements or villages out here or not. I've never been in this part of Israel. It's all controlled by us, so no worry there. From the map it looks like about forty miles as the crow flies, or maybe fifty-five or so on the road. We're heading for the good-sized town of Be'er Sheva." As Lam drove, Lieutenant Ebenezer tried to call on the long-range radio. He made the call ten times, but heard no response.

25

They drove for two hours east through the dry semi-desert of the southern Israeli countryside. The road followed a wadi that would have quite a bit of water in it during the rainy season. It must have rained a few days before because Murdock saw occasional places with running water in the wadi, and more with water holes. They turned sharply south with the gully, and then later were about to turn back to the north, still following the dry riverbed, when they heard gunshots and bullets zinged over the top of their truck. Ahead, a jeep with three ten-gallon gas cans showing to the front careened around a sharp corner and slid to a stop thirty yards directly in front of them.

Luke Howard, who had been standing in the truck bed watching over the cab, had his weapon trained on the front and he hit the trigger, spewing twelve rounds across the suddenly defensive jeep riders. The driver tried to reverse his gears, but by then three more SEALs had their weapons out firing. Both jeep front tires blew; then the folded-up windshield shattered into a hundred pieces, and four men riding in the jeep jumped off the rig and stormed into the sparse brush next to the watercourse.

Lam pulled the truck closer to the jeep.

"Keep firing at the bastards?" Senior Chief Sadler barked.

"Run them into the desert but don't hit them," Murdock said. "Let's see what they have on the jeep."

The SEALs found a box of food, two weapons, and six blankets. A few shots came from the thin brush, but a heavy volley of rounds from the SEALs drove the attackers back into the sharp sides of the wadi and out of sight.

"Grab those two cans of gas if they're full," Murdock said. "Slosh the rest of the last one on the vehicle and we'll see if we can set it on fire with some lucky-placed rounds."

The gasoline soaked the rig, and then the truck pushed the jeep off the road and they went by it fifty feet. It took only four rounds from the MP-5's to touch a spark that exploded the vaporizing gasoline into one huge fireball.

Jefferson watched the rig burn as they pulled away. "Those boys should know never to play with guns unless you're gonna win."

When they came out of the last big turn following the wadi, they were on a small rise, the largest one they had seen. The Judean hill had petered out from the north. Eb decided to try the radio again.

"High Bird, this is Grounded calling. High Bird, this is Grounded." Lieutenant Ebenezer bit his lip and looked north as if he could will someone to answer. He made the call again, and on this try repeated it three times.

A weak signal came through. "Calling Grounded. We have no record of a High Bird call. Are you using this frequency without authorization?"

"No, we're authorized out of Rama. Who is this?"

"This is Tel Aviv Air. What is your clearance? Why are you calling Rama?"

"Tel Aviv, we were on a trip into the West Bank. A helicopter from Rama took us in, and was coming back to get us when it was blown out of the sky. We have had no contact with Rama since that time about eight hours ago. Rama has one helicopter missing. We're looking for a ride out of here. We're coming up on Be'er Sheva. Can you get us transport? You should talk to Colonel Ben-Ami at Rama."

"Will do that, Grounded. Stand by."

Nothing came over the speaker. "He must be on a different frequency to get to Rama," Ebenezer said. "At last we have some contact."

Less than three minutes later the long-range radio chirped.

"Grounded, this is Ben-Ami at Rama. We lost the chopper?"

"Yes, sir. Lieutenant Ebenezer here. It was shot down by

PA gunners with RPGs just before it landed. No survivors. I'm sorry. The Authority men were out of their area; they shouldn't even have been near there."

"Your mission?"

"Mission accomplished, sir, down and out."

"Thank you." There was some dead air time.

"Grounded, you have transport to Be'er Sheva?"

"Yes, sir, a truck we borrowed from the PA."

"Your ETA?"

"Two hours max. One of our guests is wounded, rather seriously. We should get him to a hospital in town there."

"Yes, get him situated. An ambulance will be waiting for him. Then the rest of you come back here. We'll have a good after-action debriefing. Go to the airport's transient air section. An Army chopper will be there, probably about the same time you arrive. Good work, Ebenezer. We'll see you later."

"Thank you, sir. Out."

"Who the hell is your guest?" Bradford yelped. "Hell, if that's me you're jawing about, I'm fit and ugly and ready for action."

"I agree you're damn ugly, but that's not enough," Jaybird shrilled. Most of the troops laughed.

Murdock relaxed in the front seat. Should be nothing to worry about now unless these armed jeep raiders traveled in pairs like rattlesnakes and had radio communication.

"You didn't tell him about your Mossad team and it grabbing that turncoat," Murdock said.

"Not the sort of thing I'd say over a non-secure radio transmission," Lieutenant Ebenezer said. He grinned. "But it's going to be worth a month's pay to see these four gents walk into his office with that briefcase."

Murdock tried to relax. He wasn't sure it was over yet. Those marauders could still hit them hard.

"I want two men on lookout standing up by the cab," Murdock said on the Motorola. "Ed, pick them."

Even with that precaution taken he wasn't satisfied. He knew he wouldn't be until they were on board that plane heading for Rama.

The land was looking more productive. Here and there they saw settlements that led into green swatches that could be some kind of cultivation. Maybe irrigated.

By the time they came into the suburbs, Murdock realized that this must be a good-sized little city. Ebenezer told him there were over two hundred thousand residents in the town. They found the airport, and were directed to the military and transient section. An ambulance sat near a CH-46 look-alike chopper.

A darkly efficient nurse approached the truck as soon as it stopped.

"You have a patient for us," she said.

"Right back here, miss," Jaybird called, and they walked Bradford to the rear of the truck, removed one of the stake end gates, and helped him get down to the ground. He was put in a wheelchair, wheeled promptly into an ambulance with a ramp on it, and driven away at once. Murdock had time only for a quick talk with the efficient nurse. She said she would contact Colonel Ben-Ami about the patient's condition.

Only then did Murdock notice the captain's bars on her collar.

An hour later they were in Rama, had dumped their goods, and presented themselves to a half-dozen officers in Colonel Ben-Ami's special office.

Lieutenant Ebenezer took the lead.

"Colonel, before we get to the palace mission, I'd like to introduce you to these four gentlemen who return from En Gedi after some serious problems. We had reported three of them dead."

The men were greeted with shouts of joy and pleasure. One man rushed out to call Mossad in Tel Aviv and report the rescue.

The rest of the debriefing went quickly. They swore that The Knife was dead and that his support group there in En Gedi had been seriously depleted.

Lieutenant Ebenezer recommended that a permanent police presence be sent into En Gedi to maintain it as Israeli territory and to counter the strong point that the PA had just three miles away in the West Bank zone.

It was another hour before the SEALs made it back to their quarters, where Murdock enjoyed a long hot shower, a large dinner, and then a long nap. The other SEALs were fed at a special mess, and most dropped into bunks long before the next meal call.

Murdock slept until midnight, then got up, went to the soft-drink machine, and took out a Coke. He drank it, thinking about the last operation. It had worked, but it could have been better. There was no way they could know that those damn Palestine Authority men would have the Israeli radio. He finished the drink, and went back to bed. No telling what might happen the next morning.

Daylight came, and with it an order for Murdock and his planning team to be in the conference room they had used before. They were there: Ed, Jaybird, Sadler, and Lam. Murdock saw that the only other unit represented was the SAS underwater men.

Colonel Ben-Ami stood at the lectern at the front of the room. "Gentlemen, this may seem like a strange little task. Like a flotsam-and-jetsam child's story. I assure you it is not. During the past year there have been twenty-four adult deaths, fifteen children killed, and over sixty adults and children seriously injured. All because they picked up attractive items that had floated up on the beach or were found in the water.

"This problem is no accident, or series of accidents. The items are highly sophisticated and attractive death traps. We know that they are released in a pattern sequence by ships along the shore with the timing so the items wash ashore on the incoming tide. We have tried everything to stop them: intense patrols just off the surf line, surveillance of casual boats just at the incoming tide time of day, a follow-up on the makers of the items.

"The makers are in Hong Kong, North Korea, and the Philippines. We have no recourse there. The items are planted, or floated, by members of the PLO and we have a few names, but we need much, much more. It is summer here in Israel, and we will have record numbers of our residents escaping to the beach to lie in the sand and enjoy the water. We also will have a record number of deaths and tragedies, if we can't stop the booby traps."

"How long has this been going on?" Murdock asked.

"Almost a year. They come in batches and bundles. Not on every tide. Not every week. Sometimes a month between incidents. Then they might hit every day for a week. It's infuriating and frustrating. Local police have about given up."

"Have you tried the military mine-flogging machine?" Ed DeWitt asked.

The colonel frowned.

"It's a device that swings cables with weights on them in a pattern across a six- or eight-foot strip of land," Murdock said. "It pulverizes the land and explodes over ninety percent of planted mines. Should work well on these devices."

"But it would be too slow and too expensive," the colonel said. "Any other ideas?"

"What sets them off?" Jaybird asked.

"Body heat. When one is picked up and held, it takes about ten seconds of body heat from a finger or two to explode the device. They can lay in the sun for two hours at a hundred degrees and not go off."

"The best solution is to go after the ones who plant the devices," Murdock said. "You undoubtedly tried that. What results did you get?"

"Two blank walls. Both ended with the fishing boats that were used to scatter the items. Both boats were owned by a large Israeli fishing company. The officials and the boat captains and crew had no clue about the explosives."

"That still has to be the way to go," Murdock said. "Let us shadow one or two of these boats from the water. They won't see us, but we'll know every move they make. We'll have more people on the dock and on shore and in cars. We'll grab every person who even touches the boat before it goes out and after it comes back. There have to be some leads to the supply point where the explosives are smuggled on board the ship. It could be a supplier taking in lunches for the fishermen. It might be the iceman or the mechanic who works on the boat. It has to be somebody there some-where. And we'll find him. If nothing else works, we'll put men on board suspect boats as deckhands."

"Sounds good to us here at SAS," one of their officers said. "We'll be glad to share the water work. Maybe split up a half-dozen boats that could be dumping. Do they go into deep water to fish, or do they sometimes work along parallel to the shore?"

"Boats do both in almost every fishing village along the coast," the colonel said. "They want to get to the fishing grounds as quickly as possible."

The colonel pondered the situation for a moment. "All right, we'll all move back to Tel Aviv. A flight will take off from here at fourteen hundred. We'll all be on it. You're dismissed."

On the way back to their quarters, the SEALs talked about the problem. "Work it over," Murdock said. "We've got to find out how they get the goods on board the fishing boats and which one man on the boat drops the packages over the side. It could be that the boat owner knows nothing about the dirty tricks."

26

Third Platoon settled into its quarters on the air base. They were Israeli spartan with double-deck bunks, a small day-room, and a meeting room next door. With the delays getting off the ground at Rama and a mix-up in transport to their quarters, it was after 1800 before they were in their new digs. Chow followed quickly, and then they grouped around Murdock in the dayroom trying to get a handle on their new assignment.

"No way the fishing boat's captain doesn't know about the booby traps, if one of them is floating them into the beach," Donegan said. "Those are little boats, maybe twenty-four to thirty feet, and with only three men on board. How could one man hide that?"

"Easy," Jaybird said. "Three men on board. The owner or captain handles the boat at sea and drives to the fishing grounds. The two deckhands are sleeping if it's anything like a boat I worked on one summer out of San Diego Bay.

"When the one guy is supposed to be sleeping, he isn't. He waits until the boat is along a popular beach and he drops a box overboard. Inside he's set a timer to explode the box apart but not set off the booby traps. The box splits, the items float to the surface, and charge in with the tide. By that time the fishing boat is ten miles out in the Mediterranean."

"So how do the goods get on board?" Lam asked.

"Easy. The crewman, who is an Arab, packs the booby traps in a box marked 'bread' or 'fruit' or some other food-

218

stuff and nobody would think a thing about it. Once it's on board, the Arab takes that box and hides it until he needs it."

"What Jewish boat captain would hire an Arab?" Mahanani asked.

"Lots of folks," Senior Chief Sadler said. "The Israeli population is made up of twenty percent Arabs. They work everywhere. Why not on a fishing boat?"

"So it could happen that way," Murdock said. He'd been sitting in listening. "What other ways could those little bombs be sprinkled on the water?"

"Pleasure craft at the right time and right place," Fernandez said.

"How about a low-flying aircraft, drop the goods and beat it out to sea," Luke Howard said.

"Yeah, but Israeli radar would be on him like a bear on a honey tree," Ching said.

The room went silent.

"Come on, you guys. Part of the reason you're getting paid the big bucks is your brainpower. How else could these bombs be spread?"

"Private powerboat."

"A sailboat."

"Some asshole on a surfboard pretending to be fishing."

"All three of those would be so obvious the Israeli cops would be down their throats in a second," Jaybird said. "The innocuous fishing boat fits the picture and the job. Must be hundreds of them sail out of a dozen ports along here every morning."

"Senior Chief," Murdock said. "Find out which tides the explosives usually come in on. Is it the first one of the day, like they could have been planted early in the morning, or are they more likely planted during the night and come in during the night?"

"If they are scattered at night, gonna be a hell of a tough job to catch the bastards," Jefferson said.

"When do we get started on this one?" Frank Victor asked.

"Israeli cops have rented a fishing boat through private

parties," said Murdock. "They are going fishing in the morning at 0400. Lam, Jefferson, and I will be on board in deckhand outfits and with binoculars and long guns. We'll go out to see what we can see. We'll have to continue to the fishing grounds, fish some, and then come back with the fleet. Our captain and another crewman hidden on board will probably do most of the fishing."

"Good, the rest of us get to go exploring Tel Aviv," Jaybird said.

"Not so, oh, motor-mouth," DeWitt said. "Tomorrow the rest of us have several projects. We'll get assignments from Colonel Ben-Ami at 0800."

"Doing what?" Ching asked.

"As far as I know, we'll be checking out the supply operations that furnish these fishing boats with food, drink, supplies of all kinds. There has to be a contact here somewhere to help get the booby traps on board one or maybe more than one boat."

"What else?" Canzoneri asked.

"How many fishing villages and ports do you think there are along this sixty-mile strip from Haifa to Tel Aviv?" DeWitt asked. "I don't know, and any one of them could be where the explosives are coming from. It's like a giant jigsaw puzzle, showing a black orchid on a black background. We've got almost nil to work with."

"Best part so far is that nobody is going to be shooting at us," Jaybird said. "How is Bradford coming along?"

Ed DeWitt looked up. "Had a report on him from the doctors. The slug missed all the vitals. Grazed a bend in his small intestine but didn't rupture it; otherwise we'd be sending him home in a box. He'll be transferred to the base hospital here in two days."

Senior Chief Sadler looked at his notes on a clipboard. "So, we have chow at 0630 same place we ate tonight. We report here in our cammies, with no visible weapons, at our ready room at 0800. That's it. Commander Murdock will tell his men when and where. You're dismissed."

•   •   •

The next morning at 0345, Lam, Jefferson, and Murdock stared at the boat beside them at the fishing dock. They all wore used deckhand clothes like the other fishermen had on; jeans or blue pants, T-shirts with various emblems on them, and loose blue work shirts for the chill of the morning. They wore used running shoes for stability on the fish-slippery decks. The boat wasn't what they'd expected.

"This thing floats?" Lam asked. She was thirty-two feet long and made of wood that had been scraped and patched and painted for what Murdock figured could have been a hundred years. She smelled like fish from bow to stern. Twin outriggers stood straight overhead next to the skinny mast with antennas on it. The outriggers were on cables that were controlled by hand winches on the deck. A small, unpainted cabin hunched at the bow. There the real live fisherman who worked for the police made his final checks on the craft. He came out of the cabin and waved the three men on board.

"Good morning, gentlemen. My name is Ravid Sartan. I'm the captain of this magnificent craft. Welcome on board. I have talked with the Army people and know what to do. You can help or watch, but you must look like you belong to the crew so others don't get curious. For now, two of you go below, one will help me cast off."

Murdock pointed at Lam and Jefferson and they vanished below the deck. Murdock talked with the captain in muted tones. Captain Sartan was slight, with black eyes, a sharp nose, and a long face. He had a mustache and his hair was a little long. His hands and arms looked strong enough to bend steel bars, and his body was quick-moving on seaman's legs.

"We're here to do anything we can, and watch whatever we can. Let me know what needs to be done."

"Yes, they told me you'd be coming," Captain Sartan said. "We're ready to sail with the rest of the fleet. We won't do anything out of the ordinary to make us stand out. I have another crewman below who will help us with actual fishing once we get to the right spot."

"We'll try to blend in and stay out of sight and out of

your way. You know what we're looking for. Did you know the man who brought supplies on board here this morning?"

"Yes. He's been working several boats along here for ten years. Solid, absolutely trustworthy."

"He looked like an Arab."

"He is an Arab," Captain Sartan said. "You know, one out of five who live in this country are Arabs."

"I heard. You'll go out the harbor just beyond the breakers, and then, I understand, some boats go right and some go left, working just outside the breaker line before heading for their fishing spots."

"Right. Every captain has his own ideas where the best location is to fish. Some know, some don't. When one man gets a good bite, he radios it to the rest and we all move that way. Usually the bite is over by the time we get there."

"You troll or use the nets?"

"Both. The net is small and has an open mouth. We pull it in once every hour."

"Baited hooks on the trolls?"

"Right, and some flashers and feathers, anything to entice the fish to bite," Captain Sartan said. "Fishing is not good off here. The captains try to earn a living, pay for their boat, and dream of a bigger boat so they can afford longer-range fishing on the rich banks off Ethiopia. You won't recognize any of the fish we catch today."

The captain checked an old pocket watch, put it away, and went to the cabin. Murdock and a regular crewman threw off the lines, and the old diesel engine began hammering as the small craft pulled away from the dock. Murdock found a good spot just in back of the small cabin and took out the 9-×-35 binoculars. He kept them under his blue shirt. As soon as they moved up the surf line, he would have them out and watching the three or four other fishing boats near them. If any one of them threw anything overboard, he would take the name of the boat and radio it in. An Israeli coastal cutter would be on his stern within minutes.

Murdock and the other two SEALs checked every fishing boat they could see with binoculars as half a dozen sailed along the coastline at a steady ten knots. It was still dark, but there were enough work lights and deck lights on each craft to give the watchers the vision they needed. None of them saw anyone throw or drop anything overboard.

Twenty minutes later all but one of the craft had turned away from shore, heading for favorite fishing areas. Murdock helped with the net, getting it ready to let out. Then, when they began to bait the large hooks and stow them in special compartments along the inside of the rail, he worked at that too. Most baits were inch-wide "steak" slices through the backbone of a fish about an inch and a half thick.

A half hour later the ship slowed and the deckhand let out the net that trailed far aft. Then he let down the outrigger poles that held six lines each. Each line had thirty baited hooks or lures on it.

After an hour of trolling back and forth, they used a power winch and pulled in the small purse seine net. Captain Sartan came to supervise. When the net came in, they were busy pulling small fish out of the tangle of the net itself. Each fish, no matter how small, was thrown into a fish box about two feet wide, three feet long, and eighteen inches high.

When the main pocket of the net came in, they had many more fish, many of them still alive. They were dumped on the deck and scooped up with shovels into the fish boxes. When one was filled, it was lowered into a hold that was kept at thirty-five degrees to gradually chill the fish, keeping them fresh until they were back in port.

The captain looked at the three boxes of fish and shrugged.

"That pull might be good enough to pay for the diesel oil I'm burning on this run," he said. "I see why I quit being a fisherman."

When they pulled in the twelve lines one by one with hand cranks, they found fish on one out of six hooks. Some were small; three or four on each line were ten to twelve pounds. The captain was pleased.

When one line was cleaned of fish, it was quickly rebaited and let out again with a sinker of deliberate size to keep the hooks at a desired depth.

Slightly after 1600, they worked their trolling back toward Tel Aviv, and soon pulled in the lines and net for the last time. The captain shook his head when Murdock said he had hoped that they would find something.

"Wrong way to do it," Captain Sartan said. "I know these men, these boats. I can pinpoint four or five captains who might be blackmailed into helping some Arabs do this terrible thing. They are weak, they are bad fishermen, and they have large debts that they can't pay."

Murdock brightened. "Will you come talk with the Army man who is investigating this problem?"

"For Israel, I will be honored to do so. As soon as we get in and I sell the fish, I will change clothes and go meet your Army man. I have thought the small bombs must be coming from the fishing fleet. I just didn't know how. But after talking to some people I know, I think there is a pattern that we can work and men we can pressure. Yes, I think we can find a way to beat these terrorists."

"Why didn't you tell somebody before?" Murdock asked.

"Hell, I was deep in debt, trying to make the boat pay. I heard about the bombs. One even injured a friend of mine and his boy, but I was too blown away with my own problems. Then I sold the boat, got my debts cleaned up, and then the police came asking about using my boat. They told me why. So then I got to thinking. Know what I mean?"

"I know. We didn't find a thing out there today. How would they do it if it is a fishing boat?"

"Easy if you know the Mediterranean the way a fishing boat captain does. The tide takes about six hours to come in, more or less. You want the bombs on the beach by daylight or soon after that. You wait for the change of tides that start about midnight and scatter your bombs on that day about midnight. Nobody can see you at night, and there isn't much going on with patrol boats, especially when they see a fishing boat either going out early or coming in late."

"That would do it."

"Also, it would account for the bombs showing up on random days. Check the bombs and the incoming morning tide. My bet is that they would match."

Murdock and the two SEALs helped scrub down the deck and hose off the fish scales and residue. When they pulled into the dock near the other fishing boats, the boat looked like any of the dozen or more docked there.

"When and where do we go see this Army friend of yours?" the fishing captain asked.

"As soon as we get cleaned up, in non-fishing clothes, and I can make a phone call."

"Sounds good to me. I want to catch these murdering terrorists."

It was almost an hour later that Colonel Ben-Ami, wearing civilian clothes, Captain Sartan, and Murdock met in a small cafe. They had half sandwiches, coffee, and talked. After ten minutes, the colonel studied the fisherman.

"Captain, I believe you have given us a good lead here. How do we proceed? You mentioned two or three fishing boat captains who do not own their boats and are working for hire who are also deep in debt and might be open to some kind of blackmail and bribery."

"Yes, two. There may be one other. I'll go to him asking for work tomorrow and I'll be able to tell. The first one you need to check out thoroughly is Captain Ahron of the *Fishing Fool*. He's about thirty-five, works hard, isn't the best fisherman in port, and lets his deckhands get away with being lazy and sloppy. He docks on the B wharf."

Both Murdock and Colonel Ben-Ami wrote down the name and docking area.

"The next man is probably more likely. Captain Ahron is mostly just dumb. This next one is sneaky, and I wouldn't trust him with my maiden aunt. He's Gabi Zekharyah. Early fifties, bald as a bowling ball, thickset, and all muscle. Hard worker, but always trying for a big deal that falls through. He thought he had a contract to supply all the fresh fish to a big chain of hotels. He needed two boats to supply enough fish. He tried to do it with one, and couldn't meet the orders and lost the job to a competitor.

"He sails the *Gimbra II,* and docks near where we came in on the main wharf. He is loud, arrogant, and has a flash-fire temper. He would be my top suspect."

"Next we check the tide charts to see when the next high tide will hit the beaches between eight and ten A.M.," Murdock said. He explained to the colonel Captain Sartan's theory about how such a drop would take place.

Colonel Ben-Ami used a cell phone and talked to the Israeli Coast Watch. The man on duty said there would be a medium-high tide in two days that would hit the beaches off Tel Aviv peaking at six-thirty A.M.

"Gives us time to get ready," Murdock said. "Captain Sartan, we need to rent your boat again, to watch Zekharyah if he goes out of the harbor around midnight."

"I can do that, Commander. Would I be in line for the reward if he turns out to be the one and you convict him?"

Murdock looked at the colonel. "There has been a forty-thousand-shekel reward offered for catching the killers," Ben-Ami said. "That's about ten thousand U.S. dollars. It's been offered by several civilian groups. I think you would be considered, if we nail the man and he is the right one."

"Not a word of this to anyone," Murdock told the fisherman. "I bet rumors and talk spread on the dock like the mumps."

"It does. My rental today I passed off as a look at the boat by a new buyer. That's why we're meeting here well outside the fishing community, and why I asked the colonel to come in mufti."

"Just so you understand," Murdock said. "If Zekharyah is the guy, he could simply not drop any booby traps until we got tired of watching him, if he did know we were watching."

"No worry there, mate. My son's a policeman. He's told me all about those things."

They left, each going a different direction. Murdock caught a cab, and used some of the expense money the colonel had given to him and the rest of the SEALs. The shekels felt strange and looked even weirder, but they bought goods and services.

He left the cab at the entrance to the air base, showed his papers to the guard, and made it inside.

As soon as he walked into the SEALs quarters he could

sense that something was wrong. Ed Dewitt and Senior Chief Sadler had their heads together over cups of coffee. They motioned him over, poured him a cup, and Sadler scowled.

"We've got trouble, Commander. An hour ago we had word that Jaybird is in the Tel Aviv city jail."

27

"In jail?" Murdock exploded. "How in hell?"

"Skipper, the men worked with the colonel on some dishy little jobs this morning checking out suppliers to the boats. It was a total waste of time. When we got back at noon, he said the men could take the rest of the day off. If anybody wanted to go into town he'd give them passes, but they had to be back by 1800. We had some expense money that we parceled out, so the guys wouldn't be flat broke. Turns out this is an expensive town."

"And?" Murdock said, urging him on.

"Jaybird didn't come back. Just an hour ago we found out he's in jail on several charges."

"Such as?"

"They didn't tell us, Commander."

Murdock used a phone in the dayroom and called the colonel's office. He wasn't there. An aide said he might be at the officers' club. He was. Murdock called and told him the problem.

"Yes, the talkative one. It's happened before with some of my men. Be at my office in ten minutes in your cleanest cammies. No time for a dress uniform even if you had one. One of my aides and two of our military police will go with you. We usually have good relations with the Tel Aviv police."

Ten minutes later at the colonel's office, Murdock met a Captain Bildad, who arrived in a military sedan with driver.

"Commander, sorry about this," said the captain. "If it isn't too serious, we should be able to straighten it out. I have authorization to bring your man to our brig under military police escort. If it comes to that, I have a fund we can use to pay a fine or bail."

"I can't let these guys out of my sight for five minutes," Murdock began.

Captain Bildad chuckled. "Sir, they are SEALs. We know about the dangerous jobs you do, the risks that you take. It's only natural to let off steam once in a while."

"Let's hope that the city police are that understanding." The two military policemen came in a vehicle behind the captain's sedan. Murdock stewed about it all the way into town. Once there, he tried to relax. They were taken into a reception area, where a sergeant looked up the record and gave a folder to a police captain, who ushered the two officers and the military policemen into a conference room.

Introductions were made. Captain Ranon leafed through the report and looked up. Murdock couldn't read his face. He was short and solid, with a bull neck ending abruptly in his chiseled face. A small crack appeared in one corner of his mouth; then his eyes took on a tiny glint.

"Commander, you're with the U.S. Navy SEALs, is that correct?"

"Yes, sir."

"So is this lad we have in custody, one David Sterling?"

"That's right, sir. One of my best men."

"He seems to be good at several things. We have a complaint here that he was observed climbing the outside of one of our older hotels. He was on the fifth-floor level sitting on a narrow ledge, talking to the pigeons and singing bawdy songs."

"Yes, sir, that could be our Sterling."

There was an awkward pause. "Sir, what are the charges against Petty Officer Sterling?"

The captain looked at the papers again and rifled through two or three. "One charge is peeping, looking in a lady's hotel room, but that one is probably without much merit. The second charge is trespassing. It seems he did not have the hotel's permission to scale the outside of the building.

It attracted quite a crowd before it was over. That is a minor charge."

"There is more, Captain?"

"I'm afraid so. The more serious charges of exposing himself in public and lewd conduct."

"Sir, I don't quite understand."

"Your Petty Officer Sterling was naked during this climb, Commander. Then he relieved himself, urinating on the fifth-floor ledge."

Murdock shook his head as the Israelis behind him grinned and muffled the urge to laugh.

"Sir, this particular man has a tendency to get a little drunk at times and when he does, his usual conduct is to climb the outside of buildings in the buff. I can't explain it. He can't explain it. I'm sure some psychiatrist after three or four years of probing could come up with the reason. I assure you, he's harmless. He's also a highly decorated member of my platoon, where he has served with outstanding distinction for four years. He's been wounded in action three times, and has a part of a Presidential Unit Citation. He would have various military medals, but our work is covert, therefore no publicity, therefore no medals."

The police captain shuffled the papers again, closed the folder, and put it on his desk.

"Yes, I can see he's an integral part of your operation. Are you now under orders with one Colonel Ben-Ami of the Israeli Army Special Operatives Section of the Mistaravim Counter Terrorism Unit?"

"We are, Captain. Sixteen of us."

"Hmmmm." The captain looked at the papers again. "Commander, the nickname of Jaybird, the first name that he gave us after his arrest. What does that mean?"

"Sir, it's from some early American literature, folklore or local sayings. It comes from naked as a jaybird. Which, as you know, he tends to be now and then."

The policeman looked at Captain Bildad. "Sir, I would assume that you represent Colonel Ben-Ami in this situation. What does the Army have to say?"

"Captain, we have been operating with the Third Platoon

of the U.S. Navy SEALs now for about ten days. They have undertaken dangerous and highly productive raids in the Gaza Strip and in the West Bank. They have performed flawlessly, with precision, at the lowest cost of life. Petty Officer Sterling is an integral part of that operation.

"At the current time we are on a joint venture to stop once and for all the floating booby traps that our beach areas have been plagued with for the past eleven months. Petty Officer Sterling is a part of that operation. Colonel Ben-Ami requests that if the charges are not of a serious criminal nature, the man be released into the custody of the Israeli Army's Military Police and jurisdiction."

The police captain nodded at the Army captain, who took a step back. All but the policeman were standing. The cop looked over the papers again, then closed the file and held it out to one of the military policemen.

"Nothing here that should merit the incarceration of the man. He is hereby turned over to the military police, and his commanding officer, and because of his service to the nation, all records of this arrest and the incident are expunged from our databases. This session is closed. You are all free to leave. The man will be brought to you in the waiting area."

"Thank you, Captain," Murdock said. They filed out.

Captain Bildad walked beside Murdock. "Well, we won that one. I've lost here before. It's a kind of informal hearing in noncriminal cases. The MPs will take Jaybird in their car until we get back to the base; then he's all yours." The captain grinned. "How many times has this happened?"

"Not sure, but he's only been arrested four times now for it. No jail time, but there was a hundred-dollar fine and costs once."

When Jaybird came out, he wore a jail jumpsuit of bright orange. The outfit discouraged escape attempts. They never did find his clothes, which he took off and threw away as he climbed the hotel. Jaybird wasn't making jokes.

"Fucking head hurts like twenty jackhammers are having a contest," he said. He looked at Murdock, then quickly away. "Sorry, Skipper. Just got carried away. Don't know what the booze is they serve over here."

"See you back at the air base," Murdock said, a small smile showing. Jaybird did look like he was hurting. Good. Maybe it would be longer before he tried his naked climb again.

Back in the SEALs' quarters a half hour later, Jaybird had little to say. He took a shower, grabbed a can of Coke from the machine, and hit his bunk. Nobody jazzed him about it. The old hands knew better from previous experiences, and the newer men took a clue from the vets.

The Israelis had brought in a big-screen TV set and hooked it to cable. In the other end of the dayroom they had provided a CD player and a hundred CDs, mostly American artists.

Murdock sat in between with the phone. He had been talking to a weather specialist at the Israeli Coast Watch.

"Right, I want to know how many times during the past two months there were high tides that peaked between six and eight in the morning."

"I could almost tell you from memory, but I'll do a search on my tides computer file. It should have it down to the minute. Then I'll read off the dates to you. Will that work?"

Murdock said it would, and waited for the computer to do its work. Three minutes later the night man at the Coast Watch desk had the data. Murdock wrote down the dates. There had been eleven days in the past two months when the tides were high between 0600 and 0800 on the beaches around Tel Aviv.

Murdock tried to contact the bomb squad at the Tel Aviv police, but a recording said they were all out and in an emergency he should dial the general police contact number. He had to wait for morning.

About 2200 Murdock, Lam, DeWitt, Sadler, and Fernandez sat around a table in the dayroom talking about the bombings.

"No way we can just pick up the guy who spreads the bomblets," Fernandez said. "Hey, we've got to follow the trail to the guy who provides him, and then nail *him* and find out where he gets the shit and nail *him*. We get back at least three levels and we should be able to choke off the beach bombings altogether."

"Right," Sadler said. "Just chopping off the rattles won't kill the damn snake. Got to go for the body and then smash its head."

"First we stop the drops, then we go for the next step," Murdock said.

"Bet you ten to one it's some fucking A-rab who owns the fishing boat that's dumping the goods," Lam said. "Then he has complete control. He can go out anytime that he wants to."

"Our top two suspects are Israelis," Murdock said.

"That would make them traitors; they could hang. Does Israel have the death penalty?"

No one knew. The consensus was that it did not.

"How else can we hit the bastards?" DeWitt asked.

"We hit them right up the supply chain," Murdock said. "The things come from overseas somewhere, so they import them. Once we nail the delivery boy on the Mediterranean, we should be able to squeeze the name of the up-the-line sumbitches out of him."

Murdock looked around the group. Eyes were starting to drop shut. "Okay, you brain-trust guys. I'm packing it in. Tomorrow Lam and I will work the bomb squad and see what backgrounding we can do with our fishing buddy Captain Sartan on the two major suspects. The rest of you can do some training, or Ed will check with Colonel Ben-Ami to see if there are any other developmental tasks we can do while we wait for the next morning high tide."

Murdock figured he'd drop right off the second his head hit the pillow, but it didn't work that way. Jaybird kept cropping up. He'd really looked subdued after this episode. Lucky it was over here and not in the States. If Commander Masciareli, their SEAL Team Seven boss, found out about it, there would be hell to pay. He'd threatened to cashier Jaybird out of SEALs if he ever did his naked climb again. No reason he'd ever hear about it. Murdock would tell each man about the situation and pledge him to silence.

So, he had to have a long talk with the Jaybird. There was a chance that booze was getting to him. It could have turned into poison for him and set off some uncontrollable impulses in his brain. He'd have that talk with Jaybird and try to get him on the wagon for six months. With these hard-drinking SEALs, it would be tough, but not as hard as in the old days. Murdock shook his head, remembering when he went through BUD/S. It was a beer bust every other night. Yeah, he'd have that talk with Jaybird tomorrow. Take him on the trip to town to talk to the bomb squad and then the Coast Watch people. He had to get this damn timing down. It could lead to capturing the bomb spreader. Tomorrow.

28

The three SEALs sat in the conference room in the bomb squad's domain watching a five-minute TV tape about the floating terrorist bombs and how the public could stay safe around them. As the tape ended, two cops came into the room. Both wore the standard khaki uniforms and both were sergeants.

One of them took the lead. "I'm Sergeant Elkan, lead man in the bomb detail. The captain says we're supposed to tell you all we know about the booby-trap floater bombs we've been finding on our beaches." He emptied out a paper sack on the table. Spewed out were several highly colored plastic tubes, each about a foot long. Some were straight, some in the form of a U, some with a twist and curl on one end.

"These are the devils. As the captain probably told you, we're fighting a losing battle. We send a squad out on the beach every morning looking for them. Pick up the ones we find with metal grabbers like the street cleaners use. They go in our bomb box and get detonated out of town.

"The outer wrapping is waterproof. Inside there is a tiny quality of dynamite, but enough to blow off a man's hand. We're not sure why they detonate, but the secret is something in the plastic that reacts to the heat of the skin. Two fingers on the things for ten seconds and you go looking for your fingers."

Murdock picked up one of the bombs and nodded. "I'd guess these have been neutralized." He introduced himself, Lam, and Jaybird. "Sergeant Elkan, we're not here to steal your thunder or to take your jobs. We were invited to take a look at the problem and see if we can help eliminate it. I understand you have a time profile from your computer concerning the day and tide position of each of the bomb incidents during the past two months. I'd like a copy of it if I could so you can advise us about the time line."

Sergeant Elkan nodded, sorted through some papers on his desk, and laid out two of them. "These are charts for the past two months up to last night," he said. "The green shade is the incoming tide. Then you have the change, and the outgoing tide is shown in red. Each of the bombing incidents is shown with an X marking the time when each bomb was found."

Murdock and Lam studied the charts. Murdock looked up. "So it looks like your bomb finds have been in the morning when high tide peaks between six and eight A.M. Is that right?"

The two Israelis looked at the charts. "Yes, sir. The last four bombings have been in conjunction with high tide at those hours."

"High tide tomorrow comes at 0823," Murdock said.

"We have a routine patrol that covers every high tide, twice a day, no matter what hour it comes. It's helped reduce the wounded and dead dramatically."

"Any patrols offshore?" Lam asked.

"No, not our jurisdiction. The Coast Watch takes care of that area."

"Could I have a copy of these printouts?" Murdock asked.

Sergeant Elkan handed him the folder. "Yes, sir. These are some more printouts and data we've established on the type and numbers of releases of the floaters. We hope that you can help. Right now we're taking help from anywhere that we can find it."

Murdock picked up one of the defanged bombs. This one was in bright reds, greens, and yellows in an eye-catching design.

"Can I borrow one of these, Sergeant Elkan?"

"Absolutely, Commander. Is there anything else we can do for you?"

"I think that covers it right now. Oh, at a later date we might call on you to bring out a bomb box. I'm sure you have one to put picked-up explosives in and to transport them."

"We have one, and it's available seven-twenty-four."

"Thank you, Sergeant Elkan. I hope we need it." They shook hands and the SEALs left.

"A little touchy, weren't they?" Lam asked.

"Right, but they are just protecting their turf," Jaybird said. "Like some expert is called in to do a job that they couldn't get done."

"If we have any big catch, we'll call them in," Murdock said. "Remember, we're working back up the distribution line, so we have to be careful not to warn the next step up."

They found their car and driver from the base waiting for them. Murdock looked down at his cammies. "We stand out like three-dollar bills in these suits. If we're going to do any undercover work we need civilian clothes."

"They have an Air Force store out at the base that has clothes," Jaybird said.

"Let's go see what we can find," Murdock said.

On the ride back to the airfield, Lam began to frown. "Hey, whatever happened to Don Stroh? We haven't seen him for days."

"Maybe he got a real job to do," Jaybird gibed.

Murdock grinned. Now that was more like the old Jaybird. "He must have got tangled up in red tape somewhere. This joint operation has a lot of tangles."

At the store they found some jeans and T-shirts. Murdock said they could wear the same fishing shirts they had used the night before. The fishing fleet had long since sailed for the day. Murdock called their boat captain.

Ravid Sartan answered his phone on the second ring. "Captain, this is Murdock. I hope you had a good night's sleep."

"Always. I sleep like a rock. What's happening?"

"We need to do some prowling. Zekharyah is out with his ship, but I thought we could talk to some of the people he deals with, suppliers, buyers who take his fish, the usual."

"How could we do that and not get them suspicious that something is going on?"

"Can't do it. We can stroll around and watch things, but talking to them isn't a good idea. Not yet. Especially if they are involved in the bomb dropping." The line was quiet for a moment. "You have any regular civilian clothes?"

"We just bought some. We look pretty good."

"Fine. Meet me at that fish chowder cafe a block over from the wharf. I have something I want to show you."

They met at the eatery and walked down several blocks. The street became shabbier, the people less moneyed, the buildings old and run-down. It was the closest thing Tel Aviv had to a business slum.

Two blocks farther down they saw a fight. Two small Asian men pounded on an older man, who tried to fight back but didn't know how. Then one of the smaller men swung a knife, and the older man grabbed his throat and staggered sideways. Before he hit the ground the thugs had stolen his wallet and watch and run down the alley, vanishing into a ramshackle building.

"Don't worry about it," Captain Sartan said. "There was no way we could have helped him. It would only have put a spotlight on us for a dozen pair of eyes." He motioned the SEALs forward. They went past the dead man and continued on.

"Another block and we come to a hundred-yard alley that's known as The Devil's Little Acre. This is the absolute bottom for killers, robbers, con men, and those who think they can control these nefarious citizens into a group for more efficient crime.

"The police don't come here often. When they do it's in force, and they figure on losing at least two men to hidden snipers."

Sartan gave the SEALs each a floppy hat that covered their military haircuts and hid their faces.

"Nobody wants to be seen or remembered down here. Near this end of the alley is a friend of mine of long standing. He had some domestic troubles, a dead wife and her missing cash estate, and he wound up here feeling safe from everyone. Twice a month we get together to talk about the good old days, when there were fish out in the Med and a man could make an honest living. I have a pass at this end of the alley, but no farther. We call him Dr. Seuss because he draws funny animals. He has from ten to fifteen men working for him now, and he's expanding. Soon he'll move down deeper into the alley for more protection."

A man came out of the shadows of the alley. He carried an Uzi that was trained on the four of them.

He jabbered in Hebrew, and Captain Sartan spoke back to him giving his name. The man, dressed in multiple layers of old shirts and a sweater or two, nodded slowly and waved them forward with the deadly Uzi muzzle.

"What if a new man didn't know your name?" Murdock asked.

"Then the guard would use his cell phone to check."

They went past two doors and up to the third one, which had two men standing in front of it.

Murdock checked the alley—not more than fifteen feet wide, not made for cars, none present, the buildings sagging and faded and some leaning out over the street. There was a general odor of decay, rot, and dirt.

They stopped at the front of the building with the two guards. Captain Sartan stepped forward and said a few words to the guards, who both had silenced Uzis and wore clean clothes but no uniforms. One opened a door and motioned them inside.

Once past the door, Murdock was swept up in an Oriental fantasy. The air smelled of flowers, and he saw a small waterfall to his right with tropical flowers blooming in and around it. The room was large, with a vaulted ceiling, draperies on the walls, and a thick carpet under their feet.

Captain Sartan smiled as he saw the looks of surprise on the SEAL faces. Two young women in harem costumes of frilly net pantaloons and sequined tops met them and waved them forward past a woman playing a small harp and another playing a plaintive Russian balalaika. Now the walls held oil paintings that could have been old-master originals. At the end of the room a door stood open a foot, with a huge man standing guard. He was dressed like a Moorish eunuch, complete with bare chest, red sash, pantaloons, boots, and a deadly-looking two-foot curved sword. His arms were crossed. When he saw Captain Sartan, he bowed and stepped aside. The door swung open and inside, the room was starkly futuristic, with metal walls, a thin carpet on the floor, ranks of computer terminals and video screens around one wall. On the other side sat a man behind a free-form desk of highly polished cherry wood.

He stood, grinned, and held out both arms. Sartan stepped forward for the hug and kisses on both cheeks.

Murdock could still see the wind and sun deeply ingrained in the old fisherman's face. He was broad and thick, with no neck at all, with a bull head hacked from a chunk of granite that had stringy gray hair combed over the top and down one side.

"Sartan, you old bastard. Where have you been? Heard you tried to sell your boat. Does that relic still run?"

"Better than that yacht of yours, Marnin, you son of a cockroach's mother. How have you been? You're losing weight. Too many harem girls at the same time. I keep telling you that no man can handle more than two at a time and keep them both happy."

"How is my first love Jemina? I always told her she was too good for you. You kept her pregnant and barefoot and now she's going to college."

"What can a man do?" Sartan turned and waved at the SEALs. "My good friend, these are special men. They are called the masters of the sea, the avenging gods that come out of the deep; they are three of the famous United States Navy SEALs."

Marnin's eyes widened and then snapped. "Yes, yes. I saw a demonstration once in the harbor. Impressive. Men's men. Can I entertain you with men's women?"

"Not this time, you old coot. We're here on business."

"Fishing. Good. I can now afford to buy you a trawler and you can fish off Ethiopia just like the swells in the high-rent district do. I can have it here next week, you outfit it locally, and I'll pick up the tab and you can be off fishing in a month or so."

"You're not buying me a damned trawler. I told you that

before. We have more important problems." Captain Sartan reminded him about the floating booby traps. "We want to find out who makes them, who imports them, who supplies them, who buys them, and who dumps them in the surf."

"Take about ten minutes. Old friend, you don't want much." He flicked an unseen spot off the shoulder of his thousand-dollar suit, and then nodded. "These hooligan schelmps. Their bombs killed one of my men. They have a complicated operation."

"You know about it?"

"Just enough to stay away. They kill people for sport."

"Arabs?"

"What other schelmps would do this to women and children out playing in the water and on the sand?" His face worked, and a tear slid out of one eye that he slashed at with one hand.

"Can you give us a name, a starting place?"

"More like an ending. I know for sure that it is that dog of a fishing boat captain Gabi Zekharyah who does the dropping. He would sell his own mother into a whorehouse for a hundred shekels."

"You're positive?"

"A thousand percent. But if you hit him first, the rest of the operation will fall back and set up somewhere else."

"A starting place?"

"International Food and Novelties. We have citizens from a hundred and twelve different countries in Israel. Many of them yearn for foods and desserts and familiar items from their homelands. This outfit imports the stuff from all over the world."

"Including China and North Korea?"

"Yes. A good Jewish business, run by an honest and fair man. But he has a traitor in his midst and he doesn't know it. We're not sure who it is. I didn't look beyond there. The bombings slacked off and I had other vital concerns."

"The inside man is an Arab?"

"As far as we know. He sets up the buys in China. When they arrive with a special notice, he sets them aside for his specific customer and takes payment, and enters the cash into the company books so nothing is lost and the company even makes a profit on the sale. I lost one man trying to get farther. He had been watching the firm for a week, and noted certain non-employees coming and going from the back door. He phoned me one night about one o'clock and said he would have good news for me in the morning. We found his body floating in the harbor the next afternoon."

A voice sounded from one of the computers. Marnin stood at once, went to it, and sat down and typed in a few words. He came back and smiled. "Business," he said. "When one of my target stocks drops to a certain price during trading, I put in a buy order on-line. Beats the hell out of a stock broker."

He looked at the SEALs. "I know you boys are good, but be damn careful around that International Food place."

He stood. "Now, excuse my bad manners. I have guests. How about something to drink, to eat? Anything? What can I bring you?"

"Actually, we should be getting to work, some backgrounding on this International Food firm," Murdock said. "We definitely do not want to wind up floating in the bay."

"I like this boy," Marnin said. He pointed at someone across the room, and a moment later a man rolled a small cart across the room. On top was a jeweler's black velvet cloth with four square jewelry boxes setting on it.

He handed one to each of the men. "Nothing for you, but something for that special woman at home. With my compliments. If there is any enforcing kind of work you need done along the lines you've been talking about, please come and see me." He shook each man's hand and led them toward the door.

"Marnin, you old fish scaler," Captain Sartan said. "You take care of yourself."

The man who controlled half the crime in Tel Aviv smiled. "Now you can be sure of that."

Outside the front door, one of the guards walked them the fifty feet to the mouth of the alley and the more civilized street. Then he returned to his post.

"Now there is the kind of friend to have," Murdock said.

"Can we trust what he said about the foreign food importer?"

"We can trust him with our lives," Sartan said.

Lam lifted his brows. "So if what he says is true, we will be trusting him with our lives. Let's get started."

29

To get started, the SEALs and Captain Sartan drove past the big food-importing firm.

"Looks like any other business," Lam said. "Offices, big loading dock for a dozen trucks at once, and their name plastered on everything you can see."

"How can we penetrate a big outfit like that when we're looking for one individual?" Jaybird asked.

"Might not be that hard if we had time," Murdock said. "But we'd need cooperation from the owner. The man we want has to be one of the managers, or at least somebody who puts in orders to foreign markets."

"So looks like we work up the food chain here," Jaybird said. "We know the delivery outfit, and we know the one getting the goods. How many kinds of foreign foods would a fishing boat order anyway?"

"When do the fishing boats get orders brought to them?" Murdock asked.

Captain Sartan shrugged. "Most of them get supplied each morning; then they don't worry about refrigeration. Some boats on the other end of the scale get goods for a week at a time."

"So could be an 0300 delivery, three A.M.?" Murdock asked.

"That's when mine used to come. I seldom had anything delivered from International Food and Novelties."

"So it looks like that's our next hot appointment," Lam said. "Only, how do we stake out the boat and not look out of place?"

"I've seen a few street people, bums and winos, sleeping

it off on the sidewalks," Jaybird said. "You have many of them around town?"

"Too many. They get to be a real problem."

"Good, we can be three winos deep in our cups and sleeping on the sidewalk."

The SEALs agreed.

"You'll be wanting to carry firearms?" Sartan asked.

"I'm almost never without one," Jaybird said.

"We'll need some protection and enforcement ability," Murdock said.

"Better have your colonel talk to the police and get yourselves deputized, or at least get gun permits."

"Should be no problem," Murdock said. "Do any of the fishing boats get in early?"

"Three or four of them. They have contracts to supply hotels and restaurants with the fresh fish catch of the day. If it isn't caught that day, they can't advertise it that way, and the Health Administrator watches them like a hungry lion in a herd of African antelope."

"I'd like to walk past the boats, maybe past where Zekharyah docks, again, just to get the feel of the place," Murdock said.

They did. The fishing dock here was on a mole, a triangular-shaped wharf that extended out into the bay at a forty-five-degree angle, then took a turn to the left parallel with the shore, and then another forty-five-degree angle coming back toward the shore pier. It gave access to both sides of the wide dock for moorage and discharge and onboarding cargo via small flatbed electric trucks that plied the pier continuously. Zekharyah's boat, the *Gimbra II,* had its dockage midway in the third leg. Only one boat on that leg was at its berth unloading the early morning catch.

Sartan knew the captain and the crew. He told them some friends of his wife were in town and he was giving them the ten-shekel tour. They continued to the end of the mole, and watched the boats coming and going in the harbor.

"About the tides," Sartan said. "They will help boost the floaters highest on the sand, but it's the waves, the breakers, that really push the items through the surf and into shore."

"Then the bombs would have to be dropped near the surf line, or maybe inside the first wave," Jaybird said.

"Yes, otherwise a north-south current along the coast could pick up a bunch of them and send them a hundred miles down the coast."

"So the men dropping off the packages of bombs know what they are doing."

"They've had enough practice to get it down to perfection," Murdock said. "We need to chop off the tail of this snake and work back up to its head."

"How are we going to stake out this pier?" Captain Sartan asked.

Lam grinned. "Hey, that's the easy part. We can put ten men around his boat and he'll never see a one."

"On the other boats," Sartan said. "But won't the other captains warn him? This is a tight little community, and even if Zekharyah is a bastard, the other captains will help protect him."

"They would, but they won't see us either," Murdock said. "We'll be underwater waiting for him to make his move. We'll already have taken the screw off his boat so he can't run for it."

"You can do that?"

"We're part fish," Jaybird said. "Mostly barracuda."

They all laughed at that, and headed back along the concrete wharf toward the shore.

Back at the dock, Murdock asked where the delivery trucks usually stopped.

"For big shipments they use forklifts and boxes or pallet boards for the goods. Smaller packages they work with the little power tractors. Just a motor and a lift and a man pulls it along."

"Where will the truck from International Food and Novelties stop at?" Lam asked.

"They always use a big bobtail truck, because they make a lot of deliveries. It would be back here where the cross street hits the one in front of the wharf."

"What are you thinking, Jaybird?" Murdock asked.

"We take the truck up here, grab the driver, insist that he

shows us which delivery is heading for Zekharyah's boat, then we open it and check to be sure it's the fireworks. We close it up. One of us about the same size as the driver puts on his uniform and hat if he has one, and makes the delivery. As soon as Zekharyah signs for the delivery, we take him down."

"He's going to be armed," Sartan said. "Both of his men will have Uzis or some other submachine guns. A lot of fishermen could get hurt if everyone starts blasting away."

Murdock scowled. "True," he said. "So we don't take his screw off. We use a high-speed boat and take him as soon as he separates from the other fishing boats."

"I like that a lot better," the boat captain said.

"By then the fishing captains will be talking about the shoot-out. They'll identify Zekharyah's boat, and the supplier is going to know seconds later," Lam said.

"Means we have to take them both down at once," Jaybird said. "One squad on the boat, one to take down the International Food place."

"Be a lot better if we knew who we were hunting," Murdock said. "Big business like that might have ten guys who buy goods and sign orders from foreign countries. Which one is our man?"

"I know the general manager there," Sartan said. "He knows I'm out of business, but I could call him and tell him I was getting my feet under me and ask him about some supplies I used to get from him."

"Take him out to lunch; then we could drop by your table, one of us at least," Murdock said. "We can find out the specific man who orders goods from China. If there are two or three who work the China trade, we'll take down all of them and find the right one."

"Trade with China must be a haphazard thing," Lam said. "Would they order in advance and keep fast-moving goods in stock until needed? Say, toys and knickknacks and non-perishable items?"

"Seems reasonable," Captain Sartan said. "I'll get a lunch date with him for today. We could take out that end of things even before the boat sails tomorrow."

"Let's do it," Murdock said. He handed Sartan the cell phone the colonel had given him to use if he needed it. The Israeli thought a moment, took a card out of his wallet, and dialed a number on it.

Two hours later, Murdock sat with Captain Sartan at a hotel coffee shop not far from International Food and Novelties. The general manager of the firm, Kiva Nissan, shook Murdock's hand and they sat down.

"I always come here because they buy food from us," Nissan said. "They pride themselves on having at least one dish from over eighty different countries around the world."

Murdock had been introduced as a family friend in Tel Aviv for a vacation.

"How do you like our little community here?" Nissan asked.

"I've hardly had time for the ten-shekel tour," Murdock said.

Nissan ordered specialty sandwiches for them, and before the food came, Sartan turned serious.

"Kiva, I'm working with the Army and the police on a delicate matter. We need to know who in your firm handles orders to China."

"I don't understand. Food and novelties. We're not talking about hand grenades and machine guns. Two men do the work with the Chinese, but I want to know a lot more about why you need to know their names before I can help you."

Murdock spoke up. "Mr. Nissan, we are not accusing you or your firm of any wrongdoing. However, we think one of your employees may be doing a terrible thing to the people of Israel, may be causing hundreds to be injured, maimed, and killed."

"How in the world? Food and novelties?"

"Mr. Nissan, you are aware of the savage and deadly floating booby traps that have been washing up on our beaches for the past eleven months."

"Yes, terrible. . . ." He stopped. "You mean you think . . ." He shook his head. "Both of these men have been with me for years. Both have families here, both are respected."

"Is either one an Arab?" Sartan asked.

Nissan slumped in his chair. "Yes, I have tried to be even-handed about employing Arabs. They have a right to work as well as Israelis. I have twenty, maybe more Arabs working for me. To think that one of those two . . ." He shook his head again. "I simply can't believe it could be true."

"There is one way we can know for sure," Murdock said.

"How? Anything. Now I must know."

"I can tell you this, but it must go no farther. We know that one of your trucks makes deliveries almost daily to boats at the dock. The driver takes boxes to the *Gimbra II,* a fishing boat owned by Gabi Zekharyah. We are almost one-hundred-percent certain that he gets deliveries from your store, and later dumps the deadly booby trap bombs in the surf line as he heads out to fish."

The sandwiches came, and the men only stared at them.

"This is true?" Nissan asked his countryman.

"We have everything but his admission."

"How can you prove that one of my men . . ."

"When ordering from China, do you order in quantity, then break down the shipments for individual orders?"

"Yes. Mostly that way. Sometimes we do special orders; they come in with a customer's name on them and we hold them until needed. Sometimes connections are missed and we try to keep a supply on hand. . . ." He stopped again. "In our warehouse. We can check the warehouse and see if any special orders there are waiting for delivery to Zekharyah's ship."

"Mr. Nissan," Murdock said, "these are dangerous men. One man investigating this problem has been killed and dumped in the bay. We don't want anyone in your firm harmed. Can we check the warehouse without drawing suspicion?"

"Yes. From time to time I inspect the warehouse, the salesmen, even the delivery trucks. I don't think we'll arouse any suspicion. Just one of you should come with me. Mr. Murdock, it should be you. Someone might recognize Captain Sartan."

"We expect a delivery to Zekharyah's boat tomorrow

early A.M. We need to let that shipment go through. Would it be possible to check the warehouse this afternoon?"

"Yes, and I'll have the name of the salesman who ordered the goods for his boat. Then we will know for sure."

"Should I meet you at your office this afternoon?" Murdock asked.

"No. I want you to come with me now, right after we eat these sandwiches. I think I can swallow now. I'll be giving you a tour of the whole operation, so going to the warehouse will look natural. So eat and enjoy; then we'll go dig out this traitor I've been paying for the past fifteen years."

30

For two hours that afternoon Murdock and Nissan toured the International Food and Novelties operation. Murdock saw a lot more than he wanted to. By the time they came to the warehouse and shipping, everyone there already knew who he was and that he was not after their jobs. Nissan played the tour leader at every stop.

"This is where our shipments are loaded; the last delivery is the first on the truck, and the first delivery is loaded on last." They went around the truck into the warehouse.

"Here is where we store the goods until we ship them, and this is where we break down large shipments into smaller quantities for orders to go to individual retailers."

They walked up one aisle, then over. His voice lowered so only Murdock could hear it. "This is where we have our Chinese orders. They should be on these pallet boards. Yes. Here. They are separated by food and novelties." He produced a razor-blade knife, and quickly slit the tape on top of the cardboard box and opened it. Inside were cartons filled with toys, whistles, and noisemakers. The next box had boxes of pencils, tablets, and notebooks. The third box, listed as novelties from China, held packages of the long gaily colored tubes.

"Those are the ones," Murdock said. "They are bombs like the ones that have been washing up on the beaches."

Nissan looked at the numbers on the box, and some key words, and wrote them down on a pad from his pocket. "These orders went through Mr. Rafi. Let's go talk to him."

Murdock touched the .45 automatic under his left arm, and followed the merchant out of the warehouse and back to the third floor. They went to the owner's office, and Nissan asked his secretary to have Rafi come in.

"He's always been so mild-mannered. I can't understand why he would do something like this." The man who came in the office was about five feet six inches. He wore slacks, a white shirt, and tie. Murdock figured he was about 130 pounds, wiry, would be tough in a fight. He smiled, but seemed ill at ease.

"Rafi, how are the Chinese items going? I know we don't have a lot of ethnic Chinese in the city, so the food sales will always be slow. What about the novelties? They seem to have more volume."

"Yes. Exactly, Mr. Nissan. The novelties do sell better, so I order more of them."

"You've been ordering all of the novelties?"

"Yes, I specialize in them."

"Good. Let's go down to the warehouse. There's one bunch that look like they were severely damaged in transit. I want you to check them out and tell me if we should bill the shipping company or the supplier for the damage."

"Yes, no problem, Mr. Nissan."

The three of them went back to the warehouse. Rafi pulled on cotton gloves.

"I always wear gloves when I inspect the goods," he said. "That way I don't damage them and I don't get my hands cut up."

At the boxes they showed him the two they had opened.

"No damage that I can see," Rafi said.

Nissan opened the next box and exposed the plastic tube bombs. Rafi never blinked. He inspected the sides of the box, then the contents.

"No damage. I don't understand."

"Do you know what these items are, Mr. Rafi?" Murdock asked.

"Certainly. Item 14-14-12 Chinese light sticks. You bend them and break them and they light up."

"I see. So would you take your gloves off and bend one for us, as a demonstration?" Murdock asked.

Rafi frowned. "I can't do that. I never take my gloves off. My hands are highly sensitive."

"Then I'll do it for you," Murdock said, reaching for one of the colorful tubes that lay on top of the package. His hand was almost on it when Rafi knocked it aside.

"No, don't," he shouted. He grabbed two of the floating bombs and ran down the aisle.

"Stop, Rafi," Nissan shouted. "We can work this out."

Murdock ran after the man. Rafi twisted one of the tubes and threw it at Murdock. The tube hit the hardwood floor and exploded like a hand grenade, but with no shrapnel. Murdock charged through the smoke of the bomb, and saw the man heading up some steps. Rafi pulled a pistol from his pocket and fired once. It sounded like a .32. Murdock ducked behind some wooden crates, then charged up the stairs when the man vanished through a door.

Murdock went up the last few steps slowly, watched around the door casing, and dodged back as a shot slammed through the air where his head had been. Murdock wished he had put on his Motorola. He could use some SEAL backup about now.

The room at the top of the stairs was a manager's office. Across the way Murdock saw another door that was just closing. He rushed toward it, kicked it open, and leaned against the wall beside the door. A shot snarled through the opening. Murdock peered around the door from floor level. It was an outside door with steps leading down to a roof. He saw Rafi running across the roof. He was too far away, but Murdock took a shot with the heavy .45. The sound alone might scare him.

Suddenly Rafi vanished over the side of the roof. Murdock charged down the few steps to the roof and surged across it. A metal-rung ladder extended down two stories to the ground. Rafi had just hit the last rung when Murdock fired. The downward shot ripped into the side of Rafi's right leg and knocked him down. Before Murdock could move to get a clear shot at him outside the ladder, Rafi struggled to his feet and rushed toward a car in the parking lot. He was out of range of the heavy .45.

Murdock raced down the steel ladder, and hit the bottom just as the car Rafi jumped in started to move. The SEAL fired twice through the driver's-side window, then twice at the rear, searching for the gas tank. The third shot at the tank sparked a flash fire that hit the vapors in the gas tank, which exploded like a firebomb. Flaming gasoline sprayed the mostly empty parking lot. The entire sedan gushed with flames, and Murdock knew that if his first two rounds hadn't killed the bomber, then the fire had.

Nissan came to the edge of the roof and looked down. He shook his head and climbed down the ladder; then both of them stood there watching the car burn. Two other cars in the far side of the lot were not touched.

"Mr. Murdock, you better leave. We can square this with the police later. I'll do the talking. Right now I want to get those bombs out of my warehouse and turn them over to the bomb squad."

"Better tell them to bring two of their bomb buckets. They're going to need them."

"Could Rafi have done this by himself?" Nissan asked.

Murdock held up both hands palms up. "Hard to tell. Check his personnel file. See if there's anything unusual. Talk to the men he worked with. I think I'll do that right now."

Murdock went back to the warehouse with Nissan. Because Murdock was with the boss, the men all talked freely, except for two who did not speak English. Another man translated for them.

None of the men knew what was in the boxes from China. They figured just regular novelty goods. Murdock took a heavy cloth and held up one of the deadly floating bombs.

"Now I know what those are," one man said. "The booby traps on the beach that have been killing little children. How did they get here?"

Murdock didn't answer him, merely talked to the rest of the men. Before he was done, three policemen came and took away the box of bombs. Nissan found two more boxes with more of the plastic tube bombs in them.

"Enough here to flatten this whole building," one of the

cops said. He was one who Murdock had talked to earlier that day at the police station. When the goods were all safely outside in the bomb boxes, heavy steel containers that could withstand a tremendous explosion and keep those nearby safe, the cop thanked Murdock.

Then the homicide crew came and looked over what was left of Rafi. A fire truck had put out the flames before the man's body was totally destroyed. The cops ask how he'd died, and Nissan told them what had happened. They took Murdock's .45 and the .32 hideout on his left leg and drove him downtown for questioning. The homicide team had just started to question Murdock when the phone rang.

"Yes, sir. Yes, sir, I understand. Right away, sir. Right." The homicide investigator put down the phone and motioned to Murdock. "Our chief of police and a Colonel Ben-Ami want to talk to you in the chief's office right away. Follow me, please."

The office looked like a living room—plush chairs, carpeted floor, big-screen TV, table, large desk with an absolutely clean surface. Overhead recessed lighting, with the soft background of pulsing music.

Colonel Ben-Ami sat next to the desk, and behind it lounged a man in his fifties, gray/white hair, full white beard and mustache, and fiercely blue eyes over a nose that showed two breaks. Neither man stood.

Murdock watched both of them, came to attention in front of the desk, and waited for them to speak.

"Sounds like you've been busy, Murdock," Colonel Ben-Ami said. "I thought you understood this was a controlled and unified team effort."

"I understand that, Colonel."

"I also understand that your efforts have resulted in the confiscation of over three hundred pounds of the floating booby traps out of a local business warehouse."

"Yes, sir."

"In the process a man was killed," the chief said, his voice low, a rumble that reminded Murdock of far-away thunder.

"Yes, sir, I believe he died in a fire in his car which crashed."

"Crashed after you shot it several times with a .45 automatic," Colonel Ben-Ami said. "Is that correct, Commander?"

"Correct, sir."

The chief stood and held out his hand, his face breaking into a huge grin that almost closed his eyes.

"Damn glad to have you on board, Commander Murdock. You had been sworn in as a temporary military policeman, so whatever happened at that warehouse was in the line of duty. We'll need you to make a report, sit for a shooting panel which will be videotaped, but which is a formality. In a half hour you should be out of here."

"What about the boat that drops the bombs?" Murdock asked.

"He's still out fishing."

"He'll hear about this fire on his standard-band radio, and if the name of the dead man gets out, he will probably head for China."

"For once, we're ahead of you, Commander," Colonel Ben-Ami said. He smiled. "It's a good feeling. As soon as we heard about the fire and the raid here, we put Lieutenant DeWitt and six men in a fast police launch. It and another boat with SAS divers are now heading for sea in an effort to track down the boat and to bring it, and Zekharyah, back to face the courts."

"Good," Murdock said. "I'd like to get my two weapons back."

"Routine after the taping. I want to thank you again, Commander. You've solved a problem that we've had for almost a year."

An hour and a half later when Murdock was released from the central jail, he found Lam and Jaybird waiting for him, along with the colonel and his staff car.

On the way back to the air base, the colonel took a phone call. He listened, said a few words in Hebrew, and hung up. "We have a report that the two patrol boats now at sea have cleared thirty-five fishing boats. There are six more in the area they are heading for. They tell me they have a report that the *Gimbra II* owner was recently granted a license to carry an automatic rifle on board because he was afraid of pirates.

"My guess is that he also has on board submachine guns for his crewmen. They have to be in on this operation. If they have tuned in to local news stations lately, they'll know about the fire and the death and the police raid on the International Food and Novelty company. They will be ready to put up a fight."

"It might not last that long if DeWitt is in command," Murdock said.

"The problem is, they can't sink the boat. They have to bring it back with Zekharyah alive if possible so he can stand trial for treason. That's what the civil authorities want as much as the bombs to stop."

Murdock looked toward the sea. "I just wish I was out there with them. It sounds like it should be a good fight."

31

Ed DeWitt stood at the rail of the Israeli patrol boat as it skimmed through the placid Mediterranean. They were about three miles off shore, and had checked out thirty-five fishing boats in the north half of the fleet. There were only six more ahead of them. So far they hadn't found Zekharyah or his boat, *Gimbra II.*

DeWitt had brought five men from his squad, Fernandez, Canzoneri, Victor, Mahanani, and Jefferson. That was all the boat captain would let him bring on the thirty-two-foot patrol boat. The craft could do thirty knots if it had to, DeWitt figured.

They came up on another fisher. It was trolling, and the patrol boat stayed well to the port side, out of the way of the trolling lines. They moved in to fifty feet and a bullhorn sounded.

"Ahoy, just checking on your welfare. We heard one boat in the fleet had an injured man on board."

"Not here," a husky voice called from the ship. "Haven't heard any distress calls on the radio."

"Thanks, we'll keep checking."

The patrol boat geared away, and angled toward another fisherman a mile away and closer to shore. DeWitt stood at the rail with his binoculars, trying to read the name on the next fishing boat. Still too far away. He didn't know what the SEALs would do on this trip. It could be a simple arrest, with the captain put in handcuffs and a crewman told to follow them back to shore.

The fisher came up quickly at what DeWitt figured was

their twenty-five-knot speed. He checked again and then saw the name, *Gimbra II*.

"This is the one," one of the crew called. DeWitt used the Motorola and told all the SEALs to stay out of sight. He dropped below the solid rail around the front of the boat and waited.

Two minutes later a bullhorn on the Coast Watch boat came on.

"*Gimbra II,* heave to. We have official business with you."

"Heave to? No way. We're fishing here." The words came from another bullhorn on the fishing boat.

"This is official business. Heave to, now."

"We had official business last week. You checked all our papers, permits, and weigh charts. What else is there?"

"Cut your throttle and we'll tell you."

The fishing boat didn't respond. "Put a round across their bow," Captain Dagan of the patrol boat said. A rifle cracked, and still there was no response from the smaller boat.

"Last warning, Zekharyah. Come about, or we'll have to open fire on your boat."

The response this time was a rifle shot from the fishing boat that slapped into the cabin and ripped out the rear side.

"Two rounds into the cabin," Captain Dagan said.

DeWitt lifted up so his glasses cleared the rail, and watched the boat. He saw no one on board. At once two rifle rounds cracked, and the rounds jolted into the small boat's cabin, breaking a side panel and tearing through thin wood. There was no response.

"Come about and heave to, or we'll be forced to fire again," the captain said on the bullhorn.

There was no reaction from the ship. It continued forward, but now in a slight left turn that would bring it in a long arc back toward shore, now about three miles away.

DeWitt adjusted the Draegr rebreather that he and all the SEALs wore as a matter of course, and checked the boat again with his binoculars. Nobody.

He watched the boat; the gentle turn to the left was precisely the same. He went into the cabin, saw where the shot had ripped through, but not hit anyone.

"Captain, shouldn't the boat be trying some maneuvers to get away? Make some quick turns or something?"

The young Captain Dagan nodded grimly. "First time I ever had to shoot at a boat."

"Captain, I'd bet my last month's paycheck that there is no one on board the fishing boat."

The sailor frowned. "Why?"

"Otherwise he'd be taking evasive action. Dumping out the goods or trying to get away."

"So, what's next?"

"Put another two rounds into the cabin. Maybe you can slow or stop the craft."

The young captain agreed, and told his riflemen to hit the cabin twice again. They did, and nothing happened. The captain looked at DeWitt.

"I think I can stop the boat with a pair of twenty-millimeter rounds into the cabin."

The Israeli Navy man frowned, then nodded.

"Fernandez, up front. Bring your twenty."

DeWitt let Fernandez fire the first round. The twenty hit slightly to the right of center on the cabin, and blew apart the wooden frame but didn't stop the craft.

DeWitt aimed dead center on the cabin and fired. The round exploded with a cracking roar, smashing the cabin and bringing an immediate slowing of the fishing boat. A minute later it was dead in the water.

"Boarding party," the Navy captain ordered.

The patrol boat came alongside the fishing craft. Two sailors quickly tied the two together, and an Israeli with an Uzi submachine gun jumped on board the fisher and bolted forward to what was left of the cabin.

"Nobody here and no dead bodies," he shouted.

"Go below."

A moment later he was back. "No one and no dead bodies."

"Where are they?" the captain asked.

"Overboard, just after they took that shot," DeWitt said.

"They knew they couldn't outrun us or outshoot us. So they went for a swim."

"Three miles?" the captain asked.

"Easy for a swimmer," DeWitt said. "And they could have a sea sled on board. A man like Zekharyah would plan ahead. What could he do if you figured out the deal and nailed the supplier? He must have heard about the fire and the raid on the International Food distributor."

"Where would they be now?" the captain asked.

"A sea sled can make about two knots per hour. My guess is they have scuba gear, which will leave a trail of bubbles. We could go in within a mile of shore and work a picket line back and forth looking for bubbles. Once there we can drop off our SEALs every twenty yards and watch for the fishermen. We don't leave bubbles."

The young Captain Dagan looked at DeWitt and grinned. "Let's do it, go now."

He reported the situation to the other patrol boat and to his superiors on shore, who gave him the go-ahead. The other patrol boat met them at the spot and their divers went into the water. A half hour before the swimmers could have made it a mile offshore, the picket line stretched for half a mile in a direct path from the first firing of the fishing boat's rifle to the beach.

Just before he went into the water, DeWitt suggested to the young captain that he request the Army to send a company of men to patrol the beach, watching for any exhausted swimmers coming out of the water, especially any with a sea sled. That was backup in case they got by the divers.

"Done," the captain said.

Murdock went underwater, made contact with his SEALS, and they began their prowl of their sector. It was only three hundred yards wide, but was in the center of the estimated line the swimmers would take.

The Coast Watch captain went on the fisherman's network frequency, notified the boats in the area about the three missing men, and warned them that if they picked up the men out of the water, they must report it immediately. The men were fugitives and would be arrested on sight. Anyone harboring the men would be subjected to stiff fines and imprisonment.

Then the Coast Watch boat worked a line a mile long up and back, crawling along at three knots, watching for any trail of bubbles.

Underwater, the SEALs worked through the clear water. The sun was out bright and the water sparkled with the light. They stayed at ten feet, figuring any swimmers would be above them. On the second run up the three-hundred-yard course, they found a trail of bubbles. The problem was they came from below. Canzoneri followed them down, and when he came up he surfaced to report.

"Just a gush of bubbles out of a crack in some rocks down there," he told DeWitt. "Mother Nature passing air. Wouldn't be surprised if it had a bunch of foul chemicals in it."

They dove again.

On the third swing along their assigned corridor, Canzoneri swam up to DeWitt and pointed to his ears, then out to sea. They both tried to listen, then DeWitt grinned. It was a motor. It could be the sled. It was too faint to be the patrol boat's motor. They knew how it sounded. This one was faint, but coming their way.

Canzoneri swam back along the line and compressed the men so they were only ten yards apart, so they could just see each other in the water. They kept at fifteen feet now and waited. They all gave thumbs-up. Everyone could hear the motor, a thin whining sound that would come from an electric motor underwater.

Mahanani stared to sea, and looked upward in surprise as he saw it coming. The nose of the sled was down about ten feet. It had one man on the handles and two more men with scuba gear hanging on to the sled man's ankles as they were towed along.

Mahanani waved to the man on each side of him and pointed upward, then waited until the three men were directly over him. He surged upward, jerked the first man's hands off the sled, and grabbed his air hose and ripped it out of its connection. He swam for the second man, but

Victor was there ripping away at his face mask, jerking it free, then holding the man underwater as he clawed for air.

Mahanani went back to his first man and jolted him upward, bringing him out of the water and keeping the arm locked around his throat.

The patrol boat had seen the splashes; it raced in from three hundred yards away. A second man popped up, Victor with a nearly unconscious fisherman. Both men were grabbed and pulled on board the patrol boat.

Jefferson brought up the last man; he was half drowned, and the sailors on the boat used CPR and brought him back.

"We want them alive so they will stand trial," Captain Dagan said. He radioed the news that all three fishermen had been captured including Zekharyah. They went out to the drifting fishing boat, put a tow rope on it, and sailed for the harbor.

An hour later, the SEALs were back in their temporary quarters at the air base outside Tel Aviv. They had showered and were getting ready for chow when somebody yelled near the door.

Don Stroh walked in and waved. "Am I too late to go on any of the missions?" he asked. Jaybird threw his floppy hat at the CIA agent. The rest of the SEALs shouted unkind words at him.

He chuckled. "Well, maybe next time. Don't suppose any of you would be interested, but this mission is over. I've had you released from the military here. There will be a business jet here at 0800 tomorrow to pick us all up and start our homeward journey."

That brought a series of loud cheers.

"Always said that you were an okay guy," Jefferson yelled.

"The Israeli President has awarded each of you two medals. They will be noted on your record, but of course you can't wear them until you retire."

"Thanks a lot, Stroh," Fernandez yelled. "How about that ten-thousand-dollar bonus you were going to get us?"

Stroh looked surprised. "Hell, hasn't that come through

yet? I put the requisition in about two years ago. Probably still going through channels."

Three more floppy hats sailed in his direction.

He waved at them and went to talk to DeWitt and Murdock.

He shook hands with both. "You guys did great on this strange one. The President appreciates it. The Israelis are more than grateful, and I'm pleased. To show you how happy I am, the steak dinners are on me at the officers' club in about twenty minutes. We have a reservation."

32

The SEALs arrived at North Island Naval Air Station slightly after noon two days later. They'd had a holdup in London to pick up a special courier, and then another wait in New York. They dropped off their gear in the equipment room and pulled on their civvies.

"You all have three-day liberty," Murdock said. "If any of you wind up in jail, you're going to stay there until your liberty is up, so remember that. I'm going to sleep for the next three days."

Jaybird dug into his civvies, waved at the bunch, and ran for his battered '94 Chevy. It started. Good. He backed out of the lot and hustled across Coronado to the Little League field. There was no one practicing. He didn't even know what day it was. He parked and walked up to the field, then sauntered into the public rest room the city had built nearby. In the men's room he looked at the overhead where he had planted the video camera. It had to be there.

He saw it, and moved a chair over so he could stand on it and pull the camera down. He pushed it under his loose shirt and walked out of the rest room to his car. It wasn't the new kind of video camera that let you play back what you had just shot. He had to go home, get the adapter, and put the cassette into his video player.

His mind was whirling. He couldn't really use it as evidence in court. He had violated the privacy of anyone showing on the tape. But he also hoped that the camera caught Rusty Ingles with his pants down molesting at least one small boy. He needed proof, and this would be it. If he was lucky. If the sound-activation switches had worked. If there was enough light. If nothing went wrong. If they were in a spot where the camera could see them.

Jaybird drove sedately. He didn't want to get a ticket and waste that much more time. He parked, ran up the steps to his apartment, and burst inside. It was just as he had left it.

He turned on the TV, set it on Channel Four, and pushed the tape in the video player. He hit the rewind, and was pleased how long it took to rewind. He had something on the tape.

Then it stopped and he punched up the play button. The TV picture shut off, there was some lead tape, then the inside of the playground bathroom came into view. The mike wouldn't pick up much from that distance, but there were some rumbles of voices. At first there were only four young boys urinating with their backs to the camera. Then they left, and the next image was of a man and his young son using the urinals. There were ten more men and boys shown in the rest room. Where was Ingles? In the next section Jaybird saw Rusty Ingles come into the shot. Phil, one of the older boys on the Little League team, followed him. Rusty said something and they both laughed; then they urinated with their backs to the camera. Before Phil could turn around, Rusty was beside him, talking, his hand moving Phil's hands away and caressing his small penis. Phil pulled back, but Rusty said something else, turned, and his own penis was out, hard and angled upward out of his fly. The young boy giggled and looked around, too scared to move.

Rusty played with the small cock for a few moments, but it didn't grow any or get hard. Rusty said something else and they both laughed. Then Rusty began to masturbate. That was enough for Jaybird. He turned off the machine and took out the tape. He considered it a moment, then put it in a small box behind some books on a shelf in the living room.

He brought in the newspaper from the porch. It was Wednesday. Not a game day for Little League, not a practice day for his team. Rusty Ingles should be at work. Either he was an insurance salesman, or he had his own agency. Jaybird fumbled in his wallet and found the card. Yes, his own agency. Jaybird stared at the card, then at the video camera. The camera didn't lie. Ingles was a damn pedophile; he fondled and jacked off little boys. Not a chance Jaybird was going to let him continue as a coach. He had to be eliminated. How?

Jaybird knew a blast from his trusty MP-5 would do the job. He lifted his brows. That was the first time he'd thought of killing the bastard. That was what Ingles deserved. How many of the team had he fondled since the practicing had begun? None of them must have told their parents or he'd be long gone.

Jaybird kept shaking his head. "That fucking bastard!" he exploded. He went to the second bedroom and took a .38-caliber two-inch-barreled revolver from the bottom drawer. He fitted it into a holster and strapped it on his left ankle. His pants covered it fully, and made it easy for him to draw it in a rush. He still didn't like the idea of shooting the fucking queer pedophile. Something slower, much slower.

Black's Beach. Jaybird grinned. Appropriate. Yeah. That was the nominally nude beach, where the city winked at nude swimming and sunning. It was hard to get to. You had to climb down the La Jolla cliffs on a treacherous trail, or walk down from Torrey Pines State Beach to the north. It was at least a two-mile walk and most people didn't bother. Yes, the beach would be perfect.

He thought of calling Rusty and taking him out to dinner so he could talk about the team and get caught up on what they had been doing. No. He hated the thought of being with the damn queer pedo that long.

A drink and get caught up. Yeah. There was a bar in Del Mar called Harley's. They would meet there at eight, have a drink, and then outside, he'd pull the gun and make Rusty get in Jaybird's Chevy and they would drive. Jaybird had a folding military-type entrenching tool in his car that he used for getting out of sand traps. Perfect.

He made the call, got Rusty on the second try, and made the date for the drink. Rusty seemed relieved that Jaybird was home. Said he was going crazy trying to coach. He didn't know the game that well. Jaybird told him he'd take care of that for him at the next practice tomorrow.

They met at eight o'clock. Jaybird was early, and stopped Rusty outside the bar. No sense being seen with him in the bar. Jaybird said it was too noisy in there to talk, so they went to Jaybird's car to talk about the team. Once in the car, Jaybird pulled out the .38 and aimed it at Rusty.

"What the hell?"

"We're going for a little ride, Rusty. I'll explain on the way. You try to get out of the car, I'll shoot you dead. That's my job, killing people, and I'm good at it, so don't give me an excuse."

"Christ, man, what are you saying? We're friends. We're coaches."

"Rusty, while I was gone, my video camera has been planted in the men's rest room at the Little League field. Every time somebody talks in there, it snaps on and records until the sounds stop. Make you stop and think?"

"I don't know what you're talking about."

"Sure, and there really is green cheese on the moon. You're the star of the show, you fucking queer bastard pedophile. I saw you fondling one of the boys before I left. Now I've got you on tape, and I'll be glad to turn it over to the Vice Squad and let them spread your face and your pedophile name all over the newspapers and TV news casts."

Rusty gasped, then didn't say a word as Jaybird drove down from Del Mar on the coast highway and took the road to Torrey Pines State Beach.

"Where the hell we going?"

"What difference does it make to you, child molester? You're going to have fun in the water."

"Hey, I don't even swim good. I couldn't keep up with you. You're a damn SEAL."

"True. You don't have to swim."

"Oh, thank God."

"At least," Jaybird said. He parked at the far end of the strip along the surf next to the slope down to the beach. His was the only car there. No late-night swimmers and no blazes going in the fire rings.

"Out of the car slowly. I can outrun you, so don't try. I'd just as soon shoot your ass right here, but you might want to live a little longer."

"Look, man. I'll do anything you say. I'll close up my business and move to another town. I'll give up coaching. Anything you want me to do."

"I want you to walk down to the hard sand and turn left and keep walking." Jaybird carried the fold-up shovel in his left hand.

"Come on, Jaybird. I've been straight with you. It just happens now and then. I'm not a nut about it. Just a feeling I get and I got to do something about it. Like when you really need a woman."

"Keep walking."

They moved down the beach for thirty minutes, then were in the middle of Black's Beach. Absolute privacy. Hundred-foot cliffs rose in back of the beach. The tide was out and coming in. There was no good access to the beach for three miles to the south and two miles north. As private as it could get and not a person in sight.

"Right here should be fine," Jaybird said. Rusty turned toward him, and Jaybird hit him with a roundhouse right fist that knocked Rusty into the sand. Jaybird dropped on top of him, rolled him over, and bound his wrists and ankles with plastic riot cuffs he had used for years.

"What the hell? Jaybird, I don't understand."

"Right, you don't understand. That's why you fucked the little kids. But you won't do that anymore."

"I promise I won't. Get these things off me."

"No." Jaybird watched the surf coming in. He was about halfway down where he could see high tide had been that morning. It would peak about midnight. Just right.

He moved in front of the pedophile and began to dig.

"What are you doing?" Rusty screamed.

"Didn't you ever go to the beach and the kids covered you up with sand right up to your nose?"

"You can't, you wouldn't. For the love of God, Jaybird.

I'm a human being here. Just one little quirk. That's all, just one."

Jaybird went on digging. The soft sand moved quickly. There was no water yet when he was two feet down. He dug a trench six feet long, then added another foot. It was three feet deep when the seawater started coming in. He rolled Rusty into the grave, then turned him over and pulled his shoulders to the near end so his head was just above the level of the sand.

Rusty was sobbing. "You can't do this, Jaybird. You can't."

"Who the fuck is going to stop me? You're just another vermin on this old planet that the SEALs have to wipe out. It won't hurt much at first."

Jaybird used his knife, sliced the plastic strip off Rusty's ankles, and put it in his pocket.

"You keep your legs right there or I'll club you on the head with the shovel. Got that?"

Rusty sobbed and nodded. "You can't do this."

Jaybird shoveled the sand back in the hole, covering up Rusty's legs. Rusty pulled one leg out of the sand and Jaybird stepped on it, forcing it back down in the loose sand. By the time Jaybird had two feet of sand in the trench, Rusty couldn't move his legs.

Jaybird took his knife and laid it along Rusty's throat. "I should slash your carotid and let you bleed out. But not this time. I'm cutting off the band on your wrists. You let them move from your lap where I put them and I bash you with the shovel. Just like with your legs. You get it?"

Rusty didn't answer. He stared at Jaybird with wild eyes; they darted from one side to the other as if looking for a way to escape.

Jaybird continued to shovel in the wet sand. A wave lapped up near the grave, then receded. Jaybird worked faster then, and soon had the trench filled. Only Rusty's head now showed above the sand.

The next wave lapped at the edge of the now-filled trench. Jaybird dug more sand, heaping it up on the length of the grave; then he took one last look at Rusty Ingles. Ingles had stopped sobbing. His eyes were half shut, and saliva drooled out of his mouth and dripped on the sand.

The runner from a breaker hit the sand twenty feet away and rushed up toward Ingles's head. It barely lapped at his neck, then soaked into the sand, and the rest rolled back toward the Pacific.

"See that, Ingles, you bastard? Those waves are getting closer and closer. Pretty soon they will be washing into your face, and then over your head. Might be a good time to practice holding your breath. Tide will be in full in another hour. By then this spot will be under three feet of water. Just wanted you to know and to think about it, and to think about all those little boys you traumatized with your damn messing around. Just wanted you to know."

Rusty screamed. His voice came in a roaring blast of fury and anger and fright. The sound careened off the cliff and shattered in both directions up and down the coast. He screamed a dozen times until his voice turned scratchy.

"Jaybird! Jaybird! That's enough. I'm cured. I'll never touch anything young again. A promise. Dig me out of here fast, Jaybird. Please. Come on. I never hurt you."

Jaybird squatted in front of Rusty Ingles and spat in his face, then turned away and walked straight up the beach to the base of the cliff. He sat down and watched the waves roll in.

Rusty still screamed. The volume had dropped off and the raspiness had increased until now the sound came out more as a whimper than a scream.

Jaybird watched a night gull sweeping the surf line looking for chum. It passed the head sticking out of the sand, circled around, came back, and lit on Rusty's head. A sudden movement sideways by Rusty and the bird fluttered away.

The next breaker rolled in a foot deep when it hit Rusty; it broke over his head and quickly rushed back to sea.

A half hour later, Jaybird could see no sign of Rusty Ingles. He watched the tide surge in higher and higher. Just after midnight it peaked and headed back the other way. Jaybird didn't need to watch anymore. He took the shovel, folded it, and walked north along Black's Beach toward the Torrey Pines Beach parking lot.

Someone might have seen his Chevy parked there while he was gone. It wouldn't matter. Why would anyone remember it or remember his license-plate number? He knew what would happen in the surf. The outgoing tide would pull at the sand. The loose sand in the trench over Rusty would gradually wash away. By the time the last of the waves had left him, the trench would have been emptied, Rusty's totally dead body rolled out and into the surf. The trench would be filled again with sand from the waves. Rusty would be washed back and forth by the waves, and perhaps pulled out to sea. In three days he would float and begin his journey down the coast, south with the current. He probably would be found one morning where he had floated up on the beach in National City.

Jaybird drove home slowly. Several drivers honked horns at him on the Five freeway getting down to the Coronado Bay Bridge. He was thinking about Rusty Ingles. He had killed many men and some women in his life as a SEAL. This was the first time without his uniform on. The cause was as just. The world and the Coronado Little League would be much better off without Rusty Ingles around.

He parked in front of his apartment and sat there. Something had changed. The act of killing would never be quite the same again, even in a tough firefight with the SEALs. No, he wouldn't see the screaming face of Rusty Ingles as the last breaker rushed over his head and drowned out his screams. But he would remember the man, and the reason he had eliminated him from the face of the earth and interaction with mankind.

How would Jaybird change? He would be a notch less raucous, a touch less of a loudmouth, maybe a bit more patient with his fellow SEALs and with civilians who fucked up. Yes, but just a touch. He was still Jaybird. He would report to Little League practice tomorrow and be the best damn coach in the world. He would never touch one of the boys, and he would be ultimately patient with them. He was their coach, their friend, their advisor and mentor. That was a lot to live up to.

Hell, tonight had made him into a better coach, and a better SEAL, and a better man. He went up the steps into his apartment. He'd get eight hours sleep, then do a twenty-mile conditioning run, and be at the Little League field early for practice.

Damn, he could hardly wait to get there and back to coaching baseball.

SEAL TALK

MILITARY GLOSSARY

Aalvin: Small U.S. two-man submarine.

Admin: Short for administration.

Aegis: Advanced Naval air defense radar system.

AH-1W Super Cobra: Has M179 undernose turret with 20mm Gatling gun.

AK-47: 7.63-round Russian Kalashnikov automatic rifle. Most widely used assault rifle in the world.

AK-74: New, improved version of the Kalashnikov. Fires the 5.45mm round. Has 30-round magazine. Rate of fire: 600 rounds per minute. Many slight variations made for many different nations.

AN/PRC-117D: Radio, also called SATCOM. Works with Milstar satellite in 22,300-mile equatorial orbit for instant worldwide radio, voice, or video communications. Size: 15 inches high, 3 inches wide, 3 inches deep. Weighs 15 pounds. Microphone and voice output. Has encrypter, capable of burst transmissions of less than a second.

AN/PUS-7: Night-vision goggles. Weighs 1.5 pounds.

ANVIS-6: Night-vision goggles on air crewmen's helmets.

APC: Armored Personnel Carrier.

ASROC: Nuclear-tipped antisubmarine rocket torpedoes launched by Navy ships.

Assault Vest: Combat vest with full loadouts of ammo, gear.

ASW: Anti-Submarine Warfare.

Attack Board: Molded plastic with two handgrips with bubble compass on it. Also depth gauge and Cyalume chemical lights with twist knob to regulate amount of light. Used for underwater guidance on long swim.

Aurora: Air Force recon plane. Can circle at 90,000 feet. Can't be seen or heard from ground. Used for thermal imaging.

AWACS: Airborne Warning And Control System. Radar units in high-flying aircraft to scan for planes at any altitude out 200 miles. Controls air-to-air engagements with enemy forces. Planes have a mass of communication and electronic equipment.

Balaclavas: Headgear worn by some SEALs.

Bent Spear: Less serious nuclear violation of safety.

BKA, Bundeskriminant: Germany's federal investigation unit.

Black Talon: Lethal hollow-point ammunition made by Winchester. Outlawed some places.

Blivet: A collapsible fuel container. SEALs sometimes use it.

BLU-43B: Antipersonnel mine used by SEALs.

BLU-96: A fuel-air explosive bomb. It disperses a fuel oil into the air, then explodes the cloud. Many times more powerful than conventional bombs because it doesn't carry its own chemical oxidizers.

BMP-1: Soviet armored fighting vehicle (AFV), low, boxy, crew of 3 and 8 combat troops. Has tracks and a 73mm cannon. Also an AT-3 Sagger antitank missile and coaxial machine gun.

Body Armor: Far too heavy for SEAL use in the water.

Bogey: Pilots' word for an unidentified aircraft.

Boghammar Boat: Long, narrow, low dagger boat; high-speed patrol craft. Swedish make. Iran had 40 of them in 1993.

Boomer: A nuclear-powered missile submarine.

Bought It: A man has been killed. Also "bought the farm."

Bow Cat: The bow catapult on a carrier to launch jets.

Broken Arrow: Any accident with nuclear weapons, or

any incident of nuclear material lost, shot down, crashed, stolen, hijacked.

Browning 9mm High Power: A Belgium 9mm pistol, 13 rounds in magazine. First made 1935.

Buddy Line: 6 feet long, ties 2 SEALs together in the water for control and help if needed.

BUD/S: Coronado, California, nickname for SEAL training facility for six months' course.

Bull Pup. Still in testing; new soldier's rifle. SEALs have a dozen of them for regular use. Army gets them in 2005. Has a 5.56 kinetic round, 30-shot clip. Also 20mm high-explosive round and 5-shot magazine. Twenties can be fused for proximity airbursts with use of video camera, laser range finder, and laser targeting. Fuses by number of turns the round needs to reach laser spot. Max range: 1200 yards. Twenty round can also detonate on contact, and has delay fuse. Weapon weighs 14 pounds. SEALs love it. Can in effect "shoot around corners" with the airburst feature.

BUPERS: BUreau of PERSonnel.

C-2A Greyhound: 2-engine turboprop cargo plane that lands on carriers. Also called COD, Carrier Onboard Delivery. Two pilots and engineer. Rear fuselage loading ramp. Cruise speed 300 mph, range 1,000 miles. Will hold 39 combat troops. Lands on CVN carriers at sea.

C-4: Plastic explosive. A claylike explosive that can be molded and shaped. It will burn. Fairly stable.

C-6 Plastique: Plastic explosive. Developed from C-4 and C-5. Is often used in bombs with radio detonator or digital timer.

C-9 Nightingale: Douglas DC-9 fitted as a medical-evacuation transport plane.

C-130 Hercules: Air Force transporter for long haul. 4 engines.

C-141 Starlifter: Airlift transport for cargo, paratroops, evac for long distances. Top speed 566 mph. Range with payload 2,935 miles. Ceiling 41,600 feet.

Caltrops: Small four-pointed spikes used to flatten tires. Used in the Crusades to disable horses.

Camel Back: Used with drinking tube for 70 ounces of water attached to vest.

Cammies: Working camouflaged wear for SEALs. Two different patterns and colors. Jungle and desert.

Cannon Fodder: Old term for soldiers in line of fire destined to die in the grand scheme of warfare.

Capped: Killed, shot, or otherwise snuffed.

CAR-15: The Colt M-4A1. Sliding-stock carbine with grenade launcher under barrel. Knight sound-suppressor. Can have AN/PAQ-4 laser aiming light under the carrying handle. .223 round. 20- or 30-round magazine. Rate of fire: 700 to 1,000 rounds per minute.

Cascade Radiation: U-235 triggers secondary radiation in other dense materials.

Cast Off: Leave a dock, port, land. Get lost. Navy: long, then short signal of horn, whistle, or light.

Castle Keep: The main tower in any castle.

Caving Ladder: Roll-up ladder that can be let down to climb.

CH-46E: Sea Knight chopper. Twin rotors, transport. Can carry 25 combat troops. Has a crew of 3. Cruise speed 154 mph. Range 420 miles.

CH-53D Sea Stallion: Big Chopper. Not used much anymore.

Chaff: A small cloud of thin pieces of metal, such as tinsel, that can be picked up by enemy radar and that can attract a radar-guided missile away from the plane to hit the chaff.

Charlie-Mike: Code words for continue the mission.

Chief to Chief: Bad conduct by EM handled by chiefs so no record shows or is passed up the chain of command.

Chocolate Mountains: Land training center for SEALs near these mountains in the California desert.

Christians In Action: SEAL talk for not-always-friendly CIA.

CIA: Central Intelligence Agency.

CIC: Combat Information Center. The place on a ship where communications and control areas are situated to open and control combat fire.

CINC: Commander IN Chief.

CINCLANT: Navy Commander IN Chief, atLANTtic.

CINCPAC: Commander-IN-Chief, PACific.

Class of 1978: Not a single man finished BUD/S training in this class. All-time record.

Claymore: An antipersonnel mine carried by SEALs on many of their missions.

Cluster Bombs: A canister bomb that explodes and spreads small bomblets over a great area. Used against parked aircraft, massed troops, and unarmored vehicles.

CNO: Chief of Naval Operations.

CO-2 Poisoning: During deep dives. Abort dive at once and surface.

COD: Carrier Onboard Delivery plane.

Cold Pack Rations: Food carried by SEALs to use if needed.

Combat Harness: American Body Armor nylon-mesh special-operations vest. 6 2-magazine pouches for drum-fed belts, other pouches for other weapons, waterproof pouch for Motorola.

CONUS: The Continental United States.

Corfams: Dress shoes for SEALs.

Covert Action Staff: A CIA group that handles all covert action by the SEALs.

CQB: Close Quarters Battle house. Training facility near Nyland in the desert training area. Also called the Kill House.

CQB: Close Quarters Battle. A fight that's up close, hand-to-hand, whites-of-his-eyes, blood all over you.

CRRC Bundle: Roll it off plane, sub, boat. The assault boat for 8 SEALs. Also the IBS, Inflatable Boat Small.

Cutting Charge: Lead-sheathed explosive. Triangular strip of high-velocity explosive sheathed in metal. Point of the triangle focuses a shaped-charge effect.

Cuts a pencil-line-wide hole to slice a steel girder in half.

CVN: A U.S. aircraft carrier with nuclear power. Largest that we have in fleet.

CYA: Cover Your Ass, protect yourself from friendlies or officers above you and JAG people.

Damfino: Damned if I know. SEAL talk.

DDS: Dry Dock Shelter. A clamshell unit on subs to deliver SEALs and SDVs to a mission.

DEFCON: DEFense CONdition. How serious is the threat?

Delta Forces: Army special forces, much like SEALs.

Desert Cammies: Three-color, desert tan and pale green with streaks of pink. For use on land.

DIA: Defense Intelligence Agency.

Dilos Class Patrol Boat: Greek, 29 feet long, 75 tons displacement.

Dirty Shirt Mess: Officers can eat there in flying suits on board a carrier.

DNS: Doppler Navigation System.

Draegr LAR V: Rebreather that SEALs use. No bubbles.

DREC: Digitally Reconnoiterable Electronic Component. Top-secret computer chip from NSA that lets it decipher any U.S. military electronic code.

E-2C Hawkeye: Navy, carrier-based, Airborne Early Warning craft for long-range early warning and threat-assessment and fighter-direction. Has a 24-foot saucer-like rotodome over the wing. Crew 5, max speed 326 knots, ceiling 30,800 feet, radius 175 nautical miles with 4 hours on station.

E-3A Skywarrior: Old electronic intelligence craft. Replaced by the newer ES-3A.

E-4B NEACP: Called Kneecap. National Emergency Airborne Command Post. A greatly modified Boeing 747 used as a communications base for the President of the United States and other high-ranking officials in an emergency and in wartime.

E & E: SEAL talk for escape and evasion.

EA-6B Prowler: Navy plane with electronic counter-measures. Crew of 4, max speed 566 knots, ceiling 41,200 feet, range with max load 955 nautical miles.

EAR: Enhanced Acoustic Rifle. Fires not bullets, but a high-impact blast of sound that puts the target down and unconscious for up to six hours. Leaves him with almost no aftereffects. Used as a non-lethal weapon. The sound blast will bounce around inside a building, vehicle, or ship and knock out anyone who is within range. Ten shots before the weapon must be electrically charged. Range: about 200 yards.

Easy: The only easy day was yesterday. SEAL talk.

Ejection seat: The seat is powered by a CAD, a shotgun like shell that is activated when the pilot triggers the ejection. The shell is fired into a solid rocket, sets it off and propels the whole ejection seat and pilot into the air. No electronics are involved.

ELINT: ELectronic INTelligence. Often from satellite in orbit, picture-taker, or other electronic communications.

EMP: ElectroMagnetic Pulse: The result of an E-bomb detonation. One type E-bomb is the Flux Compression Generator or FCG. Can be built for $400 and is relatively simple to make. Emits a rampaging electromagnetic pulse that destroys anything electronic in a 100 mile diameter circle. Blows out and fries all computers, telephone systems, TV broadcasts, radio, street lights, and sends the area back into the stone age with no communications whatsoever. Stops all cars with electronic ignitions, drops jet planes out of the air including airliners, fighters and bombers, and stalls ships with electronic guidance and steering systems. When such a bomb is detonated the explosion is small but sounds like a giant lightning strike.

EOD: Navy experts in nuclear material and radioactivity who do Explosive Ordnance Disposal.

Equatorial Satellite Pointing Guide: To aim antenna for radio to pick up satellite signals.

ES-3A: Electronic Intelligence (ELINT) intercept craft.

The platform for the battle group Passive Horizon Extension System. Stays up for long patrol periods, has comprehensive set of sensors, lands and takes off from a carrier. Has 63 antennas.

ETA: Estimated Time of Arrival.

Executive Order 12333: By President Reagan authorizing Special Warfare units such as the SEALs.

Exfil: Exfiltrate, to get out of an area.

F/A-18 Hornet: Carrier-based interceptor that can change from air-to-air to air-to-ground attack mode while in flight.

Fitrep: Fitness Report.

Flashbang Grenade: Non-lethal grenade that gives off a series of piercing explosive sounds and a series of brilliant strobe-type lights to disable an enemy.

Flotation Bag: To hold equipment, ammo, gear on a wet operation.

Fort Fumble: SEALs' name for the Pentagon.

Forty-mm Rifle Grenade: The M576 multipurpose round, contains 20 large lead balls. SEALs use on Colt M-4A1.

Four-Striper: A Navy captain.

Fox Three: In air warfare, a code phrase showing that a Navy F-14 has launched a Phoenix air-to-air missile.

FUBAR: SEAL talk. Fucked Up Beyond All Repair.

Full Helmet Masks: For high-altitude jumps. Oxygen in mask.

G-3: German-made assault rifle.

Gloves: SEALs wear sage-green, fire-resistant Nomex flight gloves.

GMT: Greenwich Mean Time. Where it's all measured from.

GPS: Global Positioning System. A program with satellites around Earth to pinpoint precisely aircraft, ships, vehicles, and ground troops. Position information is to a plus or minus ten feet. Also can give speed of a plane or ship to one quarter of a mile per hour.

GPSL: A radio antenna with floating wire that pops to the surface. Antenna picks up positioning from the closest 4 global positioning satellites and gives an exact position within 10 feet.

Green Tape: Green sticky ordnance tape that has a hundred uses for a SEAL.

GSG-9: Flashbang grenade developed by Germans. A cardboard tube filled with 5 separate charges timed to burst in rapid succession. Blinding and giving concussion to enemy, leaving targets stunned, easy to kill or capture. Usually non-lethal.

GSG9: Grenzschutzgruppe Nine. Germany's best special warfare unit, counterterrorist group.

Gulfstream II (VCII): Large executive jet used by services for transport of small groups quickly. Crew of 3 and 18 passengers. Maximum cruise speed 581 mph. Maximum range 4,275 miles.

H & K 21A1: Machine gun with 7.62 NATO round. Replaces the older, more fragile M-60 E3. Fires 900 rounds per minute. Range 1,100 meters. All types of NATO rounds, ball, incendiary, tracer.

H & K G-11: Automatic rifle, new type. 4.7mm caseless ammunition. 50-round magazine. The bullet is in a sleeve of solid propellant with a special thin plastic coating around it. Fires 600 rounds per minute. Single-shot, three-round burst, or fully automatic.

H & K MP-5SD: 9mm submachine gun with integral silenced barrel, single-shot, three-shot, or fully automatic. Rate 800 rds/min.

H & K P9S: Heckler & Koch's 9mm Parabellum double-action semiauto pistol with 9-round magazine.

H & K PSG1: 7.62 NATO round. High-precision, bolt-action, sniping rifle. 5- to 20-round magazine. Roller lock delayed blowback breech system. Fully adjustable stock. 6-$\times$-42 telescopic sights. Sound suppressor.

HAHO: High Altitude jump, High Opening. From 30,000 feet, open chute for glide up to 15 miles to ground. Up to 75 minutes in glide. To enter enemy territory or enemy position unheard.

Half-Track: Military vehicle with tracked rear drive and wheels in front, usually armed and armored.

HALO: High Altitude jump, Low Opening. From 30,000 feet. Free fall in 2 minutes to 2,000 feet and open chute. Little forward movement. Get to ground quickly, silently.

Hamburgers: Often called sliders on a Navy carrier.

Handie-Talkie: Small, handheld personal radio. Short range.

HELO: SEAL talk for helicopter.

Herky Bird: C-130 Hercules transport. Most-flown military transport in the world. For cargo or passengers, paratroops, aerial refueling, search and rescue, communications, and as a gunship. Has flown from a Navy carrier deck without use of catapult. Four turboprop engines, max speed 325 knots, range at max payload 2,356 miles.

Hezbollah: Lebanese Shiite Moslem militia. Party of God.

HMMWU: The Humvee, U.S. light utility truck, replaced the honored jeep. Multipurpose wheeled vehicle, 4 × 4, automatic transmission, power steering. Engine: Detroit Diesel 150-hp diesel V-8 air-cooled. Top speed 65 mph. Range 300 miles.

Hotels: SEAL talk for hostages.

Humint: Human Intelligence. Acquired on the ground; a person as opposed to satellite or photo recon.

Hydra-Shock: Lethal hollow-point ammunition made by Federal Cartridge Company. Outlawed in some areas.

Hypothermia: Danger to SEALs. A drop in body temperature that can be fatal.

IBS: Inflatable Boat Small. 12 × 6 feet. Carries 8 men and 1,000 pounds of weapons and gear. Hard to sink. Quiet motor. Used for silent beach, bay, lake landings.

IR Beacon: Infrared beacon. For silent nighttime signaling.

IR Goggles: "Sees" heat instead of light.

Islamic Jihad: Arab holy war.

Isothermal layer: A colder layer of ocean water that

deflects sonar rays. Submarines can hide below it, but then are also blind to what's going on above them since their sonar will not penetrate the layer.

IV Pack: Intravenous fluid that you can drink if out of water.

JAG: Judge Advocate General. The Navy's legal investigating arm that is independent of any Navy command.

JNA: Yugoslav National Army.

JP-4: Normal military jet fuel.

JSOC: Joint Special Operations Command.

JSOCCOMCENT: Joint Special Operations Command Center in the Pentagon.

KA-BAR: SEALs' combat, fighting knife.

KATN: Kick Ass and Take Names. SEAL talk, get the mission in gear.

KH-11: Spy satellite, takes pictures of ground, IR photos, etc.

KIA: Killed In Action.

KISS: Keep It Simple, Stupid. SEAL talk for streamlined operations.

Klick: A kilometer of distance. Often used as a mile. From Vietnam era, but still widely used in military.

Krytrons: Complicated, intricate timers used in making nuclear explosive detonators.

KV-57: Encoder for messages, scrambles.

LT: Short for lieutenant in SEAL talk.

Laser Pistol: The SIW pinpoint of ruby light emitted on any pistol for aiming. Usually a silenced weapon.

Left Behind: In 30 years SEALs have seldom left behind a dead comrade, never a wounded one. Never been taken prisoner.

Let's Get the Hell out of Dodge: SEAL talk for leaving a place, bugging out, hauling ass.

Liaison: Close-connection, cooperating person from one unit or service to another. Military liaison.

Light Sticks: Chemical units that make light after twisting to release chemicals that phosphoresce.

Loot & Shoot: SEAL talk for getting into action on a mission.

LZ: Landing Zone.

M1-8: Russian Chopper.

M1A1 M-14: Match rifle upgraded for SEAL snipers.

M-3 Submachine gun: WWII grease gun, .45-caliber. Cheap. Introduced in 1942.

M-16: Automatic U.S. rifle. 5.56 round. Magazine 20 or 30, rate of fire 700 to 950 rds/min. Can attach M203 40mm grenade launcher under barrel.

M-18 Claymore: Antipersonnel mine. A slab of C-4 with 200 small ball bearings. Set off electrically or by trip wire. Can be positioned and aimed. Sprays out a cloud of balls. Kill zone 50 meters.

M60 Machine Gun: Can use 100-round ammo box snapped onto the gun's receiver. Not used much now by SEALs.

M-60E3: Lightweight handheld machine gun. Not used now by the SEALs.

M61A1: The usual 20mm cannon used on many American fighter planes.

M61(j): Machine Pistol. Yugoslav make.

M662: A red flare for signaling.

M-86: Pursuit Deterrent Munitions. Various types of mines, grenades, trip-wire explosives, and other devices in antipersonnel use.

M-203: A 40mm grenade launcher fitted under an M-16 or the M-4A1 Commando. Can fire a variety of grenade types up to 200 yards.

MagSafe: Lethal ammunition that fragments in human body and does not exit. Favored by some police units to cut down on second kill from regular ammunition exiting a body.

Make a Peek: A quick look, usually out of the water, to check your position or tactical situation.

Mark 23 Mod 0: Special operations offensive handgun system. Double-action, 12-round magazine. Ambidextrous safety and mag-release catches. Knight screw-on suppressor. Snap-on laser for sighting. .45-caliber.

Weighs 4 pounds loaded. 9.5 inches long; with silencer, 16.5 inches long.

Mark II Knife: Navy-issue combat knife.

Mark VIII SDV: Swimmer Delivery Vehicle. A bus, SEAL talk. 21 feet long, beam and draft 4 feet, 6 knots for 6 hours.

Master-at-Arms: Military police commander on board a ship.

MAVRIC Lance: A nuclear alert for stolen nukes or radioactive goods.

MC-130 Combat Talon: A specially equipped Hercules for covert missions in enemy or unfriendly territory.

McMillan M87R: Bolt-action sniper rifle. .50-caliber. 53 inches long. Bipod, fixed 5- or 10-round magazine. Bulbous muzzle brake on end of barrel. Deadly up to a mile. All types .50-caliber ammo.

MGS: Modified Grooming Standards. So SEALs don't all look like military, to enable them to do undercover work in mufti.

MH-53J: Chopper, updated CH053 from Nam days. 200 mph, called the Pave Low III.

MH-60K Black Hawk: Navy chopper. Forward infrared system for low-level night flight. Radar for terra follow/avoidance. Crew of 3, takes 12 troops. Top speed 225 mph. Ceiling 4,000 feet. Range radius 230 miles. Arms: 2 12.7mm machine guns.

MIDEASTFOR: Middle East Force.

MiG: Russian-built fighter, many versions, used in many nations around the world.

Mike Boat: Liberty boat off a large ship.

Mike-Mike: Short for mm, millimeter, as 9 mike-mike.

Milstar: Communications satellite for pickup and bouncing from SATCOM and other radio transmitters. Used by SEALs.

Minigun: In choppers. Can fire 2,000 rounds per minute. Gatling gun-type.

Mitrajez M80: Machine gun from Yugoslavia.

MI-15: British domestic intelligence agency.

MI-16: British foreign intelligence and espionage.

Mocha: Food energy bar SEALs carry in vest pockets.

Mossberg: Pump-action, pistol-grip, 5-round magazine. SEALs use it for close-in work.

Motorola Radio: Personal radio, short range, lip mike, earpiece, belt pack.

MRE: Meals Ready to Eat. Field rations used by most of U.S. Armed Forces and the SEALs as well. Long-lasting.

MSPF: Maritime Special Purpose Force.

Mugger: MUGR, Miniature Underwater Global locator device. Sends up antenna for pickup on positioning satellites. Works under water or above. Gives location within 10 feet.

Mujahideen: A soldier of Allah in Muslim nations.

NAVAIR: NAVy AIR command.

NAVSPECWARGRUP-ONE: Naval Special Warfare Group One based on Coronado, CA. SEALs are in this command.

NAVSPECWARGRUP-TWO: Naval Special Warfare Group Two based at Norfolk.

NCIS: Naval Criminal Investigative Service. A civilian operation not reporting to any Navy authority to make it more responsible and responsive. Replaces the old NIS, Naval Investigation Service, that did report to the closest admiral.

NEST: Nuclear Energy Search Team. Non-military unit that reports at once to any spill, problem, or Broken Arrow to determine the extent of the radiation problem.

NEWBIE: A new man, officer, or commander of an established military unit.

NKSF: North Korean Special Forces.

NLA: Iranian National Liberation Army. About 4,500 men in South Iraq, helped by Iraq for possible use against Iran.

Nomex: The type of material used for flight suits and hoods.

NPIC: National Photographic Interpretation Center in D.C.

NRO: National Reconnaissance Office. To run and co-ordinate satellite development and operations for the intelligence community.

NSA: National Security Agency.

NSC: National Security Council. Meets in Situation Room, support facility in the Executive Office Building in D.C. Main security group in the nation.

NSVHURAWN: Iranian Marines.

NUCFLASH: An alert for any nuclear problem.

NVG One Eye: Litton single-eyepiece Night-Vision Goggles. Prevents NVG blindness in both eyes if a flare goes off. Scope shows green-tinted field at night.

NVGs: Night-Vision Goggles. One eye or two. Give good night vision in the dark with a greenish view.

OAS: Obstacle Avoidance Sonar. Used on many low-flying attack aircraft.

OIC: Officer In Charge.

Oil Tanker: One is: 885 feet long, 140 foot beam, 121,000 tons, 13 cargo tanks that hold 35.8 million gallons of fuel, oil, or gas. 24 in the crew. This is a regular-sized tanker. Not a supertanker.

OOD: Officer Of the Deck.

Orion P-3: Navy's long-range patrol and antisub aircraft. Some adapted to ELINT roles. Crew of 10. Max speed loaded 473 mph. Ceiling 28,300 feet. Arms: internal weapons bay and 10 external weapons stations for a mix of torpedoes, mines, rockets, and bombs.

Passive Sonar: Listening for engine noise of a ship or sub. It doesn't give away the hunter's presence as an active sonar would.

Pave Low III: A Navy chopper.

PBR: Patrol Boat River. U.S. has many shapes, sizes, and with various types of armament.

PC-170: Patrol Coastal-Class 170-foot SEAL delivery vehicle. Powered by 4 3,350 hp diesel engines, beam of 25 feet and draft of 7.8 feet. Top speed 35 knots, range 2,000 nautical miles. Fixed swimmer platform on stern. Crew of 4 officers and 24 EM, carries 8 SEALs.

Plank Owners: Original men in the start-up of a new military unit.

Polycarbonate material: Bullet-proof glass.

PRF: People's Revolutionary Front. Fictional group in *NUCFLASH*, a SEAL Team Seven book.

Prowl & Growl: SEAL talk for moving into a combat mission.

Quitting Bell: In BUD/S training. Ring it and you quit the SEAL unit. Helmets of men who quit the class are lined up below the bell in Coronado. (Recently they have stopped ringing the bell. Dropouts simply place their helmet below the bell and go.)

RAF: Red Army Faction. A once-powerful German terrorist group, not so active now.

Remington 200: Sniper Rifle. Not used by SEALs now.

Remington 700: Sniper rifle with Starlight Scope. Can extend night vision to 400 meters.

RIB: Rigid Inflatable Boat. 3 sizes, one 10 meters, 40 knots.

Ring Knocker: An Annapolis graduate with the ring.

RIO: Radar Intercept Officer. The officer who sits in the backseat of an F-14 Tomcat off a carrier. The job: find enemy targets in the air and on the sea.

Roger That: A yes, an affirmative, a go answer to a command or statement.

RPG: Rocket Propelled Grenade. Quick and easy, shoulder-fired. Favorite weapon of terrorists, insurgents.

SAS: British Special Air Service. Commandos. Special warfare men. Best that Britain has. Works with SEALs.

SATCOM: Satellite-based communications system for instant contact with anyone anywhere in the world. SEALs rely on it.

SAW: Squad's Automatic Weapon. Usually a machine gun or automatic rifle.

SBS: Special Boat Squadron. On-site Navy unit that transports SEALs to many of their missions. Located across the street from the SEALs' Coronado, California, headquarters.

SD3: Sound-suppression system on the H & K MP5 weapon.

SDV: Swimmer Delivery Vehicle. SEALs use a variety of them.

Seahawk SH-60: Navy chopper for ASW and SAR. Top speed 180 knots, ceiling 13,800 feet, range 503 miles, arms: 2 Mark 46 torpedoes.

SEAL Headgear: Boonie hat, wool balaclava, green scarf, watch cap, bandanna roll.

Second in Command: Also 2IC for short in SEAL talk.

SERE: Survival, Evasion, Resistance, and Escape training.

Shipped for Six: Enlisted for six more years in the Navy.

Shit City: Coronado SEALs' name for Norfolk.

Show Colors: In combat put U.S. flag or other identification on back for easy identification by friendly air or ground units.

Sierra Charlie: SEAL talk for everything on schedule.

Simunition: Canadian product for training that uses paint balls instead of lead for bullets.

Sixteen-Man Platoon: Basic SEAL combat force. Up from 14 men a few years ago.

Sked: SEAL talk for schedule.

Sonobuoy: Small underwater device that detects sounds and transmits them by radio to plane or ship.

Space Blanket: Green foil blanket to keep troops warm. Vacuum-packed and folded to a cigarette-sized package.

SPIE: Special Purpose Insertion and Extraction rig. Essentially a long rope dangled from a chopper with hardware on it that is attached to each SEAL's chest right on his lift harness. Set up to lift six or eight men out of harm's way quickly by a chopper.

Sprayers and Prayers: Not the SEAL way. These men spray bullets all over the place hoping for hits. SEALs do more aimed firing for sure kills.

SS-19: Russian ICBM missile.

STABO: Use harness and lines under chopper to get down to the ground.

STAR: Surface To Air Recovery operation.

Starflash Round: Shotgun round that shoots out sparkling fireballs that ricochet wildly around a room, confusing and terrifying the occupants. Non-lethal.

Stasi: Old-time East German secret police.

Stick: British terminology: 2 4-man SAS teams. 8 men.

Stokes: A kind of Navy stretcher. Open coffin shaped of wire mesh and white canvas for emergency patient transport.

STOL: Short TakeOff and Landing. Aircraft with high-lift wings and vectored-thrust engines to produce extremely short takeoffs and landings.

Sub Gun: Submachine gun, often the suppressed H & K MP5.

Suits: Civilians, usually government officials wearing suits.

Sweat: The more SEALs sweat in peacetime, the less they bleed in war.

Sykes-Fairbairn: A commando fighting knife.

Syrette: Small syringe for field administration often filled with morphine. Can be self-administered.

Tango: SEAL talk for a terrorist.

TDY: Temporary duty assigned outside of normal job designation.

Terr: Another term for terrorist. Shorthand SEAL talk.

Tetrahedral reflectors: Show up on multi-mode radar like tiny suns.

Thermal Imager: Device to detect warmth, as a human body, at night or through light cover.

Thermal Tape: ID for night-vision-goggle user to see. Used on friendlies.

TNAZ: Trinittroaze Tidine. Explosive to replace C-4. 15% stronger than C-4 and 20% lighter.

TO&E: Table showing organization and equipment of a military unit.

Top SEAL Tribute: "You sweet motherfucker, don't you never die!"

Trailing Array: A group of antennas for sonar pickup trailed out of a submarine.

Train: For contact in smoke, no light, fog, etc. Men directly behind each other. Right hand on weapon, left hand on shoulder of man ahead. Squeeze shoulder to signal.

Trident: SEALs' emblem. An eagle with talons clutching a Revolutionary War pistol, and Neptune's trident superimposed on the Navy's traditional anchor.

TRW: A camera's digital record that is sent by SAT-COM.

TT33: Tokarev, a Russian pistol.

UAZ: A Soviet 1-ton truck.

UBA Mark XV: Underwater life support with computer to regulate the rebreather's gas mixture.

UGS: Unmanned Ground Sensors. Can be used to explode booby traps and claymore mines.

UNODIR: Unless otherwise directed. The unit will start the operation unless they are told not to.

VBSS: Orders to "visit, board, search, and seize."

Wadi: A gully or ravine, usually in a desert.

White Shirt: Man responsible for safety on carrier deck as he leads around civilians and personnel unfamiliar with the flight deck.

WIA: Wounded In Action.

Zodiac: Also called an IBS, Inflatable Boat Small. 15 × 6 feet, weighs 265 pounds. The "rubber duck" can carry 8 fully equipped SEALs. Can do 18 knots with a range of 65 nautical miles.

Zulu: Means Greenwich Mean Time, GMT. Used in all formal military communications.